Lauren Beukes writes novels, comics and screenplays, and has

LaurenBeukes.com

facebook.com/laurenbeukes

@laurenbeukes

Praise for *Broken Monsters*:

'Scary as hell and hypnotic. I couldn't put it down.
I'd grab it, if I were you'
Stephen King

'This is a tremendous novel, full of original
characters and stunning dialogue'
The Times

'A thriller with a rare and intriguing capacity to
make the reader think'
Telegraph

'A terrifying crime novel that places the victims
at its centre'
Marie Claire

'Deftly layered . . . engrossing'
Sunday Times

'Never exploitative . . . never superficial . . . Beukes
shows how horror can be the best way to explain
our unbelievable reality'
Guardian

'A compelling spine-chiller that keeps you hooked
to the very end'
Heat

'Following up an international bestseller is never easy, but
[Beukes] makes it look easy'
Shortlist

'I unhesitatingly urge you to buy it and read it now'
James Ellroy, author of *LA Confidential*

'Beukes is a compelling storyteller who has created strong characters in Gabi and Layla'
Metro

'Beukes has once again redefined the thriller genre'
Stylist

'Make a long flight fly by with this gripping thriller'
Grazia

'Vivid, troubling, but never less than completely engaging'
Val McDermid

'Captivating . . . *Broken Monsters* defies the standard tropes of the serial killer genre'
Los Angeles Times

'A strange and fascinating thriller'
Sunday Express

'When Stephen King calls a book "scary as hell and hypnotic", don't read it late at night in a tent in the woods . . . I regretted not having a door with a deadbolt'
Wall Street Journal

'Clever and creepy'
Sunday Mirror

'Any fears that *The Shining Girls* was a one-off are banished in *Broken Monsters*. Lauren Beukes' masterly storytelling is firmly in place'
Daily Express

Also by Lauren Beukes

Moxyland
Zoo City
The Shining Girls

LAUREN BEUKES
BROKEN
MONSTERS

HARPER

Harper
An imprint of HarperCollins*Publishers*
1 London Bridge Street
London SE1 9GF

www.harpercollins.co.uk

This paperback edition 2015
1

First published in Great Britain by
HarperCollins*Publishers* 2014

Copyright © Lauren Beukes 2014

Lauren Beukes asserts the moral right to
be identified as the author of this work

A catalogue record for this book is
available from the British Library

ISBN: 9780007464616

Set in Sabon LT Std

Printed and bound in Great Britain by
Clays Ltd St Ives plc

MIX
Paper from
responsible sources
FSC™ C007454

FSC™ is a non-profit international organisation established to promote
the responsible management of the world's forests. Products carrying the
FSC label are independently certified to assure consumers that they come
from forests that are managed to meet the social, economic and
ecological needs of present and future generations,
and other controlled sources.

Find out more about HarperCollins and the environment at
www.harpercollins.co.uk/green

I dreamed about a boy with springs for feet so he could jump high. So high I couldn't catch him. But I did catch him. But then he wouldn't get up again.

I tried so hard. I got him new feet. I made him something beautiful. More beautiful than you could imagine.

But he wouldn't get up. And the door wouldn't open.

SUNDAY, NOVEMBER 9

Bambi

The body. The-body-the-body-the-body, she thinks. Words lose their meaning when you repeat them. So do bodies, even in all their variations. Dead is dead. It's only the hows and whys that vary. Tick them off: Exposure. Gunshot. Stabbing. Bludgeoning with a blunt instrument, sharp instrument, no instrument at all when bare knuckles will do. Wham, bam, thank you, ma'am. It's Murder Bingo! But even violence has its creative limits.

Gabriella wishes someone had told that to the sick fuck who did this. Because this one is *Yoo-neeq*. Which happens to be the name of a sex worker she let off with a warning last weekend. It's most of what the DPD does these days. Hands out empty warnings in The. Most. Violent. City. In. America. *Duh-duh-duh.* She can just hear her daughter's voice – the dramatic horror-movie chords Layla would use to punctuate the words. All the appellations Detroit carries. Dragging its hefty symbolism behind it like tin cans behind a car marked 'Just Married'. Does anyone even do that any more, she wonders, tin cans and shaving cream? Did anyone ever? Or was it something they made up, like diamonds

1

are forever, and Santa Claus in Coca-Cola red, and mothers and daughters bonding over fat-free frozen yogurts. She's found that the best conversations she has with Layla are the ones in her head.

'Detective?' the uniform says. Because she's just standing there staring down at the kid in the deep shadow of the tunnel, her hands jammed in the pockets of her jacket. She left her damn gloves in the car and her fingers are numb from the chill wind sneaking in off the river. Winter baring its teeth even though it's only gone November. 'Are you—'

'Yeah, okay,' she cuts him off, reading the name on his badge. 'I'm thinking about the adhesive, Officer Jones.' Because mere superglue wouldn't do it. Holding the pieces together while the body was moved. This isn't where the kid died. There's not enough blood on the scene. And there's no sign of his missing half.

Black. No surprise in this city. Ten years old, she'd guess. Maybe older if you factored in malnourishment and development issues. Say somewhere between ten and sixteen. Naked. As much of him as there is to be naked. It's entirely possible the rest of him is wearing pants, with his wallet in the back pocket and a cell phone that won't have any minutes, but which will make calling his momma a hell of a lot easier.

Wherever the rest of him is.

He's lying on his side, his legs pulled up, eyes closed, face serene. The recovery position. Only he's never going to recover and those aren't his legs. Skinny as a beanpole. Beautiful skin, even if it's gone yellow from blood loss. Pre-adolescent, she decides. No sign of acne. No scratches or bruises either, or any indications that he put up a fight or had anything bad happen to him at all. Above the waist.

2

Below the waist is a different story. Oh boy. That's a whole other section of the book store. There's a dark gash, right above where his hips should be, where he has been somehow...*attached* to the lower half of a deer, hooves and all. The white flick of the tail sticks up like a jaunty little flag. The brown fur is bristled with dried blood. The flesh appears melted together at the seam.

Officer Jones is hanging back. The smell is terrible. She's guessing the intestines are severed, on both sets of bodies, leaking shit and blood into the conjoined cavities. Plus there's the gamey reek of the deer's scent glands. She pities the ME having to open up this mess. Better than the paper-work, though. Or dealing with the goddamn media. Or, worse, the mayor's office.

'Here,' she offers, fishing a small red tub of lipgloss out of her pocket. Something she bought at the drugstore on a whim to appease Layla. A candy-flavored cosmetic – that's sure to bridge the gap between them. 'It's not menthol, but it's something.'

'Thanks,' he says, grateful, which marks him out as an FNG. Fucking New Guy. He dips his finger in and smears the greasy balm under his nose; cherry-flavored snot. With sparkles in it, Gabi notices for the first time, but does not point out. Small pleasures.

'Don't get any on the scene,' she warns him.

'No. No, I won't.'

'And don't even think about taking any pictures on your phone to show your buddies.' She looks around at the tunnel with the graffiti that grows on bare walls in this city like plaque, the weight of the pre-dawn darkness, the lack of traffic. 'We're going to contain this.'

They do not remotely contain it.

3

Last Night a DJ Saved My Life

Jonno is yanked from sleep's deepest tar pits by an elbow to the jaw. He comes up flailing and disoriented, only to find himself fighting bed sheets. The girl from last night – Jen Q – rolls over, her arms flung above her head, revealing the sleeve of tattooed birds that runs up her chest and over her shoulder. She's oblivious to having nearly concussed him. Her eyelids are flickering in REM, caught up in a dream that makes her breath jagged, similar to the panting delight he elicited from her earlier when she was riding him, his hands on her hips. When she came, she flung her head back, flicking her mane of braids. His bad luck to catch one in the eye, which called an abrupt halt to the proceedings as he teared up, blinking in pain.

'Easy...' he says, rubbing her back to bring her out of it. He can feel the dark corona of a hangover hovering around his head waiting to slam down. But not quite yet. Perversely, the pain from the elbow jab seems to be keeping it at bay.

'Mmmgghff,' she says, not properly awake. But he's broken through the skin of her nightmare. He runs his palm down the curve of her waist, under the sheets. His cock stirs.

That's twice in one night she's hurt him. It's entirely

possible she'll break his heart next. It was the way she kept saying afterwards, 'Oh my gosh, I'm so sorry,' but couldn't hold back the giggles, collapsing onto his chest, crying with laughter while his eye streamed.

'That's not exactly a gesture of solidarity,' he complained at the time, but the soft weight of her felt sweet, her whole body shaking with laughter.

'Do you want to fuck again?' he whispers into her ear now.

'T'morrow,' she mumbles, but parts her legs to accommodate his hand anyway. 'S'nice. Keep doing that.'

She sighs and rolls over, so that he can move in behind her. He pushes his hard-on up against her ass, his fingers sliding over her clit until he realizes that her breathing has deepened because she's gone back to sleep. Great.

He flops onto his back and looks around the room, but there's not much in the way of clues. 1 x wooden ceiling fan. 1 x Scandi modern cupboard. Reedy blinds over the window. Their clothes all over the floor. No books, which is troubling if he intends to fall in love with her. Did he tell her that he's a writer?

He wonders what the Q stands for. An actual last name or a DJ add-on? Jen X would have been too cutesy, he supposes. Not her style, based on what he has to go on. Which is, to summarize this in one of the easily digestible lists he churns out in lieu of making a respectable living:

1) The set she played last night at the so-called secret party, for which a hundred people showed in a studio in Eastern Market under a T-shirt shop. He can't remember the music she was playing, but it was that time of the night when everything merges into doof-doof bass.

2) The way she danced, her braids twisted up on her head, to prevent exactly the kind of injury she had inflicted

5

on him. The first thing he noticed. She moved like she was happy. And she smiled when he caught her eye. He liked that. Not too cool to smile.

3) The way she plucked the cigarette impatiently from his mouth when they were outside, still strangers, bound only by the camaraderie of being smokers, having to stand out in the cold with the fuzzy promise of emphysema in the distant future. They'd been talking about Motown and techno. That Rodriguez documentary. The bankruptcy. All the easy conversational set-pieces. He thought she was going to take a drag, and instead she kissed him.

4) Making out in her car. There are snapshots in his memory, Instagrams really, because they're blurry round the edges: following her down a hedged-in alley round the side of a house to a detached cottage, kissing her neck while she messed around with the keys, the smell of her skin making him crazy, swearing, laughing, her sharp 'shhhh' as the door fell open and they tumbled inside.

5) The shapes of furniture in the darkness as she led him straight through to the bedroom. Both of them drunk. Or him, definitely. He could tell by the way the room went all tilt-a-whirl for a moment. Kissing, tugging off clothes. The way she felt inside.

Shit. Did they use a condom? The thought makes his stomach flop, but not for the reasons it would have a year ago.

She gives one little rabbit snore, and he ducks as she flings out her arm again. No good. He can tell by the clarity of his thoughts that he's not going back to sleep. He has become an expert on his own insomnia. Usually it's fear that jerks him awake in the middle of the night, heart racing. He leans over the side of the bed, fishing for his phone in his jacket pocket. Four forty-eight. That's later

6

than his average, which is usually around two in the morning. He should get laid more often. *No shit, Sherlock.*

Jonno does not check his inbox, even though the number above the little envelope insists that he has new messages. New voicemail too, according to the digit attached to the cartoon speech bubble. It used to be that the only icons that could inspire such terrible dread were plague signs. A black X over the door.

He opens the browser instead and looks up Jen Q. Only a couple of pages of search results, usually limited to a listing at a festival or a gig guide. A tiny profile on some music review site. But she's social media-ed to the eyeballs. All the usual suspects and even a MySpace page, which means she's probably a little older than he thought. He clicks through her selfies, inspirational quotes, self-promos. 'Xcited 2b playing Coal Club 2nite. $5 cover!' It's all surface shit, posing for the world. He knows the feeling.

His hangover is settling in. He's going to need something to keep it at bay.

He throws back the covers and swings his legs over the edge of the bed, waiting for the swirl of nausea to pass. Jen doesn't stir. She has raccoon eyes from her mascara. Cate would never have gone to bed without taking off her makeup.

It's freezing out here. He tucks the cover up over the birds on her shoulder, pulls his jacket on over his nakedness, and staggers in what he hopes is the direction of the bathroom to find something for the vice around his head.

He should write something. Anything. Take three steps in Detroit and you're falling over a story. But they've all been done by the native sons. Fuck you and your Pulitzer, Charlie LeDuff, he thinks, patting down the wall to find the light switch.

He flinches against the halogen and the reflection in the medicine cabinet – it's not even merciless, it's plain mean. He examines his face. The puffiness will go away once he catches up on his sleep. George Clooney rules: crow's feet on a man are sexy, and the patches of white in his six-day scruff of beard are a badge of experience. Jesus. Thirty-seven years old and sleeping with DJs.

Not bad going, he grins at himself. Ignoring his inner troll, which snipes, *Yeah, but she's no Cate, is she?*

You don't know that, he thinks. She could be. She could be really smart and deep and funny. I could follow her round the world, a new gig in a new city every night, write in hotel rooms.

Yeah, 'cos that's working out so well for you right now.

'Lost?' Jen says, leaning on the door, wearing a hideous blue flannel dressing gown. Looking a little puffy herself – which is charming in its own way. She is idly rubbing at her collar bone, exposing a glimpse of smooth skin.

'Oh hey. I was looking for an Advil. Or something.'

'You try the medicine cabinet?' Amused, she leans past him to pop it open on a clutter of cosmetics and medicine bottles, a packet of tampons that makes him avert his eyes like he's twelve all over again, and, alarmingly, several needles still sealed in plastic. She reaches for a bottle and drops two aspirin into his hand. 'You can use the glass by the sink. It's clean. You coming back to bed?'

'Yeah.' He slugs the pills down, following her back into the bedroom.

She shrugs the horrible robe from her shoulders like a wrestler and climbs back into bed. 'I saw your look. Don't worry about it. I've got what my grandma used to call "the sugars".'

'Uh?'

'The needles. I'm diabetic. They're back-up in case I run out of pens. What, you thought you'd hooked up with some junkie?'

'It crossed my mind for a millisecond.'

'Aren't you glad we used protection?'

'Did we?' He shoves away the pop of disappointment. 'I'm a little fuzzy. Not that it matters. Seeing as you're not, you know, um.' He is aware of how idiotic he must look, with his jacket zipped up and his cock hanging out. *Smooth operator.*

'You don't remember?' But she's smiling, the covers tucked up under her chin. 'You're hurting my feelings.'

'You might have to remind me.'

'Get in here,' she says, lifting the blanket, tilting her head at the pack of Durex on the bedside table. He's the kind of guy who can take a hint.

'What were you dreaming about?' he whispers into the perfect curved shell of her ear as he enters her.

'Does it matter?' she arches her back up against him, and right now it really doesn't.

'C'mon, wake up. You gotta go.'

'Mmmmf?' Jonno manages as she shoves him out of bed. He is confused for a moment, then he remembers where the hell he is. *Hot DJ girl. You had your cock inside her. Nice work if you can get it, boychick.*

'But it's still dark,' he protests through the sleep glaze, even as he's pulling on his socks. He stands on one of their used condoms. Squelchy even through his sock.

'Hustle. I mean it.'

'Did they start the zombie apocalypse already?' He tugs

on his shirt and realizes it's backwards. He yanks it off and starts again. She is sitting cross-legged on the bed, naked, watching him and smiling.

'You're a funny guy, Tommy.'

'Jonno.' It stings much more than it should.

Her hands fly to her mouth. 'Oh jeez. Sorry.' She starts giggling again. 'Oh, that's terrible. I'm so embarrassed.' She tips forward, burying her head on her knees. She can't stop laughing. 'Sorry.'

'The least you can do is buy me breakfast,' he says in his best indignant voice. He pulls on his jeans and buttons his fly. At least he can't screw that up.

'All right. But only if you get out of here, right now.'

He lowers his voice. '*Is* it zombies? Because if that's the case, I think we should be improvising weapons.'

'Worse than that, doofus. It's my dad.'

'Wait.' His brain is scrabbling like a dog with a small bladder at the door. He looks around again. Definitely not a teen pad. And that's a woman's body, right there. The fullness and softness and the smile lines. She sees the panic on his face and laughs harder, leaning on him, her hand on his stomach. He automatically sucks it in. *She's already seen you naked, genius.*

'You thought…'

'Zombies I can deal with.'

'I'm twenty-nine, you idiot.'

'Well thank God for that.' And that's not true, he thinks. The profile he read last night said she was thirty-three.

'I'm living at home. For now.'

'And your dad thinks you don't have sex?'

'Not under his roof. Well, on his property.'

'Ah.'

'Yeah.'

'I should probably get going then.'

'You probably should.' She is grinning madly. She nods her head at the door. 'Same way you came in.'

'But you're still buying me breakfast.'

'Not today. I've got family stuff.'

'Tomorrow, then.'

She relents. 'There's a coffee place in Corktown. I'll see you there at ten.'

'That's not very specific.'

'You'll find it.'

'I'll get a cab home, then. And see you tomorrow.' He is trying not to sound desperate.

'Okay.' She's beaming.

'All right.' He stands there a moment longer.

'You should go.'

'It seems like a very bad idea to leave you.'

'But you should anyway.'

'Okay. You know it's cute that you don't swear.'

'Go! For Pete's sake!'

He leans down and pulls her into a deep kiss. 'Okay.' He stalks down the corridor with great stealth and purpose, not looking back, reeking of eau de pussy. It's no use.

'Um,' he says, poking his head round her bedroom door. She is lying with one arm cast above her head, her eyes closed, head tilted back, and her hand between her legs. 'I'm really sorry to interrupt—?'

She sits up, not the slightest bit embarrassed. 'Would you get out of here?'

'I would. I just...' he shrugs helplessly. 'I don't know where we are. It was dark when we came in. If you could give me a suburb at least?'

11

Under the Table

TK wakes up under a table in a strange house. His feet are sticking out the end in his worn black boots. He pulled a pillow off the couch for his head, used one of the drapes for a blanket. Man has to improvise. When he was eleven, he could drink most grown men under the table, but this is not the case today. Twenty-three years living clean, and he's got the AA medals to prove it, even if they're in a cardboard box with the rest of his stuff up in Flint with his sister.

The dawn light is a drowsy gray through the table cloth. Like a shroud. No wonder he was dreaming about being buried alive. Staring up at the dark grain of the wood makes it feel like he's lying in a coffin – the luxury model you gotta fork out extra for, with the creamy exterior and the gold-plate handles and the silk-lined space inside. Not the kind he buried his momma in. But that's morbid thinking, and the day is bright and all laid out ahead of him and he's got a whole house to go through.

A different man would have slept in one of the beds upstairs, but the family took the big mattress with them and it wouldn't feel right to sleep in one of the little kids' rooms. Besides, it's one of his special talents. He's got a knack for sleeping anywhere, anytime. Worked it up in the assembly line making screws, where if you were smart and motivated and very sneaky, you could take on the work of two men for an hour or two, while the other guy caught some shut-eye, and then switch it up. Bosses didn't like it, but long as the work got done, what did they care? He finds he sleeps better if it's really noisy. Conditioning, they call it. Drills and bolts and the whine of heavy machinery? That's pure lullaby to him. The birds twittering outside to greet the sunrise don't make the cut.

Something crashes in the kitchen. He bolts upright, smashing his head on the underside of the table. Damn. Shouldn't have got complacent, even with the door locked behind him and a kind-of permission.

He tried to do it real polite. He stood on the corner across the way, while the family packed the car, loading everything into a station wagon and a U-Haul trailer. They strapped the mattress to the roof and a table to the mattress, upside down with its legs in the air like a dead bug. The kids went into the house and came out again, carrying boxes in relay, while the afternoon shadows stretched out. The wife kept glaring at him, like the foreclosed notice in a plastic folder taped to the door was somehow his fault. The kids, too. Shifty glances at him and then back at their folks, except for the toddler of course, who wanted to play in the boxes. Real cute little boy, getting underfoot like one of those wind-up toys that keeps going.

TK tried to be nonchalant about it. Taking his time to roll a cigarette and smoke it. He didn't mean to make them freak out. But he couldn't walk away and leave it to chance, either. Someone else might happen along. And sure, that seems unlikely in this neighborhood where theirs is the last house standing among overgrown lots and burned-out wrecks, and he only chanced on them because it's what he does; wander the city looking for luck. TK is no stranger to terrible coincidence. Ask his momma, and her twin sister who got her killed.

'Leave it alone,' the husband muttered, pulling on the ropes to make sure everything was tight as. But it was boiling up inside her, the whole time he waited, trying to make it seem like he wasn't.

'No,' she said, handing the toddler off to her man and striding toward TK across the yellow grass, her little fists balled up like she was a pro-footballer instead of five-foot nothing. The husband started after her, then realized she'd immobilized him by handing him the baby.

TK dropped the cigarette and ground it out. No manners in breathing your poison in someone else's face. Nor in littering, nor wasting tobacco, even the cheap stuff. He picked up the stump and pocketed it. When he stood up again, she was in his face, hands on her hips, spitting outrage. Not really at him, but sometimes people need a stand-in. He'd seen it often enough, at the shelter, at meetings. He could be that for her.

'Can't you even wait till we're out of here, you...vulture!' Her voice cracked as she said it, but the insult bounced right off him. He doesn't know much about vultures outside of what he's seen on TV, hop-hopping to get at some dead carcass. If he'd had a choice, he'd have told her he's more like one of the city's stray dogs. Because they're shameless opportunists and you can cuss them out much as you like,

14

they've learned not to take it personally. The lone animals anyway. It's when they pack together that you got a problem. Only takes one mean dog to wind up all the others into biting teeth and snarls. But he's a solo mutt and he knows how to wag his tail a little.

'I'm sorry to see you go, ma'am,' TK said, calm, looking her in the eye. 'Used to be that it was only the nice *white* families moving out of Detroit.'

He'd knocked the indignation right out of her sails. Good manners will do that; turn a situation around. You got to treat people like people. Something his momma taught him, along with how to use a gun, and what the minimum going rate for a whore was.

'Yes, well,' she said, angrily brushing at her eyes, 'tell that to the bank.'

'You don't worry about your things, ma'am. I'll make sure everything finds a good place and a purpose.'

'Thank you. I guess.' She sounded bitter. She shouted across at her husband, who was about to lock up, 'Leave it! It doesn't matter anyhow. Right?' She looked at TK for confirmation, of more things than he suspected he was able to give. But he tried anyway.

'Yes, ma'am,' he said, solemn. 'Good luck.'

'Ha!' she said. 'You're the one who's staying.'

'All right?' the husband called over.

The car doors slammed, but they left the house open for the dusk to go creeping in – along with any shameless opportunists who happened to be hanging around.

TK waited until the U-Haul lights had disappeared round the corner before heading in and locking the door behind him. Flicked the light switch, but the electricity was already cut off and he took the executive decision, one he regrets now, with the noises coming from the kitchen, to wait till morning to see what was left.

Something shatters. Glass or crockery. Which makes TK think it's not a looter. He doesn't like to use that word. That implies theft, and he's never stolen a thing in his life, not even when he was a kid and all fucked up. He's in asset reclamation and redistribution. Also career consultation, IT support, peer counseling, recycling and, when he really has to, mopping up at the party store on Franklin. Which might seem like a strange place for a recovering alcoholic to work, but it keeps him honest, and he never accepts money from underage kids looking for someone to buy them a six-pack of Coors the way some homeless do. Or as he prefers to think of it: domestically challenged.

The noises in the kitchen sound clumsy. Scuffling. Maybe a drunk. Or something else. He crawls out from under the table, feeling for the pepper spray he carries with him. Expired, but you can't always believe what you read on the side of the box. He has a blade hidden in his walking stick, a jerry-rigged thing he made himself, but pepper spray has always served him better, especially against feral dogs, long as you're upwind and not backed into a dead end, which he has been in the past, but only once. Thomas Michael Keen learns his lessons quick.

He moves quietly toward the kitchen, flicking the safety off the spray nozzle, holding it up, facing the intruder. He peeks round the kitchen door. The kitchen is in a state. Cupboards hanging open. Food spilled all over the floor. No way the woman who told him off on her lawn would leave her house like this.

A furry bandit face pokes out from behind one of the

cupboard doors, its mouth matted with bright blood. TK swears. And then the raccoon goes back to licking at the strawberry jelly on the floor, among the shattered remains of the jar that once contained it.

'Go on! Shoo! Get outta here!'

The raccoon raises its head and looks at him. He runs at it, waving his arms and yelling. 'Scoot your furry butt!'

It bristles, and then thinks better of it and dashes for the cat flap. With a swish of cold air and a thwack of plastic, it's out into the dawn, running for its life. And they both have a story to tell.

Briefly, TK considers crawling back under the table and going back to sleep until the sun's up proper, but he's shot full of adrenaline from the damn critter.

Hoping against the obvious that it's gas not electric, he checks the stove, so he can make a cup of coffee. Unfortunately, it's electric – probably came installed with the house. Worth fifty bucks if he can disconnect it and figure a way to cart it to the junk store. He's already cataloging in his head.

But a man's got to have his caffeine fix, so he spoons in a mouthful of instant coffee mixed with brown sugar and washes it down with water. The faucet sputters and chugs ominously. The city'll have turned that off too. House like this with three kids probably has a good-size cylinder, though, enough for him to have a wash and a shave and still be able to flush the toilet after he's done the necessary. You got to live on the streets to appreciate the sheer decadence of that white porcelain flushing commode.

He was a landlord once upon a time, when he was thirteen and the most together of all the dopeheads. He moved into a deserted building, pulled down the boards, put up curtains, cut the grass, paid a nice Chinese lady a cut to come by once a week to take in the rent money, 'cos who was going to give it to a kid? He got an old electrician to teach him the basics of stealing power from the circuit box without frying himself like an egg, and every time the neighbors went out, they'd fill buckets with water from the garden hose. It worked fine as long as his tenants kept up appearances, looked after the place, but you can't trust a bunch of dopeheads not to fuck up a good thing. Eventually, they'd started partying on the front lawn, and the neighbors caught on and called the cops, and they'd had to abandon their abandominium.

He was going to start up someplace else, but then his momma got herself killed, bled to death in his arms, and he got taken off the streets by the justice system. Ten years straight, and then on and off. Prison's like booze, it's a tough habit to break. He used to drown the memories with whatever he could get his hands on, which would get him in trouble all over again. Now he's learned to block it out in his head, like windows boarded up with plywood.

TK digs in the kitchen cupboards until he finds a bunch of black plastic trash bags, and then heads upstairs to go through every room with care. They've packed in a rush, leaving clothes on hangers, others tossed on the floor. He folds everything up and puts it in the bags. A pile for him, one to send to Florrie, leftovers for Ramón to pick through, and the rest they'll take down to the church.

He tries on a checked flannel shirt, but the arms are too short. Same with the suit jacket. That's the trouble with being a big guy. But the red pair of kicks he finds in a box at the back of the closet fit him just fine. Nothing wrong with them either, practically brand-new, apart from the black oil smear over the right toe. He tucks them under his arm and piles up the old broken toys and baby wipes, a half-full tub of nappy-rash cream (everything's half-full when you're in asset reclamation), and dumps it in a bag.

All he needs is to strike it lucky. Find the *one* house with a suitcase full of money. He could probably buy this place off the bank for what, ten large? Maybe less in this neighborhood. Fix it up, move his sister in, fill it up with his friends, legitimate this time.

They say possessions tie you down, but maybe not tightly enough, if you look at this town. The sum total of his stuff fits into a shoe box. Photos, a map of Africa, a pair of reading glasses, his AA medals, and an old sixty-minute cassette tape with his family talking on it, made before his little brother died. Cassettes wear out eventually. He knows he should get it digitized. He knows a bit about computers, he's a self-taught man, but Reverend Alan's promised to send him on a real course, and that's the first thing he's gonna ask them to show him how to do. Photographs, voices – those things are what you pull close when you're missing connections to people, not fancy sneakers and big-screen TVs.

The sudden hammering on the door downstairs nearly makes him crap his pants, and he hasn't even had a chance to use the facilities yet. Maybe the family had a change of heart and called the cops on him. The cops are not kind to stray dogs, even loner ones with more bark than bite.

He could probably make out the back. He's already calculating which bags are worth taking with him when he hears Ramón's voice over the knocking: 'Yo, let a brother in, it's cold out!'

He opens the door on his friend, who looks especially squirrelly today, hunched over a battered shopping cart, glancing up and down the street. His face transforms from skittish mistrust to a huge grin when he sees TK, and he waves the free Tracker phone Obama gives away to people like them so they can apply for jobs. Good for making plans to raid a house too, although Ramón insists on sending elaborately neutral texts in case it does what it says on the box, and the government *is* tracking them.

'Hey, Papi, got your message. Took me a little while to find a cart. Damn Whole Foods chains 'em up.'

'That's the problem with gentrification right there, brother. The power's out, but I found some lunch meat and cheese in the icebox if you want a bite.'

Ramón peers into the interior of the house, fiddling with the rosary beads he keeps in his pocket. His eyes dart around, finally settling on TK and the red Chuck Taylors under his arm. They're hard to miss. 'Nice shoes,' he says.

'I think they're my color. It brings out my eyes.'

Ramón looks confused.

'They're bloodshot,' TK explains.

'Right.' He snorts out a laugh, but the envy leaks through anyway.

'You know I'd give you the shirt off my back, Ramón,' TK tries again, 'but the shoes on my feet...'

'Probably wouldn't fit me anyhow.' He shuffles on the step. Which only emphasizes his soles flapping as they pull away from the bottoms of his black lace-ups.

TK sighs. Sucker. 'I never did like red shoes.' Which is not true, but hell, Ramón's face brightens like a lightbulb turned on inside it. 'Now get your ass inside already. You're letting all the cold in,' he says, helping his friend wrangle the shopping cart up the porch stairs.

The Detective's Daughter

Layla is late for her Sunday rehearsal. Blame her mother, shaking her awake at four in the morning because she has to go out to a scene and 'don't forget the code to the gun safe, beanie, just-in-case'. When she had two parents working different shifts, there was always someone home, and she didn't need a *just-in-case*, and there was always someone to drive her to where she needed to be, like rehearsals on a Sunday, because she has *a scene* of her own to get to, thanks Mom. Instead she has to wait for an hour at the bus stop, bundled up against the cold and doodling in her notebook, resisting the temptation to scribble on the bench like so many others before her. She plans to leave her mark on the world in other ways.

Doing extramurals is supposed to help bring Layla out of her shell. Like she doesn't know it's cheap babysitting so her mom doesn't have to feel guilty all the time. But she *should* feel guilty. It's her fault they moved downtown after the divorce, her fault all Layla's real friends live in Pleasant Ridge, which is only on the other side of Eight Mile, but might as well be a world away when you don't have a car.

She shoves through the double doors of the Masque Theater School and gallops up two flights of stairs to the main stage area. She's relieved to hear from the chanting – all echoey and strange in the stairwell – that they're still doing warm-up exercises. She dumps her bag by the door and looks for Cas – not hard in a room full of black kids. She slips in beside her, and falls in with the chorus of tongue-twisting vowel sounds that rise and fall. Mrs. Westcott raises her eyebrows, half-hello, half-friendly warning.

Shawnia leads the circle, raising her fist in the air to indicate that they're switching up the exercise. Black power, the speaking stick, all the rituals that count. They all stop dead and watch for their cue.

Shawnia starts flopping her body around, like she's having a seizure, and they all follow suit, trying to let go of their bones, making their limbs limp as tentacles. Layla flops her body forward so that her unruly curls brush the ground. (Which are not a weave, thank you for asking. She got them the old-fashioned way, from her mom, and yeah, that means she's a mixie and no, you can't fucking touch my hair, what do you think this is, a human petting zoo?)

'Couldn't get a ride?' Cassandra whispers. 'Bet Dorian could have given you one.'

Layla accidentally on purpose tries to smack her. But Cas ducks, making it look like part of her movement.

'Oh no, too slow!' she whisper-mocks, both of them grinning.

'Focus, please!' Mrs. Westcott yells. She says drama came straight out of human sacrifice rituals. Some ancient prehistoric tribes used to kill their chieftain every winter solstice as an offering to the gods to ensure that the spring would return, until they figured out that killing off their smartest and brightest maybe wasn't the best way to run a society. They started re-enacting the sacrifices wearing masks to fool the gods, to allow the chieftain to return as a new man, or close as.

You can inhabit a role, Layla thinks, you can reinvent yourself. She thought she could get away with it. Whole new school year, whole new school on the other side of the city, whole new Layla.

She played the divorce card on her dad to get him to buy her new clothes to fit in with the cool kids. But it was tough to keep up the act. Like dying your hair blonde, according to Cas. 'Trust me. The maintenance is a nightmare.'

Besides, it turns out it's harder to fool teenagers than old gods. Clothes maketh not the mean girl. Eventually you're going to slip up and say something colossally dorky, like you read Shakespeare for fun.

It took a week before she decided it was too much effort and blew her cover on purpose so she could go back to wearing her usual uniform of jeans and geeky T-shirts. Hard enough being the in-between Afro-Latina, who can fit in with the white kids or the black kids, but not both at the same time. But it sucked being back where she started, on the outside, eating lunch alone in the gymnateria or cafenasium, whatever you want to call it, because like all well-intentioned charter schools, Hines High was short on funds.

That was before she made friends with Cassandra, or more likely the other way round, because, let's face it, Cas is so out of her league. She's super-hot, even though she never wears makeup, with her fine sandy-brown hair, big gray-blue eyes and freckles, and breasts that make boys do double-takes. And she doesn't give a fuck about anything.

It's how they became friends, when Cas called Ms. Combrink a bitch to her face and Layla covered for her, clumsily, yelling out, yeah, she had an *itch* too. It landed them both in detention, but they got to talking and she persuaded Cas to come along to audition at the theater school. She aced it without trying, even though she sings like a frog with emphysema. Life lesson: looks plus don't-give-a-fuck confidence mean you can have anything you want – any guy, any friends. But Cas chose *her*. Which makes Layla infinitely grateful and paranoid. She's told Cas she's waiting for the day she dumps a bucket of pig's blood on her head – *Carrie*-style.

'Gross. I would never do that.' Cas was dismissive. 'If I was going to humiliate you in public, I'd be much more subtle and vicious.'

But it means she doesn't push too hard when Cas changes the subject every time personal stuff comes up. It's part of what she admires about her – that Cas is unknowable. Like Oz. But unlike that huckster wizard, you can't just pull back the curtain on Cas, because all you'll find are curtains behind curtains. It's part of her ineffable cool. But Layla can't tell her that because she'll get a big head, and she already has big boobs to contend with. It would definitely throw her off balance.

Shawnia raises her fist again for the final exercise before they launch into rehearsals proper, the cycle of gratitude. Double-clap-stamp, round the circle. 'I'm happy today,' she starts, 'because…I got an acceptance letter from U of M!' Clap-clap-stamp. Everyone whoops.

Layla has her sights set further than that. When she graduates in three years' time, she's getting out of Michigan.

She's not naïve enough to think she'll make NYU or Los Angeles, but there are other cities with great theater schools. Chicago, Austin, Pittsburgh.

'I'm happy today because I got a date for prom,' Jessie says. Clap-clap-stamp.

'Did she pay him?' Cas whispers and Layla tries to keep a straight face. Maybe because Jessie's the only other white kid in theater group, it's easier for Cas to pick on her. 'By the way…' Cas flashes her screen at her, to show her a tweet from Dorian. 'Hitting the ramp l8r. Anyone up for a skate?'

The claps continue round the circle.

'You stalker!' Layla whispers, trying to hide her delight, already calculating who she can bum a ride with to get there.

'I'm doing it for you, baby girl. For looo-ve.'

'No phones, girls!' Mrs. Westcott calls out from the stage.

'I'm happy because it's end of the weekend,' David intones and gets answered with boos, but he just raises his voice, 'which means I get to go to school tomorrow and see all my boys!' Clap-clap-stamp.

'I got a text from a boy who likes me,' Chantelle says.

'But do you like him?' Mrs. Westcott teases.

'Oh *yeah*.' Chantelle looks smug.

Clap-clap-stamp.

'I spoke to a boy I *like*,' Keith says. Clap-clap-stamp, a wolf-whistle.

'My little brother made the hockey team,' Cas says. 'More time at practice, less time to bug me.' Clap-clap-stamp.

'I'm happy because…' Shit, Layla has had half the circle to think of something. 'I'm seeing my boyfriend later.' She flushes. Clap-clap-stamp. Saying it makes it true. Or commits her to trying, anyway.

***

She didn't intend to get high. But after rehearsals, hanging around watching the boys in the skate park, the weed blunted the boredom of waiting for her mother, who kept texting to say she was held up, until everyone else had bailed to go home, including Cas, and it was only her and Dorian, who kept sliding away from her, and she had to get used to it.

He's aiming for kid sister. She wants unsisterly things. It's not *that* big an age difference. She'll be sixteen in December. But he's graduated already and taking a year out, crashing on the couches of some artist-musician friends down by Hubbard Farms while he decides if he wants to go to college. 'In the right light, Detroit's kinda like the new Bohemia,' he told her, passing her the joint, taking care not to brush her fingers with his. She wanted to reply that in the right light, he could be the Florizel to her Perdita, except he probably hasn't read *The Winter's Tale*, and he'd think she was even more of a dork.

He's not the only guy in her life who fundamentally doesn't get it. Yesterday's weekly scheduled phone call with her dad (like she's in prison or something) went badly, and it's been gnawing at her. She was telling him about her part in the play, the portable phone cradled to her ear, NyanCat a purring lump against her leg, and he was all hers for a moment, like they used to be. He even promised to fly out to see it if his schedule allowed, because the last live performance he saw was a bad remake of *The Little Mermaid* on ice, for God's sake.

'Yeah, how do you even skate on fins?' she said, blocking out the sound of her step-sibs squealing in the background.

'They managed,' William said, and she could picture his brow crinkling in amused horror. 'It was godawful, Lay, you have no idea.'

She laughed. 'Maybe that'll be me one day. The sea witch on skates.' He was supposed to retort, *Are you kidding, you'd be the lead, honey.* And then she would feign outrage and maybe she'd go on to mention *this guy* she met. It's a comedy routine the two of them have, with established rules. But then his new life butted in, like elderly neighbors cutting the music at a house party.

'Hang on a sec, Layla. No! Julie! Do not throw food on the floor! C'mon, you know you're not supposed to do that, baby.'

'Remind me again why I have to stay in Detroit?' She meant for it to sound light-hearted, just to hook his attention back to her, but he started reeling off all the same old reasons, on auto-pilot. *Just till you finish high school. Your mother needs you. I need to try to make this work. It's not easy with little step-kids.*

'Yeah, the last thing you want is your teenage daughter from your previous marriage hanging around to remind you of how you screwed up the last one,' she snapped. Which led to a long silence down the phone line.

'Hello? You still there?' She suddenly missed their DIY craft projects she threw out when they moved: the scientifically accurate mobile of glow-in-the-dark planets she and her dad hung together, the dreamcatcher he helped her weave when she was seven – inspired by the Ojibwe who hunted here, he told her – with dangling crystals that caught the light. She wondered what shiny bits of wisdom he was passing on to his new kids.

'Earth to Dad?' She tried for jokey.

He came back from very far away. 'That was a terrible thing to say Layla. I'm really hurt.' That pleading note entered his voice, the one she thinks of as PD: Post Divorce.

27

Be reasonable. 'Besides, you know your mother needs you.'

'Bzzzzz! And that's the incorrect answer! Thank you for playing!' She hung up before he could say anything else. She waited for him to ring back. He didn't. She's not going to apologize, she thinks fiercely. Not this time.

She doesn't notice the white Crown Vic pulling up very slowly alongside the skate ramp, cruising for trouble like only cops and gangs and bored teenagers do. She's lost inside her weed-fuzzed head, intent on Dorian poised on the concrete lip in that perfect moment of potential, the streetlight flared behind his head in the dusk. He shades his eyes against the headlights. His beanie is pulled low over his sideburns. 'Hey, Lay,' he calls out to her. 'I think it's your mom.' But it's like overhearing the Iranian women gossiping at the corner store – sounds fraught with meaning that don't have anything to do with her.

He tilts his board over the edge and lets gravity have its way with him. He glides down the curve and up the other side, tracing lazy parabolas through the gray slush of melted ice. If she slits her eyes, she can almost see contrails in his wake. It's beautiful. Like art. Or music, she thinks, the zipper scrape of the wheels across the cement.

'Lay,' he arcs around, catching the trunk of the tree. His breath fogs out in a cartoon speech bubble in the cold. 'Ley' means 'law' in Spanish. This is her mom's idea of an inside joke.

'What?' She's annoyed with him for breaking the magic. And then the Crown Vic gives a single *whoop-whoop* of the siren, a flash of red and blue from the lights mounted in the grille. More subtle than the bubble they stick on top, but not by much.

'Crap!' She drops the joint from her fingers. God, she

wishes her mom wouldn't *do* that. She slides down from the tree, super-aware of her body, her limbs like foreign objects that aren't quite ready to do what they're told. She tucks her hands under her armpits, not only to hide the smell of the weed on her fingertips, but to prevent her arms floating off, because right now it feels like they might drift right out of her sleeves into the sky.

'Wake up,' Dorian pokes her in the ribs, totally busting her spacing out. He's laughing at her. But not in a shitty way.

'Okay, okay,' she mumbles, her face going hot. She concentrates on the ridiculous choreography of putting one foot in front of the other. Who *invented* walking? Seriously.

He shakes his head and guides his board over to the car. He grabs on the side mirror to bring himself to a bumping stop and leans down to greet through the window. 'Hola, Mrs. V.'

'It's *Ms.*' her mother says. 'And I prefer Detective Versado. Or ma'am. As in, "No, ma'am, that's not marijuana you can smell coming off me like I've taken up residence inside a bong."'

'Legal in several states now,' he grins.

'So move to Colorado.'

'Mom!' Layla winces. 'Leave off. Please.' She opens the door to climb in the back.

'Don't you want to sit up front?'

'Nah. This way I can pretend I'm one of your perps. You treat me like a criminal anyway.'

'Well, if I catch you smoking that stuff…'

'You *won't*,' Layla retorts. Catch her that is. Especially if she can lurk in the back seat and shut down the conversation. Then she can lie down in the back and watch the streamers of lights out the window, like she used to when she was a little kid when they went out for dinner and she fell asleep in the back and her dad would lift her out and carry her into the house to install her in her bed, smelling like cigarettes and sweat and the sharp aftershave he always wore for special occasions. She feels a burn of nostalgia for that little kid and that happy family.

'Later,' Dor says now, kicking away.

'Bye,' she says, going for casual disdain, which seems to work on boys like him, along with lots of eye-liner. And tits. And being three years older, and not such a colossal dork. God, she's so screwed.

Her mother is watching her in the rear-view mirror, with that little crease tugging downwards at the corner of her mouth, the one that didn't used to be there. It's a PD thing. 'You know, there are studies that show—'

'Yeah, yeah, I *know*, Mom. Weed corrodes the brain, I'm gonna be sorry when the only job I can get is flipping burgers. Or worse. End up po-lice.'

'Sure wouldn't want that,' her mother says mildly, but Layla knows she got to her by the way she pulls away, jerking the steering wheel into a hard U-turn toward the freeway.

'I had a weird case today,' she says. Opening gambit. Layla's not falling for it. She engages super-surly mode from the drop-down menu of emotional options in her head.

'I wish you wouldn't talk to my friends.'

'Don't worry. The feeling's mutual. Dorian, anyway. I like Cas, though.'

'And don't rate them either. This isn't the friend Olympics. They don't get a score out of ten.'

'Do you *want* to walk home?'

'Dorian could have given me a ride.'

'I suppose he is cute, in that deadbeat stoner way.'

30

'Mom!' Layla dies inside. If it's that transparent to her *mother*, then the whole world knows. Which means it's obvious to Dorian as well, and that's too hideous to contemplate.

'All right, all right. Truce. I bought you some lipgloss.'

'Swell.' Layla says. She sits up, pulls out her phone and starts typing a text to Cas.

>Lay: Finally! 3 HOURS late!
>Cas: More time for loooo-oooobe with Dorian
>Lay: Excuse me?!?
>Cas: Aaargh! Loooooove. Love! Not lube! Autocorrect.
>Lay: Freud much?
>Cas: :) :) :)

'I had to use some of it,' her mother says. 'Hope you don't mind.'

'Mom, this stuff's a con. It dehydrates your skin so you have to keep applying it.'

But the thought of the soft, sweet slick of the gloss is suddenly very appealing. She presses her lips together to see how dry they are. Pretty dry. She runs her tongue along the edge of her incisors which makes her super-aware of how her teeth are part of her skull. She feels a little queasy at the thought of the exposed bone, right there in the open. The inside-out. She drags her mind back to the last thing her mom said through the warm blur of the weed. Lipgloss. Right. 'What flavor is it?'

'Cherry. Don't you want to know what I used it for?'

'Putting on your lips?' Layla says. Drop-down menu: maximum sarcasm.

'To cover the smell of a body.'

31

'That doesn't work. I saw it on the crime channel. Anyway, gross. I don't want to hear about some dead person.'

> >Lay: Disgusting cop stories #Yay #notyay
> >Cas: U like it
> >Lay: Little bit

'You sure? Not even the part where I punked the rookie? Who, unlike you, does not watch the crime channel.'

'If you're so desperate to talk about it, go ahead.'

'I shouldn't tell you. It was messed-up.'

'Or don't. Whatever. I'm not your therapist.'

'I'll give him this. He turned green, but he didn't spew.'

'That's pretty cold, Mom.'

> >Lay: OMG. She's SO immature

'Poor guy. Guess he should watch more TV.' She turns thoughtful. Enough for Layla to lower the phone. 'Poor kid, too.'

'It was a kid?'

'Like I said, it was messed-up.' Her mother glides away from the conversation like Dorian on his skateboard.

> >Lay: Shit. Dead kid
> >Cas: What! What!?!?!?!? All the deets. I wantz them
> >Lay: Later

'Someone I know?'

'I don't think so, baby. And you know we don't talk shop.'

'I thought we just were.'

'Yeah, I know. That was indiscreet of me.'

'So be indiscreet. Who am I gonna tell?'

'Layla, we haven't even notified the family yet.'

'Fine. Whatever. You started it.'

'It's been a rough day. Sorry.'

'Me too.' She throws herself back in the seat and picks up her phone again. A force-shield against parental stupidity.

BEFORE

Traverse City

He heard Louanne was back in Michigan, but it took Clayton the better part of two weeks and a lot of driving to find her. You got to concentrate driving at night, but it keeps your mind occupied.

He downs those Monster energy drinks to keep him awake and to counteract the effect of the OxyContin and some kind of super-strength Tylenol in red gel caps he buys from a dealer in Hamtramck, who gets them from Mexico, because he's wrecked his back and doctors are all full of shit.

And even though he doesn't sleep, he has dreams. Crazy dreams. Sometimes while he's driving, his brain summons shapes up out of the darkness. Like tonight. He drove through a pile of wet leaves, and it was like a mush of crows, all rotten feathers and pointy beaks.

He wonders if his old man ever saw things on the road when he was trucking long-distance across the country. He never asked him. Sometimes he would take Clayton with him on the shorter hops, to Chicago or Buffalo. They didn't talk on those trips. Clayton was too scared to say the wrong thing, in awe of the man who chewed gum non-stop because tobacco would give you the cancer, and they'd drive for hours like that, both of them silent, watching the miles peel past. Eventually his old man stopped taking him, because he couldn't miss school. But when he graduated and said he wanted to make art, his father shrugged and said, so do it then, long as you can feed you and yours.

When the cancer got him anyway, forty-eight years old, younger than Clayton is now, hiding in the recesses of his pancreas, he left his son the house and enough money to do some courses and live for a while just working on his art. For years he made the visions in his head, dragged them out with paint or an acetylene torch, and even sold some of them. He used to work in the early hours, carried by inspiration and the dwindling supply of bank notes from whatever scrounge job he'd done last. Better than any clock, those bank notes, ticking off the days until he'd have to put down his brush or his chisel or his torch.

His versatility comes from doing jobs that could feed his art. He learned how to weld working on armor-plated cars right here in Detroit before they were shipped off for the first Iraq war. Learned woodwork in a sign factory. But the last while he's had to take anything he can get to bridge the gaps, which seem to be getting shorter and shorter, because the money doesn't last as long, and the guys doing the hiring look past him to younger, stronger men. Everyone's always looking for the new thing, as if his age and experience count for shit. He's only fifty-three. He's still strong enough to work, any job you like, and he's just as good as those kids. He's got perspective.

It's what he told that shrimpy little curator Patrick Thorpe. Practically begged him for a chance to be included in the group show – got down on his knees like a marriage proposal, in the middle of Honey Bee supermarket. Patrick hemmed and hawed and said he'd have to talk to the others, but why didn't Clayton make something and they'd see.

It paralyzed him, of course. Everything he tried seemed like a dead thing under his hands. Until he heard Lou was back. Lou and Charlie. It's good to be driving with a purpose, but that's the easy part.

The talking was hard. Asking people if they'd seen a redhead in an old silver Ford Colt with a kid with her. He had to make up stories. They didn't like that he was just a dad looking for his kid. Because that came with a big ugly question mark: what did you *do*? Nothing. That's the problem. He let her go.

He went to the diner where he and Lou first met, and the manager said that she'd been back working her old job, but he had had to let her go when he caught her stealing singles from the tip jar. He heard she was living out of her car now, a real shame, but what was he supposed to do?

It gave Clayton a lead though, because there are only so many places a woman with a kid and no home but a car can go. He tried all the RV parks around Detroit, and then further out. In Muskegon, he found a lady who'd been renting her a trailer who said she'd got a letter from Lou promising to pay the month's rent she skipped out on if she'd forward her mail to a Mail Boxes Etc. in Traverse City. She gave him the thin wedge of envelopes (bills, all bills) to pass on to her direct. Such a sweet little boy, the landlady said.

He tried to josh with her, about how he wanted to teach Charlie to use a welding torch, when he was a little older, of course, because a little kid might burn his own face right off, but the words came out wrong, and the woman frowned and said maybe it wasn't Traverse City, maybe it was Grand Rapids. And she should probably hang on to the mail after all, but it sure was nice to meet him and good luck finding Lou, and could he please remind her about the rent.

After that, it was easy. The Mail Boxes Etc. was right next to a Walmart and there, in the parking lot, was the silver Colt, nestled up next to a shiny new RV with lace curtains and cream trim parked next to a row of trees clinging to their last leaves.

Across the lot, the glass storefront beckoned, a shining portal into the land of anything you want, 24/7. Come in, come in, it's all in here.

Clayton knows you can camp overnight outside a Walmart, no trailer-park fees required. You could see the whole of America that way. A pilgrimage for the restless and the lost.

He pulled in next to the shopping carts corralled between the railings and turned off his truck. He sat there for a moment, under the corn-colored lights, listening to the engine tick over, noticing how the dark puddles were full of reflected neon.

Sleeping in cars, he thought. That's no good for anyone. They could come home with him. Her and Charlie. He'd have to tidy up, but he's got the room to spare.

He swung open the door of his truck and climbed down. Her car still had a crumpled bumper, same as when he met her. Both of their vehicles were a little battered, he thought, just like they were.

Lou was in front, her seat tilted right back. Funny how you can recognize someone just by the shape of their head. He thought he spotted the kid in the back of the car. Mop of curly hair among the rubble of their life. Boxes and

40

blankets and crap. A CD boombox on top, the blue LED display the only light in the vehicle.

He tapped on the Colt's window. Once, twice, his knuckles freckled with white scars and the beginnings of liver spots and old cigarette burns from back when he thought that might help.

'Hey Lou,' he said. 'It's me.'

She shifted, then sat upright in alarm. The stripe of light across her face and her wild red hair made her look like a girl in a music video, only not as pretty.

'Roll down the window,' he said and she did, but only a thin slice, enough for him to hear the kids' lullabies playing on the CD.

'What are you doing here?' she whispered, probably harsher than she meant to.

'I came to say hello.'

'Oh no,' she said, louder, tilting her chin to get her mouth closer to the crack of the window. 'Get your ass out of here. I don't want to see you. You hear me, Clayton Broom?'

'I was in the area.'

'Detroit's four hours away.'

'Maybe I live here now. It's a nice place, Traverse City.' He'd only seen what he drove through to get here, the night lying heavy on the empty streets. That's when the borders are the most porous between the worlds, and unnatural things leak out of people's heads and move freely.

'You're lying again.'

'I joke around a little, I'm a joker.'

'Ain't funny, Clayton. Wait.' She struggled with her seatbelt. He thought that was a strange thing to do, clip yourself in to a parked car. Maybe it was to hold her in place for sleeping. Like men strapping themselves into bunks on ships.

She yanked up the knob of the lock and eased the door open so she could slip out. The light inside was busted. She was wearing tracksuit pants, a green sweatshirt, and woolly pink socks. She was going to get them filthy out here.

She took his arm in a C-clamp grip, and steered him away from the car, right under the light, so he could see how much the color in her hair had faded. She used to dye it deep red, like hotel carpets, but the henna was growing out, showing brown and gray roots. Calico cat. Like the one that used to live with them when he was squatting with all those young artist kids in the building overlooking the kosher butchers in Eastern Market.

'Why are you here?' Lou demanded. 'Middle of the night.'

'It's not okay for a man to look up an old flame?'

'Flame.' She laughed, but the sound was as brittle as the neon light of the logo. 'What we had was a matchstick, Clayton. Burned out, like that.' She snapped her fingers.

He tried again. 'I wanted to see how you are.'

She put out her arms and performed a clumsy pirouette in her socks. She stumbled, which made his heart break a little more. 'You've seen,' she said. 'Now you can take off.'

'You're living out of a car, Lou.'

'Only for now. I had a place. I'll get one again. I got a job interview here next week.'

'Here?'

'You never met someone who worked in a Walmart before?'

'How is Charlie?'

'Fine. He's fine.' She turned cautious.

'I want to see him.'

'You don't got no business with him. Besides, he's not even here.'

42

'Where is he, then?'

'Around. Visiting.' Her eyes skipped to the car. One blue, one brown, the most striking thing about her sharp little face. Just like that calico cat. It used to claw and bite if you tried to pick it up. He shut it up in the cupboard above the sink once, as a joke. It broke plates. Scratched one of the girls up when she opened it. Hard to say who was more mad, the girl or the cat. He was sorry she got hurt, but it was funny as hell.

He tried again. 'I brought him a present.'

'What kind of present?'

'*Now* you got time for me?' He smiled, even though he was annoyed by the flash of greed that lit her up. She saw that he'd noticed, and got pissy.

'You want to come here, get me up in the middle of the night? Best you have something to make up for that.'

He felt sorry for her. All this need in the world. He tried to remember when he last slept.

'It's in the truck,' he said, still hoping he could save this. 'Lemme get it.'

She rubbed her arms and stared out across the rows of empty bays to the store entrance. A street-cleaning machine was chugging along across the road.

'You want my jacket, baby?'

'I want the present and then you can go.'

He pushed her a little. 'No "how are you? Good to see you?"'

'You wanna play like that? Okay. How are you, Clayton?'

'Well, to tell you straight, Lou, I'm doing pretty bad. It's the dreams again.'

'Not this fourth-dimension shit again.' She pinched down her arms, as if checking she was still there. 'Ain't nothing

43

but your messed-up head.'

'I don't even have to be asleep. Sometimes I dream with my eyes open. I see things. Maybe some people are more open to it. I think some places the walls are thinner, like a cheap motel.'

'You should probably go find one of those. I'm tired of talking. It's late. I want to go back to sleep with my boy.'

'No, wait, please, Lou. Lemme get his present, okay? *Please*. I came all this way.' He went over to the truck and lifted it out of the footwell: a stout metal barrel made from an old muffler, with stumpy legs and a pointy head with pert ears and a snout. It still made him laugh to look at it. He turned, expecting her to share his delight. 'Here. I made it specially for Charlie.'

'What's that s'posed to be?'

'A dog. Every kid needs a dog. Look, it can bark and wag.' He demonstrated the clever hinge he put in the jaw that opened and closed, the bouncy spring of the tail.

'That don't look like no dog I ever saw, Clayton Broom. That'll put the fright into him. Probably cut himself on it, too.'

'I smoothed off the edges, don't worry. I wanted to let it oxidize so it would look like it had brown fur to match Charlie's hair.'

'He got red hair.'

'You got red hair, baby.' He laughed. 'Right out of the bottle. Charlie takes after me. My hair was brown before it turned white.'

'Don't you know nothing?' Her eyes went silvery with tears.

'Hey, hey, baby, it's okay.' He tried to put his arms around her, but she shrank away.

44

She used to laugh at his jokes. He's sure she did. He told her the story about the cat in the cupboard and she laughed and laughed. The prettiest waitress at the diner, he told her, even if it was a lie. He offered to drive her home one night after work, stuck around until her shift was over, even helped her mop up the floor, turn the chairs around. He took her back to her place, where she knocked back a half-jack of vodka and cried on his shoulder about her shit-heel ex-husbands. Two already and her the wrong side of forty. He told her about the world under the world, and that scared her a little, but it made her come closer too. They were both lonely and afraid and there's nothing wrong with what happened next. Only natural.

'I want to see him, Lou,' Clayton said.

'He's not here.'

'Who's in the back of the car then? Yoohoo, Charlie-boy!' He waved at the little boy shape sitting up among the boxes and the lumpy bags. Two years old. Exactly the right age. He and Lou were together before she took off for Minneapolis with that Ryan guy. He'd done the math.

'Mama?' The car door swung open, and Charlie slid out, rubbing his eyes. Clayton filled up with unbearable pride at how beautiful he was, this little boy. Better than all his art. The masterpiece of human biology. It's a goddamn miracle is what it is.

'Charlie, it's all right, sweetheart. Get back in the car. Go back to sleep.'

'Who's that?'

Clayton stepped toward him, to ruffle his curls. 'I'm your—'

'No,' she cut him off. 'You and me, we did it once. Barely. Shit, I was so drunk.'

'All it takes,' Clayton said. 'Birds and the bees, Daddy puts his penis in Mommy's vagina, and the stork comes calling.'

She covered the kid's ears. 'You don't talk that way in front of him. He got *red hair*, you lunk. Like his *dad*. Like Ryan. He's not yours, dummy.'

The lace curtain on the RV twitched, a woman's face peeked out.

'No,' he shook his head, hard. 'That's not true.'

'I'm fucking telling you, you lunk. What's wrong with you?' She shoved at him again. Just like that little cat.

'Don't push me!' He caught her skinny wrists, and Charlie let out a wail like a siren. It was all going wrong. Like everything always went wrong.

He was blinded by a flashlight in his eyes.

'Everything okay over here?' It was a security guard.

He let go of Lou's wrists and shaded his eyes to be able to see the man. It's got so he can't trust in things to stay the way they're supposed to be.

'Everything's fine, Wayne,' Lou said, putting a flirty little kick in her voice. 'But my friend hasn't bought anything yet.'

'I just got here,' Clayton explained. 'Five minutes ago.'

'Sorry, sir, overnight parking is at the manager's discretion.'

'What's that supposed to mean?'

'It means you gotta *buy* something,' Lou said. She sounded sorry. She always had a temper. But it was gone as quick as it came. 'It doesn't matter what. It'll take you five minutes. Then Wayne here will be happy and we can sit and talk. I promise.'

'You on first-name basis with all the security guards round here?'

'Wayne looks after us. You too, if you go buy something.'

'Store policy, sir.' The security guard puffed up.

'All right, all right. I'm going. You want anything, Lou baby?'

'Um...' she said, looking at the bright door across the parking lot.

'Cigarettes?' he offered. 'An Energade? A pop or something for Charlie?'

She swiped at her eyes, rubbed the back of her hand off against her sweatshirt. 'Yeah, all right. And a lighter. Or matches. Matches are safer for Charlie. I can give you money.'

'Don't worry about it. I'll be right back. Don't go anywhere, okay?'

'Where would I go?'

The guard, *Wayne*, walked with him to the door, as if he just happened to be heading the same way.

'She's a nice lady. I don't want any trouble,' he said. He'd tucked his flashlight into his belt next to his pepper spray.

'Me neither,' Clayton said. He felt terribly tired, and the pinch in his spine was back. 'Are you in love with her?'

'What? No!'

'Because she's living out of a car? You think you can judge her? Because she's got a kid? Is she not good enough for you?'

The guard shook his head. 'Man, you gotta understand. You are here on my say-so. I don't know what your problem is with your lady, but you need to sort it out peaceable or you're both vacating tonight.'

'Don't take it out on her.'

'Just saying. You got to act civilized.' The glass doors slid open to release a blast of warm air, like an oven door. 'Here we go, sir, happy shopping.'

Civilized. It's the end of civilization, he wanted to shout at the guard. The whole country falling apart, the rich getting richer and the poor camping out in their cars – if they're lucky. And inside here, it's all slick and white with fluorescent lights and colorful packaging on the shelves of plenty – but it's all empty, he wanted to scream. All this shit is nothing. But he kept a hold of himself, steered himself between the aisles and the Halloween decorations and picked up the things he needed: cigarettes, a bottle of water for the truck, Skittles for Charlie, and soda. He found a pair of shoes in the kids' section. Sneakers with superheroes on them, although he wavered between Batman and Spiderman. What did Charlie like? He didn't even know.

It didn't matter, he thought. Even if Charlie was Ryan's kid. He could step up. Every kid needs a father figure, a stable home. Not a car.

'Will that be all, sir?' the cashier said with a smile as automatic as the sliding doors. He managed to say thank you and get out of there.

But the parking space where he'd left them was empty. He closed his eyes. In case this was one of his hallucinations. But the car was still gone when he opened them. He stood there, the plastic bag with his purchases dangling from his hand.

'She took off,' said the woman in the RV, leaning through the lace curtains, as if he couldn't see with his own eyes. Crowing about it.

'I can see that,' Clayton said, trying not to cry. 'I'll give you these smokes if you tell me which way she went.'

She eyed the shopping bag and turned Judas quicker than you can change the channel. 'Took off east. Back roads, I reckon.'

'I reckon you'd be right.' He tossed her the pack of cigarettes.

'Menthol,' she said, disgusted.

He might be able to catch her if he hurried. How far could she have got in that rattletrap car?

He roared through the deserted streets, through the suburbs with their neat little houses and manicured lawns, and onto the road out of town. A dull noise filled his head, like static on the TV swallowing up the rest of the picture, the same way fog was coming up from the lake, a white drift lapping at the edge of the tarmac. The needle on his accelerator leapt up to 60, 70. He lost himself in the driving, caught somewhere half-asleep, half-awake, the truck gulping down the miles of dark road.

Until he came round the corner on a road in the woods, and saw her tail lights up ahead, between the trees and the fog. He drove up right behind her to make sure, close enough to see the galloping silver horse on the badge on the trunk. He flashed his lights to tell her to slow down. He just wanted to talk.

He saw the silhouette of Charlie's wild curls twist round in the passenger seat. She rolled down the window and stuck out her hand, waving for him to pass, even as the Colt sped up. He accelerated until he was right behind her and then veered out so that he could pull up next to her, winding the window down. He could hear her transmission screaming. No way she could keep this up. The needle nudged up to 80, 85.

'What the hell are you doing? You're gonna trash your *house*, Lou,' he yelled. It was the wind that pricked tears in his eyes.

She gave him the finger, stabbing it into the air. Then she lost control of the car. The Colt swerved violently and her mouth pulled into a perfect O of surprise. He looked back at the road, just in time to see feral eyes glowing in the darkness and then something leapt up like a shadow and punched a hole through the windscreen, coming down hard on the canopy above his head.

He ducked instinctively and let go the wheel, and the truck shot off the road, bounced heavily through the ditch and plunged into the woods with a sound like cheap wall-paper ripping right through.

Leaves, he realized, not wallpaper, and branches thrashing against the windows. He tried to pump the brakes, to steer a course through the dark foliage, veering away from the big trees that loomed up in the mist, the ones that would crumple the truck like an accordion, obeying the laws of velocity. He didn't want to die like this, alone in the woods.

Branches snapped off against the truck and the thing on top flopped around obscenely, thudding against the roof. He let go, let the truck steer where it wanted, let the woods take him.

He watched in the rear-view mirror for Lou's headlights, because surely she would come back for him, but the road was far behind him now, the trees shrinking his view of it, like a porthole.

The truck slowed and finally came to a stop, kissing up against a huge black willow and rocking back, leaving scrapings of paint on the bark. Clayton felt a sense of terrible calm looking out through the spiderwebbed cracks in the windscreen and the gray fog. There are limits, he thought. Something soft and heavy slid off the roof of the truck onto the ground.

He got out the truck. Gravity felt different. Walking on the moon. Lou was probably making her way toward him right now with a flashlight, picking her way along the trail of devastation his truck had left through the undergrowth, holding Charlie's hand because she wouldn't leave him in the car. Charlie would be sucking his thumb, Clayton thought, trying to be brave for his momma. The thought of that frightened little kid made his heart break. He'd make it up to him, reward him with Skittles and the Spiderman sneakers. Hell, he'd go back and buy the Batman ones too, and it would become a family story they would tell at Thanksgiving. 'Remember that time Uncle Clay crashed his truck in the woods and we had to go looking for him in the fog.' (He wouldn't ask the boy to call him Dad, not if he didn't want to.)

'Lou! Hey, Louanne, I'm over here,' he shouted into the gray, the restlessly shifting trees. But there was no flashlight, no answering yell. They're not supposed to be out here, none of them, so far from *civilization*. Strange things can happen if you stray off the road.

He could hear a rasping breath. Shadows moved in the mist, or maybe it was all inside him, his own breath. He kept his hand on the truck because the fog was so thick he didn't know if he would be able to find his way back if he let go. His fingers were numb. The flecks of paint marking the tree started wriggling into the wood like maggots. They burned from inside, spreading to other trees.

'Louanne,' he whispered. 'Charlie?' He listened hard, trying to hold his own breath. He felt as if something was walking with him, that if he put his hand out, he would touch its shoulder. He thought about all the things in his toolbox in the back of his truck that he could use as a weapon.

He worked his way round to the front, where the noise was coming from. The pale streamers of the headlights lit up swirls and ripples of bark, and a trembling flank, brown fur with white spots.

51

He didn't think Lou was coming. He thought maybe she had turned into that vicious little cat, and carried Charlie away by the scruff of his neck.

The deer raised its head and looked at him with black eyes.

'It's all right,' he said, kneeling down, putting his hand on the animal's warm neck. He could feel the life and strength of it under his palm. It panicked at his touch, kicking out, trying to get to its feet. But there was too much wreckage inside.

He felt like he was falling into its eyes. There were doors opening in the trees all around him, a door swinging open in his head.

Not yours, he thought. Nothing's yours.

'It's all right,' he said again, stroking the animal's neck. It shivered at his touch, but it didn't try to kick again. He didn't know why, but he was crying again. Fat tears slid down the side of his nose and onto its hide.

'I know how to do this.'

I dreamed I was a dream of a dream.

MONDAY, NOVEMBER 10

Detroit Diamonds

The window of Rocket Coffee gives Jonno the perfect view of the hollow shell of the Michigan Central Train Station. The Acropolis of Detroit. Some genius suggested preserving the iconic ruins. That's what everyone's here for, anyway. To gawp at the broken buildings, take their portraits. The only difference between the hipsters breaking into abandoned buildings here and the middle-aged tourists in socks and sandals in the Colosseum is that the former use more filters on their photographs and the latter have audio guides. Not a bad idea, actually. He could do that – write audio tours. The problem, he reckons, is not the obsession with ruin porn, it's that everyone is trying to figure out what it all *means*. It's the human condition, obsessively reading too much into things.

Like the fact that she is forty-six minutes late. And that's thirty-one minutes longer than you should be expected to wait for any girl, unless she's a certified supermodel or the producer on the biopic of your awesome life, according to '10 Rules For The New Gentleman's Guide To Dating' he churned out for some shitty men's site last year. It's all chum to pull in the likes. But eyeballs are more fickle than sharks, and the economy is still in the gutter, and he should be writing a post-post-modern *Moby-Dick*, not trying to come up with smarmy listicles faster than everyone else. But try getting paid for *that*.

Oh, he's been published in obscure literary magazines with a subscriber base of eight, not including the publisher's mother, or the complimentary contributor copies. All the wannabe writers desperately reading each other's stories, as if they could generate enough energy in a magnetic feedback loop that it would draw some of those damn eyeballs over here. But it's all shit. Even his stuff. It's only because he has realized that she's not coming that he can even consider this. Because this is such a disaster, it mitigates his Total Failure As A Writer.

She's not coming.

The despair cuts through the caffeine poisoning. He's already had three cups of coffee, at first because he felt smug, sitting in the window bar, waiting for the hot DJ girl. That was before the Great Wake-Up Call, and then he lost his place when he went back for the third flat white, and now he is wedged in the back, near the bathroom, perched at a little round table that seems specifically designed to be emasculating.

But she was *beaming. At you. Apparently.*

Fuck the beaming. Fuck this depressing ghost town of a city. Fuck his career. He should write a melt-down memoir. An anthem for his generation. Bret Easton Ellis with more man-child ennui. Then she walks in the door, and he swears to fucking God that all the atoms in the room recompose themselves around her. She's wearing jeans and snow boots and a puffy jacket in an electric turquoise that matches her eye-shadow, with jangly earrings and her braids tied up in an elaborate croissant twist.

'Hi,' she says, slinging her bag down onto the table, recklessly enough that he has to grab for his cup. 'Sorry.'

'You say that a lot.' He's grinning. He can't help it.

'Yes, well,' she shrugs. 'What, you didn't get me one?'

'Half an hour ago!'

'You want another?' She indicates his cup, still three-quarters full and he finds himself nodding, even though a fourth will probably tip him into heart-attack territory, like that kid who died from chugging energy drinks. But coffee is natural.

So is herpes.

'But to go, okay?'

'What about breakfast?'

'We'll get pastries. I want you to show me round town. Show me *your* Detroit.'

'What does that mean?'

'Whatever you want it to. Personal perspectives on the city.'

'All right,' she says, with the same tolerantly amused look she had when he walked in on her with her hand between her legs. Definitely love, he thinks.

Inside her jazzy little blue Hyundai, she clips in the radio face and heavy techno blasts out, a whining buzzsaw with a frenetic beat. He winces. It sounds like the grinding teeth of machines on methamphetamines. Good name for a prog rock band. Machines on Meth.

She notices and laughs at him through a bite of almond croissant. 'You were dancing to it on Saturday night.'

'I was drunk!'

'Want me to turn it down?'

'Please.'

'You're a funny guy, Jimmy.' But she flicks the volume knob.

'Jonno,' he corrects.

'I know. I'm messing with you. So, where do you want to go?'

'Back to your place?'

'Not possible.'

'Then mine.' Although the thought of his grubby rental apartment gives him a fresh twist of resentment. And panic. His scattered underwear, the empty pizza boxes, the soggy towels balled up on the floor. He would need an hour, no three, to make it presentable. Actually, probably easier to burn it down.

'Not yet,' she says.

'Then somewhere you like.'

'It'll be cold.'

'I can take it.'

'You going to write about it?'

'Maybe. If it's good.'

'Isn't journalism dead?'

'That's what they tell me.'

'You should start your own video channel. Get advertising.'

'That's what they tell me too. It all keeps changing. I don't know how anyone's supposed to keep up. It's like learning to salsa in the middle of an earthquake.' That's not bad. He should write that down. It would be a good essay. Scratch that, an easy essay. More chum. Maybe she'll open him up to something. He always thought a muse should be sex on legs.

'You're old is the problem,' she says, flicking the turn

indicator. She's wearing black-and-yellow striped fingerless gloves. Her nail polish is chipped.

'Thanks for that.'

'Relax,' she says. 'I'm teasing.'

They drive past the yacht club and she points out the old zoo, all shuttered up, the animals long gone. Maybe they joined in the white flight to the suburbs.

They pass the long stretch of the main beach. Dishwater waves with white caps are worrying the gray sand. He remembers being a teenager in Rhode Island, lying on his stomach to hide his semi, watching the girls rub coconut oil into their skin, or run shrieking into the waves. Such an assortment of girls. It seemed then that they were all available to him, that he could work his way through all of them, the same way he was going to be able to travel to all the different countries, try his hand at different jobs, all the branching possibilities. Keep your options open, his parents told him, but they didn't tell him that growing older is about your options shutting down, one by one.

It's baking in the car. He struggles out of his jacket and pushes up the sleeves of his sweater. *Do men get hot flashes?*

'You're going to have to put it on again,' she warns him, pulling over into a small parking lot opening onto the grass.

'What, here?'

'You asked me to take you somewhere special to me. Belle Isle is happy childhood memories. What?' she challenges. 'You wanted to go urban exploring? Check out the ruins of the American Dream? Maybe you wanted to whack golf balls off the roof of the Packard Plant. Oh wait, I know. You wanted to harvest corn with your *own hands* from an urban farm in the middle of a dirt-poor neighborhood?'

61

'Could be fun,' he says defensively. But she's right. He's read all that shit. It's *all* been done. The original stories are mined out, and all that's left is fool's gold. Or, more appropriately, Detroit diamonds, which is what locals call the blue glass on the street from broken car windows. He feels anxiety slamming into him like the gray waves on the river.

'You been to Secret beach?'

'If I had, would it still be a secret?'

'Come on, grumpy pants.' She swings open the door and the cold snaps like a rubber band against his face. She leans in. 'You asked me to take you somewhere I like. Not somewhere you could find a blog post.'

'Maybe that's a blog post in itself.'

'Very Zen of you.' She slams the car door and starts walking out to a wannabe lighthouse in the grass. He scrambles out after her, pulling his jacket on.

'Hey!' he shouts. 'I hope you're not luring me out here to kill me!'

She turns, walking backwards so he has to jog to catch up, and gives him the wickedest grin. 'Keep up the oral and I won't have to.'

It takes them about twenty minutes of tramping along the path to get there. His jacket is useless against the vicious little wind. They turn off the path to tramp through waist-high weeds and springy bushes, until finally they push through, and the grasses part to reveal a scrubby stretch of beach and a narrow channel of dark water that opens onto the river past the bend.

She spreads her arms like a magician's assistant. 'Secret beach,' she says. 'Also called hipster beach.'

Also vastly overrated. There's no story here.

'What do you think?'

I think I'll say whatever will get me into your pants again. *Which is the trouble, isn't it, boychick? Talking your way into things?* Like petite Monique. Who had a screw loose. Emphasis on 'screw', which allowed him to overlook the 'loose'. She used to crawl under the table at fancy restaurants to blow him. His cock stirs in his pants at the thought. Or Trish, who had a kid. Although he didn't like the kid, and the kid didn't like him. Which is fair enough, because the kid was old enough to see him for what he was, just another tourist stopping off at MILF Island for a cocktail and a picture on the beach before moving on to less complicated destinations. Or Cate, who was everything he wanted. *Until...* Shut up. Stop it.

'It sure *is* secret,' is what he manages. The wind nips and tugs at them, rustling through the grass.

She frowns. 'It's hard to get a real sense of it in winter. They don't really like people coming here. There are no lifeguards, and there's a bad rip current just off the point. A kid drowned there a couple of years ago.'

'What's that?' He points at the columns of black stones, improbably stacked on top of one another, adorning some of the bigger rocks.

She shrugs. 'Art.'

That's a generous description. 'Are they glued together?'

'No. I think that's the idea, that they're not. The craft is in balancing them.' She frowns at the cairns. 'Hey, these are different to the ones I've seen before. Help me.' She grabs onto his hand for purchase and hefts herself up the rock to see.

'Yeah, look. There are faces. Sort of melted together. Neat.'

'I'll take your word for it.' But he can make out the roughest of features hollowed out of the stones, shallow eyes, stretched mouths, as if they're screaming. *How romantic.*

'Woah,' Jen Q says as her boot skids out from under her. Her shoulder slams into the artwork, if that's what it is – if there's a reason it's stacked up out here and not in the Detroit Institute of Art. The column topples like Jenga and the stones plop-plop-plop into the water. He's still holding her hand, and yanks her back to safety. She comes down on top of him, bringing them both crashing to their knees in the wet sand.

'Jesus. Remind me not to take you into a china shop,' he says. Which sets her off again, shaking with laughter. He holds her, freezing damp soaking into his jeans, warm girl in his arms.

This could be alright, he thinks.

Just don't fuck it up.

Writings on the Whiteboard

The quote of the week (written in red marker on the white-board in the detectives' meeting room): 'It's not very neighborly.' It came from a witness statement regarding one Mr. Jackson Brentworth of Livernois Avenue, fatally shot over a borrowed fly mower that wasn't returned. Best part was the damn thing had never even been taken out of the box. Now Mr. Brentworth is residing *in* a box forever and ever, amen. Not very neighborly at all. Man shoulda returned the lawnmower, am I right? The leaden mouths of the general public sometimes drop gold nuggets.

Half of Homicide is here for the briefing, waiting on commanding officer Captain Joe Miranda. Gabi is pinning up the official photographs provided by Evidence Tech. Every angle on the body, every scrap of material recovered from the scene, including trash. Only way the streets get cleaned up these days.

Her partner, Bob Boyd, is picking at his teeth with his fingernail and examining the gunk he scrapes off with forensic interest. His size is useful on the street, although his bull-neck is starting to go wobbly around the edges, and he sweats a lot through the shiny suits he wears to impress. Gabi knows all about it because she gets to share a car with him. In summer, she tried to give him subtle hints, like pulling up outside a laundromat and demanding he go wash his fucking shirt or she wouldn't drive another inch. He doesn't approve of her dressing down, jeans and sweatshirts, but then he didn't have to deal with some knucklehead leaking all the female officers' bra sizes when they got measured for bulletproof vests.

She's pleased to see Ovella Washington, even if she has her head in her own case file, making a real point about it. She's got a lot of hours. She worked Vice before they started running morality out of individual precincts, and Robbery before she transferred to Homicide.

Luke Stricker looks even more brutish since he shaved his head, the kind of guy you would expect to be on the other side of the handcuffs. It complicates matters having him on this, but he's one of the most competent cops on the force. And competence is very attractive. Especially now.

Mike Croff is ticking off the seconds by making little popping sounds with his lips. He notices her annoyance and freezes, mid-pucker. He widens his eyes with cartoonish innocence, turning it into a whistle. Peter and the Wolf. *Doo-doo-di-dit-dit-doo*.

Oh yeah, and young Marcus Jones, sitting on the edge of his seat at attention, his straight-out-of-the-academy eagerness undone by his ridiculous hair style; cornrows with a little rat's tail. She *almost* feels bad about the lipgloss stunt. Turns out he wasn't such an FNG after all, called it in on his cell phone instead of the radio, so the press only got wind of it after the meat wagon was already loaded up. Nothing to see here, move along folks. Saved her ass, and in return she's got him saddled with a dumb nickname. There's already a picture on the noticeboard, his personnel photo badly photoshopped onto Tinkerbell's body, surrounded by fairy dust.

Joe Miranda sweeps into the room and starts talking as if *he's* been the one waiting around. 'All right, let's get this on the road already. Versado, you landed this show, you're running with it.' He sits down on the end of the desk, slicks down his wave of black hair, and knots his hands.

'Yes, sir.' Gabi goes to the whiteboard and uncaps one of the marker pens. 'Officer Jones, if you could run us through your report?'

'Don't forget your magic unicorn, Sparkles!' Bob Boyd cups his hands around his mouth. The good detectives, finest on the force, titter. All except Ovella Washington, whose focus tightens on her file.

Marcus Jones aka Sparkles, now and forever, stands awkwardly, thrown off his game.

'Relax,' Gabi says. 'Just like in the report. But if there's anything you left out the paperwork, now's the time to fill in the details. Start at the beginning.'

'Okay. Right. I was straight off a shooting called in at Vernor and Clarke, round two a.m. Sunday morning. I'm on my own – my partner's in hospital with a burst appendix. By the time I get there, no-one's seen anything. Found some shell casings in the grass, but they could have been from yesterday. Or last week.'

'Cut to—' Gabi prompts.

'Right, right.' He frets at his merit ribbon. It's cute that he wears it. 'So's I get back to my car – and there's a call about illegal dumping down by the river.'

'Well, that's an emergency,' Boyd says.

'It would have been if it was our body being dumped,' Miranda says with calm authority. He's not called 'Ol' Blue Eyes' for the shade of his irises (which are, for the record, Italian-brown), but for his Sinatra cool.

'So I take a shortcut under the bridge near Mexicantown and I see it. Him, I mean. First I think it's an animal. Roadkill or something. But then I see his face. It's clear he's…gone. I keep driving—'

'How is it clear, officer?' Luke Stricker jumps in. Harsher than necessary, Gabi thinks. Cut the kid some slack. She should talk.

'It's in his eyes. There ain't nobody home.'

'You could see all that from your car?' Miranda asks. 'Could have been shock. Kid could still have been alive. You could have got an ID from him.'

Gabi steps in. 'We know he died offsite, sir. No blood at the scene, and the prelim report from the medical examiner indicates that the body was in cold storage for a day or two before it was dumped. It's going to take them a little while to establish time of death, but he was long gone by the time Officer Jones found him.'

'Next time you check before you drive past,' Stricker says. 'Especially with a kid.'

'Yes, sir.'

'Why *did* you keep driving, Officer Jones?' Gabi says.

'Maybe I woulda done it different if my partner was there, but I thought maybe the killer was still nearby. I was looking for a car pulling away, someone running. I called it in on my phone while I was driving. Got half a mile and then turned around. I couldn't leave him lying there.'

'That was good thinking, using your phone,' Miranda says, mildly. 'None of you boneheads would have thought of that.'

'A lot of civilians got police scanners,' Sparkles says. 'I didn't want rubberneckers. It didn't seem right.'

'It's good protocol,' Gabi says. 'We can almost guarantee there will be another body, and when that turns up, let's keep it on our mobiles.'

'The department gonna pay for my minutes?' Croff moans.

'Oh, spare me!' Washington looks up from her file at last. 'When there's another body, there's another body. We all got plenty of our own to deal with. I'm sorry this little boy got killed. It's horrible. But it's one murder. Why should you get all the resources?'

'Washington!' Miranda warns. But Gabi doesn't blame her. There are cases that catch all the attention. Kids especially. The whole department was obsessed with that little girl who got raped and murdered downtown several years ago. But in the meantime, there's a killer who's been gunning down prostitutes for five years. Washington's been following him since her Vice days. Same MO every time – shoots them in the face. Thirteen down and counting, a baker's dozen of hate. Never any witnesses. Nobody wants to talk. And besides, the feeling is that it's just a bunch of whores. 'City should put him on payroll for pest control,' she's heard some of the dickheads in this very department say.

'Just like your killer, Ovella, this is unlikely to be a once-off. There's a good chance of another mutilated corpse turning up. Might be six months, might be tomorrow. Our guy's probably done practice rounds in the past.'

'I'll take that,' Stricker says. He likes the pitbull work, the kind you can dig your teeth into.

'I need *everyone* on it.' Gabi picks up the black marker and tries to write 'John Doe' on the board, but the ink

69

gives out halfway. 'Goddammit.' She tries another pen.

'Shouldn't it be John Fawn?' Croff jokes.

'What?'

'The deer. It wasn't a doe.'

'All right,' she concedes, rubbing out 'doe' and replacing it with 'fawn'.

'John Yearling,' Boyd musters. 'Unlike you pussies, I spend time in the woods.'

'Bambi,' Stricker says.

And that settles it. There is that frisson of rightness, everyone smiling and nodding. Coffee and black humor: the fuel that keeps cops going.

'Very cute,' Miranda says. 'I hear anyone referring to this body as Bambi in public and I'll put you on traffic duty forever. Do not write that down, Versado.'

'Yes, sir. Sorry, sir.' She scrubs 'Bambi' and goes back to 'John Doe'.

Under that, she writes:

ID the body
Find the murder scene
Motivation
Murders with similar MOs
Boyd: Hunting associations, park rangers, nature clubs

'Aw, shit,' her partner complains.

'Us pussies couldn't possibly interview big bad hunter types,' Gabi mocks. 'You've already got an in.'

'That's true. But season's in full swing. You got a million registered hunters in Michigan alone. You want me to go through all of them?'

'You could start with the ones with any kind of record for violence.'

'Apart from shooting widdle animals, you mean?' Croff

says in an Elmer Fudd voice, working his hustle for all it's worth. Every department has workers and slugs, and Croff is definitely Team Mollusc. He lets Stricker do the hard stuff and relies on his smart mouth and leaning on his connections for the rest.

'Domestic assault charges. Unnecessary cruelty to animals. Shooting out of season.'

'Was it a white-tail or a black-tail?'

Gabi takes the photograph off the wall and hands it to Boyd. 'White. That any help determining where the animal came from?'

Boyd puts on his glasses and squints at the photo. 'Means it's from a local population. Black-tail would have been better. He would have had to bring it in from Oregon or Canada. It would have been much easier to trace.'

'There are deer on Belle Isle,' Sparkles says.

'Those are European,' Boyd scoffs. 'Fallow deer. This animal is definitely a white-tail, five months old.'

'How can you tell?'

'Hasn't lost its spots yet,' he says smugly, tapping the white flecks on the flank.

'And fawning happens in May or June,' Washington says. 'Don't make out like it's rocket science, Bob.'

'So we know it's probably from Michigan state, and probably killed recently because the age matches up, more or less.'

'Unless the killer has a freezer full of dead fawns,' Stricker says.

'Point,' Gabi says. 'It's a good fit. Did he get lucky on the first go, or is there a pile of dead deer somewhere of all the ones that didn't match? Bob, I want you to add taxidermists to your list.'

'Give me a break! I've already got a million hunters. Where the fuck am I supposed to get that?'

'There's probably a professional association,' Stricker says. 'Look on the Internet.'

'That sounded a lot like you volunteering.'

'Sure. I'll take it.'

'Fine,' Gabi says. 'And look into associated stuff too.'

Stricker: Taxidermy. Circus freak shows. Other

She can't help thinking that 'other' is not a bad category for their relationship. The divorce rate among cops is high. Not un-coincidentally, high levels of interdepartmental affairs, too. The bosses will turn a blind eye if you keep it on the down-low. She didn't get involved in any of that while she and William were still trying to work things out. But here she is now, screwing brutally competent Detective Stricker on those days their off-duties coincide.

'All right, so what's the motivation? Apart from being a sick fuck?'

'It's on display. He wants attention,' Washington says.

'Not like he put it up on a pedestal on the riverwalk.'

'But she's right. He did want it to be found. He's not trying to cover it up. Kid and an animal.'

'*Black* kid and an animal,' Washington points out. 'What's that say?'

'Could be racially motivated.'

Washington: Race crimes / local hate groups

'What about Satanists?' Croff says. 'Could be an occult murder.'

'Sure.' Gabi rolls her eyes.

'Or voodoo hoodoo shit.'

Satanists. Occult. Voodoo hoodoo shit

'You good with that, Ovella?'

She folds her arms, revealing glittering fingertips – the diamanté appliqués on her nails lead a lot of people to underestimate her. 'Because I'm black? Or because I'm Catholic?'

'Satanists are usually white,' Boyd chips in, trying to be helpful.

'That's racist,' Croff grins. 'You're insulting Satanists of color.'

'You wanna throw in the Michigan Dogman?' Washington complains.

'Knock it off,' Gabi says. 'We need warm bodies on the phone calling the other precincts and districts on broadly similar murders. Don't let anyone try to dump their cold cases on you.'

'Can I sit down now?' the rookie asks.

'Not yet, Sparkles. Was there anything else you noticed at the scene?'

'There was no blood or nothing. And he looked real peaceful. I think he didn't even see it coming.'

'Don't speculate on that until we have more facts.'

'Forensics?' Miranda pushes.

'I'm going to see the ME after this,' Gabi says. 'The dismemberment would have been fatal and there was a wound to the back of his head, near the base of his skull.'

'And the glue holding the two parts together?'

'I've put in a priority request for identifying the bonding agent. Industrial, probably, which should make it easier to trace. But testing is going to take a few weeks unless we can get a lead.'

She writes in her own name.

Versado: Autopsy / Adhesive

'ETA on the results?' Miranda asks.

'Six to ten days. Would have been longer, but we piqued their interest. It's a nice change from bullet wounds and semen.'

Sparkles is still musing. 'There was a lot of graffiti at the scene, but I guess that's normal.'

Gabi scans the photographs. 'Might be worth checking out the tags.'

'What, the killer left his signature?' Croff snipes. 'Wouldn't that be something?'

'Like the idiot who murdered his wife and posted the picture on Facebook?' she says, honey-sweet. 'Or the knucklehead who robbed the gas station on Dearborn two weeks ago still wearing his McDonald's namebadge? Criminals do stupid things all the time.'

Suspicious graffiti tags

'You got an ID on your kid yet?' Miranda asks.

'Stricker and Boyd started on that this morning.'

'Pulled all our missing kids reports and put in a request with the other precincts. Got about a hundred we're going through. Ditched the girls already, working through the boys. Lucky it was cold out, so he looks like he looks.'

She knows what Luke means. Preserved. Couple of days in July, and he'd be swelled up like the Michelin Man. She had that once with a teenager pulled out the water after three days. Her mother kept saying, 'Nah, nah, that ain't my baby. My baby ain't fat like that, my baby ain't got those chubby cheeks.' It took two hours to persuade her otherwise, and she only succeeded because of the tattoo of the seahorse on the girl's ankle. Gabi gets it: you don't want to believe. Not in real life.

'We could hand over the kid's photo to the press,' Boyd says.

'We are not releasing the photo,' Miranda says.

'Doesn't have to be the whole thing. Crop it to a head shot.'

'You gonna make me repeat myself?'

'Just saying.' Boyd scratches his beard.

'We'll give it another day. It's going to be traumatic enough for the family without seeing it in the press.'

'Can I come with you to the medical examiner?' the rookie says. 'I found him. I feel like I should see him through.'

'Fine by me, Sparkles,' Gabi says. '*If* your precinct commander signs off on it. But you better know that if you're in, you've bought a ticket for the whole ride. I will use you.'

'Thank you, ma'am.'

'Ovella, can you get on the Michigan Intelligence Center? Mike, you've got a friend in the FBI, right?'

'I don't have any friends, Gabriella, you know that.' No, just three kids and a happy marriage to a human resources manager. It's what makes him such a colossal wise-ass. He can afford to be.

'If you could talk to someone with access to a better database than we have, that would be helpful. And it would be worth a beer.'

'Make it a six-pack.'

'Okay, people, everybody clear? You find anything, you let me know soon as.'

'What if we run out of minutes and have to radio it in?' Sparkles asks.

'Use a code.'

'How about "Faline"?' Croff says, tapping away at his smartphone.

'What's that?'

He turns the screen to show them. 'Bambi's girlfriend in

the movie. And that's you now, isn't it, Gabriella?'

There's enough laughter that she lets it go. 'Fine. Faline it is. Everyone else, we're calling in to all the precincts. Similar stiffs, MOs, any connections. Start local, go as far as it takes. Biggest priority is identifying the boy and finding the rest of him. The deer too.' She writes it down. The marker gives out on her halfway through 'find the rest'. She throws it at the wall.

'Is there *one* fucking pen in this precinct that writes?'

BEFORE

History of Art

Clayton disappeared into the work. Otherwise he had too much time to think, about his cracked windshield and the dent in his grill and the blood on the tarpaulin in the back of his truck. Everything was so muddled in his head. The memories were like silverfish, that skittered away into dark corners. It was easier to look away than try to grab hold of them.

(Don't look in the refrigerator.)

Besides, the work was flowing. He was inspired. Like he hadn't been since he was twenty years old, when he was too young and too stupid to have doubts about what he was doing. He could slip away into it, like diving into the deepest part of the lake: the same pressure in his head, the tightening in his ears, the hurt in his chest, aching for air.

When he surfaced, blinking in the fluorescent light in the basement, hours had gone by. Days maybe. His body reasserted itself with all its tiresome urges. His stomach roiled with hunger, his back ached, his hands were cramped, with fresh calluses. But he had new work, in new materials, finally making use of all the things he had squirreled away in his basement over the years; pieces made of clay and wire and newspaper and reclaimed wood. Strange and beautiful work, like he'd never made before. The sculpture he'd promised Patrick languished untouched in the yard. It seemed brutish and clumsy now. But he couldn't be sure. He couldn't trust himself to judge. He could be going mad, he decided.

The last time he had black-outs was nearly ten years ago, when he was drinking too much at the squat in Eastern Market. He'd hustled his way in among the youngsters, because it felt alive and vibrant: a real arts scene, like Paris in the twenties, or New York in the seventies, nineties Berlin. But he didn't fit in. He was too old, his work was too strange, he didn't know how to talk to the endless stream of girls, with their tattoos and bright hair, who came to hang out, to pose for portraits or be photographed, usually topless, sometimes naked.

He never took to acid or any of those other drugs, although they were going around among the kids. Coke, speed, mescaline. The late-night parties where he was always the odd one out, sitting on his own on the couch. They would come and sit right next to him and not talk to him. He would drink to make it bearable, and wake up oblivious to whatever had happened the night before, stumbling out into the shared living space to ice-cold vibes. He would spend the day miserable, waiting for someone to finally confront him about what he'd done. Some inappropriate thing he'd said, some dumb practical joke that everyone had taken too seriously.

But he hadn't been drinking. Or sleeping, or eating, or taking his pain pills. He avoided the refrigerator, the thin Plexiglas shelves yanked out and set beside it. He also took care not to look at the black stains on his wall, which seemed to swell when he passed them. A trick of the light, mold from the newspapers piled up in teetering stacks in the hallway.

He opened a can of beans in tomato sauce, poured it into a dish and put it in the microwave. The device hummed and the glass plate turned round and round and round until PING. He was reassured by the normalcy of this, even if the act of eating seemed repulsive.

Spooning the food in, chewing the soft pulp, his tongue rolling it back toward his throat, swallowing – it was all automatic, like he was functioning on the muscle memory of someone he used to be. He patted his pocket for cigarettes and realized he didn't want them, the chemical taste in his mouth, the way they sucked away his breath.

He felt unlike himself. 'Unlike.' He said it aloud. Words sounded strange. The meaning unraveled. It was as if Clayton was the skin and bones he pulled on.

He had to get out of the house. He had to talk to someone. Show them what he'd done.

(Don't look in the refrigerator.)

He had to fire these clay figurines – the ones he doesn't remember making, but that seem familiar. It's why he doesn't normally work in clay – because he doesn't have an oven, but he reckons Miskwabic Pottery would let him use their student kiln. He used to help pack tiles into boxes and move big bags of wet clay for Betty Spinks in exchange for pottery lessons.

He packed up the figurines and took them out to the garage, ignoring the cracks webbed out across the windscreen – he'd have to get that fixed. He hauled the tarp out of the back and flipped it over to hide the rusty stains.

Yanking up the garage door, some part of him expected

it to open onto nothingness. But it was a bright late-autumn day, the low cloud cover catching the sunlight and spreading it around.

He drove past rows of wooden houses with peeling paint and overgrown grass, the bare trees reaching up their branches as if to rip a hole in the sky, and took a shortcut through Indian Village, where the houses got a lot nicer, and all dolled up for Halloween, with pumpkins in the windows and spooky floss draped over the big old oaks and elms lining the driveways of the historic homes.

He pulled into the gravel parking lot of the cosy Tudor-style building and nudged the truck right up against the fence under the tree near the road, away from the other cars, to make it harder to spot his broken windscreen.

The fat security guard held open the door for him as he carried his load in, warm air wafting out.

'Help you there, sir?'

'I'm fine,' Clayton said. It *almost* felt true, here in this bright shop with its shelves of arts and crafts tiles with their iridescent glaze. Historic buildings all over the city were decorated with Miskwabic mosaics, hallways turned into geometries of light, cornerstones and edgings marked out in bright patterns. But they don't sell anything like that here. Instead they have 'gift tiles', botanicals and devotionals and simple geometrics, the city skyline, a Tigers D, street numbers, a little ballerina girl, pumpkins for Halloween. You take all the beauty in the world and you boil it down to kitsch, he thought.

Inside, a family was browsing while a hipster with wild hair talked them through the history, paying special attention to the twenty-something daughter. Betty was behind the counter, her graying hair in a loose plait, wearing a red sweater and a necklace of colored beads. She looked up at the sound of his voice, peering over her glasses at him. 'Knock me down. Clayton Broom, where *have* you been hiding yourself?'

'I got this,' he said, lamely, indicating the box in his arms.

'I can see that, sweetie,' she replied. He'd always thought of her as no-nonsense apple pie. 'You want to bring that in back? Hey, Robin, when you're done flirting, can you mind the register?'

'Sure, Betty.' The youngster with the twists of hair nodded at him in a friendly way, but his attention was already swinging back to the daughter, who absolutely *had* to look at the earrings in the display case. Clayton watched them circling each other with the documentary dispassion of someone who had never got that right.

Betty marched through to the firing room, past the two industrial kilns sitting alongside each other like a history lesson – the old brick oven with the burn marks down the front beside the aggressively shiny steel kiln – to her office.

She cleared a space on the desk, shoving her files onto her chair, so he'd have space to set down the box. 'Now, what have we got here? Can I take a peek?' But she was already folding back the cardboard flaps and taking out one of the figurines, a woman with a bird's head, like a skinny Degas ballerina, her arms flung wide as if she could lift off. There were a flock of them in the box, with various faces. 'Hmmf,' she said, but he could tell she was impressed. 'You been practicing?'

'Trying new things,' he said.

'That's important. I got my little god-daughter to try pottery, and now her parents are complaining they haven't got room for all her masterpieces.'

'Me too. I don't have space. I've been on a...binge. It all came out of me. It keeps coming.'

'Well, that's great. You got some of the muse pixie dust to share around, you let me know. I've been experimenting, too. What do you think?' She gave a self-deprecating nod at the workspace countertop, where an elaborate vase of overlapping folds glazed in delicate greens and whites running to dusky pink at the tip sat next to a decrepit old laptop. 'I've been playing with shapes in nature. Flowers, insects, sea anemones.'

Clayton examined the tulip vase, the twirl of petals unfurling from the base. 'It's pretty,' he managed and then blurted it out. 'I think I have a brain tumor, Betty.'

Her eyes softened. 'That's a big jump, honey. Have you seen a doctor about this?'

Clayton shook his head. 'I don't trust 'em. They all work for the pharmaceutical companies. But my old man died of pancreatic cancer. I know the signs. I've been feeling shaky, and I've been seeing things. I can feel it inside me, Betty, like an octopus in my head, getting its tentacles into everything.'

'Sit yourself down, Clay. You want a cup of coffee? Tastes like gasoline, but it'll perk you up a little.'

He sank down into the seat by the door, lower than he expected it to be. She set the clay figure carefully back into the box, careful not to damage it, then perched on the edge of the desk beside him.

'You been sleeping?'

'I don't know.' He corrected himself, 'Must have. I've been dreaming. Bad dreams. People with papier-mâché heads. Monsters in the woods.'

'You've been neglecting yourself, honey. You should go home and get some rest, eat some food, then go see a doctor. Get some tests done. I'm sure it's not a tumor.' She gave his shoulder a hard squeeze. He could feel how strong and bony her fingers were, like coral. 'You get yourself home and take care of yourself. You got someone who can help you?'

He nodded, fighting back the tears. Sympathy was the worst. Betty was savvy enough to see it. She closed up the box and changed the subject to brisk business. 'Well. You leave these with me, and I'll get them fired in the student kiln. Call you when they're ready to come and glaze, unless you want to leave them raw, which could work for these. You want to pay now or COD?'

'I'll pay now. Can't guarantee I'll have the cash later.' He stood up to fish crumpled notes out of his pocket.

'Up to you, sweets. Twenty bucks. You want to pay me now, that's fine. You want to pay me in kind later, that's good too. God knows the storeroom needs cleaning out. We got boxes of stock in there, I don't even know what's broken, what's last season.'

'I'll pay now, I'm flush.' It was a lie, but he didn't want to owe her. He smoothed the note out on the desk, ironing the creases flat with his fingers. The moth-wing texture of it got into the back of his teeth. 'You ever think about how rigid the world is?'

'Clay isn't. This material we work with, I mean, not you.'

'But I'm rigid, too. We're all locked in to what we are. Take this,' he held up the note.

'I intend to, sweetie.'

'It's nothing. But people believe in it. Money makes the rules. This is what things *cost*. This is what you have, where you are, what you are, what you can be. Money is a dream that has made itself definitive.' He was caught up in it, his tongue doing a million miles an hour. It happened sometimes when he hadn't seen other people for a while. 'Do you know that story about Michelangelo?'

'That he was homosexual?'

'Not that. About the Pieta, the Madonna and Christ. When he finished sculpting it, he struck it and cried out, "Now speak". He expected his art to live. But it didn't. How could it?' He was on the point of tears again.

'I think God's the only one who gets to breathe life into mud, sweetie. And you're wrong, about being locked in.' She patted the box full of bird girls. 'You see this, Mr. Smartypants? You see how far you've come, how much you've evolved as an artist? Late-bloomer, sure, but you've transcended *yourself*, Clayton Broom. Don't come here talking about rigid.'

He nodded, trying to remember how to look happy, the precise facial muscle arrangements. 'Thank you,' he managed. But he wondered if this was really what he wanted after all.

Trajectories

There are trajectories that cut through our lives, Gabi has found, that link things together. Sometimes those are literal, like the scar under Bambi's arm.

A few years ago there were so many unclaimed bodies at the Wayne County morgue that the city had to rent a truck to store them all in, piled three-deep like a short stack. Only pancakes don't get toe tags. It wasn't that nobody loved them enough to come get them; the families had to save up to be able to pay for their funerals.

Now they've opened an additional pathology lab up at the university, and Bambi is enough of a novelty to get special priority. The new facilities still smell like dead people and preservatives and cleaning products and that peculiar metal tang you can taste in the back of your mouth. Hearts still make the same wet slop sound when they land in a bucket full of organs. The corpses on the metal tables are still uninhabited shells.

'Foreclosed people,' she observes to Marcus. The rookie nods sagely, missing the joke. He's got a long way to go.

Boyd digs in his ear with one finger. 'I think they're more

human like this. When you shoot an animal, you can only really appreciate what made it an animal when it's gone.'

'That's beautiful, Bob, especially considering you still shoot them anyway. Can you quit picking at yourself?'

'It's itchy.' He wipes the wax off on his pants. 'I saw an ad for ear candles in a magazine. Do you think that works?'

'Why don't you try it and report back?'

There is a small crowd of people in scrubs gathered around her stiff. She can tell it's Bambi by the six-inch dip in the sheet between the constituent parts of boy and deer.

Dr Mackay is poking around under the sheet, talking in a low voice. He looks like he's from another century, with deep grooves in his forehead you could play like an LP record if you had a turntable. He keeps trying to retire, and they keep asking him to come back. There are two cops at the back, craning their necks to see.

'Move it along, boys. This isn't your case.'

'We just wanted a look. That's some crazy shit, Detective.'

'Yeah, yeah, this takes the crazy-shit cake. Now hop.' Boyd makes as if to move toward them, and his bulk is enough to get them going.

'You letting every sightseer in, Dr Mackay?' Gabi snaps. 'Should we be charging?'

'They got a body in here, same as you, Detective. Little more clear-cut than yours.' He sounds as if he blames her personally. 'And the others are students. There's a lot of interest in this, as you might imagine.' He nods at the serious young people in scrubs. 'You're excused.'

Boyd pinches his nose. 'Didn't you wash him?'

'We've flushed the body several times with the high-pressure hose. What you're smelling is the contents of the bucket. Stomach acid, gall and feces. Stuffing. Your killer

88

didn't do a particularly good job.'

'You need some lipgloss, Sparkles?' Boyd teases Marcus, who is breathing hard through his nose.

'No thank you, sir. I'm mostly interested in the autopsy.'

'Aren't we all,' Gabi says.

Mackay flips the sheet, revealing the corpse, already laid open. Human excavations – the casual violation of the body's integrity. They all peer into the abdominal cavity. 'Very inefficient. See here, where he cut through the stomach. He made a hell of a mess.'

'It's not a hunter,' Boyd says. 'Hunter wouldn't do such a half-assed job of gutting something.'

'Unless he was in a hurry. Besides, I'd venture that there are a lot of amateurs running around the woods with semi-automatics who wouldn't know the front end of a deer from its ass.' Gabi nudges the bucket beside the table with her shoe. It's full of wadded-up paper and a flaky fabric, sodden and reeking. 'What did you mean by stuffing?'

'Newspaper at a guess, although we'll need to send it for testing. It was used to fill the cavity, probably to keep the shape after he removed the organs before he stuck it back together.'

'Had to look right,' Gabi ventures.

'Why newspaper?' Sparkles says.

'What he had lying around. I'm pretty sure it's not what professional taxidermists use. What *do* they use? Sawdust? Emulsifying foam?'

'Don't ask me,' Boyd shrugs. 'You put Stricker on that.'

'I believe they make casts,' Dr Mackay says. 'Now, here's your fatal wound.' He points out the blood-crusted hole halfway up the boy's neck. 'Blunt trauma severed the verte-brae. Could have been a hammer and chisel, but there was a massive application of force, and the bruising around the area suggests it was mechanical, probably pneumatic. I'd guess it was some kind of nail gun, which is something I'm telling you, not putting in the report because it's speculation. If you could bring me the nail, that would be wonderful. But as you can see by this tissue damage, he dug it out. Possibly with pliers.'

'How hard is it to get a nail gun?' Gabi asks.

'Hardware store sells them over the counter,' Boyd says. 'I'll run a check.'

'Now, this is the really neat part,' Mackay says. 'You see the seam where he was joined to the deer? I had to cut through it, but you can see in the cross-section, here, how the tissue has fused.'

'What does that mean?'

'Like the kind of gluing a plastic surgeon might do, but not quite. It's extraordinary really; a chemical reaction has caused the proteins to break down and mesh with each other. Think of it as a flesh weld. I've mailed some colleagues about it.'

'Welding. Nail guns. We got fuckin' Handy Manny on the loose,' Boyd says.

'I like how he tried to hide it by brushing up the fur. It's a nice touch. Oh, I do have something else interesting for you. You'll like this.'

'Oh boy,' Gabi says.

Mackay raises the boy's skinny limb to reveal the soft private folds of the armpit, with its first tufting of pubescent hair. It feels somehow more invasive than seeing him laid open and Gabi's first instinct is to look away.

'Look,' Mackay says, so she has to. Bambi has an old scar on his tricep. A pucker of scar tissue just above his

90

armpit, like a tiny daisy. 'Here's where the slug went straight through. He was lucky. Inch to the right and it would have re-entered the body, gone into the chest cavity.'

Not so lucky this time, Gabi thinks.

Studs and Holes

'Stop messing around, he's no good.' Cas leans over Layla, her chest brushing against the back of her head, and takes over control of the mouse.

Her best friend is wearing a plastic cat mask, because that's what the toy shop had in stock. They needed some kind of disguise, and they were cheaper than the Guy Fawkes masks, which are all manufactured in a sweatshop in China anyway. The mask makes Cas look like she's a crazy-hot superhero: the Kitty Avenger, whereas Layla just looks like a dumb-ass. As per usual.

'Hey. Maybe I *wanted* to talk to him,' Layla says as Cas clicks away from the cute boy with scruffy hair and glasses. Little on the plus side, but hey, not like Lay's any kind of super-catch either. Ask Dorian. Just thinking his name tugs at her insides.

'That's not what we're here for,' Cas says. 'And, please. Those glasses were so faux.' She clicks next, next, next, through the live camera feeds. A girl playing guitar, mumbling a song off-key through the fall of hair over her face. A little kid sprawled in rumpled Batman sheets playing video games, who doesn't even look up. Probably forgot he left the program running. A guy with acne speckled like constellations across his face, who grins into the camera when he sees them and raises one hand, but Cas has already clicked away.

'It's gross how they don't even tidy up,' Layla complains. Even though it's reassuring to know that everyone's a slob. Everyone's messy life hanging right out there in the open, like their own private reality TV show. You can't look away. The roulette of human connection.

'Did *you* tidy up, Miss Priss?' Cas snaps.

'I'm naturally cleanliness-inclined. And get your boobs off my head. Can't you put those things away?' She shoulders her, half-heartedly.

'Can't help it. They got a mind of their own.' Click. Click. Click. Next. Next. Next.

'They should have a national flag and a constitution,' Layla grumbles. 'I really have to do my homework.'

'What homework?'

'History assignment. Belgian colonialism in the Congo.'

'You *picked* that,' Cas accuses. 'No way Mr. Jeffries assigned that.'

'I want to know about my history.'

'I'm more worried about my present. And you're only half African-American. Congo, my ass.'

'Da-mn,' Cas pauses. A man with architectural cheekbones is putting on makeup, thick glitter eye-shadow and fake lashes that curl up almost to his eyebrows.

'Hey sweeties,' he says, a little wistful. 'I like the get-up. Want to keep me company while I get ready?'

'Sorry, Ru Paul. We're on the prowl,' Cas says. Next.

'She seemed cool.'

93

'Yeah, okay. We'll see if we can come back later. God knows you need makeover tips.'

And then Cas hits what she's been looking for. Not so hard to find. Layla's surprised it's taken them this long. He's been clicking through too, lying in bed with his shirt off. His face is wide open. Naked. Like the pale sausage hanging out of his jeans, only semi-erect. But he perks right up when he sees them.

'Well hello there, soldier,' Cas says in her best Lana del Rey purr.

'Hi,' he manages. They've watched quite a bit of porn. Layla has seen a lot of penises. But they're still endlessly fascinating in their variety. Like messy rooms.

'What's with the masks?' he says.

'All the better to show you our tits,' Cas says in that sultry put-on voice, and Layla has to stop herself from laughing out loud. 'What's your name, baby?'

'Why?' His hand is jerking up and down. His teeth are bared in a smile-grimace.

'So I can scream it later when I'm thinking about you.'

'Gavin,' he says. 'Now.'

'Do it now?' Cas cocks her head at Layla, exaggerating the gesture so the meaning still comes through, even with the mask, as if she can't quite believe what she's hearing. 'You mean *right* now?'

'Your tits,' he gasps, his hand a blur. His cheap camera doesn't have enough resolution to cope. 'Show me…'

'You first.' Cas leans right into the camera, shrugging her shoulders together to amplify her cleavage.

'What?'

'Show me *your* tits.'

He slows down, uncertain. 'You want me to…'

'Show me your tits, baby.' She leans in with a sexy little growl. 'Show me that man nip. That makes me really hot. I bet you got tight little ones, like studs, am I right?'

'What?' he repeats. His hand slows.

'Studs. Little shiny metal things on shoes and jackets?' Layla adds helpfully. 'Kind-of military fashion thing?'

Cas bumps her with her shoulder, telling her to cut it out, stick to the script. But Layla's bored of the script. The petty humiliations Cas insists on.

'Uh. What?' Some of the blood flow seems to be rerouting back to his brain along with the realization that they're not going to deliver.

'You keep saying that,' Cas mocks. 'What. What. What. Am I not enun-ci-a-ting clearly enough for you? Don't sweat it, big guy. Well, can't really call you that, can I? Smaller-than-average guy. But hey, it's not your fault you have a retarded-looking cock.'

'Fuck you. Fuck you bitches.' He tucks himself back into his pants, reaching for his mouse with the other hand to click away. But not before Cas manages to get in the last word.

'Not with *that* thing, thanks. But don't worry, Gavin, we've been recording this. You're going viral tomorrow.' It's a blatant lie, but he doesn't know that. He goggles like an asphyxiating fish. 'No, wait—'

Cas shuts the window down and flops onto Layla's bed, barely missing NyanCat, who opens one eye warily and then wraps her tail over her nose. 'Oh my God, that was classic. Clas-sic. Right?'

'Yeah, well,' Layla shrugs. Then perks up with indignation: 'And you can't say "retarded", Cas.'

'C'mon, he had it coming, and please, bitch, it's just a

word.' She rubs the cat on the top of her head with her knuckle. 'Don't you think so, Nyan, baby?' She lifts the cat up and nuzzles her face. NyanCat treads the air, panicky, and then goes limp and submits, purring. Typical. Not even felines are immune to Cas's sheer force of personality. 'I know what will cheer you up,' she says.

'Watching a movie?'

'Doing another one!'

'Hello, homework?'

'Doesn't this count as sociology? Gender studies or something?'

'Yeah, sure, I'm going to include it in my college application essay.'

'You probably could, you know, if you put the right spin on it.'

'I'm not some bag of dicks on SpinChat, Cas. You can't play me.'

'Hey, girls.' Her mom creaks open the door.

'Mom!' Layla rips off the mask, which she knows only makes her look guilty. 'You're supposed to knock!'

'So you can click away from the porn? LOL.'

Layla winces with genuine pain. 'Oh God, Mom! No-one actually *says* that. What do you want?'

'Hey, Ms. Versado.' Her friend gives a cheery wave, still wearing her mask. She perks up around Layla's mom like boys do around Cas's chest. 'We were rehearsing our lines.'

'With masks?'

'It helps us get into character. It's a theater exercise,' Cas says glibly.

'I was going to offer you cocoa.'

'Yeah, right, Mom. What do you *really* want?'

'I need some help with my computer. And then I can

bring you cocoa. If you're actually doing your homework and not messing around on the Internet.'

'What's wrong this time?'

'It's not connecting. And the machines at work don't.'

'Don't what? Finish the sentence, Mom.'

'Work. They don't work. You *are* in a mood tonight. Is it boy trouble? Because, you know, YOLO.'

'Mom! God. Okay, I'm coming. Just please don't speak any more.' She shoves away from the desk. 'No prank posting from my accounts, okay?'

'Would I do that?' Cas bats her eyelids. 'Bye, Ms. Versado!'

Layla flings herself down at her mom's laptop in the living room. 'What's wrong with it?'

'I'm looking for pictures of dead bodies and all I'm getting is cartoons.'

'Okay, there's your problem. You had safe search on. Just type in your search again. What is it?'

'Dead bodies plus animals.'

'I am *not* typing that. What are you looking for specifically?'

Her mother sighs. 'Unusual corpses that might have been reported in the last few years. Animal-human hybrids. Strange taxidermy projects in Michigan or surrounds.'

'Is this the kid?' Layla glances at the Nikon camera her mom uses to take her own crime-scene photos, the card reader plugged into the USB port.

'It's a case, Lay. Don't ask questions.'

'Don't you have a police database for this?'

'Sure,' she says, dripping sarcasm. 'As useful as always. I've put in a request to the Michigan Intelligence Center.'

'And your fancy new computers?' The new Public Safety

Headquarters looks like it belongs in TechTown, all gray and blue concrete and glass, with a parking lot big enough to accommodate news vans. Inside there's a proper reception area with comfy couches and glass cases of memorabilia and trophies, meeting rooms with AV facilities, a gym with TVs above the treadmills, a real coffee machine – and the detectives' desks in depressingly identical gray cubicles.

Layla feels almost nostalgic for the old precinct on Beaubien, where she'd hung out, sometimes doing her homework in the corner of her mom's office with its wood paneling and dappled glass and big black filing cases and a computer that was only good for holding down paperwork. And, yeah, okay, revolting stained floors and the awful interrogation room the size of a broom closet, where people wrote messages on the walls like 'Emmie, I'm so sorry, I didn't mean for this to happen, God is love, please God help me.'

She remembers how shocked she was, at thirteen, seeing a photo tacked up of a dead naked woman laid out like a starfish, the camera aiming right between her legs. Someone had written 'Killer: Spongebob Squarepants?' in ballpoint across the top of it. Her mom had pulled the picture off the noticeboard, the red thumbtacks popping out and rolling across the floor. 'Sorry, beanie. Ignore it. Dumb cop humor.'

She knows all about that. She comes from a long, proud line on her dad's side. Her great-grandpappy was a firefighter, his son was a sergeant, and then her dad turned traitor and went private security, even though it's safer, better paid, with benefits. She knows she's supposed to continue the family tradition because po-lice is in her blood, but as far as she's concerned, it's just testosterone. Like the mind-control parasites you get from cats. Toxoplasmosis.

If life is all determined by chemical signals, hers are telling her to move on, little girl, right on out of Motor City. Anywhere but here. Anything but po-lice.

'Our fancy network got a fancy virus,' Gabi says. 'Someone was downloading porn and it had a spartan or something.'

'Trojan,' Layla corrects automatically.

'All Greek to me.'

'Mom!' Layla cringes.

'The IT guys swear we'll be back up tomorrow, but in the meantime...'

'Can't you just fire all the useless cops?'

'There would be nobody left. Come on, beanie, you're always telling me you can find anything on the Internet.'

'It's like the universe that way. Constantly expanding,' Layla says. 'But it's mainly creeps and freaks, Mom, I'm warning you.'

'I think my killer would exactly fit those criteria.'

She pulls up the search results. 'Well, here we go. Animal-human hybrid corpses. It's all yours.'

'Great.' Her mother puts on her glasses and squints at the screen. *Island of Dr Moreau*, the East River Monster, 25 Creepiest Real Science Experiments, that horrible mouse with the ear growing out of it, a two-headed squirrel in a dress and twirling a parasol, among 307,000 other results that get even weirder.

'What is—?' Gabi cocks her head. 'Oh. Right. Is that supposed to be his tail or a tentacle?'

'I'll exclude furries and hentai in your search terms. Unless you think that's going to be helpful?'

'No. No I don't think so.'

'You're going down a nasty rabid hole, Mom. Good luck.'

Layla nudges open her bedroom door with her hip, carrying black coffee for both of them, because cocoa is for little kids, to find her friend looking suspiciously thoughtful, scrolling through a forum with some very dubious gifs.

'Hey, you'll never believe what my mom just said – oh sweet baby Jesus, you had so better not be posting pictures of me to some bugfuckcrazy porn site.'

'Depends,' Cas grins. 'Got any of you when you were ten?'

'What the hell are you doing?'

'Catfishing.'

'We're not doing that.'

'But little SusieLee's already got two messages.'

'You need another hobby. Ideally one that involves making very finicky, time-consuming things to sell on Etsy.'

'Like homemade tampons with girl power slogans?'

'You are disgusting.'

'You like it.'

'Yeah,' Layla admits. 'Bitch.'

'Slut.'

'Love ya.'

'I know.'

I dreamed I was a man.

TUESDAY, NOVEMBER 11

Scar Tissue

The old bullet wound in the kid's armpit gives Gabi something she can work with. Six hundred and forty-seven non-fatal shootings in Detroit last year. But the city's not so soul-decayed that a six-year-old kid catching a stray bullet from a gang war doesn't make the news. Not yet, anyway. It helps that the ambulance broke down en route and the officers on the scene had to drive the kid to the hospital in a patrol car. Five years ago, which meant it took some digging, but there is a trail of paperwork that leads right back to him.

His name is Daveyton Lafonte. Eleven years old. He has been missing since Friday afternoon. The parents filed a missing persons report with the 10th Precinct, who were not answering their phones when Gabi had Sparkles calling round to every police station yesterday. Blame it on bureaucratic failures, lack of resources, lack of funding, lack of giving a shit.

They drive up to the house in Ewald Circle with the bad tidings. It's her and Bob Boyd, who is surprisingly good with grief (he credits the suit), and Sparkles, who is getting a crash course in terrible conversations you never want to have, but will, over and over again.

Gabi has found that small talk works like stepping stones to bridge the shock of the gap between 'I'm sorry to inform you that your son has been killed. May we come in?' and the brutality of 'I need to ask you some questions'.

The hows that come in between. Skirting round the issue. Using technical terms. 'Lateral bisection.' 'Possible hunting accident.' 'There was a dead animal on the scene.' Testing them to see what they know, how they react, because the parents are suspects too. The paralysis of disbelief that she has to penetrate. The official script only gets you so far.

'Do you have a recent picture of him?' Gabi asks the parents as gently as she can. On the piano, next to a goofy candid shot of the boy peering through the grill of an oversized hockey helmet, and a school portrait, three-quarter profile, looking hopefully to a future he'll never see, there's a photograph of Daveyton with the disgraced former mayor, who is now doing jail time.

She picks it up. The kid looks worried by the attention, or maybe by Kwame Kilpatrick's expression, brow furrowed, mouth open, speechifying. Maybe his kid instincts told him the mayor was a rotten, corrupt thug.

'We were all real proud at the time,' Mrs. Lafonte says, taking the frame out of Gabi's hands and putting it back on the piano. She readjusts it, angling it just so. 'He shook us all by the hand. Didn't mean so much to Davey, though. He wanted to meet Steve Yzerman. Always loved the Red Wings. Kwame promised he'd set it up. He wanted to play hockey, but all that equipment is expensive.'

'Mayor promised our boy wouldn't get hurt again,' Mr.

Lafonte says. He is sitting bolt upright on a black leather recliner that's not designed for it.

Mrs. Lafonte makes a strangled bird sound in her chest. She doesn't seem aware of it, as if her body is something detached from her. Marcus looks down at his shoes, stricken. There's a dreadful pause.

'Can I get you some coffee?' Daveyton's mother asks, clutching at social ritual.

'No, thank you.' Jesus, she hates this part of the job. 'Do you play?' She indicates the piano.

'Used to,' Mrs. Lafonte says, grateful for the question. 'I performed with the Detroit Symphony Orchestra once. But that was before the arthritis. Always hoped Davey would pick it up. But he was more interested in those little fighting critters. What are they called?'

'Pokémon?' Gabi suggests. 'My daughter liked those.' Layla was three or four, so they only caught the tail-end of it, but she remembers hustling her past the toy aisle. There were so many things they tried to control, her and William. It was easier when Layla was little. When they could simply change the channel on Barney. They had long debates about whether to let her play with Barbie or toy guns, and why there wasn't a police officer Barbie *with* a toy gun. But then Layla started developing her own tastes and opinions, and the whole world came rushing in at her, and there was nothing they could do to shield her from it.

'Battle Beasts,' her husband says, dully.

'Battle Beasts! That's it. You get the toys, but you're supposed to have a fancy phone that they can interact with, to fight other kids. Are you sure you don't want something to drink?'

'This is too much,' Mr. Lafonte says. 'I can't—'

'The first few days are critical. Why don't you point Officer Jones to the kitchen, and he can make us *all* some coffee. And maybe you could show us Daveyton's room?' They're looking for signs of an unhappy home, the markers of violence, hidden doors, secret rooms, locked basements, the smell of blood or bleach.

'No, no, I'll make the coffee. I think I should keep busy, don't you?' Mrs. Lafonte flashes them a brittle smile. 'You get on without me. I'll be right back.' But she drifts up the stairs leading up to the second floor. Marcus moves as if to go after her, to steer her toward the sunlight coming in the kitchen windows down the hall, but Gabi shakes her head. Leave her be.

'Could we see his room?' Gabi tries again.

'Are you sure it's our boy?' Mr. Lafonte says, daring her to be wrong about this thing they have brought into the house.

'You'll need to identify him. I think maybe it should be you, Mr. Lafonte. No need to put your wife through that.' She looks him in the eyes. 'But yes, we're sure.'

He lets go of hope like a helium balloon. It seems to have been the only thing holding him up. His shoulders hunch over and he tilts forward, his whole body crumpling. 'We moved up here to get away from all that,' he says. 'After the shooting. It's a good neighborhood. This isn't supposed to happen in *good* neighborhoods.'

'Bad things happen everywhere, Mr. Lafonte. Forgive me, but I have a list of routine questions I need to go through with you. You won't like some of them.'

'My son is dead, Detective—'

'Versado,' she fills in for him.

He waves the name away. 'You think your questions can hurt me?'

So she goes through them, systematically. Where Daveyton was last seen. Who he was seen with. Did he have any friends who might have been a bad influence? Any gang-related activity? Any adults who showed a special interest in him? Did he have any hobbies? Had he mentioned any encounters with strangers? Any medical conditions? Was he on any medication? Or drugs? Any trouble at school or in the neighborhood?

'In this neighborhood?'

Behind him, Mrs. Lafonte plods down the stairs, carrying a plastic laundry basket, and vanishes into the kitchen. Routine, like small talk, to find your way back, because the most risible thing about death is that life carries on.

'You got any hunting buddies?' Boyd asks.

'No. Why would you ask that?' Mr. Lafonte is getting more and more confused.

'You ever take him out into the woods?'

'What is this?' Outrage jerks Mr. Lafonte's spine upright.

'We're trying to cover all the bases, sir. All lines of enquiry. It's possible it may have been a hunting accident.'

'What happened to my boy?' He stands up. 'I want to see him.'

'You will, Mr. Lafonte.' Not like she has, of course. The Lafontes will get their son all cleaned up, with a plastic sheet for modesty to cover where his legs would have been. They'll be able to tell immediately though. The visibility of absence.

'I want to see him *now*.'

There is a screeching grinding sound from the kitchen. Marcus reacts before any of them, running toward the noise. Beat cop instincts. Gabi and Boyd are out of practice. He stops, frozen in the doorway at the sight of Mrs. Lafonte, her teeth bared, squashing a plastic dinosaur into the protesting garbage disposal. There are shreds of tiger-striped blue plastic around the sink. She's forcing it in, the protesting blades whirring near her fingertips. The toy grins idiotically with its bulging eyes, even as the soft plastic rips under the blades. The laundry basket is full of toys.

'Stop, Mrs. Lafonte.' Gabi pulls her hands away. 'Please.'

'Oh, I'm sorry, honey.' Daveyton's mother turns to them, smiling vaguely. Shock makes people do strange things. Gabi remembers one woman who jumped off her porch and sprinted around her house three times as if she could somehow out-run the bad news. Mrs. Lafonte holds out the shredded plastic. 'Did you want them for your little girl?'

The Skin You're In

Knock knock. Who's there? Clayton. Clayton who? Clayton gone away not coming back, all eaten up on the inside by the dreaming thing he let into his head that didn't mean to get trapped here, drawn out by the raw wound of the man's mind, blazing like a lamp in one of those border places where the skin of the worlds are permeable, *exactly like* the walls of a cheap motel if the walls of a cheap motel can sometimes turn to a meniscus you can push right through by accident. It only wants to get home, and it doesn't know how.

The dream navigates the city in Clayton's body, pulling on his thoughts like strings in a labyrinth to guide it through the streets. His muscle memory manages the brute mechanics, shifting the stick, applying the brake, obeying the rules of the road.

All the rules. All the definitives. Car! Tree! Traffic light! Bus stop! Things are only one thing even if they are categories, species, of themselves, because the names lock them in even more specifically. Elder! Poplar! Oak! Black Gum! White Cedar! Basswood! It feels suffocated by the rigidity of the world. And yet...there is evidence of the dreaming everywhere. There is a world beneath the world that is rich and tangled with meaning. Clayton knew this.

Clayton's thoughts are fuzzy things, flickering beneath the surface, keeping them both alive. It has to hold onto them, to steer him through the world, to make the words in Clayton's mouth come out in the right order.

The ghost nerves sometimes fire in the reconstructed flesh, like when he passes by the corner café and his hand flies to his mouth in an automatic gesture for cigarettes. Or his head turns to watch a woman's hips rolling as she walks down the street ahead of him.

There are other places with strong personal associations, layers of meaning mapped onto the city that make it more navigable. They pass a hospital and the dream is struck by Clay's memory of the smell of the detergent. Bundled-up sheets, stained with shit or blood or urine. The fierce heat of the laundry and the rush of steam from the dryer doors. He got fired from the hospital for stealing a stained sheet, pinning it up at an exhibition. He called it 'Sick'.

The dream takes comfort in Clayton's memories. It seeks them out, and that they are not exactly as the man remembered gives it hope, that perhaps the world *can* be twisted and bent.

It can sense the unconscious currents beneath the city, like the gas pipes that puff thick plumes of steam into the streets.

There are lines of associations. There are nested fears. The giant black fist suspended on cables in the square among the high-rise buildings, a monument to the boxer Joe Louis, but also to power and fear. The curved towers of GM's headquarters nearby, a cluster of glass dicks nudged up together for safety, every window lit up, thrusting defiantly into the darkness.

The currents are crude and subtle in the billboards shouting slogans that say one thing, but mean another, tugging at desires and anxiety, but also alive in the graffiti, the squiggled tags that writhe with look-at-me, acknowledge-me, I'm-here.

And art, most of all.

The dream and Clayton sit on a cool marble bench in the central courtyard of the Detroit Institute of Art, which Clayton never visited because he didn't like the formality of it, when he thought art should be rough and ready, and they stare at Diego Rivera's giant frescoes of men and machinery and feel the churning beneath. All the galleries are like that, dreams seething beneath the surface of the paint, under the skin of the bronze statues. Clayton was so close. But he didn't know how to cut through.

The dream thinks it does. You need life to make life. 'The birds and the bees', to steal a thought from the man it is inhabiting.

Eventually it has to leave the art museum. The needs of the body are a nagging constant. So they are behind the wheel of the truck when it sees the boy, half-collapsed against the side of the bus stop, his head resting against the scuffed-up Plexiglas. It stops the car and watches the boy sleep. There is no-one else around. The boy stirs and his leg kicks out, once, reflexively, like a rabbit or a dog. Or another kind of animal.

It climbs out and goes to get something out of the toolbox the man keeps in the back.

It remembers this from a dream Clayton once had.

'Get up!' Shaking the limp boy by his bare shoulders, his skin still clammy from overnighting in the freezer in the basement. The boy's head lolls back on his neck, and the dream weeps with frustration, its tears shattering like glass on the cement, among the detritus in the tunnel, the trash and condoms, the old tires, bits of chalk left over from a mural of a girl's face, smiling down on them with serene encouragement in the quiet and the dark.

It brought him here to unveil him, close to the physical border between Canada and the United States, in the hopes that borders overlap.

It can't understand what's wrong, why he won't get up, maybe wobbly at first on his new legs, like a faun, before he begins to bound and leap and fly, and then his very being, the fact of him, will rip through the skin between the worlds, let them slip away, back home. Or bring all of the dream crashing in on them.

It has been so very careful, so patient. Flesh is messier, and has its own challenges, but it is not so very different to working in metal or clay or wood. It followed the instructions on the package of chemicals very carefully. A day to prepare, a day to bind. Maybe that was its mistake. The choice of materials, the freezer, keeping the deer in the refrigerator, the plastic wrap mummifying the boy, suffocating him. Perhaps he opened his eyes in the ice chest, battered his hands against the lid, perhaps he has already come and gone, and it missed its moment.

It strokes the bristly hair of the legs that run to the smooth skin of the boy's belly, the scoop of his navel. It cups one of the small, sharp hooves, takes one of the child's hands and laces his slim fingers between Clayton's clumsy ones. It squeezes, gently. An admonishment. Get up now. Stop playing. It's not funny. Words it knows from Clayton's head.

114

But the boy is a dead, empty thing. It has done it all wrong. This stupid head, these stupid hands. It tries to remember how it came through, the man in the woods and the lure of uninhabited spaces – a vacancy that dream can rush in to fill, a door to step through.

'I'm sorry,' the dream says with Clayton's mouth. And it is, for both of them.

About to climb back into the truck, it hesitates and picks up a piece of pink chalk from the ground. It draws the rough outline of a door, the chalk snapping in Clayton's thick fingers. But it is persistent. Because maybe, next time, the door will open, and the boy will climb unsteadily to his hooves and take lilting steps through.

The dream will try again.

Anywhereland

There's no such thing as by the book, Gabi knows. Every case defines itself. But you start with what you know. Work backwards. Fill in the gaps. Daveyton did not arrive home between four and five p.m., when he usually does on a Friday. He left school around three, according to the science teacher who was supervising the hang-out that day, which is what Humboldt Middle School calls their aftercare, confirmed by the footage they've retrieved from the security cameras. The school can't afford to maintain their library, but they have surveillance cameras and metal detectors. Priorities.

Usually, he would walk to the bus stop (public transit: the school does not have its own bus service) with a friend in his class, Carla Fuentes, but she had a dermatologist appointment, and her dad picked her up early. Which means he went missing somewhere in between school and home. It's the worst place of all, that anywhereland.

The parents have been interrogated separately and together, with a lawyer and without, and referred for counseling. They were both at work at the time of their son's disappearance.

Lucky to have a double income. Juliet Lafonte works as an administrator at a doctor's office, although her arthritis makes her a slow typist. She has witnesses to her whereabouts all Friday.

Paul Lafonte works dispatch at a printing warehouse. His alibi is golden, complete with a time sheet with his signature on it. His company had already printed a stack of 'Missing' brochures, which the parents have been stuffing in mailboxes around the neighborhood. They will have to print new ones. Not 'have you seen this boy?', but 'did you?' The finality of past tense.

They canvass the Lafonte's neighbors, Daveyton's teachers, the principal, trying to establish his whereabouts on that day, who he hung out with, if there were any adults who had shown an unusual interest in him.

She gets all the familiar platitudes that fail to sum up a life. He was 'a good kid', he was 'well-liked', he 'worked hard but he messed around in class sometimes'. His favorite subjects were math and social studies.

'Was there anything unusual about him that I need to know?' Gabi asks the principal.

The woman frowns. 'He dwelled too much on the shooting. It made him a celebrity. I didn't like it. Any excuse to show off his scar. He made up all these stories. He said he was a superhero, the bullet was radioactive and it gave him powers, and then he jumped off the bleachers to prove it and broke his arm. Then he wrote an essay about how he got shot because he knew too much. He'd overheard the gang boss planning to whack his mom because they'd been using her as a cover to smuggle drugs in her piano. He saved her life, but they broke her fingers – and that's why she can't play anymore.'

They talk to some of his school friends, with their parents' permission and a counselor present. Gabi asks Carla Fuentes about the route the kids took to the bus stop. Was there anywhere they liked to stop along the way? A detour or shortcut they liked to take? The little girl blinks throughout the interview. 'Is he really dead? Really, really?'

The kids have more questions than answers. So do their parents. The rumors are already spreading.

It was a new initiate in the gang that shot him, coming back to finish him off. It was the janitor, who has a prison record for armed robbery from ten years ago, and this is exactly why schools shouldn't hire ex-criminals. And one which might lead somewhere: the father wanted to pay off his gambling debts with the insurance money.

Gabi and Boyd leave Sparkles to mop up the paperwork and compile a list of names to follow up, and go out to walk the route Daveyton would have taken to the bus stop.

The sun is feeble, the sky a washed-out blue. They pass by a used-car dealership and a gas station, an empty lot, the burned-out husk of an old university residence, the scorched roof caving in above the red brick and ivy. A poster in an empty window promises cash for gold.

'Lotta fuckin' places you could grab someone and drag 'em inside,' Boyd observes. 'We're going to have to come back here.'

'Have we phoned the bus company yet to check if the driver remembers Daveyton?'

'I put your puppy dog on that.'

'That's unkind, Bob,' Gabi says, but Sparkles does have a waggy-tail eagerness that's tempting to exploit. 'Fair amount of traffic,' she checks her watch. 'Lunchtime. Wonder what it's like at three p.m. on a Friday.'

'Quieter.'

They reach the bus stop – Plexiglas scratched up with graffiti and stained with rain and dust. The wooden bench is partitioned into four parts with metal railings to prevent anyone from lying down. Initials and swearwords have been crudely carved into the wood. Several boards are missing from the last seat. Cigarette butts litter the ground, smoked down to the filter. Boyd peers down the road, left and right, checking out the run-down apartment block opposite, the parking lot across the way. Gabriella crouches down by the bench.

'Bob.' The urgency in her voice makes him turn. 'Here.' She indicates a fine spatter of brown on the glass, low down, butt-height if you were sitting. Or head-height if you had managed to contort yourself into a position where you could sleep. Or if someone had pulled you off the bench and shoved you on the ground and stuck a nail gun to your head. 'He did it right here. Full view of the street.'

'Motherfucker's either got balls of steel or he's dumb as pig shit.'

'Carpe diem. It was opportunistic,' she says, playing it out. 'He was driving round looking for the right victim.'

'One that would fit his deer pants. Sizing them up.'

'Spotted little Daveyton waiting for the bus. Maybe circled round for another look. Pulled over. Might have tried to get him in the car first. Offered him a ride.'

'It was vicious cold on Friday,' Boyd agrees.

'Mmm. Smart kid like that wouldn't have gone for it, and our killer couldn't take the risk. No, he parked in front of the bus stop to obscure the view, went right up to him. Maybe didn't even bother with conversation, just shoved him down and nailed him in the head. Loaded him in the car and drove away.'

119

'I would say that the blood drops over here and here,' Boyd points to the faintest drops on the ground, 'would corroborate that theory. Nail straight into the brain – there might not have been that much blood. If he didn't remove it on the scene, it could have kept it sealed in tight.'

'Our sick bastard's also a slick bastard. We need to lock this down. Get statements from the people who live in that apartment block. Get this blood tested and ID-ed. Don't radio it in!' she snaps as he reaches for his belt. 'Cell phones only.'

Boyd rolls his eyes. 'Whatever you say, Versado. This is going to turn into a shit-storm however we play it.'

The Bright

'Two weeks in Detroit already and you haven't done the Packard Plant?' Jen teases him. 'Just what kind of out-of-towner journalist are you?'

Good question, snipes his troll.

'I spent most of that time getting drunk,' Jonno retorts, which makes it sound like he was out partying, instead of holed up in the studio apartment (easy walking distance to downtown) that he rented from a web designer on AirVacancy for four weeks. The plan was to get the lay of the land, buy a car, find a more permanent place to live, maybe take a bartending job, meet cool people, and start his brand-new life. His host had diligently left a pile of city guides and local newspapers on the table, but he couldn't face the Detroit Institute of Art or hip Corktown, and when he went for a walk, he got as far as the liquor store and scuttled back home.

He needed an adjustment period. He needed to fortify himself. Once he got as far as the French restaurant adjoining the lobby downstairs, where they were showing Fellini movies with subtitles. He drank eight martinis and the cute waitress, who might have been interested in him before he got sloppy drunk, had to help him into the elevator. This is grief. This is loss.

This is rotting in a stranger's apartment feeling sorry for yourself for being a pathetic idiot who sucks at forward-planning.

He should have thought it through more. But he was in too much pain to think clearly. He was in free-fall from what happened in New York. Until Jen Q.

Jen-Jen-Jen.

His muse, his savior, his Joan of Arc with braids. It was fate, forcing himself to go out on Saturday night. *You're rushing into things. The Amazing Rebound Man.*

Now that he's got an in into the city (and okay, wheels), Detroit's a whole other place. Everyone knows Jen Q. She is cool and popular and she opens doors to the parts of the city everyone knows – and then breaks them open to places he didn't imagine.

'So here we go, the biggie,' she says, pulling under the corridor bridge of the Packard Plant: over two miles of broken-down factory.

'The number one Death-of-America pilgrimage destination,' Jonno says. But he's impressed despite himself. The sprawling waste of it. Broken bricks and concrete pillars holding up the sky. Everything is choked with weeds and graffiti. The word 'fuck' appears a lot, which seems appropriate.

They drive past a fashion shoot in a gloomy interior full of rubble, a wiry guy holding up a bounce board to better direct the light at a girl with big eighties hair in a bikini top and short-shorts, standing defiantly against the cold among the pillars of a caved-in factory floor, the sky leaking in behind her.

Some old hobos are watching from a doorway opposite.

'Local perverts?' Jonno says.

'Don't be so judgmental. They live here. They collect old junk, clean it up and sell it on eBay. God knows what's going to happen to them if this place ever gets redeveloped.'

'That's an amazing story, can I talk to them? I could write about that.'

'No,' Jen snaps. 'Leave them alone. Everyone's done it. You know what's worse than fifteen minutes of fame? The same fifteen minutes again and again, and it doesn't change anything. They're still living in an abandoned building, still scraping by.'

They're all hustlers, Jonno thinks, all still figuring themselves out.

'Hurry,' she says, pushing him into the abandoned theater. They've parked across the road so as not to attract attention. You might call it urban exploration, but it's still trespassing. 'Put this on.' She hands him a face mask. 'For the asbestos.'

'Great,' he says, sarcastically. But it *is* great. He feels inspired in a way he hasn't for years, and if that means he dies from some horrible lung disease in ten years' time, so be it.

The theater is like a cathedral inside, the same sense of peace and awe. *Or maybe it's just that it's cool and quiet, and your footsteps echo.*

He hadn't expected to be so moved by it all. The rows of chairs curved to face a stage that has caved in, the rotted remains of curtains hanging bedraggled on either side. One red velvet chair has been yanked from its row, like a bad tooth, and set up in the center of the stage. You can see the appeal. Haunted by civilizations past. A reminder of mortality. This too shall crumble and fall.

'Want to go up to the balcony?'

Jonno looks, warily, at the flight of stairs under a land-slide of rubble and dust. He thinks about how it might give way under him, send him sliding back to where he came from.

'Nah.'

Jen sweeps him on to an early dinner party at a loft apartment owned by two guys who made millions off a website, Text Regrets, where people post messages they wish they hadn't sent. They seem like clever fictions, even though the guys swear they're all real.

'You're just mad you didn't think of it first.' Jen nudges him in the bathroom, handing him her car key to snort a bump of coke off.

Of course he is. And because the more texts he reads, the more he finds it's all there. Not just rude messages about blow jobs accidentally sent to your mom, but pathos and bathos and comedy and the richness of human experience. In a text. What hope does he have? The world is condensing, attention spans narrowing to tiny screens, and there are people who are wittier and smarter, who know how to write for those nanospaces. He wants to sink into despair, but the cocaine won't let him.

They sit down for dinner at a long table, with big dogs galumphing round the kitchen and splashy art pieces on the wall. A young guy with wild dreads who works at the local historic pottery, a lady lawyer, an architect, a Google engineer, and a couple of cute promo girls on a roadshow for a hip sunglasses brand, setting up pop-up stores.

On the other side of the table they're talking about art and Jen's diabetes, after she pulls up her cream sweater and shoots up right there, pinching the flesh at her waist and clicking the insulin pen against it. He loves that she's so don't-give-a-fuck-about the procedure and the questions that rise up around her. He loves the contrast between her dark skin and the pale wool. He wants to reach out and pinch her waist himself, with possessiveness and lust. But he is stuck with promo girl, who's telling him how they hand out free samples to innovators and connectors.

'You're spreading the virus of consumer desire,' Jonno observes. They've reached the point in the evening where they're talking at each other.

'I miss my dog,' the cute brunette says. 'We've been on the road for eight weeks now. I want to go back to New York already.'

'I'm from New York,' Jonno says. 'Can I get a pair?'

'Oh,' she says. 'Sorry, I don't have any with me. Maybe tomorrow?' But her pitying smile says maybe never. She turns to talk to the architect about dogs.

They catch the tail-end of an art exhibition, where everything is tired and the same – the same anti-consumer bullshit, Ronald McDonald in jihadi gear and Mickey Mouse in the role of Saturn eating his children. A gumball machine marked 'Reality Check' dispenses candy shaped like the red pills in *The Matrix*.

'Cute,' he says. 'How did they *ever* come up with that?'

'Are you this jaded about everything?' Jen says, ruffling his hair. 'Oh, hang on, I have to say hi to Simon.' She shimmies over to talk to a lithe young man with a lumberjack beard and tattoos on every available surface. Jonno pours some of the gelatin sherbet pills into his hand, trying to act like he's not checking out this Simon guy. He swallows a pill in the hope that someone might have laced it with molly – that would be experiential art – but he suspects that all he's going to get out of it is a red-stained tongue. Maybe this is the thing about getting old – that nothing is new any more.

'It's all the same,' says the man standing next to him, examining the grotesquery of Mickey Mouse about to gobble up a child with sharp pointy teeth. 'Nothing's original.'

'I was thinking the exact same thing,' Jonno says, happy to find a comrade in cynicism, until he sees it's some crusty guy with a shock of white hair in a rumpled brown blazer. Jen is still talking to Simon, her hand on his arm, firing a spike of jealousy down his spine, which he tries to cover with blather. 'Like where is the art that's going to change the world? It's undiscovered.' Like the amazing undiscovered novelists of the world, he thinks.

'Maybe it's waiting to be found,' says the white-haired man. His blue eyes are intense, drilling into Jonno.

'Yeah, but it can't wait! You have to *make* the connections, you have to get it in front of the right audience. It's all about the eyeballs. Always the damn eyeballs.'

'Hey, Jonno,' Jen interrupts, 'this is Simon. I was telling you about him earlier. The séance?'

Jonno vaguely remembers snippets of a conversation on the other side of the dinner table while he'd been trying to score free shades from promo girl. Something about an artist who killed himself in the caravan he'd customized.

'Yeah, bro. We had beer and naked girls, we did a barbecue in the bathtub – all the things he liked. I was the Ouija board.' He lifts up his shirt to reveal the tattoo of old-fashioned type and the all-seeing eye on his chest. 'His spirit didn't show up, but we think he would have appreciated it.'

'Now *that's* original,' Jonno turns to say to his new friend, but the crumpled man has wandered off, and Simon has more coke, even though Jen abstains this time round. So much for the party girl.

He's pretty trashed by the time they end up at an apartment block in the city center at three in the morning, where a cluster of party people are standing shivering in the cold, waiting, for what he isn't sure, but they have to join the line. There is texting. Regrets, maybe. Or instructions, because a man leans out an upstairs window and throws out the keys, attached to a plastic bag so they come parachuting down, like one of those army-men toys.

The girl in front catches the keys and opens the door onto a staircase lined with graffiti that winds up and up, and they all traipse along gamely. It reminds him of Williamsburg in the 2000s, the edgy-as-fuck parties in the warehouse district. Someone has drawn the outline of a door on the wall next to a crazy cartoon cat giving them the finger. 'Knock-knock, are we there yet?' Jonno says, rapping his knuckles on the chalk outline.

'Come on,' Jen says, nudging him. 'Two more flights.'

The party is weird. A dark room with people milling half-heartedly on the dance floor. Someone in the back sells them two beers for five dollars. Jen takes a turn on the decks and Jonno slinks off to the enclosed balcony among a jungle of pot plants, trying not to feel lonely and old. A skinny Thor-lookalike with long blond hair and a Viking nose offers him a bump off an LP cover and they get talking.

'This is the Detroit I want to write about,' he says, feeling urbane as fuck. 'Tattoo séances and nutty street art and text-message millionaires. People don't even know this is happening.'

'Of course we know it's happening, shithead,' Anorexic Thor says. '*You* don't know it's happening.'

But he won't be put off. It feels like this is something, something real and he could be a part of it. The drug has his tongue. 'Have you noticed how dim this room is? We're all trying to keep the dark at bay by surrounding ourselves with it. This city,' he says, inspired, 'this city is all about the people, who have to burn against the dark. It's the bright against the blight.'

'Or we keep the lights off so we don't alert the cops,' Jen Q says, draping her arms over his shoulders. She kisses the top of his head. 'Come on, time for bed. I think you've had enough.'

Higher Power

Some shelters make you play musical chairs. Move around, table to table. Same with recovery programs, TK has found. It's all about getting to know one another, but he reckons it's a bit like taking off your pants. You have to expose yourself, naked for all the world to see. You stand up and you say *I'm a drunk. I'm an addict. I'm a murderer. I'm a whoreson.* It's supposed to be only part of who you are, but it seems to him once you take that label, you're stuck with it. Some words are stronger than others. It's…what's the Hollywood word for it? Your elevator pitch.

He's been looking into this stuff, reading websites on how to write a screenplay. But all that advice on how to get ahead in Hollywood involves a cash lay-out. Buy the book. Do the course. Have a professional reader give you notes on your synopsis. Same as the how-to-be-a-day-trader sites he was looking at seven years ago before the whole economy came crashing down around their heads exactly like a giant robot movie.

Life does that too, and the support programs, they want you to appeal to a higher power for help. Your call. God,

Jesus, Buddha, Krishna, Muhammad. Whole damn catalog to choose from. TK chose his chair.

'You can't choose a chair, TK,' Celeste told him at that same meeting. Crack addict, hadn't spoken to her only daughter in ten years after stealing her ATM card and taking her grocery money, but there she was lecturing him about God.

'Sure I can. I can feel it right now. My higher power's presence supporting me – right under my ass.' Which cracked up the room, and the counselor slapped him on the back and shook her head. But he was dead serious. You can't tell him there's any God would allow the kind of shit he's lived through. Kids having to avenge their mommas. Public defender who barely even looked at him, let alone got his side of the story. What happened in jail after that. God who'd let that happen to a kid? That ain't somebody he wants to be palling around with. He'll take his chair, thank you, ma'am.

So it's not that he doesn't believe in God, it's that they don't see eye-to-eye. He'd never tell that to these people though, the ones lining up outside St. Raphael's in the shadow of Comerica Park, shabbier than the crowds they get here during a game. Some of them can spare him a smile, but some of them don't even have that in them. There's a way back from that place, if you can find it, if you can find your chair.

TK goes down the line, slapping hands in greeting. 'Hey there, good to see you. We open at eleven. You hang in there.'

The church calls it a soup kitchen, but mostly they don't serve soup. They do sandwiches and hotdogs and chili in winter, and they hand out chips and sweets, whatever's going spare from local grocery stores, sorted into brown paper bags by the volunteers. He's overheard Reverend Alan talking about how it's getting harder to pull in donations.

When TK was a kid, he thought that living in a free country meant you got stuff for free. He got disabused of *that* notion real quick. He used to hate the old men pulling him aside on the corner: 'B-ooooy! I got something to tell you.' He didn't want to hear it. Had to learn the unfairness of it all first-hand. You think the world comes down to basic math. One plus one. Life for a life. But apparently that don't add up in the US justice system, no matter what the Bible says about eyes and teeth. It took him a long time to figure it out and now, pushing sixty, he's got his shit together, he's got it down, and none of them kids want to listen to him. He's become that old man. 'B-ooooy! I got something to tell you.'

Ten minutes after the doors open, people barely sat down with their food, and Lanny is already complaining up a storm, bitching about pretzels when he wanted crackers. Used to be an ocular surgeon, he says. Which is a fancy term for eye-doctor, because doctors need long words as much as they need scalpels and lasers and white coats. Lanny says he could take care of that bump on TK's eyelid, if his hands didn't shake so much. He says it's Parkinson's, but TK knows a drunk when he sees one, and not just by the half-jack of Carstairs White Seal he slips out of his pocket to spike his coffee.

You get all sorts in here. Not only ocular surgeons. Anyone can find they've been standing on the trapdoor when they thought they were the spotlight attraction.

'Lanny, Lanny,' TK says, slinging his arm around the man. The problem with being a self-appointed trouble-shooter is it means you got to deal with the damn trouble.

131

'Lanny, my man, it's nothing. Here, you swap with me. I got some crackers.'

Lanny is still grumbling. 'They don't treat me right, TK. Man has a right to crackers.'

TK walks him over to the table where Ramón and his lady Diyana are sitting with their hands clasped together tighter than a clamshell, staring at each other like lovesick teenagers. But unlike teenagers, they've seen enough to know how rare and precious their feelings are.

Diyana is easy with the smiles these days. Used to be that she hid her mouth with a hand to cover up her one black tooth, but she's kinder to herself since she and Ramón got together. Love will do that.

'Nice shoes, Ramón,' TK says, noting the red high-tops with a wink and a twinge of regret. He sees he's shaved too.

'Thanks, TK.'

'Lemme see?' Lanny demands.

'Like the ones I had when I was nineteen,' Ramón says, sticking his foot out from under the table, twisting it one way, then the other, for them to admire. 'Only those were white.'

'Gonna get soaked with the first snow,' Lanny grumbles.

'Then I'll switch to my boots,' Ramón shrugs.

Lanny is already bored of the conversation. 'You know they gave me *pretzels*? Did you get pretzels or crackers?'

'Lemme get you a hot dog. That'll make up for it, right, Lanny?'

TK is heading for the line when he sees a lost-looking man lurking by the door. Long white hair tied back in a ponytail, face as crumpled and ill-fitting as his brown blazer. Mid-fifties, TK would guess, although the street has a way

132

of making people look older. His features are gaunt and also saggy, with scooped-out cheeks and soft folds gathered up under his jaw, but his pale blue eyes are as sharp as a box-cutter a kid might pull on you in the street. All sorts, TK reminds himself, but he automatically checks his hands to see if he's holding. Man with eyes like that in prison is a man with intent. Or a tweaker.

But the man is holding only an empty plastic cup, aiming for the table with the Kool-Aid. The back of his hands are pocked with little scars, like the ones you get in the screw factory, when splinters of metal filings shear off and stick into you and you got to pick them out with tweezers after your shift when you should be having a nice cold one. If you still had a job. If you hadn't sworn off the drink.

'Hey there, you okay?' he says, trying to set him at ease. It's one of the things he does, gets newcomers settled in. 'You need something I can help you with?' The man's expression spasms, trying out different combinations. Ah, TK thinks, autistic. That's easier to handle than psychotic.

'I'm looking for someone.' He speaks hesitantly, dragging the words out like someone trying to control a stutter. 'I thought it was Louanne. But it wasn't. Not the boy, either. He couldn't get up.'

'You got a name?' TK prods, gently. 'If it's someone who comes here regular, I'll probably know them. If not, I can help you look them up on the computer. White pages, Facebook. You can find pretty much anyone these days.'

'I don't know,' he says, looking round the big hall, people clustered round the big tables with the cheery tablecloths. 'Someone. It's very raw here,' the man says, rubbing the white stubble on his cheeks up and down, up and down. 'Everyone is broken.'

133

'Hey, now,' TK bristles, 'people get banged up a little. But they're good people. Why don't you come sit with us for a bit.' He keeps talking – it helps with ones like this, sets them at ease. 'This place is like the movies! You got everything: drama, action, romance, hard times, good times, coming back from the dead times. You know they filmed all the *Transformers* movies here? *Robocop*, too. I reckon it's about time they did a movie about people instead of machines,' TK says. 'Explosions and fighting robots and shit. What's that got to do with the heart?' He pauses. 'I know I'm going on, but point is, you can't judge people by the outside. Like the Bible says, the body's just a vessel. Not that I'm religious or nothing. You know they make you choose a higher power when you go through the twelve steps? You know what I chose?' He gets ready to launch into his tale, honed like a comedy routine.

'A chair,' the man answers.

TK reels. 'I told you this before? Have we met?'

'I can see things inside. Like shadows on the wall. People are messier. But I can see the chairs. I can see your momma.'

'That ain't none of your business. Here.' TK puts a brown lunch bag into his hands as they reach the front of the line. 'Pretzels all right with you?' He shoves his tray at Big Dennis, who is dishing up today. 'You want a hot dog too? Two with the works for me, please. No, wait, make it one ketchup, one mustard, onions on the side.' He can't remember what Lanny likes. There is bad weather brewing behind his temples. Might be a fit coming on. Black Sundays he calls them, although they strike on any day they feel like.

'You shouldn't eat that,' the man says.

'You see a salad bar round here?' It comes out sharper than he'd intended.

'Do you know what that's made out of?'

TK is dismissive. 'Sodium, fat, whole bunch of chemicals with long names that probably gonna give me cancer. But it ain't killed me yet. Besides, it's not for me.'

'Scraps.'

'Sure. Lips and assholes. Still tastes good.'

'Intestines, fat, organs. Bits they scrape off the bone and spray off the floor of the slaughterhouse with hoses, and then they pulp it up in vats until all you have left is pink slime.' The man recites it like a nursery rhyme.

'Hey, now, you wanna be vegetarian, that's all right, but we got a rule here about preaching…'

'Pink slime. That's all you are inside. Like you said, vessels. You have to open them up.' He grabs hold of TK's arm, the gleam of revelation in his blue eyes. 'You need to come with me. I got a truck outside.'

'I suggest you let me go, boy,' TK says, coldly. 'This isn't that kind of place. I don't go that way.' He wrenches his arm free. 'You want a pick-up, you choose somewhere that ain't a church. I think you should take your meal and go now.'

But halfway back to his table he turns to see the man dangling the paper bag from his hand, looking down at the ground, all – what's the word from that comic TK likes so much about the little kid and his imaginary tiger – discombobulated. That's it. He looks utterly lost. TK calls to him, 'You should maybe think about coming in for counseling, man. Thursdays.'

Back at the table, Lanny's chair is vacant.

'Men's room,' Ramón says. 'Said he might be a while. Pretzels upset his constitution.'

'All right. Guess I'll leave this for him, then.'

'You okay, Tom?' Diyana's the only one who can get

away with calling him that. 'You look upset.'

'I'm fine. Need to take my medication is all.' TK's annoyed with himself. The man brought up all kinds of wrong in him, and he can feel the pressure building inside his head. 'I'm gonna go in back and get it.'

The offices behind the hall are usually locked up. Trust is a luxury item, like designer shoes and fancy coffee. You have to be able to afford it. But the room where they store the tables and chairs is always open. No-one's tried to make off with the furniture yet – and no-one thinks to look in here, which means a man can take a nap undisturbed, if he's so inclined.

He eases between the stacks of chairs, and then crawls under them, bunching up his jacket to use as a pillow. Ten minutes shut-eye, to ward off the storm clouds and lay low from his new friend.

TK comes out of the darkness fighting. Diyana and Ramón are standing over him, looking worried, while Big Dennis is trying to stick a plastic serving spoon between his teeth.

'Get that shit out of my mouth, man. Don't they teach you anything?'

'Didn't want you to bite your tongue off,' Dennis says.

'Best thing with a seizure is to put a pillow under a man's head and let him get on with it.'

'All right, all right, TK. I'm sorry.'

'Don't be hard on him, Tom. He's was trying to help.'

TK sits up, blinking. The light is too bright. It feels like it might set him off again. His head is full of ghosts of tortured metal and sheets blooming with bloody flowers. 'What happened?'

'You had one of your fits.'

'I know *that*. I mean, what the hell happened to all the chairs?'

'We thought you did it,' Diyana looks around, puzzled.

The chairs are arranged all around him in perfect circles, a bull's eye with him at the center. But that's not even the most disturbing part. It's that someone's gone and turned them all upside down, legs sticking up in the air like dead bugs.

'Not me, man,' TK says, leaning over his knees, feeling nauseous. 'Not me.'

The Art of Fishing

The extra-credit Future Promise class Layla signed up for is canceled. *Por supesto!* But no-one has bothered to inform them. Double *por supesto*. Suits her, it was lame anyway. 'Entrepreneurship! Creative economics! Personal brand building! How to capitalize on social media!' Sponsored by the Detroit New Business Association. The lecturer, who was barely older than they were, spent the last class explaining how to set up a Facebook page for your business, skipping over what kind of business that should be. She got the idea he was kinda hoping they would know.

'Why can't you just go private?' Layla said this morning, when her mom told her it was probably going to be another late shift.

'Because I believe in helping people, not hunting down bogus insurance claimants for some corporation,' her mother snapped. '*Unlike* your father.' She repented immediately. 'Goddammit. I'm sorry, Layla, that was a shit thing to say. But I don't know why you have to always push me.'

More than half the class bails when it becomes obvious

138

that no-one is coming. She follows the stragglers to the gymnateria; a cluster of the cool kids. She only knows a couple of them by name: CeeCee Wallace, in her fur-lined boots and denim skirt with a fox tail clipped on the back, and Travis Russo, who slams his body around as if it's a new car he's learning to drive.

He goes off to shoot hoops with one of his boys, while the girls sit on the edge of the stage, swinging their legs and tossing out easy gossip about a bunch of people Layla doesn't know, which makes it hard to have an opinion. Who got with who, who is a slut, who's cheating on who, who's causing drama. She tries to turn it into a theater exercise, studying them, filing bits of dialogue and the way the intonation goes up at the end, what they do with their hands. She never knows what to do with her hands. This is probably why so many people smoke. Why they get fucked-up at parties. A beer is something you can hold onto.

She thinks about the props Mrs. Westcott has asked them to bring to rehearsals at the Masque to help them get into character. She wishes she had something to help her get into Layla-who-totally-fits-in.

There is a lapse in the conversation after they all agree that Abbie is a cheating whore. Layla tries to break in, having rehearsed the line that will make her seem witty and cool and deep. 'Hey, don't you think—' she stammers as they turn their attention on her. 'Smoking. It's such a primitive ritual, gathering round the fire.' In her head, she had used this as a way to move on to Plato's shadows on the cave wall, and how do you know what's really real? Like global warming, or your folks breaking up, or Abbie turning out to be such a cheating whore. You can't trust things to stay stable. Because a turkey thinks everything is peachy until the farmer comes along with a hatchet. But now her spiel seems horribly lame and pretentious.

'Yeah,' CeeCee says. 'And 'cos nicotine is totally addictive.' The others laugh and the circle closes around itself again. A cell that just repelled a virus.

Travis dribbles the ball over. 'Is that your friend?' he says with real interest as Cassandra strides in through the double doors, looking around for her. She has a way of walking like she's in a heist movie, her coat flapping around her and her evil Hello Kitty backpack slung over one shoulder.

'Yeah,' Layla says, grateful for the rescue, but also a little stunned that Travis is talking to her. She bundles up her stuff. 'I gotta go.'

'What up, bitch?' Cas calls across as she scurries to meet her.

'Class was canceled,' Layla explains. The stragglers have all gone quiet. She can feel their eyes on the back of her head, and she's grateful for the bubble of untouchable cool Cas carries around with her.

'Hey, aren't you—?' Travis starts to ask.

'No,' Cas says, dismissing him. 'C'mon, slut, we're going to miss our bus.'

'We could always ask for a ride.' This is a time-honored tradition at high school, making nice to the kids who have their own cars, but Layla hasn't had the guts to do it before.

'With those jerk-offs? I'd rather walk. Besides, you're going to get your license in a month, right?'

'Assuming I pass. And then I still have to get a car.' Layla has to walk at a clip to keep up with Cas, but she is already more herself. Her friend brings it out in her. Her own personal power-up.

They pass by the rows of dented lockers and the bathroom

140

that reeks of marijuana, and crash out the doors into the parking lot. It's a point of pride that Hines High doesn't have metal detectors – a testament to the quality of education and the faith the school has in its students. Which didn't prevent them doing a spot search of the parking lot for drugs this morning.

'How was extra math?' Layla asks.

'Mathy. Don't know why I bother. I'm going to be a waitress anyway. You know what they say, big tits, huge tips. Watch out, Hooters.'

'Doesn't your dad want you to go to MIT?'

'Sure, and he wants to revolutionize social media too. Doesn't mean it's going to happen. Run! There's the bus.'

'It's a sad indictment of society…' Layla pants as they sprint for the stop, 'that your boobs will probably get you further in life than my brains and talent.'

'Not forgetting my fine ass,' Cas says, barely out of breath, ignoring the bus driver's scandalized look as the doors hiss open and she swipes her card. 'Besides. I'd rather be a happy Hooters waitress than a depressed out-of-work actor.'

'Who says I'm going to be out of work?' They head toward the back.

'Really?' Cas grabs the pole as the bus lurches into the traffic and gives Layla the perfect model-scout head-to-toe evaluation over her shoulder. ''Cos there are already *so* many roles for actresses of color in Hollywood. I'm just saying, you better start saving for your nose job. Get your boobs and liposuction done while you're at it. Skin-lightening even.'

'Oh yeah? Well Detroit doesn't even have a Hooters, biatch.'

'I could start my own franchise. Or maybe a competing rip-off brand. Tooters.'

'Or an ass-centric one. Pooters.'

'You're so disgusting, Layla Jane Stirling-Versado.'

She grins. 'You like it.'

They grab seats in the middle, by the second set of doors, because Cas gets car-sick. 'Any new news on Dorkian?'

'I texted him. He didn't even reply.'

'Burn. You see the girl he's been posting to on Facebook?'

'What? No!'

'Some party on Saturday. She's coming from Los Angeles. An artist or whatever.' She pulls it up on screen – the whole conversation laid out for everyone to see.

>Looking forward to finally meeting you at Dream House! xxx

TimTam Linden. 'Artist. Fashionista. Trouble.' In her profile picture, she has ash-blonde hair in a sharp bob that flicks up at the front and a short-short fringe. Mod does punk. She's so cool, Layla could die. They flick through her photographs – heavily filtered pictures on the beach, posing with some vaguely famous-looking people, pictures of lights on a building.

'We have to go,' Layla says.

'To the party? My parents will never let me.'

'No, listen. We get a cab. You tell them you're sleeping at my house, I'll tell my mom I'm crashing at yours.'

'You're insane.'

'I'm in love.'

'Like I said.'

Cas's phone makes that super-annoying chipmunk noise

she's set for her MChat alert tone. She sits upright and elbows Layla in the ribs.

'Damn motherfucker!' Cas shows her the phone. The old lady sitting opposite them wearing a knit cap with a woolen rose on it scowls at them.

'It's okay. I didn't need my spleen anyway. What is it? Did his relationship status just change?' Layla snarls, grabbing the phone. The chat window is open.

>VelvetBoy: Hi, SusieLee2003. You having a good day? :)

'I don't know what I'm looking at. Who is VelvetBoy?'

'Who do you think, dummy? A friendly stranger who wants to talk to little SusieLee.'

'Seriously?' She takes in the username, the profile pic Cas found somewhere of a tubby little blonde girl, twelve-ish, sitting on a fence, grinning to show a slight gap between her teeth, holding a sunflower. 'Is that photostock? No-one's going to be stupid enough to fall for that.'

'Someone just did.'

'Oh my God, we have to reply.' Layla thumbs over the keyboard.

>SusieLee2003: Hi back! :) Its OK so far. Wish it wuz summa!
>VelvetBoy: You're obviously not in California then?
>SusieLee2003: Michigan! SO cold. Cant it just snow already?! Where r u?
>VelvetBoy: That's a very pretty name. Is that your real name?
>SusieLee2003: Is that yours? :)

>VelvetBoy: LOLOLOLOL No. :)

'Oh God, so gross,' Layla says.

'Keep going! Don't lose him.' But there's an edge to the way she says it.

>SusieLee2003: Velvet is romantic :) It makes me think of soft things.

'Like my vulva!' Cas says, gleefully. Rose Hat Lady jerks in her seat and gives them the eye-daggers. 'What?' Cas says to her. 'You've got one too!'

>SusieLee2003: Like kittens. And pretty dresses
>VelvetBoy: Party dresses. With ribbons.
>SusieLee2003: Like the Kardashians!
>VelvetBoy: I don't really like that show.
>SusieLee2003: Me neither! Theyre so rich + fake!
>VelvetBoy: You don't know how refreshing it is to hear someone your age say that.

'You should mistype more words for authenticity,' Cas says.

'For your information,' Layla says, getting into it now, 'it's part of her character history. Little SusieLee is very precocious and happens to have won the spelling bee three years in a row.'

>VelvetBoy: You're a beautiful girl, SusieLee.
>SusieLee2003: Thats easy for u 2 say :(
>VelvetBoy: It's true. Beauty comes from inside. I wish all girls knew that.

>SusieLee2003: U dont have boys teasing u
>VelvetBoy: Why would boys tease you?
>SusieLee2003: They say Im fat. And stupid and ugly
:_(
>VelvetBoy: You're not any of those things.
>SusieLee2003: How wld u know? u dont evn no me
>VelvetBoy: You can tell a lot from the way someone
talks. I can tell you're kind and clever. Tell me about the
real you. Inside. That those stupid boys don't see.
>SusieLee2003: Ummmm :{ Like what?
>VelvetBoy: Things that make you happy. What do you
want to be? How old are you?
>SusieLee2003: I like music. I'm learning to play guitar.
>VelvetBoy: That's great. Hey I got a spare music voucher
as a promo thing. Do you want it?

'Bingo,' Cas says.

>SusieLee2003: SRSLY?!?!?! That would b awsum.
>VelvetBoy: No problem! I'll email you the code.
>SusieLee2003: OK! Wow! Tx! <Hugs>
>VelvetBoy: Can yuo do me a little favor?
>SusieLee2003: idk? Depends.
>VelvetBoy: It's not a bigge ;) Please send me a video of
you playing guitar. I'd love to hear one of your songs.
Or send more photos. You have a beUatiful smile
>SusieLee2003: Oh no! I can only do chords. Not even
a real song yet.
>VelvetBoy: Sorry! Typos. Don't put yourself down. Believe
in yourself. I do and I only just met you. Chat soon! I'll
send that voucher as soon as I get youtr photoas, ok?
<Hugs>

Layla hands Cas the phone back. 'Well that was fun. And…I feel really dirty.'

'So where the hell are we going to find a video of that same kid playing guitar, genius?'

'What?' Layla laughs. 'We're not going to send him anything. Except maybe a "you're busted, pervert" message.'

'Why not? More of his time we take up, the less time he has to chase after actual little girls.'

'You want to go full vigilante?'

'Oh my God, yes.' Cas bounces in her seat in excitement. 'We should *meet* him.'

'No way. And you don't know he's a perve for sure. He could be a kid himself. A lonely kid who knows what it feels like to get bullied. Maybe he's just reaching out, and we're the assholes.'

'Really? You *really* think that?'

'No,' Layla admits.

'So. Motherfucking game on, motherfucker.'

Layla glances out the window. 'We missed our stop.'

'Christballs.'

Playing the Game

Everyone lives three versions of themselves; a public life, a private life and a secret life. Watch any kid and how he acts with his friends at school. Ask his momma what he's like at home. Try and get her to believe the same kid robbed the corner store. 'Not my boy,' she'll say and she's right. Because *her* boy wouldn't do that. But we are different things to different people in different contexts.

Take Gabi and Luke. In the precinct, they're professional colleagues. But here in his neat little house in Highland Park, they're fuck buddies, no strings attached, which allows her to keep it compartmentalized away from Layla and the shredded remains of her personal life. It's exactly why cops end up sleeping with each other. Who has time to meet new people?

The first time was in the back of her car, late one night, after the whole department went out to celebrate a conviction in the Granston case. It was Joe Miranda's idea to go fowling – bowling with a football – hurling the ball down the lanes. They got pretty trashed, enough for management to ask them to keep it down. She gave him a ride home.

They didn't quite make it that far.

Now it's sex on demand, their respective schedules allowing. It's stress relief. It doesn't mean anything. It could be worse. She could be an alcoholic or popping valium. But that would require her to talk to someone to be able to get a prescription. Luke doesn't expect her to talk. They very specifically don't. There are unspoken rules. They don't let it interfere with their work. They don't discuss where this is going.

She loves what he does to her, the way he makes her lose herself, the world tipping away, and she likes being able to do the same to him, the way his tight control unravels. Who's the perfect cop now, she thinks, as he comes, the force of it racking through his whole body.

'Don't look so pleased with yourself,' he says afterwards, reaching for the Nicorette gum he keeps on his bedside table, along with the condoms. Not quite a post-coital cigarette.

'Can't take pride in my work?' Her phone rings and she rolls over to look at the screen. William Stirling. She groans.

'You need to get that? I can go into the kitchen.'

'It's my ex,' Gabi says, hitting reject call. 'He wants Layla to come to them for Christmas, seeing I get Thanksgiving, and I don't want to talk about it right now.' She doesn't say the obvious, that she doesn't want to be alone over the holidays – any of them.

'You'll still have to deal with it later.'

'Yes, but I can fortify myself with a drink later. How about you? Do you get on with your ex-girlfriends?'

'We having a personal conversation now? Because that's okay if we are.'

She props herself up on her elbows and lets her hand drift over his stomach. They're both in good shape for their age, but they're not young any more. There's a softening to their muscles. It's true about her conviction too. Experience has filed the edge off the hard truths she believed in when she was younger. 'You think getting older makes you more empathetic?'

'No. I think most people become more unyielding in their beliefs.'

'You're more unyielding right now,' she says, giving his cock a friendly squeeze.

'You're changing the subject.'

'I can see how you made detective.' She kisses him. 'Don't screw up a good thing, Stricker.' She checks her phone. 'We've got another hour before we have to leave.'

'What should we do with all that time?'

'I have some ideas,' she says, swinging herself up to straddle him.

The problem with chemistry is that it tends to blow things up. And she is already a chain of reactions building up inside.

Sometimes the stupid, simple things work. Ringing all the doorbells of an apartment block until someone hits the buzzer. She has seen cops claim to be cable-repair guys, electric-meter readers, pizza-delivery people: whatever it takes to get inside the building. It's not regulation. But you gotta do what you gotta do. Sometimes you only have to ask.

There are a hundred games running in Detroit every night, from dice throws on the corner to ballers playing high-stakes poker in a location that switches every week. Tonight, it's above a Kurdish restaurant on Greenfield.

The place has kilims on the walls and low brass tables and huge lamps with geometric shapes cut into them. It's quiet tonight, if you discount the number of men in suits who walk straight through to the beaded curtain at the back. The few patrons who are here tonight know enough not to make eye-contact.

The beaded curtain leads onto a passage that opens to the kitchen and the bathrooms and a closed door, manned by a thug with a clipboard and bulges in all the right places, most noticeably, a gun-shaped one tucked into his pants.

You don't get in to a game unless you have a ticket. The tickets are matched up to names on a guest list at the door. No match, no entrance. It's how they keep the cops out and, more importantly, the kind of chancers who would try to pull down a robbery. You'd have to be pretty fucking stupid to mess with the Russians, but Gabi knows that in Detroit, people will pull the trigger for a can of Pepsi, never mind a hundred large.

'You're not on the list,' the bulging man says, not even bothering to look at the clipboard. He can smell the cop on them.

'We're here to see Timor,' Luke says. 'You can tell him it's Stricker.'

'You can wait out back, through the kitchen. He wants to talk to you, I'll come get you. If he doesn't, you can take off. 'Cos I know you ain't here for trouble.'

'No doubt.'

He waves them into the kitchen. The chef glances up from arranging an elaborate meze platter: fat, shiny green dolma and thick swirls of hummus. A far cry from her own cooking skills, which mainly involve reheating things, although she has taught herself to use the barbecue since William left. Gabi realizes she's ravenous. They usually stop for a grilled sandwich after sex. It's not romantic, but she's not after romance.

The chef shakes his head, disappointed in them for being here, and that puts paid to her ordering takeout.

They stand outside by the trash cans in an alley that smells of garbage and stale piss. Luke pops a square of nicotine gum into his mouth, and offers the packet. Gabi shakes her head.

'You really think your man's going to see us?'

'In private, yeah, once he's got the game settled. He's curious. Same as everybody.' Luke smooths his palms down his pants. 'This case you pulled, Gabi...it's messed up.'

'Worst thing I ever seen.'

'I got a call about a dead baby once. When I was still doing patrol.'

Gabi winces. 'I got it. You don't have to say any more.'

'No, it was worse than that. Hear me out,' he says, but he's wearing a funny little smile.

'Better have a happy ending.'

'Listen. We get to the house, abandoned, boarded up, and my partner refuses to get out of the car. She doesn't want to see it. She's almost crying. She begs me to go in. Bargaining. Week's worth of paperwork if I don't make her come with me. And I don't want to see a dead baby either, but someone's got to go.'

'So you do.'

'With no back-up, except her crying in the car. I'm pissed off. Call said the baby was in the basement, so I go down the stairs one at a time, swinging my flashlight back and forth, one hand on my gun, in case some crackhead jumps me, and there it is. Just like the call-in said, a dead baby. Little naked head poking out among all the trash. I can taste puke in my mouth. Because you see some shit. But dead babies.'

'Fuck.'

'But it's worse than that. There's another one.'

'What the hell case was this? I don't remember this.'

'And another one. And another one. And another one. The whole damn basement is full of dead babies.' He's grinning. 'Only they're not babies, are they? They're baby dolls. Some crazy bastard had filled up his basement with baby dolls.'

'Ah.'

'I went back to get my partner. I said you have to come see this, and I drag her out of the car. Cried all the way down the stairs, and then screamed and then laughed and then she hit me. Transferred to a desk job a month later. Thank God.'

'And the dolls?'

'I guess they're still there. Someone should go find them, clean them up, donate them to a daycare or something. Doesn't your ex have kids?'

'You are an awful human being,' she says, laughing.

'Detroit's finest,' he says. 'Do you hate him?'

'William? No. It was no-one's fault, we just let it slide, and then it was too late. Got caught up in work and running after our kid, and we were doing different shifts – looking back, that was the kicker, you know? Ships in the night. My parents wanted me to move back to Miami after we got divorced, but it felt like that would be giving up.'

'I've noticed that about you.'

'That I'm persistent?'

'Stubborn.'

Her father sends her a link to every news story on violent crime in Detroit, like she's somehow unaware of it in her job. Twenty-two-year-old Renisha McBride shot in the face by a white homeowner, the school that chose to break up a fight between two girls with pepper spray, the warehouse trading in human body parts.

She begged off Thanksgiving in Miami this year because she knew they were going to apply the thumbscrews. Pestering her to take a nice job in special prosecutions investigations, perhaps, and they'd have invited a gentleman of their acquaintance to join them for dinner – who just happened to be single and something benignly professional like an accountant or a lawyer.

'You ever think about moving?' Luke asks.

'After busting my ass for eight years to get to Homicide? But I have thought about Ann Arbor. Small college town. It would be good for Layla.'

'Not much excitement in Ann Arbor,' he observes.

'Thing is, I don't actually believe in justice. It doesn't happen. Not enough. Rapists walk on a technicality. Money buys you out of problems. The wrong guy goes down for murder. Remember that detective who was closing cold cases by fingerprinting homeless people and doctoring the evidence files? People are corrupt and lazy and bad at their jobs.'

'That's a cold statement right there.'

'Not all of them. Some of them are just overworked. You make the arrest, you file all the evidence, and the prosecution screws it up because they're sitting with forty other upcoming trials and they can't give it their full attention. Or the case is delayed because the DNA hasn't been tested, but it's sitting on someone's desk waiting to be analyzed. But what are you going to do? Give up? Walk away from all this?' She makes a sweeping gesture to take in the garbage and the alley, turning it into a joke because they're both getting worked up. 'It's like parenting. You do what needs to be done.'

The door opens behind them and the light sends a cluster of cockroaches scuttling for the cover of darkness. 'He's ready for you,' says the thug.

He ushers them through the beaded curtain and up a narrow flight of stairs, past a closed room buzzing with men's voices, a little drunk, a little reckless – the swagger that comes around money. He knocks once on the door at the end of the passage and swings it open onto a bedroom with a huge photograph of Mecca on the wall above the bed.

Timor is sitting on the bed, smoking. His eyes are too small for his face, which gives him the look of a chubby rat, with a graze of stubble and dark hairs springing from the collar of his shirt and the cuffs of his tailored shirt.

'I give you ten minutes, okay?' he says, in a clipped Russian accent. 'Because I want you to know I don't have anything to do with this. We will clear the air and then you can go fart in someone else's house.'

'Paul Lafonte,' Gabi starts. 'We found your number in the recently dialed list on his phone.'

He interrupts her. 'Yes, he owes me. Two hundred dollars. You think I would put pain on a man for two hundred dollars? Does that make fiscal sense? A broken arm does not help make the payments on my boat.'

'You strike me as the kind of man who doesn't make payments.'

'It's a recession. What can I say?'

'What kind of boat?'

'You know boats? A Beneteau First 30.'

'My father taught me to sail. He skippers a yacht in Miami. Sunset cruises, corporate events. He doesn't own it, though. The upkeep is too expensive.'

'Let me ask you, then, Miss Detective. Would your father throw someone overboard for breaking a champagne glass?'

'If it was damaging to his business and he needed to set an example.'

154

Timor gives her a pitying look. 'Mr. Lafonte cannot hurt my business. He is a small fry and I am the...king lobster. I am very sorry for what happened to his son. It's a terrible thing.'

'So you know what happened?'

'The boy is dead. Isn't that enough?'

'Not in this case. There are some – unusual – specifics.'

'What are these specifics?' He twists one of his heavy gold cufflinks.

'I'm afraid I can't get into that with you, but I need to ask you something. Forgive me being forthright—' Gabi starts.

'No, no, I like a forward woman,' he leers, his mouth full of shining white caps. 'You would like to come sailing one day? It would be my pleasure to have you. See what your father taught you.'

'And go swimming with the fishes? No thank you.' Gabi smiles thinly. 'Russians are known for sending a message. Brutal ones. Cutting off hands and feet. Decapitations. There were feet washing up in Canada a while ago. Would have had to be dumped from a boat.'

'Gabriella,' Luke warns.

Timor sneers. 'I have heard these things too, and maybe some of it is true in other cities. I can't speak for every Russian. But we do not kill children. We are not fucking Mexicans! Not even the narcos would do something this stupid. Bring down the police. For what? Two hundred dollars? You tell Mr. Lafonte that as a sign of goodwill and compassion, I forgive his debt.'

'That's magnanimous of you.'

'I am a generous man,' Timor says, but the atmosphere has turned colder. 'I will wave to you from the deck when you are pulling some dead drunk out of the water, then.

Now, if you will be kind and excuse me. I have a poker game to return to.'

In the car on the way back, Stricker taps the steering wheel with his thumbs, a bass-line of annoyance. 'You shouldn't do that.'

'I know I pushed, but he wasn't about to have us whacked. As he said, it's not worth sabotaging his business.'

'I mean you shouldn't flirt. What's wrong with you?'

'What?' Gabi laughs at the preposterousness of it. 'He invited me on his boat. I shot him down. What do you think the appropriate reaction would have been?'

'This is why female cops get a bad reputation.'

'You could have said exactly the same thing.'

'He wasn't looking at *my* tits.'

'You're putting this on me?'

'Do you know what Mike Croff calls you?'

'Sure. He's told me to my face. Twofer. Latina *and* a woman means I get all the advantages, right? So the department can look more progressive.'

'Threefer. Because you're all that, and pretty too.'

'Well, don't you say the sweetest things. You're not so bad yourself, Stricker. You could be the department poster boy. What does that say about you?'

'Mike says the media is gonna *love* you when it comes to the press briefing. You play it right, you could be heading on up the chain.'

'What do *you* think, Luke? I don't deserve to be OIC? I didn't earn this?'

He keeps his eyes on the road, the deserted streets spottily lit up by half-working streetlights. 'You were first on the scene,' he says, coolly. 'Cards fall where they fall.'

WEDNESDAY,
NOVEMBER 12

Branches of Enquiry

If Gabi had to give the debriefing a score, it would be a D-minus. Lots of leads with no concrete answers, petty bickering because everyone wants this and everyone is tense. Not even the box of donuts Sparkles has the initiative to bring in from Heidi's Kitchen eases things.

Approximate time of death: somewhere between three and five p.m. on Friday afternoon, probably at the bus stop, which, despite the police tape, has already been turned into a memorial, with bunches of flowers and teddy bears tied to it.

Cause of death: a very precise blow to the back of the neck, which severed the vertebrae. Could be a nail gun, or the kind of bolt gun slaughterhouses use on livestock before they slit their throats. Twenty-nine slaughterhouses registered in Michigan, ten within the city limits, mainly round Eastern Market. Two hundred and seven hardware stores in Detroit alone. They're doing tests on pig skulls with various instruments to try to narrow it down.

Results on the adhesive and the blood found at the bus stop are still outstanding. She has put in another priority request.

In the meantime, she's gone back to the case files of the original gang shooting Daveyton was caught in, but it was a drive-by, and the shooter was never identified.

Unfortunately, the history makes the story sexier for the media. There are already calls coming in, begging for details. The parents have requested that photographs not be released to the press in their entirety.

'Straight up,' Joe Miranda says, quietly, so everyone has to pay attention when he talks. 'The journalists have to toe the line on this one. They can show what we tell them to and not a hair more.'

Ovella Washington has compiled a depressingly long list of individual members of racist hate groups in the state. 'Online posturing, mostly,' she says. 'A lot of "Trayvon-had-it-coming" and "Renisha-deserved-to-die" and generally feeling sorry for themselves and whining about how the black man is keeping them down. Daveyton's name came up on the forums only once – "One less nigger to worry about." If his killer was a crazy racist, he's not bragging about it online. The neo-nazis are more worried about running drugs. They'll talk the talk, but I don't think they'd want to risk bringing the police down on them with a stunt like this.' She taps her file with her glittering nails. 'In conclusion, I think it's highly unlikely it was the work of an organized group, but it could have been a loner within a group.'

'So we can't rule out that race might be a factor.'

'There's a lot of hate out there. What you can do is get me some brain bleach to get the horrible shit I had to read out of my head.'

'What about the Satanists?' Boyd says.

'Couldn't find any. There is an all-female roller-derby

160

team called Satan's Hotties. They don't believe in God or Satan and they definitely don't do any occult rituals.'

'Then it's a dumb name,' Boyd mutters.

'I've also spoken to local members of the Wiccan and pagan communities, who were frankly offended. I've got the address of a local botanica if you want to talk to a santeria priest. They sacrifice animals sometimes.'

'Sacrificing goats to kids doesn't seem like such a big jump to me. That voodoo shit gives me the creeps,' Mike Croff says.

'Man, you are one dumb, uncultured motherfucker if you think voodoo and santeria are the same thing.'

'Oh, touchy. You a believer, Ovella?'

'Manners, both of you,' Miranda says mildly, but it's enough to get them both to shut up.

There's a sullen silence, and then Marcus volunteers, 'I went back to have a look at that graffiti where the body was found, like you said, Detective Versado. There's a mural of a teenage girl's face painted at the end of that tunnel, so I looked into it. It's a memorial – one of her friends painted it after she fell off a roof and died.'

'Okay, so?' Gabi asks.

'Well, Daveyton died. Or nearly died the time he was shot. Could be a link. The killer could be making a statement about dead kids. It doesn't have to be race-related.'

'Seems like a reach. Sorry, Sparkles.'

'Thought I'd tell you anyway. There's also a pink square drawn in chalk on the wall, close to where the body was. Has to be recent, because chalk would wash away.'

'Good work,' Gabi says, 'I'll make a note.' Actually, she's impressed – they have to go wide at this stage. The kid could be a contender.

Stricker chips in, a little frosty, she thinks. 'I found you a taxidermist. She's been in Cleveland, teaching, but she just got back if you want to talk to her.'

'I definitely do,' Gabi says. They might even have lab results back by then.

'I also spoke to the sideshow people. They got a fire-breathing act and contortionists and acrobats and puppets. They do not have a freak show. The manager asked if they should consider it.'

'Now would be a bad time to start. How are the hunters' records looking, Boyd?'

'Great. Real great. Only nine hundred and ninety-eight thousand four hundred and fifty-three licenses to go!'

'That's not what you're really doing.'

'Nah, I'm looking at hunters with animal cruelty raps. It means they've killed buck out of season or shot under-sized animals. Two arrests in October, but there are a handful every year. I've put the word out about any unusual kills, hunters going for yearlings. But you also got to remember that there are fifty thousand car accidents a year involving deer. Our man could have hit it by mistake. Or on purpose. What I'm saying is the deer is a bust.'

'What about its stomach contents? Any unusual flora?'

'I'll go back to the ME,' Boyd grumbles.

And she's retrieved the bloody newspaper that was used to stuff the cavity and scoured every page. Random sections ripped from the *Detroit Star* over the last few years. Sparkles is going through the subscription list and cross-referencing against their other leads.

Now that the word is out, several precincts have phoned in with cold cases that are not vaguely related. 'But it's a black kid,' they whine, trying their luck. 'It's a man with an old bullet wound. Her body was found in a field where deer were grazing.'

They still have not found the rest of the remains.

The mayor's office has sent someone over to take an official statement. They are hoping that the DPD will be able to handle this with due care and sensitivity to the family, and without panicking parents of school-going kids everywhere.

'In other words, can we please make sure we don't get another corpse with a deer's ass sewed onto it,' Miranda says, and shuts it down for the day.

Opening Up

Jonno has spent half his life chasing the next big thing, trying to find a new hook, a new angle, a new spin, but now he realizes that people don't want novelty – they want the reassurance of familiarity. No-one wants to be challenged, no-one wants to have their minds blown. There is an insatiable appetite for affirmation. Back me up here, bro. Help me keep believing the thing I already believe.

The wise man gives the people what they want, more of the same, slightly repackaged. Look: it's exactly the same shit you've seen before, but this time with a different camera angle and more explosions! Emphasis on camera angles. It's easier to catch people's attention with moving pictures, Jen has assured him, and he hopes to hell she's right, because he's just dumped the last of his savings on an expensive laptop with editing software and a fancy lens for his iPhone.

He might be aging as well as George Clooney, but the camera does not love him in anything like the same way. The screen shows him a face that he doesn't recognize in the mirror, softening under the chin, his ears bigger than he realized. Old man's ears. He'll be growing hair out of them next.

If it was just his male pride, he might be able to get over it. Men don't need to be pretty to be on screen like women do. But the words don't come out right either. As soon as she points the iPhone at him, he fluffs it. He's tried writing the script beforehand, but his delivery is flat. He can't say the words the way he knows they sound on the page. It's some malevolent distortion in the camera. Revenge, because technology knows he hates it and it reciprocates the feeling. But he's trying, fuck knows he's trying. He's standing in front of a house that's been turned into whimsical sculpture, plastic leaves coating the walls, Adam and Eve holding hands above the doorframe. This is not his thing.

'Detroit's art scene is…ergh. Shit. Take it again. Okay. The city might be dying, but Detroit's art scene is burgeoning—'

'Don't use that word,' Jen interrupts him.

'What?'

'You're trying to be too clever. This isn't writing.'

No shit, Jonno thinks and gives her a salute. 'Yessir, Marshall McLuhan!'

'Too clever again. Try smiling.'

She holds up the mic, like an ice cream cone, and he bares his teeth obediently.

'Less fangs,' she says. He tries a different smile, which seems just as fake. He tries to put a spark in his eyes that will reach right through the screen and keep people watching for longer than the first twenty seconds, which is when most people click away, she's told him.

She's done all the research about viewing stats and advertising, and how if you get more than a hundred thousand views, YouTube will let you use their studios, maybe send you a fancy camera. She has shown him videos of people playing video games, for Christ's sake, who pull in a hundred K a month in advertising and a pretty boy in South Africa who makes a million a year with cutesy prank videos about his dog or how much he hates the beach.

'High culture then,' Jonno complains.

'He gets flown round the world. He does mall appearances. Girls scream like he's Justin Bieber.'

'That's not me, baby. That's never going to be me.'

'No, but you're smarter than him. You have something to say. You just have to *say* it.'

She's set up the video channel, even designed a logo for him, in between waitressing and DJing. Which is more than he's accomplished this week.

Sure, he's sent out story pitches to all his old contacts and some new editors, too. The problem is he didn't just burn his bridges when he left New York, he blew them up and napalmed the river.

You can miss a deadline or two, even three. You can fail to reply to increasingly frustrated, angry, disappointed emails, as long as you get back to people eventually, grovel, cite personal tragedy. (And that's true, he thinks, fiercely, before his troll can get a word in. It *was* tragic. It *did* fuck him up.) But to fail to deliver after they've granted you clemency? And become a repeat offender? He's on a dozen shit lists. It would take a miracle to get him back into writing, which is the only reason he's let Jen talk him in to this.

The up side: she's spending more time at his place, which means he has to keep it tidy. Which in the peculiar psychology of humans immediately makes him feel better about himself (not like he doesn't know this: '5 Quick Fixes To Instantly Boost Your Mood'). Getting laid also helps. The downside is that he feels like now he has to carry all her expectations.

When really what you want is for her to be carrying your *expectations. Little Jonno or Jen junior. Hey, have you asked if she has the genetic kind of diabetes?*

He was the one who wanted out. He accused Cate of getting pregnant on purpose to catch him. Like he was the fish of the day – and such a great prospect at that. Self-employed writer, living in a shitty apartment in Queens and thinking about moving to Jersey because the rent was getting too expensive, creeping up on forty with nothing to show except sixteen thousand words of the great American novel – which he refused to let her read.

Meanwhile, she actually had a career. Brand manager for an upmarket fashion e-tailer. She managed to get him commissions for their content portal: 'The Tweed Resurrection' (actual title they used), the best-kept secret breakfast spots in Martha's Vineyard. Which helped pay the rent until he missed a deadline because he was hungover, and got snarky with the editor via email. And the truth was, he resented having to rely on Cate's goodwill.

He wanted her to go for an abortion. It was the sensible and responsible and absolutely right thing to do. They'd only been dating for eighteen months. And sure, maybe he'd made a dumb joke about all the free shit they'd get if they married, but he didn't mean it like that. Not yet.

He looked up all the information online. Easy-as-pie. If it was six weeks, they could have it taken care of right away. *Like a mafia hit.* He tried to tell her about it in their neighborhood vinoteq, how you could insert some pills and forty-eight hours later, problem solved. They could order pizza, watch some movies – he'd take care of her.

'You make it sound like a date,' Cate said. 'Or a bad bout of 'flu.'

Through the windows, they could see a film shoot under-way in a sectioned-off part of the street with cameras and cranes and a lunch table set up under an awning.

'Wonder what they're shooting?'

'Car crash,' she said, pointing out the dented BMW with a motorbike lying next to it. A hefty man was showing the actor in black leathers how to roll across the bonnet of the car. Again and again. This is how you do it.

'Like our relationship,' he tried to joke.

Cate rolled the stem of her glass between her fingers. She'd ordered sparkling water, not wine. 'I'm keeping it,' she said, her gray eyes clear. 'I'm thirty-eight, Jonno. I might not get another chance.'

Over the next six weeks, they broke up, got back together, broke up again. He said some shitty things. Accused her of using him as a sperm bank. She retorted that he was the last man on earth she would have *chosen* to get sperm from. He demanded a paternity test. She said only if he signed a waiver that if it turned out to be his child, he rescinded all rights to see it.

Fear makes you ugly.

She went to the first scan without him, sent him an audio file of the heartbeat. Like white noise or the rush of traffic. It was nothing, he told himself. Good luck with that, he texted back.

He woke up next to some girl he'd picked up in a bar, and had his big revelation. He'd been trying to make it for twelve years in this city, and this was all he had to show. This crummy apartment with no kitchen sink, so he had to wash the dishes in the bath, and a girl from Cincinnati, not-quite-pretty-enough-to-be-a-model, with the same hungri-ness in her, wanting in to all of it: the bright lights, the parties, those secret breakfast spots he wrote about for other people. It's all a lie, he wanted to tell her. They've got bouncers for people like you and me. We might get in the door, but we'll never be part of that world, not really. He'd been trying for so long. New York wasn't made for creative people anymore, and maybe there came a time you needed to give up your fantasies and concentrate on the important stuff.

Like love. Like a family.

And then, just when he figured out what he really wanted, Cate miscarried. No pills from Planned Parenthood required. The body's way of dumping a non-viable fetus. Like bad stocks.

Twenty per cent of women miscarry in the first trimester. Millions of people go through this every day, she told him. It's part of the human experience. That made it worse – the pain wasn't even unique.

She got over it. He didn't.

He became obsessive, trawling through all the pregnancy sites: 'At eleven weeks, your baby is now the size of a fig.'

Or a lime or a muscadine grape, whatever the fuck that is. All those edible babies. One point six inches. The hurt seems bigger than that.

He begged her to take him back, in a fucking Starbucks near her work. Cate was composed even while she was crying. He tried to explain. He cataloged all the ways he'd been stupid and scared, and that it was the process he had to go through to get here. He was committed now. They could try again. She leaned over the table to take his hand in both of hers and said, 'Oh God, Jonno. I think we've dodged a bullet, don't you?' And then she got up and put twenty dollars on the table to cover their coffees – way too much and, besides, he'd already paid at the counter – and walked out of his life, and didn't return his calls or texts or emails – all the ones he tried not to send.

It all unraveled after that. He'd open up his computer and the blinking cursor was so fucking oppressive, he'd click away to his browser. Jesus, why did they have to make it blink?

He played online games and watched a lot of porn. The games got dumber. The porn got darker and more fucked-up. He recognized this as a symptom of his own numbness. He listened to the audio file of the heartbeat of a ghost.

He let the phone ring and ring. He didn't call his friends back. He didn't call his parents or his sisters. He missed a whole slew of deadlines. He missed payment on his rent. Two months in a row was all it took.

He came home to find the locks changed and his stuff in boxes outside the front door. Half of it had been stolen already. He dumped the rest on the steps out the front of the building, took his laptop and a bag of clothes – the nice stuff Cate had scored for him as part of her employee freebie benefits – and bought a last-minute plane ticket to the most fucked-up place he could think of.

If he'd been braver, maybe he would have got into hard-core drugs, fallen from grace and ended up literally in the gutter. But this felt like more of a dramatic statement. A pilgrimage of failure to the country's Mecca of ruined dreams. His friends thought he was nuts. He sent them a group message and didn't reply to any of theirs. Fresh starts don't come with expired relationships attached.

He didn't really expect to find anything here, though. He didn't anticipate falling in love, let alone getting the chance to reboot his whole life.

If he can just get it right for the damn camera.

'Okay. Okay. Are you rolling? I'm here in the Powerhouse District in Detroit, where artists are working on the Dream House project. It's taken three months of preparations to transform these rat-traps—'

'I don't think you should say rat-traps,' Jen interrupts him. 'It sounds disrespectful.'

'Fine,' he says, brushing his hair back. 'Pick-up?'

'Okay, but fix your hair.'

He smooths his hair, takes a breath and starts again. 'I'm here at the Powerhouse District in Detroit, where a group of visionary artists have spent the last three months working hard to transform these derelict *death-traps*,' he raises his eyebrows for emphasis and she pouts at him, 'into astonishing works of art.'

'Maybe you should do it less like a local news channel. People like humor.'

'You didn't like my death-trap joke?'

'They want to see you, Jonno. You have to let them in.'

'I hate this.'

'We'll edit it. Start with an image of super-weird art with music and a voice-over. It'll be cool. Trust me. Okay, look at me, not at the lens, it'll seem more natural.'

WWCD. *What would Clooney do?* Good question. He sticks out his jaw, raising it to hide the flabbiness underneath and cocks his head, just a little. Attitude. That Clooney insouciance, like he's just goosed the bride.

'These are the things you know about Detroit,' he says, counting off on his fingers. 'One. The whole city went bankrupt. Two. It's full of derelict death-traps that look pretty if you photograph them in the right light. Three. Eminem.'

171

Jen nods vigorously and mouths 'Awesome.'

'But there's a group of exciting young artists who aren't letting any of those things get in the way of their vision.'

'I'm Jonno Haim.' It sounds good. 'And I'm going to walk you through the preparations on the Dream House project. Hopefully without breathing in too much asbestos or having the roof cave in on me.'

'Cut.'

Jen flings herself onto him and covers his face with kisses. 'See! I knew you'd be brilliant.'

He kisses her back. He loves her enthusiasm, her faith in him, her sweetness. He always was a good bullshit artist.

And he really hopes Cate sees this.

Stuffed

The media are in high spirits at the press briefing. Child abduction and murder will do that. Especially when the victim was already a mascot of Detroit's plucky survivor spirit, with a drive-by shooting merit badge. Because if it's not a little blonde white girl, you need a human-interest angle. The DPD have released Daveyton's name and photograph, and offered a reward for more information. They have not disclosed all the details. Gabi can't *wait* for the newshounds to find out the *real* angle.

She hates this. She didn't become a cop to stand in front of cameras and journalists popping up and down from their seats like groundhogs with questions, and Luke's words in the back of her head. *Threefer.*

'Did the killer choose Daveyton specifically?'

'At this stage, we don't want to comment,' she says, sticking to the script the mayor's office gave her.

The camera flashes going off make her feel like she's having one of those paparazzi experiences you can rent for your prom or your wedding. Red carpet, limo, men with cameras chasing after you. Pop-uprazzi.

'Is it true that the body was mutilated?'

'I can't comment on that.'

'Is this a serial killer?'

'So far, this is a once-off.'

'Where are the parents? Are they suspects?'

'They're in mourning,' *you asshole*, she thinks but doesn't say, but it comes through clear enough. 'They've released a statement, which we've printed out for you to collect at the door.'

'Should we be closing the schools? Are our children safe?'

The mayor's aide, Jessica diMenna, steps in, smooth as a single malt, with hair the same honey color. 'The mayor's office is meeting with all district schools and community leaders. Humboldt Middle School will be closed for a week to allow the faculty and students to process this tragic loss and to attend Daveyton's memorial service. We're confident that our police force will bring the monster who did this to justice. I'd like to emphasize that it's so important that we remain calm and that we continue our lives as usual. I think it's what Davey would have wanted.'

Gabi studies the floor. She suspects that what Daveyton might have wanted is a chance to have a fucking life.

'That went okay,' Jessica smiles, posing for one last set of photographs, one hand on Captain Miranda's shoulder, one on Gabi's. The model of confidence that everything will be alright.

Gabi can't stand it. She excuses herself as soon as she can. She thinks about texting Stricker – maybe a quickie will get the anxiety out of her system. But they're not talking outside of the detectives' briefing room at the moment because she's still angry with him. Worse, he might be right – maybe they *are* grooming her. She can still feel

174

Jessica's hand on her shoulder. Screw Stricker, she thinks – metaphorically, if she can't in person. And screw them all for putting her in this position when she's just here to do her job.

Boyd's car is parked outside the taxidermist's house, a neat little two-bedroom in Livonia, across the highway from the strip mall.

'How was feeding-time at the zoo?' Boyd asks, the window sliding down to release the witchy aroma of coffee.

'Messy,' Gabi says. 'Did you happen to—?' But Marcus is already leaning over to hand her a takeaway cup. She reaches for it gratefully. 'Oh, you can definitely stay, Sparkles.'

'Sorry, it's got a bit cold.'

'Yeah, sorry I kept you waiting.'

'We were too scared to go in without you,' Boyd says, ringing the doorbell. 'Hey, what did the taxidermist say to the cops?'

'I don't know, what?'

'Get stuffed.' Which is the moment Maxie Lautner opens the door.

'Oh, hi! I thought I heard voices.' She does not look like a taxidermist should.

For starters, she is cute. Early twenties, petite with blonde hair and one of those bull nose-rings, which Gabi has always thought were the stupidest of all piercings. It would be easy to grab and twist it, bring her to her knees. Cop-think: all the ugliness in the world.

The girl clops ahead on wedge boots like hooves, leading the way into her living room. It's a tidy little house, if you can look past the creepy dead critters everywhere; rabbits and mice, mostly, although there are several deer heads and a young kangaroo poking its head out of an embroidered denim pouch with the words 'home is where the art is' cross-stitched in gold.

Sparkles bends to examine the glass display case full of little skeletons. There is a two-headed rabbit under a glass dome, standing upright, one paw raised as if pointing at something just behind her head. Gabi resists the urge to turn to look.

'It's all legal, before you ask,' the girl says.

'Why would you say that?'

Maxie glances warily at Marcus's uniform. Her voice does that up intonation, which makes every sentence sound like a question. 'I've had problems with the cops before. I guess it was my own fault. I was working on an adult kangaroo in the garage and there was blood running down into the street, and my neighbor must have freaked out. Next thing I know the cops show up and walk into my garage, and I'm holding a scalpel over a bloody corpse? The one cop starts squealing, "Oh my God, I can't handle this right now." Like what is she going to do if she finds an actual murder?'

'Where the heck did you get your hands on a kangaroo?'

'Mostly I buy dead frozen rabbits on the Internet, but my friends will call me if they spot fresh roadkill, and this guy knew a guy who worked at a zoo? So when their kangaroo died, he arranged to ship it to me on dry ice.'

Actually, Gabi reckons, the most unbelievable part of the story is that the neighbors called it in at all. Most people can't be bothered. Blind eyes, like the glazed glass beads staring out of the two-headed rabbit.

'Did they book you on a hygiene violation?' Marcus asks.

'Nah,' Boyd says. 'Hunters are allowed to process meat at home. Long as they got a license.'

Maxie brightens, eager to show her credentials. 'I have

a taxidermy license, issued by the Department of Natural Resources. It's somewhere.' She opens a drawer in an old-fashioned roll-top desk, and digs around. 'Covers domestic animals and roadkill. Only thing you can't do is endangered. Like this guy phoned me to ask if I would do a bald eagle for him and I was all like, that's a federal offense? You could go to jail for ten years for that, it's a two hundred and fifty thousand dollar fine.'

Boyd gives a low whistle. 'That's a lot of green.'

'I know. You'd have to be so stupid.'

'I like your two-headed rabbit.'

'Oh thanks. I'm proud of that one. The art is in making it as lifelike as possible, but sometimes it's fun to play around and create gaff animals. Like the Feejee mermaids from the Barnum Bailey circus? They're my favorite. Half-fish, half-monkey.'

'You hear of anyone doing humans? Someone's granny or grandpa?' Boyd asks.

'There are those realistic toy babies,' Gabi says, thinking of Luke's story about the dolls in the basement. 'They're popular with women who have miscarried or lost a child. You ever hear about someone who does that with real babies?'

'Oh man, that would be so sad.' Maxie sits down on the couch, clasping her hands in front of her. 'Having your own baby embalmed and taxidermied? No, that is seriously illegal. Way more illegal than a bald eagle. You have to be a registered mortician to work with human bodies.'

'And you don't know anyone doing that?'

'Okay, taxidermists are into twisted humor. And the weird stuff sells, you know? There's a shop in San Francisco that keeps bugging me to do more two-headed rabbits. Or mice in Victorian clothing with teeny parosols. But I've never,

ever heard of someone doing anything with a real person.'

'You know anyone who specializes in deer? Or deer gaffs?'

'Oh, everyone does deer. They're boring. I like working with small animals. They're very tricky. Pretty much every class I teach, someone pokes the mouse in the stomach and it explodes. You have to make such a small hole to get the skin off. It's like peeling an orange. A really gross orange.'

'What do you do to keep the shape?' Gabi asks, thinking of the newspaper they pulled out of Daveyton.

'Well, you can either make a plaster cast of the body and fill it with foam rubber or, what a lot of people are doing now, especially with smaller animals, is you just make a little mummy out of tape or string in the same shape as the animal, and then ease the skin back on. Use a little embalming fluid on the paws and the nose to keep them from cracking and you're done.'

'How about the seams?' Boyd asks. 'You use superglue, something like that?'

'No, you stitch it. Very, very carefully, from the inside with fishing line. With most animals the fur covers it up. If you were doing a reptile or a fish, you'd cover it with clay and airbrush it.'

'But you *could* use superglue?'

'If you didn't know what you were doing. I guess so. Oh, but you were asking about deer gaffs. I think I might have seen a picture of a fawn with dove wings on the Internet.'

'Do you think you could find that again? Identify the artist?'

'I think it was someone in Croatia. He does a lot of beautiful gaffs.'

'I'm going to show you some photographs now,' Gabi says, moving into formal mode. 'You have to be aware that

178

this is part of an active investigation, and that you are not to disclose any information about this to anyone.'

'That's heavy.'

'It's a murder investigation. Do you agree to these terms?'

'Sure, of course. I said on the phone. It's like being a doctor, right? Total confidentiality.'

Gabi does not point out that a DNR license is not quite the same as a medical degree.

'It's very graphic. I'm warning you.'

Maxie shrugs. 'I work with roadkill.'

Gabi hands her the photographs. She's picked them carefully. None of them show Daveyton's face.

'Woah,' the girl says, paling, which makes the holes in her nose flare red. 'That's fucked up.'

'Does this look like the work of anyone you know? The guy in Croatia?'

She shakes her head. 'No. Definitely not.'

'Anyone doing anything similar? With monkeys or rabbits? Practice runs?'

'No. Not like this. This isn't the work of a taxidermist. You'd never cut through the body like this – halfway through? You slit the skin down the back, along the dorsal muscle, or do a ventral cut down the stomach to peel it. You're not working with the *meat*.' She shudders.

'What if he was in a hurry?'

'No way. It's going to rot. The whole point of taxidermy is to try to get as much of the flesh out as possible. You want to keep the first couple of layers of skin, because it dries around the follicles and stops the hair falling out, but not more than that. This guy isn't a taxidermist. He's not even trying to be. I mean, you could watch how-to videos online. This person didn't have a clue.'

Faygo and a Gun

The nightmares have been coming every time TK gets some shut-eye. God's way of prodding him to think about his family more, if he held any truck with God. So even though it's only been a coupla weeks since his last visit to his momma, he goes again. He has a whole ritual he follows: he takes her a mini bottle of Jim Beam and a Faygo Cola, has one sip and pours the rest out on her grave. It doesn't count as breaking your sobriety if you're honoring the dead. Hard to believe more than forty years have passed. Still feels as fresh as yesterday.

He wasn't called TK then. He was Tommy. Or Tom or Tee. The night she died, he'd taken his little brother and sister out trick or treating. It was Florence's first Halloween, dressed up like a ghost in an old floral sheet. When she complained, he'd told her that girl ghosts wear flowers. Leroy was a vampire with a cape made from an old sweat-shirt TK had cut the sleeves off, and two smears of red lipstick at the corners of his mouth. They'd even wandered up to a white neighborhood to see the decorations and knock on the doors. The candy was better, but they also got some ugly looks. So he was in a bad mood when they got back to the house. He saw the door standing open, and he knew, he just *knew*, something was wrong.

The little kids were bickering over a Snickers bar. 'Wait here,' he told them.

'But I'm tired,' Florrie said.

'I said, wait here. Or I'll confiscate your candy. You won't see none of it.' Florrie started crying, that high-pitched whine of hers that turned into big gulping sobs. But he couldn't do nothing about that. He went inside to find his momma half on the floor, half on the couch, blood everywhere – on the white fluffy carpet she was so proud of, soaking through her clothes. He had to scream at Florrie and Leroy to stay the fuck outside, like I tole you, goddammit.

He tried to pick her up, but she was like a sack of sawdust. There were bubbles of blood on her lips. She whispered, 'Love you, my baby, love you.'

'What happened, Momma?'

'Ricky,' she said. His name shouldn't have been the last thing in her mouth.

Her twin sister's boyfriend. That was some soap-opera bullshit. Got the wrong woman. Killed the good twin. Only his momma were bad, too. Both of them, fucked-up women hanging round evil men, having more kids than they could look after.

He carried a piece since the age of nine so he could be her protector, fetch her from the bar where some man would be making demands that he weren't willing to pay for. TK learned to dread the screech of the payphone in the hall or some kid calling his name from down the block, *Tommmeeeeee*. But he headed down there anyways, .38

tucked into his pants at two in the morning to negotiate with some drunk-ass nigga who was getting too hands-on.

Leroy tried to poke his head in to get a look-see. 'Go to Uncle Lewis's,' TK shouted. He went to get the gun from behind the photo albums on the shelf.

'Where you going?' Florrie said, clinging to his pants as he locked the door and tried to walk down the steps. 'Don't go, Tommy.'

'Gonna get a grape Faygo down the store,' he said, pushing her away. Some part of him believed it, too.

'Don't go! Don't leave us. What about the candy?' She set Leroy off too. Both of them standing there bawling, but only thing he could do was just keep them out the house.

'Go to Uncle Lewis,' he repeated, but he didn't stay to see if they followed his instructions.

He didn't make it to the store. Got to Ricky Furman's house – he knew where he lived – and stood outside, watching the back of his head as he sat in front of the TV like nothing had happened. *The Munsters*. The theme tune still makes his blood rush away. The front door was unlocked. He walked right in, grabbed him and pulled him backwards over the couch, tipping the whole thing over, and shot him four times, right there in his living room. He don't remember any of that. It's all dark red, like looking at the sun through your eyelids. Like coming up after a seizure. He was the one who called the cops.

I think I just shot someone.

Only it wasn't just *someone*. It was the cocksucker who stabbed his momma again and again, until all the life ran out of her.

***

182

The can of Faygo he brought last time is lying in the grass next to her grave, under the shade of the paradise trees. He tried to get Leroy a plot nearby, but by that stage it cost too much. He had his little brother cremated after he died of a heart attack three years ago, and sprinkled the ashes on his momma's grave, so they could be together.

He sets the can on top of the grave and borrows a bust-up deck chair from a few gravestones away. No-one will mind if he uses it, long as he puts its back where he found it. He lowers himself down – his knees ain't what they used to be – and the canvas protests like it might rip, but it holds.

'See, Ma,' he says, 'my higher power's still lookin' out for me.' He tries not to think about the chairs clustered round him in the storage room at the church. Circling the wagons.

'How you been, Ma? Florence sends her love. I spoke to her on the phone yesterday. She's not working for that telemarketing company any more. She used to memorize the scripts, but now they say you got to use the exact wording for legal reasons, and that it's too expensive to print Braille manuals. I told her she should sue them for discrimination, but you know what Florrie's like. Too sweet to litigate.' He nudges the can with his toe, thinking about how Florrie smiles with unmoderated joy, because she can't see that most people bank their happiness like it's something you might run out of.

'Still working on getting a house, still putting something by, and waiting to hear if I'm gonna get that grant. The city works so slow, Ma. I got my eye on a place that's real torn up. I reckon I can fix it, given a year and some helping hands – and then I'll move Florrie down, out of that home for the blind in Flint. Have to do it over the summer, though, when the weather's better.'

183

He rips up some of the more obstinate weeds. 'I feel a lot of weight, Ma. On my chest. Not like a heart attack, don't worry. I'm looking after myself. I ain't gonna go the same way as Leroy. Sometimes it feels like you're carrying the whole world, you know? Guess you don't. You were just a dirty whore who didn't care about no-one but yourself. But you're still my momma. Never loved and hated someone so much at the same time, Ma.'

He sinks into quiet and swipes at the can with his foot with none of the violence he feels. 'Anyway, thought I would come by.' He stands and folds the deck chair. 'You look after yourself. Leroy, too. And don't you worry about me, Ma.'

On his way home, he takes a leisurely stroll down through Delray, where the prairie is sweeping in between the houses guarded over by flat-painted angels. World needs more angels, even plywood ones. A yellow dog barks at him from behind a chain-link fence, all possessive ferocity and no damn balls. Just like the gang-banger kids. They think a pistol equals cojones. That's why they tuck them in their pants. But a man should think with his guts, not his junk.

He crosses over to get away from the dog, heading toward the shuttered-up brick cube in pastel pink that is the only building left standing on this block. The rest is broken cement and grass and weeds and trash people have dumped here. Always tires. And usually a kids' scooter. Pretty much guaranteed. He'll poke around to see if there's anything salvageable. One day, he thought he'd found a human leg bone. Even called the cops, who were as freaked out as he was until the detective arrived and identified it as a cow bone. 'You thought maybe André the Giant died in this field?' TK didn't feel so bad about it because the officers

184

had been scared sick, too. They bought him a burger afterwards and laughed about it.

The faded peach building is a strip club. Or used to be. BARENAKED LADIES the sign reads, or would if some of the letters hadn't fallen off. B RE AKED L DIES. Hell, if that ain't a sign, then the sheriff's notice on the door – 'Foreclosed. Assets seizure' – definitely is.

The doors and windows have been boarded up, but sometimes they get lax round the back. Especially if they ain't planning on returning. TK moseys round the side of the building. Sure enough, someone has already cracked the doorframe, still attached to the deadbolt, but no longer to the door. It's not breaking and entering if there's no breaking involved. TK opens the door onto darkness, which becomes absolute when it swings shut behind him.

He goes back outside and scuffs around until he finds a piece of broken concrete to prop open the door and let in some light. He still has to feel his way round while his eyes adjust. Past the bathrooms, the smell of old piss. He steps confidently forward into the main bar and smashes his hip into the edge of a pool table.

'Shit. Ow!'

He pulls out his phone and uses it as a pathetic excuse for a flashlight. The place has already been gutted. Bottles smashed. Brass taps ripped right off the draft beer barrels. Probably zinc underneath. Place like this wouldn't have expensive fittings. He picks up a broken pool cue from the table. He was never a boy scout, but it's good to be prepared anyhow.

He's looking for the stairs to the dressing rooms. Back when he was a stupid yapping dog of a man right out of prison, he had a stripper girlfriend. Or he thought she was his girlfriend, but he was just another mope buying a little human attention. He knew the girls kept their stuff in the dressing room, and that the boss's office was behind that. He's willing to bet whoever broke in here didn't make it that far.

He climbs up onto the stage and can't resist grabbing the pole and swinging his weight round it. 'Baby, baby,' he laughs at himself.

There's a metal tik-tak sound in the gloom behind him.

TK turns quick, smashing the pool cue against the pole for effect. The clang reverberates through the empty club. 'You get the hell out of here, or I will break you! You hear me?'

He waits and listens. But there's no follow-up. No curious critters this time. He steps behind the DJ booth and pushes the curtain aside to reveal a door. At first he thinks it's locked, but he pushes hard against it and it gives way on to a narrow staircase that must have been hell to do in high heels.

Upstairs is a narrow attic, untouched apart from the broken glass across the floor where some fool decided to throw rocks through the window. Sheriff missed these assets, which means it's fair game, TK reckons. He has to stoop to go in under the rafters.

The four narrow dressing-room cubicles are surrounded by lightbulbs. One of those see-through plastic high heels is lying forlorn on its side. Your prince ain't never gonna find you now, he thinks. He runs his fingers through the tangle of red and platinum-blonde wigs on the counter, until he sees the speckle of rat droppings and snatches his hand away in a hurry.

The door to the office is standing open, but so is the safe behind the desk. The boss obviously had time to clear out the cash, even if he didn't take the booze. The disappointment

186

tastes like stale tobacco in his mouth. Or it might be the smell up here. He won't lie to himself – he was hoping for a tote bag full of Benjamins, like in the movies.

But then he turns round and jackpot: a flat-screen TV mounted up in the corner. Perfect condition. Even has the remote in a plastic holder mounted on the wall next to a handwritten sign that says 'Personnal who do not replace the TV remote will be fined'. He fires off a text.

>TK: R. Barenaked Ladies, DelRay. Bring a screwdriver.

They'll need one to get the TV off the mounts without damaging it, and a trash bag to carry it in. Don't want to get robbed, especially in this neighborhood.

He goes through the drawers in the girls' booths while he's waiting for Ramón to call him back. He finds dried-out makeup, a hair pick, a sequined bikini top. He leaves that alone – he wouldn't want some stranger pawing at his under-wear. He also finds a photograph of a little boy squinting into the sun on a bicycle on the Riverwalk. Why did she leave it behind? It bothers him. He's getting a little choked up about it, when he hears the same tik-tak sound from downstairs.

'Ramón?'

There's no answer. He picks up the pool cue and makes his way carefully down the stairs.

His friend is standing in the gloom, facing the wall, his palm up against it like he wants to push through, his other hand working his rosary beads. It sends a cold prickle all the way up TK's spine into the base of his skull.

'What are you doing?' he calls out, louder than he intended, but hell if he isn't freaking him out, standing there staring at the goddamn wall.

187

'It's a door,' Ramón says, but his voice is high-pitched and distant. 'I think I can open it.' His hands work over the beads.

'No. Don't you do that,' TK says, hurrying down the stairs. Maybe he trips as he climbs down off the stage. Only possible explanation. Because next thing he knows, one of those metal bar stools hurtles right into Ramón and knocks him down, breaking his contact with the door, which isn't a door at all, just a chalk rectangle someone's drawn on the wall.

'What the fuck you do that for?' Ramón says, climbing unsteadily to his knees, rubbing his hip where the stool struck him.

'It was an accident. Knocked it as I came down.' From halfway across the room. TK eyes the bar stool suspiciously as he pulls Ramón to his feet. 'I was wrong about the TV. It's got a big old crack.'

'You got me down here for nothing?' Ramón sulks.

'Yeah, sorry. I'll make it up to you. C'mon, let's get out of here. It's too sad, man. Too sad.' He hustles him out into the bright sunlight, away from the drawing on the wall. But Ramón keeps looking back.

Flavor of the Month

Gabi is going over the photographs again when a cardboard folder slides slowly down over her screen, complete with sound-effect. 'Sha-bloooo00op,' Mike Croff says, leaning over the edge of her cubicle, like the cat who got the canary *and* an airtight alibi.

'Better be good, Mike,' she says, taking the folder. It's the one thing she misses from Beaubien – offices with doors.

'Are you prepared to have your mind blown?' Croff pops his fingers in a slow-mo simulation of an explosion.

'Sure, blow me.' She means it too, after what Luke told her.

'That's funny. You said "blow me", and you don't have a dick.'

'Unless you have the other half of my kid, it's going to have to be pretty damn spectacular.' She pushes back on her chair. Her old chair had give, it would let you lean right back, this one is ergonomically designed with lower lumbar support that somewhat ruins any attempt at don't-give-a-shit cool.

'I got something *beautiful* from forensics.' He takes Boyd's chair from his desk and straddles it the wrong way

189

round, setting his chin on the backrest and watching her.

'About time,' she says, tapping the folder, not opening it, not wanting to give him the satisfaction.

'It's not superglue and it's not Dermabond, which plastic surgeons use to glue together skin edges, especially on kids who have face-planted into the edge of the table. It's also not Fibrin, which you would use to seal blood vessels.'

'Thank you for that.' She opens the damn file already and skims it, trying to get ahead of him. Amino acid chains. R group bonding. Denatured. Enzymes.

'What the fuck is "transglutaminase"?'

'That's where it gets really interesting. Ever hear of Wylie Dufresne or Heston Blumenthal?'

'Jesus Christ, Mike.' Gabi sits upright in her chair – easier with lumbar support. 'You got an ID?'

'Don't you wish. You want me to hand you your whole case wrapped up with a bow? No, they're chefs who make seriously pretentious food. Molecular gastronomy.'

'You *are* wasting my time.'

'Ah, but it's the trickle-down effect. Except, unlike the economy, it actually works. Cooking techniques make it down the food chain.'

'Can we skip ahead to the good bit?'

'Transglutaminase. Also known as meat glue. Fancy restaurants, the kind you and I can't afford, my dear, use it to make concoctions like, I don't know…bacon shrimp crème brûlée. The nasty steakhouse on the corner uses it to stick raw off-cuts together. Tell me if this sounds familiar: "It works by melting the proteins, bonding the muscle and fiber together seamlessly."'

'What's the availability? Have you run down local trans-glutiminate suppliers?'

'I can't do all your work for you, Versado. And by the way, it's transglutaminase. Call yourself a detective.'

'I'll call you something in a minute.'

'Is that Spanish for thank you?'

She gives him the finger.

'Oh, that translates in any culture.'

It turns out you can order meat glue the same way you can order dead rabbits for taxidermy – via the Internet.

The rain clatters on the metal of the containers on the trucks packed in tight formation with the rat-a-tat of automatic gunfire, forming puddles under the tires, with rainbow slicks of oil. It drips down the back of Gabi's neck, because the supervisor at Halston & Sons: Protein Specialists is not enthusiastic about the idea of letting them in, especially because they came through the yard, because sometimes you don't want to go through the front door.

'This again?' J. Halston (according to his namebadge) is not happy to see them. One of the sons, or more likely a grandson. 'All our workers are registered and union. And we had a health inspection last month. I got the certificate above the front desk in reception. If you'd come in that way, you'da seen it.'

He has an accountant's face and a boxer's build, as if his job description includes being able to pound a side of beef into submission with his fists. His shaggy eyebrows under the hood of his raincoat have descended right down over his glasses, like storm clouds in corn country.

'We're not here about that,' Boyd says, rubbing at the collar of his jacket where the cheap fabric is clinging to his neck. 'You could be serving up rat meat and that'd be none of our business.'

191

'What did you say to me?' Young Halston is electrified with outrage. 'We provide the meat for six out of ten of the best-rated burgers in the whole damn country. You check the reviews. Those are our white tablecloth customers in New York City and LA.'

'I'm sure your meat is exactly what it says on the label,' Gabi soothes.

'Damn right it is.' He shakes his head. 'Rat.'

'You're on the list of customers in the Detroit area for Tengu suppliers, for a product called ActivTG.'

'Yeah, so? Flavor of the month. That's FDA-approved. A lot of the meat industry uses it.'

'Traces of it were found on a murder victim, and we're trying to trace where it might have come from.'

'Is this about the little boy? Who was found with, what was it, animal remains?' The storm cloud over his eyebrows lifts. Gabi can almost see his mind doing cognitive circus tricks. She heads him off before he grabs for the trapeze.

'Our victim was found in a dumping-ground for all sorts of things. We're following up all the leads right now.'

'Oh man, that was awful. That little boy.'

'You have kids?' It's a cheap shot, but it works. Experience brings people together. War. Terrorist attacks. Parenting.

'Flew the coop already,' he shrugs.

'You got a photo?' she says, pushing her luck.

He takes out his phone and flicks through, realizes it's getting wet and finally summons them into the loading dock, where they don't need to shout over the drum of the rain, and – more importantly – it's dry.

The loading bay is stacked with refrigerated cases marked with the Halston logo, while workers in white overalls and hair nets and gloves bustle between them with packs of meat bound up in plastic wrap. It certainly looks FDA-approved, but it's more than hygienic: it's sterile, totally removed from the reality of the animals going in the other side.

He shows her a photograph of a blunt-faced girl in a slinky prom dress. 'That's my oldest. She's working the phone lines in our depot in Chicago. My boy's just finished high school.' He skips to a photograph of a young man posing with his arms folded across his chest, going for hardcore and failing.

'Good-looking kids.' Gabi is ready with her reciprocal offering. 'That's mine. She's a handful. Wants to be a Broadway star.'

'Grieg wants to be a nurse.' He grimaces.

'You bring them up to be independent-minded and look what happens,' Gabi commiserates.

'So, what kind of animal was it? The remains you found?'

'We don't have those lab results back yet,' she bluffs. 'We're mostly interested in getting more information on this Activ stuff. You said you *do* use it here?'

'We do what our clients want. Bespoke meats. Whatever cut or portion size you want. We do private labels too. We've had more call for specialist products recently.'

'Like what?'

'Sausage without the casing. Things like that.'

'Turducken?' Boyd offers.

'Not yet. You think that's going to be a thing?'

'In medieval times they used to stuff suckling pigs with birds.' She only knows this because of Layla and her delight in choosing the most obscure history projects. Cat-worship in Egypt, medieval torture devices.

'We don't do that,' although she can see he's considering

193

it. She guesses you have to stay on top of the trends. There's only so much you can do with meat.

'But you do all kinds of animals here?'

'We slaughter our own sheep on site, but we get in other meat from around the country.'

'Do you ever use bolt guns?' Boyd asks, because forensic tests have been inconclusive so far and they can't rule it out.

J. Halston Jnr swats the question away. 'No, we stun them and then slit their throats. Bolts are for cows.'

'How about deer? Your website says you do venison too.'

'Sure do. We get the meat in. Same as beef and chicken and pork, and we've done ostrich on special order a few times. Less cholesterol.'

'But you don't get the actual animals in?'

'Not alive, no, ma'am,' he says like he is explaining to a three-year-old. 'We get the carcasses, already prepared, and then we cut them up.'

'You know, I've never seen a real live meat-packing operation,' Boyd says.

'We've got a video on our website you can watch. State-of-the-art machinery to get the right cuts and analyze the meat for impurities.'

'Would you mind if we had a look around?'

'That would violate our health code.' He widens his stance.

'We could get a warrant. How long would that take us, Bob?' Sometimes the word alone has enough weight to bludgeon through hesitancy.

'Dunno.' Boyd scratches at his belly. 'Coupla hours? Real pain in the ass, though.'

'Come on,' Halston protests, 'half the slaughterhouses in the state probably use Activ. Restaurants, too. Heck, you can buy it online. You gonna serve warrants on everyone?'

Gabi pretends to soften. 'Well maybe you could give us a list of your employees who have access to it?'

'I can do that. But I can also tell you that it gets delivered to our front office in a box of sealed one-kilo foil baggies, straight from Tengu. Once that box is opened, it's possible someone could have lifted one of the bags without us knowing about it.'

'Kilos?'

'It's a Japanese company. They work in metric.'

'So almost anyone could have had access to it.'

'It's not hydrochloric acid. You don't even need gloves to work with it. Totally safe, which means we don't keep it under lock and key.'

'Any incidents in the workplace? Disgruntled employees? Unusual behavior?'

'Used to get guys in off the street to work a few shifts, but you know, we want to manage it better, work with the unions. Jobs are too precious.'

'And they've had problems with immigration,' Boyd whispers in her ear.

'Can I speak to your personnel department?'

'If you insist,' he says, crabbily.

They come away with a list of employees for the past five years, including temporary workers (but not the illegals, Boyd points out), and a bag of meat glue for testing.

The Man Who Ate the World

Patrick Thorpe stands on the doorstep and listens to the electronic chime going off somewhere deep inside the house. Three times the charm. No-one can say he didn't try to get hold of Clayton. The man doesn't answer the phone. He doesn't have an email address. He doesn't even come to the door.

The curator starts walking back to his car, a little ashamed that he feels relieved, and then annoyed that he should feel bad when Clayton basically forced his way into the show, begging him on his knees in the middle of Honey Bee grocery store, his arms full of piñatas. He felt sorry for him – someone who's been around the scene that long having to pack shelves at the Mexican supermarket. But pity isn't a good enough reason to sacrifice the overall caliber of the show, and although Detroit has its share of outsider geniuses, he's not sure Clayton Broom is one of them.

The door squeaks behind him and his relief pops like a bubble. Patrick puts on a smile as he turns. 'Oh, hey, Clay. "Hey, Clay." That rhymes.' He laughs to cover the awkwardness, Broom peering out at him through the crack of the door. There's something wrong with his face. It's gone slack, like he's had a stroke or contracted Bell's palsy. 'I didn't think you were home,' he tries again.

Clayton opens his mouth, his lips gold-fishing, as if he's dragging his brain up from deep underwater. 'I was working.'

'Doing some welding?' Patrick guesses, gesturing at the mask shoved up on his head, the thick overalls and gloves.

'Other things, also.'

'That's wonderful.' He fidgets. 'Listen, you got a minute?'

'I'm busy.' Clayton moves to close the door.

'It's about that.' Patrick puts a hand on the doorjamb. 'The show. I wanted to talk to you. I don't have your cell-phone number.'

'Don't believe in them.'

'That's cool, that's cool. We get too hung up on them. All you see is people staring at their screens all day. Sucks us right in. Can I—?'

Clayton backs away reluctantly and Patrick steps into a gloomy corridor lined with teetering stacks of newspapers and arrangements of stones piled up on top of one another. It smells terrible, like damp and rust. There is black mold growing up the walls. 'You, uh, redecorating?'

'It's Clayton's father's house, *my* father's house.' He chews on the words like tobacco, something he has to spit out. 'It's his old furniture. He's dead.'

'I'm sorry to hear that.' He keeps talking, rattled. He didn't realize Clayton was so far gone. Maybe it's the claustrophobia of the house, the stacks of old magazines that have made him nuts. Maybe it's contagious. 'Planning some papier-mâché? This stuff's a fire hazard. You should be careful, man.'

'I got an extinguisher.'

'So, talking about flammable,' Patrick squirms. 'I've been discussing it with Darcy, you remember Darcy, co-curating on

197

Dream House, and I have to tell you the truth, Clay, we're a little worried. The praying mantis dragon thing you're working on? Well, firstly, it's been done before. With the Gurgitator.'

Clayton lights up. Seems like somebody's home, after all. 'I helped make that. I hinged the jaw so it could open and close.'

'Yeah, absolutely. Impressive. Fire-breathing dragon-bus stopping traffic all the way down Gratiot!' He shakes his head at the drama. 'It was a huge hit at Burning Lakes, too.'

'They didn't invite me.' Clayton sinks back into himself.

'Oh. Well, I hear tickets have got real expensive. But hey, originality is tough. You know that, you've been on the scene long enough to see all the trends come round again. You're practically an art historian.'

Clayton's mouth tightens, like a twist of a screw. 'You think my work isn't original?'

'No, no. We *love* your work, you know that, Clay. But we're worried about the fire. We've got installations going up in these old wooden houses, and call me crazy, but a sculpture with a propane tank that shoots seven-foot flames into the air might be a little dangerous. We don't want the party to get shut down for breaking some city fire ordinance. I mean, maybe, if you're willing to do it *without* the flame-throwing, we can still consider it. But I'm not sure what your schedule's like, if that's going to throw you off?' He tries to downplay the hopefulness in his voice.

'I'm not doing the praying mantis any more.'

'Oh.' Patrick wilts with relief. 'Oh, that's a shame. Because the party's on Saturday. So…does that mean you won't be doing anything, after all? We'd still love to have you come along. I can put you on the guest list. No obligation, though. If it's too disappointing that you couldn't deliver something for the show, no-one would blame you if you didn't want to—'

'I've been working on something else. I'll show you.'

'Well, okay, I mean, I'll have to discuss it with Darcy,' he chatters, following Clayton through the house, stepping over a pile of black garbage bags by the door that have attracted flies even in this cold.

'What's in the refrigerator?' he says, spotting the Post-it on the door that reads 'Do not open'.

'Nothing,' Clayton barks. 'It's broken.'

In his head, Patrick is riffing that funk number: 'Won't you take me to…crazy town.' He's going to lay this on Darcy and make his escape a.s.a.p. 'Clay, I don't think this is going to work out. You know how strongly Darcy feels about the cohesion of creative vision. We can't randomly slot in another piece like art is interchangeable—' and then he sees it. He puts his fingers to his mouth. 'Oh. Oh my God.'

The garden is never going to recover. The yellow grass has been obliterated by cement dust and spark burns from the welding torch. The praying mantis languishes in the back, a crude thing lumped together from old car parts, with hand-saws for claws and three pairs of mismatched mannequin legs protruding from its carapace, reflector-light eyes and mandibles that open on a hinge so it can blast fire from the propane tank in its belly. But that's not what he's looking at.

He hesitates and then steps forward, picking his way between the figures occupying every space in the yard. Twisted bodies made from cement or coils of wire or welded combinations of wood and metal or clay. An army of the beautiful deformed, from miniatures to monsters in every medium imaginable.

'Oh my God,' Patrick says again, taking everything back in his head, all the doubt, the cattiness. This could be huge.

Clayton could be the new Tyree Guyton. 'How long have you been working on this?'

'I don't know.'

He's already writing the catalog copy in his mind. Dehumanizing distortions, the obliteration of self, with a nod to Francis Bacon or Steven Cohen. Heck, David Bowie.

There are vaguely human shapes in clay, with gaping mouths, arranged in a cluster, half their heads sheared off. They are all twisting their necks like corkscrews to look toward the house. A flock of roughly cast bronze female figures, with jabbing bird's heads and disturbingly elongated arms flung back behind them, are arranged along an old log.

A Christ figure with a beatific expression raises one sculpted hand in blessing, but his mouth is fitted with hinges and gears, and his robes, made from rags, are flowering with mold from being left out in the rain. A woman created out of wire covers her eyes with her hands with black tar oozing between her fingers, frozen in place.

And then he comes upon the blob. It's a malformed lump of molten plastic and candle wax that has bubbled up in protest under the welding torch, forming blisters like plague boils, scorched and distended and pinched into the semblances of faces with wax layered on top: a fat man growing extra heads from his belly. His mouth is gaping wide with nails for teeth, rammed up through his jaw, the round metal heads jabbing out the bottom. There are toys and junk embedded in his flesh.

'This is...amazing, Clay.' Patrick is jagged with excitement. 'We have to talk. After the Dream House show. There's a gallery in New York looking for new work. You should do a solo exhibition. It would have to be in the right venue, though. You'll need a big space to let the work breathe.' He hesitates, his mind racing through all the possibilities. 'Has anyone else seen this?'

Clayton shrugs.

'Can we have *him*? The fat man? Does he have a name?'

'No.'

'Untitled? The Blob? The Man Who Ate The World?'

'Call it whatever you want.'

'He'll fit beautifully. There's an attic room in the Lust House – all the buildings are themed. We were going to fill it with a kiddies' pool with condoms and plastic balls scrawled with swearwords. But this is so much more powerful.'

'Will people see it? It needs *eyeballs*.'

'Don't worry about that. We're expecting four hundred people. There's some video guy who wants to film it too.'

'Do you...' Clayton looks confused, struggling with himself. 'Do you want to be part of it?'

'What do you mean?'

'I need someone. I could make you something.' He sounds so hopeful, it's almost unbearable. No wonder. All these years of rejection. And hey, getting in early before the market catches on? That's not a bad idea at all, Patrick thinks.

'You mean a special commission? I'd love that! But right now you need to keep your focus here. Don't second-guess yourself, okay? This is the best work you've ever done. Oh, wait. Will you need help moving him?'

'I got my truck.'

'That's great. That's amazing. I can't believe how far you've come. This is your breakthrough, man.' He claps Clayton on the shoulder and is repulsed to find that his jacket is crusty, the texture of cockroach wings. Patrick snatches his hand away and concentrates on not wiping it on his jeans. 'This is your breakthrough, man.'

Botanica

The woman with skunk hair, black with white streaks, standing behind the counter in front of a wall of candles and glass bottles is not happy to have the police in her establishment.

'No. Sorry,' she says. 'I don't know anyone who does witchcraft. We sell blessings here.'

'I see that,' Boyd says, picking up a fat white wax cylinder with a label that reads 'Pussy licking candle'.

'I don't judge my customers,' she sniffs. 'I order in what they ask for. Rich people have psychiatrists. These people come to me. I listen to their problems.'

'Maybe you listened to a customer saying that they practise santeria. Or lucumí or vodoun?' Gabi says.

'We'll go with any kind of witchcraft,' Bob agrees. 'Especially if there's sacrifice involved.'

It's times like these that Gabi wishes her parents had taught her more Spanish. They were so dead-set on naturalizing themselves, and her especially, that it was always English, English, English. She grew up in Kentucky, where they pretty much *were* the Hispanic community, and only moved to Miami when she was sixteen. It was her first real exposure to Cuban culture, and for a while she ate it all up. The cuisine, the language, the boys.

'You're scaring off my customers.' Skunk-hair shoos them aside to let a slight, bedraggled man with red shoes through. He puts down a candle on the counter. 'Triple Strength Lottery Win'.

'That'll be five dollars,' the owner says. 'You have a fine day, Ramón. Good luck. Give my best to your lady.'

The man leaves, setting the heavy oriental bell clanging sonorously.

'How do you do that in good conscience?' Boyd says, leaning on the counter. 'That man doesn't have five dollars to spare.'

'I sell mindfulness and self-reflection. He lights that candle, every time he walks past it, he's thinking about it. Maybe he buys a lottery ticket, or maybe he's thinking about money so he applies for a job. I sold him a love candle and he tells me now he's with someone, very happily.'

'What's this?' Gabi says, holding up a paper pouch with a handwritten label that says 'wolf's heart'.

'It's not really a wolf's heart.'

'Can I open it?'

'Only if you buy it.'

'Do you normally sell animal parts?'

'No.'

Gabi holds up another pouch, a narrow twist of paper. 'Then what's this "black cat bone?"'

'Excuse me.' A woman in white with strings of colored necklaces and a white scarf wrapped around her head emerges from a small curtained-off booth at the back of the shop. She looks decidedly pissed off, Gabi decides. It's something in the way she moves, her bracelets jangling. 'I heard you talking—'

'You tell 'em, Iya! Scaring my customers off.'

'You're asking about animal sacrifice and santeria?'

'We're making enquiries—' Gabi starts.

'Like you're some podunk ignorant cops from the country,' the woman says, inflamed.

'Now hold on there,' Bob says, 'we may be podunk, but you don't gotta insult us. I'm Detroit city born-and-bred.'

'What did you find? Some shrine in the woods with bones and antlers that scared you? That's palo monte, not santeria. Or kids copying nonsense they've seen on TV.'

'I'm sorry. We've got off on the wrong foot. Can we start again? I'm Detective Gabriella Versado, this is my partner Bob Boyd. Can we talk about this in private somewhere so we can be *less* ignorant? It's about a murder investigation where the body was found with animal parts.'

'I do consultas in the back. We can talk there. But only until my next appointment arrives,' she says crisp as frost on grass, leading them to the curtained booth.

'Thank you,' Gabi says, taking a seat behind the low table, Bob wedged in behind her so they can close the curtain. 'I saw a sacrifice once – *ebo* – with my uncle in Miami. A chicken.'

'You're lucky,' the santera says. 'It's a very spiritual experience, an animal sacrificing its life for you. You should be respectful of that divine gesture.'

'I know you also kill goats sometimes too. Would you ever do deer?'

'We only sacrifice goats and rams – no cows, pigs, horses or deer – and tradition dictates that we eat the animal afterwards, so there would be no remains. We believe in...

karma, for lack of a better word. When you do harm to other people, in one way or another, you're also harming yourself. Performing witchcraft is only going to cause problems for you.'

'Like violence,' Gabi muses, 'it has a way of playing pass the parcel.'

'That's a nice way of looking at it,' the woman says, re-evaluating her.

'Can I show you a picture and you can tell me what you think?' Gabi slips the photograph of Daveyton out of her jacket pocket and puts it face-up on the table.

She glances at it and flinches. 'What I think? It's psychopathic! This is the work of someone who is very disturbed.'

'Not palo monte?'

'No.' She flaps her hand at Gabi to take the photo away. 'Palo monte don't mutilate living people, and there would be no ritualistic purpose in mixing a human body with a deer body. It doesn't make sense.'

'So what do *you* think this is, looking at the photograph?'

'You've got someone with a bad head. A crazy person.'

'What does that mean,' Gabi presses, 'a bad head?'

'In our *patakis*, our folk myths, we believe that we come to the world with a destiny we picked for ourselves in Arun. Obatala creates the human body, but you have to get your head from the potter who molds them out of clay in his warehouse. On a good day he makes beautiful heads, but sometimes he gets drunk and makes a bad head. It's a divine defect. There's no way to tell from the outside, but once you've chosen your head, you have to live your destiny.

'Most of us have a medium head. It's not perfect, but there is enough good in there that with the help of the orichas you can be pulled to the good side. But people with a bad head are so damaged they can't be fixed. There's no remedy, the only thing you can do is stop them and recycle them back into the universe.'

'So we've got your blessing to shoot this guy dead then? I'll be sure to explain that in my report,' Boyd quips.

The santera ignores him. 'You know, Detective, there is a lot of dark energy attracted to you because of the nature of this crime. You have to be careful. It makes you vulnerable to bad things happening to you or your loved ones. You should let me give you a blessing, or cleanse you.'

Bob snorts. 'Yeah, I'll skip, thanks. We done here, Versado?'

'I'll take it,' Gabi says, mainly out of politeness but also remembering the teenager she once was in Miami.

'Whatever.' Bob pushes through the curtain. 'I'll wait outside.'

The santera picks up a bundle of bay leaves and brushes them over Gabi's body, sweeping over her while she murmurs a prayer in another language. Yoruba, she guesses. It's over in a few minutes.

'Thank you.' She tries to convince herself that she feels lighter, but that's just the smell of the herbs. She's too old and jaded for magic.

'You should take a talisman for protection. *Asabache*, jet, will help repel evil.'

'Ah, but that's the problem,' Gabi says, 'I'm not trying to repel it, I'm trying to find it.'

Walled Gardens

Cas's apartment block has a coffee shop in the lobby and a gift store because it's a historic building, one of the highlights of Detroit's architecture, with genuine Miskwabic tiles, elaborate floral designs on the exterior and gold art-deco patterns in the entrance hall. It's a beautiful place to live, but more than that, it's prestigious. There's even a doorman who remembers her name, just like the story about the little girl who lived in the hotel in the kids' book Layla used to love. But he's not old and gentlemanly in a suit with brass buttons. He's in his twenties, in an aubergine-colored dress shirt that's the uniform around here, with a skinny mustache, and he's kind of checking her out. 'Hi, how you doing this afternoon, Miss Cassandra. And it's Miss Layla, right? Nice to have you back with us.'

'Hey, Javier!' Cas waves as she walks straight to the beautiful old elevator and jabs the button repeatedly.

'Hi.' Layla ducks her head.

'You need anything, you just ring down.' He leans out from his desk to say it with a special intensity, like he really, really means it.

'Was he hitting on me?' Layla says as the elevator doors close behind them.

'How long have you been alive? Every man is hitting on you always. But don't feel special. It's how management trains them up. Apparently "have a nice day" doesn't sound sincere any more.'

'That's terrible.' But she can understand it, how words can get worn down like shoes.

'Why, are you into him?' Cas asks.

'Not unless he's an arty skater boy way out of my league,' Layla says breezily. 'Why, are *you*?'

'Boys. Gross.'

'Girls?' Layla prods.

'Hey, chicken, I love you, but not like that. I'm just flying solo.' Cas pulls a ridiculous sexy pout at the gold mirrored walls. 'Besides, I am also out of your league. Ow! Don't hit me.'

The old elevator rattles them up to the fourteenth floor and Layla thinks how it's weird that Cas isn't into anyone. Maybe she's asexual or trans like Eric Redding (formerly Erica). Going to a super-liberal charter school means that kids are open about who they are, but also that everyone is up in everyone else's business. Even before she started the semester, she knew about the girl nicknamed Chlamydia (for obvious reasons) from the online gossip about her. Shakespeare would have it wrong these days. It's not the world that's the stage – it's social media, where you're trying to put on a show. The rest of your life is rehearsals, prepping in the wings to be fabulous online.

There's a red roller suitcase by the front door, which means that Cas's mother, Helen, is either coming or going. She wears smart suits and high heels and twice a week she flies to flat parts of the country with wheat fields and silos, doing labor resolution for a grain company. Layla doesn't think she's ever seen Gabriella in heels. Maybe in the wedding photos – which have been relegated to the basement along with the other souvenirs of the life they used to have.

Cas's mother is thin and beautiful. Her makeup is always flawless and her blonde hair looks like she just stepped out of a shampoo commercial.

'It's formaldehyde,' Cas told her once. 'This special hair treatment which is like seriously poisonous. And she's only skinny because of ballerina syndrome.' She sighed in exasperation at having to explain. 'You know. Bulimia and anorexia sitting in a tree, P-U-K-I-N-G. Don't worry, there's an app for that now.'

'For anorexia?' Layla was shocked.

'Probably. But I meant for counting calories. And offsetting them against the ones you burn on the treadmill. My mom spends like an hour in the gym every single day. And she does like this power walk thing through the airport. I swear she'd use weights if they'd let her take them in her hand luggage.'

'Cassandra, is that you?' Her mom looks up from her laptop in the living room.

'Hey, Mom. We were just talking about the doorman.'

'Is he new?' her mother says, going through the motions, but her attention drifts back to her screen as if its tied to a sinker.

'Same one as always. We were just talking about how *cute* he is.' Layla realizes Cas is baiting her mother.

'Mmm-hmm,' Mrs. Holt says vaguely, but Layla notices her shoulders tighten.

Her father is cooking in the kitchen. Layla thinks of him

as hipster sitcom dad – sweet and funny, but somehow tragic. He's shaved his head to hide that it's balding. 'Is that Lay with you? You pulling in for eats?'

'Thanks, Mr. Holt. Only if it's no trouble.'

'Are you kidding? You're our favorite dinner guest. And it's Andy, please. Shrimp pasta with chili good for you?'

'Sounds amazing,' Layla says.

That's what Layla envies. The almost normal. And sure, stats will tell you that divorce is normal, but she wants this. A home with two kids and two parents and something good on the stove, the smell expanding to fill the whole house.

Her parents always planned to have more kids, but they were busy and a friend of theirs got shot and they got freaked out, and in the end they just never got round to it.

'Is Ben home?' Cas says, peering around for her kid brother. He goes to a different school, for reasons Layla hasn't been able to ascertain. Special needs or something, although there doesn't seem to be anything obviously wrong with him. Cas has assured her it's because she hasn't spent enough time with him, but for all her bitching, she's insanely protective of him.

'He's at practice. Be back by half past.' Her dad is a tech-preneur. Name a major company in Silicon Valley and he's 'pulled a stint' there – his words. It's why they moved from Oakland, California. Detroit is friendlier to start-ups: lower overheads, tax incentives, hungry talent, cheap office space in TechTown. He's bought into the city's revitalization 'with bells on'. Layla loves hearing him talk. It's another language, where any word can be verbed. She and Cas have a secret drinking game they play during dinner, taking a sip of juice every time he uses techno jargon like 'angel-investor'.

'How's Crater going?' Layla asks him, trying to remember

210

the name of his big start-up project.

'Curatr,' he corrects her automatically, rolling the trrrr.

'Please don't get him started,' Cas complains.

'I still don't know if I get it. So, it pulls in all your social media to one place?'

'Yes, it's an aggregator. It pulls all your feeds to one platform.'

'Aren't there social networks that do that already?'

'Right you are, missy!' he says in some kind of cheesy British accent, and she's almost relieved she's not the only one with dorky parents. 'But the difference is that Curatr is an anti-social social network. It's a private diary, only for you and the people who are really close to you. It's about giving you kids back some privacy, a space that's yours alone, and totally safe. It's tied in with our other offering, Walled Garden reputation management, using a subscription model to better customize SEO.'

'I don't really know what that means,' Layla says, although she thinks that was an upcoming module in Future Promise. Search Engine Optimization: Hitting Your Target Audience.

'It means we partner with the major search engines to promote results you approve and push down ones that might be damaging.'

'Like doing a duck face when you were twelve.' Or being nicknamed Chlamydia, she thinks.

'Yes.' He shifts uncomfortably. Maybe he doesn't know what a duck face is and assumes it's something worse. 'Think of it as having your own publicist. We can't get rid of anything forever, but we can push it four pages back on the search results. Maybe as much as ten.'

Cas yawns dramatically. 'Dad, can we eat in my room? We have homework.'

Her father is stung, but he covers it up. 'No problemo. Two times desk dine-ins coming up.'

'Three please,' Helen shouts from the living room.

'Oh no. Someone has to eat with me!'

'Your son will be home soon.'

And on cue, Ben comes in the door, frowning intensely at his phone from under the flop of his sandy hair, and jabbing at the screen. Cas bounds up to him and snatches it out of his hands.

'Whatcha looking at?' she demands. 'Message from a girl?'

He flushes and tries to grab it back from her. 'Hey c'mon! Phones are private!'

'Big sister privileges.'

'Give it back! Iza!'

Cas examines the screen, then tosses it back to him, satisfied. 'Shut up, dumb-ass. I was just teasing. Here's your stupid phone with your stupid game.'

'Aw man, you messed up my high score. Thanks a lot!'

'I'm just making it more challenging for you. I'm like an extra difficulty setting. You should be grateful.'

'Whatever.' He brushes his hair away from his face, and she spots the bruise under his eye. She grabs his face, yanking up his chin to get a better look. 'What the hell happened to your face? Because if someone did this to you, I will fucking kill them.'

'Chill. It's hockey. I caught Jimmy's elbow at practice. You gonna go ballistic when someone body-slams me on the ice? 'Cos then you can't come to the game.' He's genuinely alarmed. 'Dad! Tell her she can't come if she's going to be such a freak.'

'Like I care about your game anyway.'

'Does that mean you're not coming?'

'Of course I'm coming. Layla too. We've made cheerleader outfits and signs to hold up and everything. "Ben, Ben, he's our guy, watch him go: super-fly!"'

'Mo-ooom!'

Their mother does not look up from her laptop. 'Would you two please stop winding each other up?'

'You going to sit and eat with me, Benjamin?' their dad says.

'Do I have to?'

'Nope. We can all eat in different places round the house, all plugged in to our devices and not talking to each other.'

'Isn't that the whole point of your business?' Cas says.

'No,' her father sighs in exasperation. 'It's creating new tools that facilitate new ways of expressing ourselves in appropriate ways.'

'We *are* expressing ourselves. Just not with the people in this room. Can we go now? Because homework?'

'Yes, all right,' he deflates. 'But only because you have a guest. Tomorrow night we're sitting at the table like a real family.'

'God, they kill me,' Cas says, flinging the door shut and flopping backwards onto her bed. She reaches over her head to dock her phone in the speakers, and some sickly sweet shoegaze spills out. 'You're so lucky that your mom's so uninvolved.'

'Yeah, it's terrific,' Layla deadpans. 'You white people. My parents would never let me get away with this kind of shit.'

'Do you miss your old man?'

'I don't know. Sometimes.' All the time. The weird trivia, the geeky projects, being able to hang out together and do nothing. She never realized what a luxury that was. She's had just the one stilted conversation with him since Saturday's disaster call. 'Come on, shove over,' she says, climbing onto the bed.

Cas's room is chaos and beauty, wallpapered with pictures ripped out of magazines or printed out. A goth girl in an elaborate lace dress with even more elaborate hand-carved prosthetic legs, a lightning storm over a volcano, abandoned theme parks, misty cliffs. She has a chandelier made out of origami cranes and fairy lights. It's like her whole room is a Tumblr of things that make her happy.

'You know you could just put this up online. It would be a lot easier to manage,' Layla says, glancing over the wall to see if there are any new pictures since she last visited a few weeks ago. A photograph of horses' silhouettes in streaks of sunlight, an illustration of a plump lionfish mermaid with poisonous quills, a girl with her hair dyed in a cascading rainbow.

'Online's not real,' Cas says, bored. 'Besides, I have to share the PC in the living room with Ben.'

'But you don't have a Facebook page or anything,' Layla persists.

'Too much effort. It's designed to make you insecure about the amazing better life everyone else is having. You're just feeding the machine.'

'It's an anxiety engine.'

'What I'm saying. You of all people should quit. You're anxious enough as it is.'

'Am not.'

'You worry if the shrimp my dad got are frozen? Maybe they're crawling with salmonella.'

'They would be killed during the cooking process.'

'Are you sure? Aren't bacteria more invincible than

214

Superman and cockroaches put together?' Cas prods her.

'Super-roach!' Layla says, trying to distract Cas because she's succeeding in freaking her out. 'I bet someone has dressed up a roach in a superhero outfit. We could check online!'

'Like I said, computer's in the living room.'

'What's your wifi password? I'll look it up on my phone.'

'My dad's got spyware. Did I mention he's super-paranoid?'

Cas's dad nudges open the door with the toe of his sneaker, balancing the tray. The food smells amazing, like a restaurant.

'Come on, Cassandra,' he berates her. 'You know how I feel about closed doors.'

'Sorry, we didn't want the music to disturb you.'

'I'll just turn the TV up,' he says, glum. 'It's not like we're having a family conversation.'

'Thank you, Mr. Holt.'

'Mmmm, thanks Dad,' Cas says, hustling him out of the room. He leaves the door ajar. 'This is why we do this shit at your house.'

'Why are your parents such control freaks?'

'It's because I once tried to off myself.'

'Seriously?'

'Or they're worried they're going to bust me touching myself. Or making like my mom.' She holds up two fingers for emphasis and then pretends to stick them down her throat. 'Blaaargh.'

When she was a kid, Layla entertained all those pop-star princess fantasies. That there had been a terrible mix-up. She was a changeling, and one day her true parents, who were either New York socialites or Hollywood movie stars, would come to reclaim her. Or her owl would fly through

215

the window with her scroll from Hogwarts.

She thinks about how Ben calls Cas 'Iza', how little they talk about her old school and her life in Oakland.

'Can I ask you something serious?' Layla picks around the shrimp.

'Serious like Dorian? Or serious like climate change? Because I'm sad for the polar bears and shit, but I don't see how we're supposed to make a difference on an individual level. Although I think using public transport helps.'

'Cas.'

'Yeah, fine. Ask whatever you want.' She's gone as still and tense as her mother did earlier. It's in her shoulders, even though she's stirring her noodles with her chopsticks, head down, intently digging for one last shrimp. Funny how body language can be genetic.

'Are you in witness protection?'

Cas laughs and her whole body unclenches. 'Yeah. Exactly. You got us. Don't tell anyone. Pass the soya sauce.'

'I mean it, Cas.'

'Like my dad was a whistleblower on insider trading software and we've been on the run ever since? And my mom's really CIA, which is why she flies around so much?'

'Fine, okay, it sounds really dumb when you put it like that.' A terrible thought occurs to her. 'Wait. *Did* you try to off yourself?'

Cas puts down her noodles and gives her a look full of contempt and pity. 'Hasn't everyone?'

THURSDAY, NOVEMBER 13

Open Wide

'What is it with graffiti in Detroit?' Jonno says into the microphone, standing under a beautifully detailed black-and-white paste-up of a wild boar, three stories high. 'Like Coney Island dogs, stray dogs and hipster facial hair, it's freaking everywhere.'

He strolls toward the camera, Jen matching his pace, walking backwards. He passes a little old lady carrying a bright pink purse.

'Tags, tags everywhere, but there's also some serious work to rival big international names like Banksy and Blek Le Rat, or Faith47. And what do we have to thank for the explosion of street art in the city?'

He pauses for dramatic effect. 'The high crime rate.'

There's a pause, then a man in a ski mask runs up to the old lady behind him, and snatches her purse. She shrieks in dismay.

'Cut!' Jen yells. 'Simon, you have to come in earlier.'

Simon slinks into shot, his ski mask pushed up on his head, looking sulky, and hands the old woman her purse back.

'This is stupid,' Jonno complains. He hates being here at all; he's decided there's a *vibe* between Simon and Jen, the residual energy of people who have slept together.

'I think so too,' the mugging victim chimes in. 'I would never give up my bag that easy. I should struggle, maybe I could hit him with it a few times before he gets away.'

'Relax, Jonno, it's cute,' Jen says. 'We can always cut it if it doesn't work. And sure, Ivy, if you want to ad-lib, go wild.'

'Great. Now the old lady gets more of a say than I do,' Simon bitches. Everybody wants to be a director.

'We want it to be funny.'

'It's not funny, it's tragic,' says Jonno.

'That's even funnier.'

'Fine. I'll pick up and maybe Simon can hit his fucking cue this time?' He still hates this, even if, it turns out, he's pretty good at it when he warms up. It reminds him of his mother, who was a nurse in an obstetrics ward. She hated inserting catheters, so she did it as quickly and efficiently as she could, which meant she got called to do *all* the catheters.

And he's kind of flattered that Jen is so serious about it. She's been designing a two-second intro sequence for his channel with an animator friend (male, of course), and they've worked out a schedule of what they're going to film, focusing on the art scene: this new street art, the Dream House party on Saturday, a pop-up dinner with the cool glitterati in a secret location next week. This might even work, Jonno thinks.

The Dream House prep video they did got 788 hits in the first twenty-four hours. They watched it spread, and it was amazing how each new view was a little shot of validation. This piece they're filming now isn't just about art, it's about the weirdness Detroit has in spades, which is what people are hungry for. They might even reach a few thousand views. It's about building your audience.

They repeat the scene. This time Simon hits his mark, the little old lady they lured over from her porch to be part of the scene for fifty dollars screams hysterically, and Jonno walks forward, improvising on the script they wrote this morning. 'Detroit's police department has bigger problems to deal with than street art. So you get major artists, sick of being arrested in California, moving to Detroit. Their loss, our gain. Here, no-one hassles you.'

He ignores the tussle that has broken out behind him and Simon's yelps of 'Ow, shit! What is wrong with you? Get her off me!'

'There are household names on the scene. Revok. Nekst, Pose, Elya. The Smooth Wizards League, Loaf.' According to Jen at any rate, he's never heard of any of these fuckers, and that's not including the oh-so-edgy art students or the white-trash weed dealers who like to think they're being creative, throwing up tags. 'But some prefer to stay mysterious, like whoever is behind the wooden Delray Angels, a heavenly host of painted plywood that some believe watch over one of the D's most forlorn neighborhoods.'

'Great! Cut there,' Jen says. 'We'll edit in footage of the angels later. *Forlorn,* Jonno?'

'Oh come on! Give me something, sometimes.' He shouts back at the scene behind him, where their would-be mugger is curled up on his haunches with his arms wrapped over his head. 'Hey, Miss Ivy! You can stop beating Simon now.'

Everyone wants to be in the movies. Everyone wants their fame time. He holds the camera out the window as they drive to film cut-aways of Detroit scenery, his scarf pulled up over his nose to protect him from the icy blast of wind.

'Did you bring food?' Jen says from the driver's seat, and he digs in the bag at his feet and hands her the sandwiches he made this morning.

'I can't eat this.'

'What?'

'White bread and jelly? Are you trying to kill me?' She's smiling, but there's also a baffled woundedness there. A look that says 'I thought you were paying attention'.

'Shit, sorry, baby. I wasn't thinking.' But how's he supposed to remember all this crap? Maybe that's an article right there: '10 Things You Should Know About Dating A Type One Diabetic'. Like how going out to dinner is a joyless exercise because food is something to be managed not savoured, or how your sex goddess's insatiable libido might suddenly crash along with her blood sugar.

'Don't worry about it,' she says, breezily. 'We can get something en route.'

Scott, the photographer, is waiting in his car, the windows fogged up. He climbs out, lanky and bearded, his beanie pulled down low on his forehead. 'I was just about to bail on you guys.'

'Sorry, babe! We had to stop to grab a bite.' Jen kisses him on the cheek, but Jonno can't tell if they have a vibe or not. 'Don't worry, we won't keep you long. If you can tell us what's going on, introduce yourself, and then you and Jonno are going to walk into the building together, okay?'

'All right,' he says. 'Okay, I'm Scott, I'm a sculptor and photographer, and I work a lot in these abandoned buildings.'

'Tell us what you found yesterday,' Jonno interrupts.

'I've been doing some follow-up work, revisiting places

I've photographed before to see how they've changed. I came back here and...'

'Cut,' Jen says. 'Now you're going to walk us inside.'

Scott rubs at his beard. 'I have to say, I prefer being on the other side of the camera.'

'I feel you, buddy,' Jonno says. 'But you're doing great.'

'This way.' Scott leads them into the broken-down strip club, propping open the door with a piece of concrete.

'I'm filming,' Jen says, shining a hand-held light on the two men. 'You can carry on talking if you want.'

'You were saying, you came here a couple of days ago?'

'Yeah.'

'Can you say that as a sentence?'

'I came back here on Tuesday, as part of a follow-up series I'm doing, and I found this graffiti. I've been noticing it a lot over the last few days, all around town.'

'And reveal!' Jen says.

She swings the light onto the wall as Scott and Jonno step to either side. There is a chalk door drawn on the wall.

'What we're looking at is a crude rectangle drawn in chalk on the wall. Do you have a name for them?'

'I call them ghost doors. I think they're kind of memorials to where people have died, or something has happened. You can feel it, can't you? There's a particular energy here. A lot of the great earth-works of Detroit – the burial grounds of the ancient indigenous people – were destroyed in the process of industrialization. And now, many of those factories have been abandoned or demolished as well. Like the Solvay Process plant, which was built on the site of the Great Mound of the Rouge, the largest mound in Detroit, and now it's just this flat patch of dirt – a toxic brownfield. It's wild: ghosts of the industries on top of ghosts of the

223

natives – we've got thousands of years of ghosts here. Some people have ghost towns, we have a whole ghost city.'

'Cut. That was amazing, Scott. Thank you.'

'It was fun.' He runs his hand over the chalk door. 'They do creep me out, though, the way they've just sprung up overnight. I heard there's one down by the tunnel where that kid was killed, but the cops have got someone stationed down there. I couldn't get near it. This going up on YouTube? Let me know when it's up.' He raises his camera and snaps off a photograph of them, which annoys Jonno – it's like he has to have the last word.

'They with you?' Scott says, pointing at a raggedy couple, holding a candle, frozen in the doorway.

'*Perdón*, we're sorry, we're sorry,' the scruffy little man says, flapping his hands as they both start backing away.

'No, wait!' Jen darts after them. 'Hi, can we talk to you? We're not the police, don't worry. We're making a movie.'

'El video,' Jonno tries a bastard attempt at Spanish, miming winding a camera reel – as if that means anything any more.

'About the graffiti,' Jen says. 'Is that why you're here? For the door?'

The woman tugs at the man's arm. 'Papi, I don't think this is a good idea.'

'Please. Five minutes,' Jen implores.

'Can you tell us your name on camera and why you're here today?' Jonno says to the man with all the wear of the streets engraved on his face.

'My name is Ramón,' the man says. 'This is my girlfriend, Diyana.'

Jen quickly pans the camera to take in the shy woman with the plaited hair, who is hanging back.

'We live on the street, and when it gets too cold we go to the shelter or a friend's house. I used to be a motor mechanic. I could fix up anything. Ford. General Motors. Chevrolet. Pontiac. But these new fancy cars. Built by robots, you need to be a robot to fix 'em.'

'What's that you have with you?' Jonno interrupts.

'It's a blessing candle from the botanica.'

'And what are you going to do with it?' Jesus, Jonno thinks, like pulling teeth.

'We brought it to the door. For a prayer for luck and good fortune.'

'What are the doors?'

'You get here at the right time and place, when that door opens? That door will take you anywhere you want.'

His ladyfriend pipes up, 'But maybe you don't want to go where that door takes you. You only think you do,' but she shrinks when Jen turns the camera on her.

'I've heard some people call them ghost doors.'

'I don't know. You call them what you like.'

'What do you have to do to open them?'

'I hear different things. You have to be here at midnight, full moon.'

'Have you tried it?'

'No, brother. I don't want to mess with that stuff.' Ramón crosses himself.

'Then why bring the candle?'

'Sometimes you got to appease the spirits. Keep them happy.'

'Can we film you lighting it? Maybe the two of you together?'

'All right,' he nods, as if this is reasonable. He bends down in his bright red keds and flicks a plastic lighter over the candle in front of the chalk outline.

225

'Just stay there for one more moment. Can you close your eyes, as if you're praying?'

'If you want.'

'And don't talk. Don't even nod your head. Just stay there. Five more seconds. Three, two, one. Thank you.'

Ramón straightens up, hands on his knees. 'Was that good?'

'It was beautiful. Really touching. It's great to show the more spiritual side of the city,' Jonno says. 'Now, if we can just get one of you and Diana holding hands and sort of holding up the candle together. No, don't smile. Look serious. That's it. Perfect.'

He gives them ten dollars each.

Catfish on the Menu

'It's not too late,' Layla says, clutching the raft of flyers they printed out at her house. 'We could just hand over his IP address and email to Anonymous or whoever. Pedobear. Bullyville. *Catch A Predator*. There are people who deal with this stuff.'

'Like the cops?'

'My mom would kill me.' But it's not just her mother she's worried about. Her dad would freak. Because what they are doing is the very antithesis of 'be reasonable'.

'Stop whining. It's going to be epic. We're in a public place. We've got masks. We're going to put it on YouTube, for real, and the guy is a twisted fuck who totally has it coming.'

'I feel sick.'

'That's the nausea of justice about to be served.'

'Feels like just plain nausea to me.'

Cas smiles at a woman stepping out of the tanning salon. 'Excuse me, ma'am?' The sun-beds on the poster on the door look like torture cabinets to Layla, the ones with all the spikes. She thinks about all the UV rays stabbing into you, the black bloom of melanomas spreading under your skin.

Cas gestures for one of the flyers and sticks it in the woman's face. 'We've lost our VelvetBoy. Have you seen him?'

'Is that your cat?' The woman takes the flyer and peers at it.

'Well, he likes pussy. But only if it's underage.'

She recoils and shoves the flyer back at them. 'That's repulsive.'

'That's just how we feel, ma'am,' Cas calls after her, cheerfully.

Lost: One Pedophile
Name: VelvetBoy aka Phil
Likes: Video Games, Pre-Teen Chat,
Asking Little Girls For Naughty Photos.

They'd argued about the wording and whether to include his full name and the photograph they'd found on his Facebook profile, which was under the same email address. How dumb can you get? Layla almost feels sorry for him. It's like he's living in the past, before the NSA and PRISM and flying killer robots in the sky. He's the kind of guy who would fall for an email scam.

They cased the joint two days ago to establish the best positioning for 'Operation Pants Pulldown'. Which is not what they're actually planning to do, Cas has promised. It's metaphorical. And because 'Operation Exposure' sounded like some kind of Arctic survival documentary.

She shoves Layla into the path of an older woman in a belted purple trenchcoat, head down against the chill.

'Have you seen our—' Layla starts, but she can't bring herself to finish the sentence. She jabs the flyer out, mutely. The lady gives her an apologetic smile.

'Oh no thank you, honey, I'm a Lutheran.'

He said he lived in Bloomington. He said he was going to be in town on business for a few days, and hey, maybe they could meet. That would be fun. He could buy SusieLee a milkshake. He could pick her up. Luckily, they managed to talk him out of that. He's supposed to meet them, well, *her* – SusieLee – at the table under the painting of the blue lady at the pancake place.

>SusieLee2003: U cant miss it.
>VelvetBoy: What if that space is tkaen?
>SusieLee2003: U'll c me. LOL!

Layla talked Cas out of using his full name.

'I want him to be ruined.'

'There are libel laws, dumb-ass.'

'Excuse me! Sir!' Cas skips over to a man taking out the trash. 'Sir? Have you seen our pedophile?'

It's the proximity. The closer they get, the more it feels like someone filled her up with burning lead, but it's having the opposite effect on Cas. She is giddy.

Philip Lowe. 43 years old. Electrical contractor. 131 friends.

'Not for lo-oong,' Cas had sing-songed, right-clicking his profile photograph to save-as. It showed him grinning widely into the camera, lakeside somewhere with water and trees behind him, holding a hamburger like a trophy, and giving a big thumbs-up. Layla spent ages studying it, searching for some sign in his face: a villainous glint in his eyes, receding hair, a criminal brow. But he looked normal, sweet, maybe a bit goofy. *Nice.* He had a small splat of mustard on his shirt. Inhuman monsters who prey on little children shouldn't be allowed to spill mustard.

'What if it's just a game?' Layla pushed Cas. 'This stupid thing he does online.'

'Intention is nine-tenths of the law.'

'Possession.'

'Probably that too. X-rated materials of minors on his hard drive. We should raid his house. Do you think we could get him to bring his computer with?'

They've got SusieLee's MChat account set up on both their phones now, so that Layla can reply to him. He messages her several times a day. It's exhausting. She wanted to send him a private message this morning to say 'Don't come. It's off. And by the way fuck you.' But she knew Cas would see it.

Layla would have preferred to set some sort of trap. The kind you can fall into, with spikes at the bottom. She still can't believe they're doing this. Maybe she could fake an injury. Twist her ankle. That wouldn't be enough for Cas. Maybe if she stepped in front of a car pulling away from the curb and let it hit her – she'd choose a compact obviously. They'd have to go to hospital. He'd wait around and finally realize that he'd been had, and that would be the end of it.

Her phone buzzes in her pocket. Cas is humming to herself as she sticks pages under car windscreen wipers like club flyers. 'Dah-dah-dah. Gonna be a good, good day.'

Layla checks the message surreptitiously, hoping he's got cold feet.

>VelvetBoy: I'm here! Are tyou still conging?

The typos give him away. Intention doesn't count for shit, but action does. He's waiting in a coffee shop for a little girl he believes is lying to her mom about going to her cousin to play. He is excited about it. He's ready to take her away in his car. She still feels sick about the whole thing, but now she is angry too. Outrage is a coat she can wrap herself in. She types back.

>SusieLee2003: Conga! I <3 conga

There is a long wait. The dot-dot-dots that mean he's writing a reply. Deleting it. Starting again.

>VelvetBoy: What does that mean? LOL?
>SusieLee2003: Im teasing! Means on my way! Order me a strawberry pls? :)

'Was that him?' Cas says. 'It's still on, right?'
'It's fucking on.'
'Good.' But she says it without her earlier conviction.
'You okay?'
'Yeah, yeah. Peachy. Let's just get on with it.'
'Mask.' Layla hands her one of the plastic cat faces. She pushes her own back on her head.

They stop outside the diner. They've picked a table visible from the street through the window.

'I can't look. Is he there?' Cas says. Her skin has turned bright pink, making her freckles fade out. Sweat is beading her nose.

'He's hiding behind his menu.'
'Maybe this is a bad idea. What if he turns aggro?'

What if he does? What if he has a gun? Or a knife? Layla has seen photographs of every variety of wound in the forensics manual her parents kept trying to hide – like

231

she couldn't find more gruesome photos online. But she knows it's not like in the movies. One bullet can kill you. A lucky stab with a screwdriver can cripple you for life. Falling off your bicycle can cause brain damage. You don't want to get in a fight if you can help it.

But then the waitress puts a frothy pink milkshake down in front of him, and he gives her a curt little nod, just the top of his head showing above the menu – and that seals the deal.

'No turning back.' She takes Cas's hand and tugs her inside.

The doorbell tinkles, incredibly loud. Everything seems loud. The clatter of plates in the kitchen. The hum of the heating. He glances up sharply from the menu and she can see him look them over and dismiss them, *too old*. He ducks down behind the menu again.

'Anywhere you can find a place, sweeties,' the waitress calls out to them. 'Be with you in a sec.'

'Thank you,' Layla says. 'But I don't think we're going to eat.' She pulls the mask down and starts for his table, but Cas pulls her up short.

'What are you doing?' Layla hisses.

'I can't.' Cas looks like she is about to burst into tears. Her mask is still perched on top of her hair, like the world's stupidest hat. 'I'm sorry.' Her shoulders start shaking.

Layla is cold with certainty. She feels like another person. 'I'll do it.'

'Excuse me,' she projects, striding across the diner, so that everyone looks up. She plucks the menu out of his hands and tosses it aside. It makes a very particular plastic filip as it hits the floor. Which is funny, because that's his name. She has to bite back a bark of laughter.

He smiles up at her, baffled. 'What's up with the mask?

232

This a hold-up?' He raises his hands: 'Don't shoot.' He still looks nice, and that makes her even madder. How dare he have smile lines?

'I thought we'd need them. But we don't,' Layla says. She peels off the cat face and drops it on the table. It smiles up at them benevolently. 'Because unlike you, Phil, *we* don't have anything to hide.'

His brow furrows. 'Do I know you?'

She holds up the flyer at arm's length, right in his face, and recites the lines, loud and clear. 'Excuse me. We've lost our pedophile. His name is VelvetBoy. Have you seen him?'

'Fuck,' his face flushes different colors, like a cartoon. Then he bursts up from the table. For a moment she thinks he's going to stab her, but he pushes her instead. The milkshake goes flying, glass exploding across the floor. She falls backwards and puts the heel of her hand down onto a shard.

'Ow, fuck!' She looks for Cas, but there's no sign of her friend. The entranceway is empty. There's no-one to stop Phil as he bangs open the door, setting the doorbell jangling again, leaving a slim fold of leather on the plastic seat.

'What the hell are you playing at?' The waitress pulls her up. 'You're bleeding,' she says, as if this is the worst crime in the world.

'Did you see where my friend went?' Layla pulls the piece of glass out of the fleshy part of her thumb. Hand-fat, Cas called it once. Where the hell did she go?

'You gonna pay for that breakage? You can't come here and chase away my customers. Are you high?'

Layla is indignant. 'He's not a customer, he's a pedophile!'

The waitress stares. 'Is this some kind of joke?' The rest

of the kitchen has come out to see what the commotion is about. Other customers are hovering. Layla feels the rush of righteousness.

'You saying the guy who was just here is a pedo?'

'Yeah, we bust him online. Soliciting a minor.' She feels like a true-blue bad-ass.

'He's taken off,' the chef calls from the door.

'I *knew* he looked sketchy. The moment he came in here, I said to myself, "Melissa, there's something off about this one. Grown man ordering a milkshake."' People are unreliable witnesses. They can talk themselves into anything.

'Hey, I drink milkshakes,' an old black guy with peppered hair says, indignant. 'You saying I'm a pervert?'

'I know this guy,' the other waitress says. 'I saw him come in here last week. Wasn't he with a kid? I'm sure he was.'

'A little boy,' the first corroborates.

'No, no I don't think so,' Layla says, pressing a napkin against her bleeding hand. This is getting out of control. The nausea of justice.

'Judge a man by the dairy products he drinks.'

'Did you escape from him, honey? Is that what happened? Like in Ohio?'

'Oh my God,' a customer half-screams.

'Call the police!'

'Please don't.' She is suddenly exhausted. All the adrenaline and righteousness have been sucked right out of her. And where *the fuck* is Cas? 'Don't,' she says again, with as much authority as she can muster. So far as she can see there's only one way out. Drop-down menu: maximum bullshit.

'I *am* the police.' She tries to summon up the image she had of her mother when she was a little kid and still thought she was a hero. All in blue, with her hair pulled up and the light behind her in the doorway, the Virgin Mary with a gun.

'It's a sting. Undercover vice. Don't worry. My partner's probably got him by now.'

'You look awful young,' the chef says, suspicious. Galleo, she remembers.

'That's why it works. I'm twenty-three.' The lies come easily. All she has to do is open her mouth and they're already there, fully formed.

'I told you I've seen him!' the waitress says.

'No, it's his first time here. New location every time, that's why we had to go through all these hoops to get him. The masks were part of his thing. Sick bastard.'

She has to get out before they ask to see her badge. She's stuffing the flyers in her jacket before they can take a look, along with the black leather wallet Phil left behind.

'What was he going to do with you?' Their faces are hungry with grotesque curiosity, reminding her of Greek tragedy masks, the ones you can turn upside down into a smile.

'I—' She pulls her phone out of her pocket, acting out the fake incoming call decoy. But there *is* a message, from Cas, that has come in sometime during the big inquisition.

>Cas: Sorrysorrysorry

'That's my partner now. We got him!'

The diner burst into a smattering of applause, like when they went to visit her grandparents in Miami and everyone clapped after the plane landed.

'I have to go do the paperwork on this.' She pulls a twenty out of her bag and presses it on the waitress. 'This

235

is for the broken glass. Thank you all, and I'm sorry again for the inconvenience.'

'Don't you want our statements?' The know-it-all chef again. She wishes he'd stayed in the kitchen.

'We've got a ton of dirt on this guy already, but maybe you could take down everyone's details for me, and I'll send an officer if we need statements.' The chef fluffs up with importance. And then because she feels she has to say something else: 'Bye now.'

The bell on the door clangs cheerily, and she's never been so happy to be hit in the face by wind chill.

She walks briskly round the corner and then starts running, not slowing until she's five blocks away. Panting, she pretends to study the poster of a very brown butt in an electric green thong in the window of the tanning salon as she thumbs over her keypad. She thinks about the unlikelihood of their friendship, why Cas picked her, why she's so secretive and aggressive.

>Lay: WTF? Where r u?

Her phone rings straight away.

'Are you okay?' Cas's voice sounds like she's taken a cheese grater to her throat.

'I don't know if I should talk to you.'

'I'm sorry! I didn't mean to leave you like that. I freaked out.'

'I noticed.'

'How did it go? Are you okay?'

'Well, I'm bleeding.'

'Oh my God, Layla. Should I call an ambulance?'

She relents. 'It's a scratch. You didn't even see it, did you?

236

I can't believe you didn't stick around.'

'But are you okay?'

'Stop fucking asking me that. In fact, don't fucking talk to me.'

'I *said* I'm sorry.'

'I heard you.'

'Are we still friends?'

'I'll let you know.'

There's silence on the other end of the line.

'I'm hanging up on you now, Cas. Don't call me, okay?'

She hits end-call and rams the phone in her pocket. It buzzes almost immediately. Twice. Fuck's sake.

> >Cas: Im RLLY sorry. Ill explain. Pls 4give me? Love u bitch

And one to SusieLee's chat account:

> >VelvetBoy: FjuckcyiuafuckagfyouafuckgtyouaFUck

She deletes them both.

Unseasonal Flowerings

It takes a little while for Betty Spinks to notice the knocking, like a dog pawing to be let in. What bothers her is that it's not the front door. Which means it's not one of her employees, nor some persistent and illiterate customer who can't read the sign that clearly says 'Closed'. It's coming from the back door to the courtyard where the student kilns are, yet that outside gate is kept locked at all times.

She shouldn't have let Donald go home early. It's store policy that the security guard has to stick around until they're all cashed up and the day's proceeds are locked in the safe. But he had a pressing engagement, literally, because he was planning to ask his girlfriend to marry him over dinner at a fancy steakhouse at the Greektown Casino, and he wanted to go home and freshen up first, so she'd wished him well (she's not bitter about love or her bastard ex-husband, not at all) and sent him on his way.

That's her first thought, naturally. Her ex. She snatches up the aluminum bat she's kept under her desk ever since the incident at the Tigers game when Peter screamed at her in front of everyone and grabbed her face so hard it left bruises on her cheek and jaw, bad enough that she was able to press charges, because all the times he'd punched her in the stomach had never left a mark. She got a restraining order now, but the bat is handy insurance.

'Who's there?' she yells at the door. There's a long silence.

'It's Clayton. You called.'

She huffs in relief and sets the bat down on the shelf. 'God's sake, you scared the life outta me!' She unlocks the door and swings it open in welcome. 'About time. I've been calling you since Halloween to come and collect your stuff. But what the hell are you doing in the yard?'

'I'm sorry. I still have your keys,' he says, holding up the keyring. 'You never took them back from when I used to help you out.'

She smacks herself on the forehead. 'I wondered where they'd gotten to! Come on in, honey, get yourself inside outta the cold. Might even still be some coffee in the pot.'

'Thank you,' he says and shuffles in, closing the door carefully behind him.

'Your pieces came out beautifully, even unglazed. Couple of them cracked, but that's to be expected. I hope you don't mind, I put one of the girls in the gallery. You've already had an enquiry from someone who wants to buy her, if that's something you want to do.'

'No.'

'You don't want to sell your work?' She turns, surprised, and sees a funny regret on his face. She recognizes it: It says *it hurts me that I have to do this*. She steps back. She's too far from the baseball bat, but there are other things she could use. Throw tiles at his head, keep him busy until she can hit the alarm, get out the door. She is calculating the location of her car keys. 'Why are you here so late, Clay?'

239

'I don't need the bird girls. I'm done with that. I came to see you.' He is distracted, running his hand over a row of the botanical tiles, fleur-de-lis in iridescent turquoises. 'I've been thinking about you. About all the natural forms.'

'What are you doing?' she says, trying to keep her voice level. The pattern is moving – it looks like there's something nudging up under the glaze of the tile, which has to be a trick of the light, the shadow of his hand. But all the tiles on the shelves are reacting the same way, luminous colors swirling, the surfaces bulging.

A green tip pokes up from a tile, like a shard, or an arrowhead, which makes her think of the indigenous peoples who lived here and made pots of their own. Miskwaabik is the word for copper, her brain supplies, uselessly. But it's not an arrowhead, she realizes, it's a tightly folded bud, emerging from the pattern on the tile. It opens as she watches, unfurling into delicate pinks and whites, deep meaty red on the inside, the petals falling open like a secret revealed, the whole shop bursting into flower all around her.

'What is this?' she murmurs, leaning on the counter. Her legs feel weak.

'A dream,' he says, stepping up to her, cupping his hand behind the base of her head, under her hair, tilting her chin down, while a tropical jungle springs into bloom around her.

'It's…a miracle,' she says. Something hard digs into the back of her skull. A gun, she thinks.

'You will be,' he says. There is the hard click of a trigger and the whole color spectrum flashes through her head. It's beautiful, she thinks in that instant before the blackness leaps up.

Cheese Dreams

Layla gets home to a dark house. Typical. Her mom is too busy chasing after dead kids to worry about the live one she's got at home.

>Mom: Bad day. Late one tonight. Fishfingers in the freezer. Do your homework. Love you.
>Lay: LuvU2
>Mom: ! :)
>Lay: Yeah yeah big revelation. When are u going to b home?

She hopes that doesn't sound as needy as she feels.

>Mom: Very late. I'm sorry. Sleep tight sugarbean.

Layla tears up at the nickname. It's the adrenaline crash after the diner scene. It would be swell to be able to talk to someone about it, she thinks, sucking her wounded palm. 'Why, yes, I am feeling sorry for myself, thank you for asking,' she says to no-one in particular. She goes to get a

Band-Aid from the bathroom, flicking on all the house lights as she goes. Let her mom just dare complain about the utilities bill. She pads back to the kitchen and yanks open the freezer. The box of fishfingers is singular. There's only one miserable crumbed hake sliver rattling around in there all by itself. Like her in this house.

Screw this. She phones for pizza. 'Stuffed crust, triple cheese with extra artery-hardening please.' The person taking her order doesn't hear her or get it, or both.

'Extra anchovies coming up.'

'Fine,' Layla sighs, because not even the pizza guy is listening to her, and reads off her mother's credit-card number from the pinboard next to the kitchen window.

'Half an hour, okay?'

'Better than emergency services response time.'

'What?'

'Never mind.'

She hangs up and taps in the area code for Atlanta and listens to the line ring and ring. She hangs up and tries again. This time someone answers straight away.

'Dad?'

He sounds harassed. 'Hi sweetie, this isn't a good moment. I've asked you not to phone at bed time.'

'Sorry, I forgot.' She pictures him reading to Julie and Wilson, one tucked under each arm. 'What are you going to read them?'

'I don't know yet. Wilson! Do not put that in your mouth! Sorry, Lay, can I call you back later?'

'You should read them *The Shrinking of Treehorn*. I always loved that one.'

'I don't know if we have that.'

'I can bring you my copy. You left it here.' In a grand

gesture of charity, she had packed up all her old toys and books and written a DIY card covered in sparkles and glitter:

For my new little brother and sister. I loved these things. I hope you will too.

She found the box still taped up amongst the miscellaneous junk her mother had stacked in the basement when she went looking for the TV remote, just after they moved. The envelope was unopened and grubby.

'Wilson! I said, don't eat that! Sorry, baby. I'll call you tomorrow. Love you, bye.' The phone reverts to dial-tone.

'Yeah. Great. What happened to later?' She chucks the phone on the bed, barely missing the cat, who opens one eye, stretches wide, then curls up like a furry comma, tail dangling off the bed. Layla scratches her head. 'At least you're here for me, Nyan. Sorry I called you a dumb name that went out of date in five minutes.'

Layla messes around online. She finds pictures of cockroaches dressed up in clothes. One of the earliest examples of stop-motion animation by an entomologist with a sense of humor. God, she loves the Internet, even if rainbow toaster cat memes come and go faster than new electronic currencies and ideas auto-cannibalize into remixes of remixes, Disney Princesses as My Little Star Wars Superhero Pony.

But eventually the bugs start to gross her out. The Black Plague wasn't spread by rats, it was fleas. Cockroaches are vectors for horrible things, flies vomit onto your food.

She switches over to Facebook, but Cas is right, it only makes her feel anxious. Photos of her friends from her old school, Emily and Jade, at a Halloween party two weeks ago.

>Thanks for the invite! she types and then deletes. She tries for something less desperate.

243

>You know I'm only five miles away, not like in the next state? ☺

That won't work either.

>Looking hawt, sexy zombies, she types and hits post. Like, hey, remember me.

God, she cannot wait to get her license, and, somehow, a car. Maybe she can guilt her dad into it, the same way she guilted him into getting her a smartphone against Gabi's wishes.

She clicks over to Dorian's page, to see if he's posted new skating videos. Not because she's a stalker. Not to see if he's still talking to that LA artist girl.

Which he is. They're making plans, right in front of her. The hurt is like being punched in the heart. She's angry with herself for being so pathetic.

She switches over to Phil's page. But it looks like he's wised up and deleted his profile. She checks on her phone and types in VelvetBoy. 'That username does not exist,' MChat informs her. Good. Maybe he's been scared off for life.

And that gives her something more useful to do than obsess over Dorian. Clean up after herself.

She deletes all the chats and clears her history of every search related to 'pedo-baiting' and 'how do you know if someone is really a pedophile?' and 'how to report a pedophile'. Even if the NSA has already recorded everything and added it to her file, she can do due diligence for her mother's sake. It's all about plausible deniability. But she keeps the SusieLee account. Just in case.

She goes outside and puts the rest of the flyers on the barbecue, drowns them in lighter fluid and tosses a burning match into the middle. The pages flare into orange flames, before the edges brown and curl up around Phil's hateful nice face. She watches the soft black ash drift into the night, her injured hand throbbing. The doorbell goes while she's gathering up the scraps, and she only just catches the pizza guy as he's climbing back in his car.

'Hey! I paid for that,' she shouts at him.

'You can't do that, not answer the door,' he complains. 'I thought I was being set up for a robbery. You're lucky I don't blacklist your house.'

She takes the pizza to bed with her, realizing she hasn't eaten since breakfast. Cheese makes the world a better place, Cas has observed. One of the holy food groups along with bacon, and ice cream, and bacon-flavored ice cream. She doesn't care about the grease stains on the covers, or that NyanCat pokes her nose into the box to lick at the pepperoni.

She falls asleep sometime after midnight, her mom still not home, and dreams restlessly about having to do her driver's test. But the words scramble on the page, and the steering wheel turns to smoke under her hands, and the car goes smashing through the wall and onto the stage in the middle of the performance. Everyone is angry with her and Mrs. Westcott is shouting at her, calling her a little fake. She gets out of the car and realizes she's naked. She can't remember her lines and everyone is laughing at her.

She tries to explain, but when she opens her mouth, little fish come streaming out and flop around on the stage, growing bigger and bigger until they turn into spiky rainbow creatures with mouths that open like tunnels, full of spiny inward-facing teeth, and they gape to swallow her whole.

FRIDAY, NOVEMBER 14

People Who Live
in Gingerbread Houses

There is a pair of shoes neatly placed in front of the kiln at Miskwabic Pottery. Ladies' rubber boots. Red with ladybugs on them. The feet are still in them, little hard nubs of gray, swimming in blood. *The ankle bone's connected to the foot bone.* A red smear down the kiln door. Bloody drag marks from the back door. The showroom is full of colorful tiles smashed on the floor like puzzle pieces, along with a florist's worth of dead flowers.

From outside, the pottery looks like a twee little pub ripped out of the English countryside, complete with chimney and wooden mock-Tudor frames, and set down in Detroit. Back here, though, it's as creepy as hell.

There's a machine behind her that looks like the ribcage of some terrible beast. The back door to the outside yard is standing ajar – probable access point. They'll need to dust it, Gabi thinks.

In front of her is the kiln and whatever's inside. It's huge, shaped like a sarcophagus, with a curved roof and chalky white bricks, scorched in places, and gas canisters and pipes down the side. A heat gauge pokes out jauntily from the side. It's framed in black iron, with a metal rod handle, and rails to pull it out on, marked with yellow and black hazard stripes. Old-school industry, this.

Gabi thinks of all the fairytales she used to read Layla. Hansel holding out a chicken bone instead of his finger to prove that he wasn't plump enough to go in the oven. Not yet. Cannibalism and murder and terrible parents. They all got sanitized. Kids can't cope with the darkness, supposedly, but how else are we supposed to wrestle with it? How else are we supposed to prepare for *this* moment when you have to open the door not knowing what's behind it? The dread prickling her scalp. Animal defense. Primitive fear.

Of course, for most people, death behind the door, the monster within, are purely metaphorical. Gabi gets the real fucking deal.

'Is there a trick to opening this?' she calls out to the arty kid who was unlucky enough to find the body. Or the crime scene. Because as of yet, there is no body. Unless you include the feet. But there will be.

'No—' the kid chokes out. He is hovering in the entrance, his arms wrapped so tightly across his chest he might snap a rib.

'Any chance anything is still alive in there?'

'Not if it's been running. It gets up to a thousand degrees.'

'And now?'

'It's cooled right down. It's safe to open.' It's obvious he's hoping she'll do it. She's tempted to draw her weapon. Images of melted things clawing their way out. Why don't you check if the oven is hot, my dear?

'Let's get it over with then,' Gabi says, taking hold of

the handle. She can feel residual heat through the bricks. Boyd braces himself on the other side. 'One. Two. Three.' They pull hard on the bar and drag the door forward, heavy and steady on the tracks, opening the door a crack and then all the way.

The oven yawns. Gabi moves around cautiously as a breeze whirls in from the back door, puffing greasy ash right into her face.

'Jesus.' She reels back, rubbing frantically at her eyes.

'It's okay, it's all right,' Boyd says, and shouts to the youngster, 'Get a wet cloth!'

But she's not waiting. She yanks her shirt out of her pants and uses it to wipe her face. 'Fuck's fucking sake.'

'You done?' Boyd asks.

'Swearing? No. I still got some left. Motherfuck.'

'Whenever you're ready.'

'Give me one fucking second, okay?' She takes the wet cloth and scrubs at her skin. Christ, she hopes she didn't breathe any in. 'You never got remains on you?'

'Not once. I'm careful, see.'

'All right, I'm ready.' She shoves the kiln door wider with her elbow, holding her breath. It's dark inside, and it doesn't help that they are between the light and whatever is inside the oven. She clicks on her flashlight.

'Jesus,' Boyd breathes. The shape in the oven is not human. Some kind of insect or sea creature, she thinks. All spiny appendages and sharp ridges. A carapace. A clay exoskeleton arranged around the space where the body should be. There are spindly extra legs protruding outwards from the torso, six on one side, eight on the other. A helmet over the absence of the skull, caved in over the eyes, sausagey tendrils hanging down where the jaw would be, like on a caterpillar. The breastplate rises to a sharp point in the center. There are fanciful curls around the arms, leaving gaps where the flesh melted away, like dead coral.

'This is some shit,' Boyd whistles.

'Serial now,' Gabi says. 'The feds will want in.'

'If it's the same guy.'

'You don't think it's the same guy?'

'It's not a deer is all I'm saying.'

'Two different killers leaving fucked-up bodies round town? We *really* have a problem.'

'No dead flowers on the other body.'

'He's getting more elaborate.'

'You have to tell the mayor's office.'

'Fuck's sake.'

'Fuck,' Boyd agrees.

'Okay. Tell me this. Where are the bones?' she says. 'Even crematoriums leave bones.' She's thinking of her grandfather, the white chips in the ash they threw into the ocean, off Havana, the only time she'd ever been. Appropriate for a fisherman.

'Kilns burn hotter,' the boy says, peering in past them, his lips trembling. 'Not a lot of people know that. Oh God, poor Betty.'

'But *some* would,' she seizes on it. 'Did the killer know? Was this the result he was going for, melting the bones away? Or was it a mistake?'

'Mistake,' Boyd says. 'He would have wanted to put her on display.'

'I think so, too. So did he get interrupted? Or did he not know?'

'Jesus, Betty.' The boy is shaking. He shouldn't be in here, Gabi thinks.

252

'Back up now.' Boyd goes over, putting his bulk between the kid and the thing in the kiln. 'Stand there, against the wall. Deep breaths, and for God's sake don't puke in here. What time did you say you got in?'

'Seven. I was out all night, figured I'd get an early start. It's quiet here in the morning. I…had a girl with me. She gave me a ride.'

'Where is she now?'

'She took off. She freaked out. I have her phone number.'

'You're sure this is Betty?' Gabi nods at the remains in the oven.

'Those are her boots. She's the manager. Betty Spinks.' He's shaking.

'When we're finished here, you're going to show me her office and start making up a list of everyone who has keys to the building, anyone who might have a problem with her, any enemies she might have had. And I'm going to need you to point out anything that looks out of place to you. How long have you worked here?'

'Three years,' he says, miserably. He points at the side of the kiln. 'That's not supposed to be there. That drawing.'

Gabi moves around to where someone has drawn an uneven rectangle in pink chalk. It gives her the dreads.

'Hey, Gabi,' Boyd calls. 'Look at *this*.' She joins him at the gaping mouth of the kiln and he points at the curve of clay where the woman's shin would have been. There is a mark baked into the surface.

'Perfect fingerprint,' she notes.

'Home and away, now, right?' Boyd grins.

The Suck

Holding on to a grudge is one big suck. It sucks that she is lonely at school and her fresh attempt to make an incursion into the Future Promise gang has been deflected with crushing disinterest, like she wasn't the girl who had a whole diner conned into believing she was an undercover cop.

It sucks that Cas keeps trying to catch her attention in history class while she checks her phone under her desk with misgiving, surfing the local news sites for some mention of Cop Impersonator Girl and the Pedophile, which is how she's captioned it in her head.

It sucks getting the increasingly bugfuck crazy messages VelvetBoy2 is sending from his new profile to SusieLee's account, which she's kept active because it's the only way she has to keep tabs on him. Like what if he works out who she really is and comes after her? And there's no-one she can talk to about any of this except Cas.

She's managed to get through the day without running in to her, but they both have to go to rehearsals at the Masque. Layla slouches up the steps to the theater school like the beast heading toward Bethlehem in that poem. Is she awful for thinking that the worst part is that she's going to have to go to the art party all on her own?

It's a relief and a disappointment that Cas isn't even there when she gets inside. There's the buzz of kids doing warm-up exercises, rehearsing lines, going through a box of shoes and trying them on. Most of them are dressed up, she realizes, the boys in high-waisted pants and button-up shirts, dapper hats and sharp shoes, the girls in fifties skirts and blouses. Keith is tottering around in a pair of heels and a yellow shirtwaister dress, melodramatically misquoting Blanche DuBois: 'I want magic! Yes, magic! I try to give that to people. I don't tell truths. I tell what *ought* to be truth.'

'Cut that out, please,' Mrs. Westcott chides affably. 'You're going to destroy those shoes.' She spots Layla and jerks her thumb at the ceiling. 'Go upstairs and find something that fits you and your character. Which reminds me...' She raises her voice to address the room: 'Everyone, please remember to bring your props on Monday. Something that anchors you to your character. Their favorite book, a piece of jewelry. Be creative.'

Layla tramps up to the attic room, a flurry of girls passing her, all dressed up and high on the excitement of it. It's crazy how transformative clothes can be – but she guesses that's the point of army uniforms. She pushes open the door and finds Cas alone, in her bra and a tight pencil skirt, picking through the box of clothes in disgust. Her face is the same flustered pink as the silk blouse in her hand.

'Hey,' Layla says, icicle-cool, not willing to be the one to make the first move.

'Hey,' Cas says, hurriedly getting to her feet, striking a pose with her hand on her waist and flapping the sheer blouse. 'Do you know there is not one single thing in here that fits over my boobs? It's like they didn't have full-busted women in the fifties.'

'Maybe that's what the Detroit riots were really about.'

Cas looks miserable. 'Can we skip to the hugging-I'm-so-sorry-part?'

Layla goes over and leans her head on her shoulder.

'Missed you, bitch.'

Cas pulls her into a bear hug, squashing her face into her chest. 'You fucking cow. I missed you too.'

'Can't. Breathe,' Layla gasps. 'Mammary. Suffocation.'

'Serves you right. Do you know what you've put me through?' She releases her and Layla comes up for air. 'You drooled on me.' Cas swabs at her bra.

'Cas. I'm sorry I was a bag of dicks.'

'Lay. I'm sorry you were a bag of dicks too.' They're grinning at each other. 'And I'm sorry *I* was a bag of dicks.'

'You were a truckload of dicks! A whole convoy of trucks loaded with dicks crossing into Canada.'

'That's a lot of dicks. Do you think you need a permit for that?'

'I think Canada probably has an embargo on dicks.'

'That's why they're so nice. No dicks allowed.'

Silence barges in between them.

'So, yeah,' Cas says, snuggling up to awkward, like she's really hoping to change the subject.

'No. Come on. What the hell *was* that? Do you know him? He didn't…when you were little?' She's played it out in her head, but she can't bring herself to say it.

'Jesus. No!'

'Okay.'

'I know I said I would explain or whatever. But it's—Shit, Lay. Can we go easy on each other for a little bit? I'll tell you soon, I promise. I know that sounds lame. But I can't face it right now. I mean, I can't even find an outfit that fits me.' She looks so stricken, Layla lets the anger burn out. In the end, forgiveness is like letting go of a rabid cougar you had by the tail.

'Did you kill someone?'

'Not yet.'

'Then I guess it can wait. But you *are* going to have to make it up to me.'

'What's it going to take? Flowers? Chocolates? Flowers *and* chocolates?'

'You have to come with me to the art party.'

'All right. But *only* if we can get you some new clothes. And they can't be black.'

'Black is the symbol of perfect democracy. All the colors united as one.'

'Give me benevolent dictatorship any day.'

'You'd be a terrible dictator, Cas.'

'By terrible, you mean awesome.'

'Awesome for you.'

'Yuh-huh. I'm a dictator. That's all I care about. Jeez. You really don't get politics, Lay.'

'So...do you want to hear about it?'

It sounds mental when she tells it, of course.

'They seriously believed you were undercover? Lucky they didn't have any cop customers.'

'Coffee's not shitty enough. But it was weird. They were so ready to lap up whatever I said. It was like *The Crucible*. Have you read it?'

'I might have seen the movie. Was Tanning Chatum in it?'

'No. It's about mass hysteria and the Salem witch trials.'

'With robot Nicole Kidman and all the creepy kids with

257

white hair who look alike?'

'No! Fuck's sake. Do you pay attention to anything?'

'Okay, okay. Hysteria. Witch trials.'

'They really, really wanted to believe. I can see how it would be easy to be a con artist. Or, I dunno, start a genocide.'

'One of those careers is probably healthier than the other one. I guess people want a little drama in their life. They want to feel special. You gave that to them for one afternoon. You're going to look back on this as the highlight of your acting career.'

'I hope not. Speaking of drama…'

'I've been getting the messages too. What are we going to do?'

>VelvetBoy2: Fuckyoubgthcfingyoujkillyou

>VelvetBoy2: Cunt.

>VelvetBoy2: Ha, ha, you got me. Funny joke.

>VelvetBoy2: Hey, SusieLee, I meant what I said. About you being a special girl. I didn't realize how special. You're a smart cookie. Wont you answer me? Please. We should talk. I'm sorry if I freaked yo uot. It was a silly game. Friends?

>VelvetBoy2: Wyhat do you want? Money? I don't have money. But I can make a plan. Yu want more game coucher?s

>VelvetBoy2: Vouchers. (Spelling!) :)

>VelvetBoy2. Cunt. Cunt. Cutn. Cunt. Cunt. Cunt. Cunt. Cunt.Cunt.Cunt.Cunt.CUNT. CUNTCUNTCUNTCUNTCUNTCUNTCUNTCYUNCUNTCUNT

Mrs. Westcott sticks her head in. 'Girls? How long does it take to find a costume? On stage in two minutes, please.

Everyone else is waiting on you.'

'Yes, Mrs. Westcott,' they chime together.

'Hustle, please.'

'This might work,' Layla says, handing Cas an emerald-green blouse with a bow at the throat.

'Layla Stirling-Versado, ace wardrobe assistant,' Cas says, doing up the buttons. 'Is there no end to your talents?'

'You should wear a skirt more often,' Layla says, admiring her friend. 'You look amazing.'

'Not gonna happen. Here.' She hands her a ruffled black dress with a cinch waist. 'You should wear this. In fact, you should borrow it for the party.'

'Mrs. W. would kill us. Besides, I thought you said no black?' Layla slips out of her sneakers without unlacing them and yanks off her jeans.

'It's got polka dots, it doesn't count.' She watches Layla folding her clothes. 'Why do you think VelvetBoy is being so crazy? Why doesn't he just walk away?'

'Because he left this behind.' She pulls out the black leather wallet from her bag. She's thought about throwing it in the river, but that seemed like letting him off easy. One hundred and thirty-nine dollars. She's counted it, but hasn't been able to bring herself to spend it, even when she was fifty cents short of a soda at lunchtime. 'Bank cards. Social security. His driver's license. Everything.'

'Shit a brick.'

'I think we should tell my mom.'

'You can't! She'll kill you. She'll tell my parents! They'll ground me for life.'

'It's okay. I'll take the blame.'

'You don't understand. Forget going to the art party, forget the Masque, they'll ban me from seeing you, they'll probably pull me out of school. We'll have to move again!'

'GIRLS!' Mrs. Westcott shrieks from below.

Layla, still in her underwear, automatically goes for the door, and Cas grabs her by the arm and drags her back.

'Are you mental? You're not dressed yet. Or were you planning to go on stage naked?'

Victimology

The obvious suspect for the murder in the pottery should be the abusive ex-husband, Peter Morrow. And wouldn't it be perfect if it turned out he had a direct line to Daveyton Lafonte because maybe he plays illegal poker games with Daveyton's dad, and maybe he hunts deer – sometimes out of season because rules are for pussies – and maybe he does restoration on old houses for a living so he carries a nail gun around with him.

Maybe he's not *just* the kinda guy who would grip his ex-wife's face so hard during a drunken altercation in public that he leaves bruises on her jaw, but the kind of sick twisted fuck who would glue a kid onto a deer and turn his ex-wife into some kind of undersea nightmare and bake her in her own oven.

It would tie things up nicely, but unfortunately none of it is true.

He's the manager at an electronics store. He was out drinking with his buddies at a sports bar downtown. They can back up his story, as can the waitress, who got stiffed on the tip.

They're still running the fingerprint they found on the clay through all the national databases, Michigan State, the NCIC, but they take his fingerprints for comparison anyhow, and there's not even one point of intersection.

And Gabi can tell in the first five minutes of the interrogation that he is your garden-variety domestic-violence schmuck who uses his fists to work out his anxieties about what a pathetic loser he is.

Peter cries and snuffles when they make him look at the photographs. 'I can't,' he moans. 'I can't.' When he reaches the one of her boots, he sobs and gags. Boyd hands him the wastepaper basket and he spits into it for several minutes. 'My wife. Who would do that to my wife?'

'Ex-wife who has a restraining order on you,' Boyd points out. 'This an act of revenge? You didn't want to cough up for alimony anymore? You hire some sicko to do this for you?'

This time he does puke. They'll turn up hardcore pornography on his work computer at the store he manages. Nothing illegal, but bad enough to get him in trouble with the HR department.

Back in the briefing room, she runs through what they know. She writes on the board with the brand-new pen that Marcus had got her earlier from the local stationery store.

'This just got a lot bigger and uglier,' she says to the assembled detectives and honey-blonde Jessica from the mayor's office, who is poised on a desk at the back, typing into her BlackBerry with ominous diligence. 'We can assume that this is likely the work of one killer, rather than two different ones with similar interests in the same week – and that our friend is either an artist or somehow involved in the arts scene.'

Artist

She circles the word. 'He wants us to see this, he wants recognition for what he's doing. Which is why we're not going to give it to him. We are not releasing the photographs to the press under any circumstances.'

'The mayor's office agrees.' Jessica looks up from her phone.

'If he's an artist, it explains why the victim profiles are so different,' Boyd says. 'We think he's an opportunist. He grabs Daveyton because he's looking for someone to match up to his deer. He goes after the Spinks woman because she's already there in the pottery. Maybe he knows her.'

'He's trying to make it easier on himself,' Gabi elaborates. 'Which means he's already thinking about it, planning it out. We believe he may have been interrupted, that he would have liked to put the body on display somewhere, and that he didn't intend for us to find it inside the kiln, despite the boots arranged outside it.'

She checks her notes. 'Robin Mitchell, an employee, opened the store early this morning, at seven, and found the body. Well, the feet. There are witnesses to his whereabouts all night.'

'Including his lady friend who fled the scene,' Boyd says, to chuckles from the guys.

Gabi ignores them. 'We suspect that the killer heard him and slipped out the back.'

Fingerprint

'Our best piece of evidence right now is the fingerprint we found on the clay. We're running it through State and NCIC. We've obviously already eliminated Mitchell, the other employees, and, unfortunately for us, the ex-husband with the domestic assault charge and the restraining order.'

'You could also ask to run the fingerprints through

military records,' Stricker says. And is it her imagination, or does he look contrite?

'You volunteering?'

'Sure. Some companies that require background checks take fingerprints as well. Hospitals, security companies. But technically we don't have access to that.'

'I got ways around technically,' Mike Croff butts in.

'I think this is sensitive enough without bringing privacy issues into it, Croff.'

'You want to catch this knucklehead or worry about some nursie who gets upset you looked at her file?'

'No, she's right,' Jessica says. 'We keep this clean, please.'

Gabi taps the board.

The scene

'Evidence Tech is still working it. There's no sign of forced entry. The alarm company says that Spinks didn't hit the panic button. This means she opened the door.'

'Or maybe your killer was already inside?' Washington says.

'We found an aluminum baseball bat on the counter near the back door. Mitchell confirms that it belonged to Spinks.'

'So first she's worried about whoever's there, but then *she puts her weapon down*,' Boyd says. 'So either he's the most charming harmless-looking motherfucker on earth—'

'Or it was someone she knew,' Gabi picks up. 'Maybe both. We're working with the staff to compile a list of former employees, students, artists who have exhibited there. Problem is that sometimes we only have first names, so it's going to be a few days of compiling and then running the full names through Accurint to get their birth dates and social security numbers so we can run criminal history checks.'

'Put Tinkerbell on it,' Croff says.

'Sparkles, Mike. And he's already on it. Right now, we're narrowing it down to people who have been arrested. If we find something else interesting, someone who had a beef with her, or someone who did something unusual or weird or creepy, we'll prioritize that.'

'What's in the courtyard?' Stricker asks.

'Student kilns and also some tables and chairs where the staff have lunch in summer. The security guard, Donald Synder, who left early, says the gate to the courtyard from the parking lot is kept locked – and there's no sign of force.'

'You fingerprint him?'

'Of course. No match. He's real torn up. Blames himself.'

'Maybe he should,' Washington says with the cynicism that comes from long years of dealing with little mistakes that end bloodily. 'You sure he remembered to lock the door?'

'It's possible he forgot, but the killer seems to have known where to find wet clay and how to operate the kiln, which suggests a familiarity with the premises and the equipment. So a member of staff or someone who made use of the facilities. We're compiling a list of people who might have had a key.'

The body

'We don't have anything to work with here, apart from her feet, which were sawn off post-mortem, we believe, with piano wire, which is used to cut clay. He would have been able to find this on site. There's a lot of blood in the kiln room, which would suggest that he prepared the body there. Her body melted right down to the bones, so we don't know if she was killed the same way as Daveyton because we don't have her skull to examine. However, there is a blood spatter on the wall broadly similar to the one we found at the bus stop where we believe Daveyton was killed.'

White / silver truck

'Robin Mitchell reported that there was a pick-up truck parked outside the pottery when he arrived, not in the parking lot, which is locked overnight, but on the street. It was not there when Boyd and I arrived on the scene. He says he only noticed it because the windscreen was banged up, like it had recently hit something. He didn't get the plates and he's not sure of the color. It may have been white or silver.'

'Something like a deer, maybe?'

'Could be.'

Dead plants

'This is the curveball. And that's saying something with *this* particular homicide. The floor was covered in organic matter. Dead plants. Flowers and vines. I'm no gardener, but they looked exotic to me. We're getting a botanist to identify them. The staff and the security guard confirm that there were no flowers or plants on the premises when they left.'

'He ordered them in? Funeral flowers?'

'We're following up with local florists to see if anyone made a delivery. But these weren't fresh flowers. They looked like they'd been dead a while. So if he brought them in, where did he get them, and why did he bring them? They're only in the store, not in the area where the ovens are – kilns, I mean.'

Chalk drawing

'And here's the clincher, which links our two bodies together. Both of them have this drawn on a wall somewhere near the body. Sparkles, you started in on the graffiti, I want you to follow up. Find out if it means anything. Gang sign, movie reference. Is anyone else doing this, or is it peculiar to our killer? Ask Bob for help if you need it.

Okay, any questions?'

Jessica sticks up her hand. 'What are you doing to resolve this as quickly as possible?'

'Everything we fucking can. Ma'am.'

What's Due

The doorbell is a wheezy mechanical bird call. Clayton ignores it, but it goes off again, digging under his focus. He recognizes it, like the sound of the microwave ping, as an electronic absolute, calling him back from where he's been.

He's not sure where that is. He has troubling pictures in his head. He can't keep one thing in mind because he keeps getting distracted. He finds himself taking on the shapes that he's working on. He has to pull himself together, feeling his face with his hands to remember what he looks like.

The doorbell rings and rings. There is knocking. Then pounding and shouting.

'Clayton! Hello? You alive in there?'

No. No, it doesn't think so. Only for a moment. Now he's gone again, retreated into a corner of his mind, frightened by the sight of the blood. It has dragged the remains from the refrigerator upstairs down to the basement, and taken the other set from the freezer in here. It is time to prepare them.

The dream has no interest in the slight man tramping round the side of the house, or the woman beside him. It can see their legs from the slit window in the basement. The woman is wearing blue heels. Darcy – it hauls her name and face out of Clayton's memories. He recognizes her from the squat on Eastern Market.

Something is happening. It's to do with the doors it has marked in all the quiet places Clayton knew about – the dreaming places where the walls are thin. Something is building like a wave. Tsunamis pull all the ocean back before they come crashing in.

Their voices carry. They're tugging at the back door, which is inclined to get stuck. You have to pull the handle down and toward you. It returns to its work, their talking so much background noise. The flesh is harder to work with now that time has passed and the seams have puckered. It won't be able to use the meat glue again, it realizes with dismay.

'Well, where is he?' It's the woman's voice.

'Maybe he forgot. Went out of town. How the hell do I know? Help me with this door.'

'It's locked, genius.'

Its attention is jerked by the contempt in her voice. Clayton knows that tone well. It makes the man inside flinch.

'God, Darcy.' It's Patrick speaking. 'Can you not be such a cow about this? I was trying to do a good thing for a man who is actually extraordinarily talented and overlooked, and I don't know why—' he tapers off. 'Shit.'

'Do we still have the kiddie pool?' Darcy says, her high heels clopping past the window strip back toward the car. 'We can go back to plan A.'

Patrick's lace-ups go scampering after her. 'I just can't believe he would do this to me.'

'Believe it.'

269

It listens to the car start up, the petulant squeal of tires as they pull away. Clayton feels panicky relief that they're gone, that they didn't find them down here, red-handed. The dream doesn't care about that. It returns to the work, considering its choice of materials. It will not make the same mistakes again. It was interrupted with Betty, and besides, that was too private.

It needs an audience. It needs to reassemble the broken pieces. Like the lady said: Go back to plan A.

SATURDAY, NOVEMBER 15

The Mouth Feel of Secrets

'You're up early, bean.' Gabi is wearing her detective's uniform: jeans and hoodie, but is still padding around in the slippers Layla bought her that make your feet look like big clumpy yeti feet with claws. 'You want some coffee?'

'I didn't sleep well.'

'Again? You've seemed off lately.' Her mom puts her palm on her forehead. 'You coming down with something?'

Layla feels undone by this little gesture of love. 'Maybe.'

It's killing her not to tell her mom. The secret feels like moths fluttering in her mouth, bashing against her teeth. But she can't face how angry Gabi is going to be, and even worse, how disappointed. The high-level discussions with her dad that will follow, strategizing what to do about her. Never mind dragging Cas into it. *We'll have to move again.* She's diligently deleting VelvetBoy2's messages, jumping every time her phone vibrates. 'How's the case going?' she mutters.

Gabi grimaces. 'Good, I suppose. We have another body.'

'That's good?'

'We got a perfect fingerprint, if we could only match it. We have a solid idea of the killer's profile. It feels like we're closing in.'

'I'm proud of you, Mom. I mean it.'

Gabi chokes on her coffee, looking both pleased and shy. 'Thank you. That means a lot. I'm proud of you, too.'

But you wouldn't be, Layla thinks, if you knew.

'I know it's been crazy,' her mom continues, 'but I'm going to make it up to you. As soon as this is all over, we'll do something really fun together.'

'We could go sailing,' Layla says, with as much enthusiasm as she can muster, because she thinks this will be something Gabi wants to hear. Judging by the smile on her mom's face, she's right. 'Like you and Grandpa did. You can teach me.'

'I know a Russian gangster who might let us use his boat.'

'Seriously?' Layla isn't entirely sure if she's shocked or impressed.

'I think he might want me to sleep with him first though.'

'Mom!'

'I'm kidding.' And it's almost okay again. Look, things can be normal. They can joke around, and her mom has no idea she is being eaten alive on the inside.

'Maybe you should start dating,' Layla says, and is it her imagination or does Gabi look briefly sad?

'Maybe after I catch this bastard. Hard to be romantic when you're dealing with corpses all day.'

'But that's what you do every day.'

'Nothing like as bad as these ones. Listen, I was thinking maybe you should stay with Aunt Cheryl this weekend. She can come pick you up. I'm going to be working long hours, and it's not fair on you. You don't spend enough time with your cousins. Family is important.'

Layla's heart sinks. Her dad's super-evangelical sister stays out near Bridgeport, and she has a party to sneak off to. 'I'm staying at Cas's tonight!' she says, a little too quickly. Piling lies on top of lies. If she stayed with her aunt, they'd drag her to church on Sunday morning, and she would burst into flames just crossing the threshold.

'Oh,' Gabi says, surprised at her vehemence. 'Should I call her parents?'

'Mr. Holt's crazy busy at work, I'll get him to call you this evening.' She's hoping that by then Gabi will be so wrapped up in the case she won't notice that she hasn't got a confirmation.

'Perfect. I'm going to head into the office. You need a ride anywhere?'

'No, I'm going to chill this morning. Practice my lines. Oh God, that reminds me. I need an ashtray.'

'Layla. Is there something you want to tell me?'

Yes. Yes. Fuck, yes, Layla thinks. 'No,' is what she says. 'It's for the play. We need a prop to help us get into the role. My character seems calm, but she's this hot mess inside. I think she probably smokes to keep up the façade.'

'Look in the basement. My old one might still be there. Remember it? Or were you too young when I quit? It's this art-deco piece, like the inside of a seashell, beautiful colors.'

'Awesome. Thanks, Mom.'

'As long as it's just an act and you don't take it too far. What's it called,' her mother snaps her fingers, 'when actors put on forty pounds for a role, or run out and get real tattoos?'

'Method acting. This Russian actor Stanislavski came up with it.'

'No method, okay? Or Russians. Definitely stay away

275

from the Russians, especially ones with boats.'

'Got it,' Layla says.

Gabi downs the rest of the coffee and checks her gun before she slides it into the holster under her arm. This is the moment to tell her, Layla thinks, right now, before she walks out the door, back into the nucleus of the case.

'Hey, Mom!' she yelps, and Gabi turns – but she can't do it. 'I meant it,' she says. 'You should start dating.'

Gabi leans against the door. 'I tell you how to run your love life, beanie?'

'All the time!' Layla protests.

'That's because you're a minor. Have fun with Cassandra. Stay off the streets, okay?'

She comes back a moment later, cursing. 'You couldn't tell me about the slippers?'

'I was hoping you'd make it all the way to the precinct.'

Can't See the Would

The exhibition houses are marked by the Dream House real-estate signs on the lawn, spread over a five-block radius, but the party seems to extend to the whole neighborhood. All the doors are open, people have set out tables in their front yards under heater lamps, selling spiced wine or beer from the keg, $2 a cup, $1 refund if you bring your cup back. There are food trucks serving gourmet coney dogs and falafel. A sound system has been set up on a porch and a DJ is spinning sunshiny house music that summons up sandy beaches and bright cocktails.

'Gives you an idea of what it could be like, huh?' Layla is wearing a silver sequinned sweater that Cas picked out for her at the thrift store, teamed with a black skirt, gold-spangled tights and flat boots.

'You can't make me look at the art. Or take it seriously.' Cas is wearing her usual get-up of a baggy hoodie and jeans and no makeup, even though she did Layla's for her. Big black punk-rock eyes with like five layers of eye-liner and bright red lipstick that she can't help tonguing at, even though it's probably laced with heavy metals and toxic chemicals. She's going to die of lead poisoning.

'I feel like a disco ball,' she complains, but only half-heartedly.

'Dorian always struck me as a disco kinda guy. You look amazing. Now please shut the fuck up and stop licking your lips. It makes you look like a mental case.'

Layla pulls up short. 'Oh shit, Cas. I dreamed this.'

'What? Waiting in line to see some crappy art as the worst ever cover for trying to get laid?'

'No, idiot. The fish.' She points out the paste-up on the side of the house, two storeys high. It's of a fish with fluttery translucent fins, striated with rainbow colors, covered in spikes and with a deep tube mouth of circular fangs like a lamprey or the pit monster in *Star Wars*. 'This is so weird, Cas. It's exactly the same.'

Cas is unimpressed. 'Maybe you dreamed it because you saw it.'

'I've never seen this before.'

'Slut, please. It's on the invite.'

'Bullshit.'

'Give it to me, I'll show you.' Layla digs the flyer out of her handbag. The image shows the place in front of them with its cheery sign: 'Dream House: An MCity Projects Party.' And Cas is right. It's not taken dead-on, so you can see some of the side of the house, the wall slanting away at an oblique angle and the fish mural half-cast in shadow.

'Lodged in your subconscious like a splinter, along with sweet, sweet dreams of Dorian going down on you.'

'Cas!'

She laughs and flicks Layla on the forehead. 'Jesus. You *are* in love. Hopeless. So where are we going to find your boy?'

'He said he'd meet us here.' Layla looks around. 'He's

not outside, so I guess we go in.'

'One at a time,' the man at the door says. One of the artists, Layla guesses, going by his paint-spattered overalls and the screwdriver sticking out of his pocket. His hair is plastered with sweat, as if he just finished working. The sign outside the house reads 'Can't See the Would'.

'We're together.'

'Okay, then. It's all on the ground floor. Please go straight through, so other people can have the same experience. Don't go upstairs because the stairs are rotten and we're all about having a good time, not falling through the floor. The live performance kicks off at eight. Enjoy.'

He ushers them in and closes the door behind them. It's gloomy in the entrance hall, although they can hear the murmur of voices deeper in.

'Like a ghost house,' Layla whispers because the muted acoustics seem to demand it.

'Or a tunnel of lo-ooove.' Cas steps forward and a thrum of bass judders under their feet. 'Shit!' She grabs Layla's arm in fright.

'I think that's the "experience".'

'Cute.'

'It's rigged to different floorboards.' Layla walks forward, setting off another deep vibration under them, like the whole house is purring. She is pleased with herself for working it out. 'Pressure plates.'

'Scared the fucking crap out of me.'

'It's pretty cool. You know haunted houses seem that way because of subsonics.'

'For once I wish we could just go somewhere without you turning it into a big fat lecture.'

'Same with church organs. The way they make the hair

on your neck stand up. It's the frequency. Too low to register on our aural spectrum. But you can feel it on some level, in your bones, and it gives you the heebie-jeebies. Or a case of the holy-moleys.'

'I always thought oral sex was aural sex. Sticking it in your ear.'

'Are you even listening to me?'

'Unless you're saying, "Cas, can I get you a drink, my dear friend", then no.'

'You don't drink.'

'They have Chinese bubble tea. I saw a cart.'

The door opens behind them and the artist pokes his head in: 'Can you move all the way in, please? There are other people waiting.'

They walk deeper into the house, through a room wall-papered in monochromatic symbols – an alien's idea of Arabic, perhaps, where musicians are setting up a keyboard and a saxophone and a big glossy double bass, and into a huge section with a stylized black-and-white forest of trees painted on the walls.

'Yargh. Makes my eyes go funny,' Cas says. The effect is amplified by thin black and white branches planted in the floor. People are milling between the sticks with glasses of spiced wine and beer and chatting, apart from one white-haired old guy who is edging round the room, staring into the forest. Their voices bounce around the space, which draws Lay's eyes up to the ceiling. The floor above has been ripped out to make the space double volume. 'That's why it sounds so echoey,' she says, nudging Cas.

'I don't think he's in here. We should go look for him outside.' Cas tries to turn her round, but it's too late, Layla has already seen Dorian – her heart does a fish-flop – and the girl he's with. She's changed her hair, but it's the one from Facebook. Dorian keeps touching her – her wrist, her arm, her shoulder, as if he's compelled to check that it's all in place.

His hair is mussed up in that effortless way that takes hours, and she's not the only one who's been raiding thrift stores. He's wearing a tuxedo jacket with the sleeves rolled up over a seventies T-shirt featuring orange and green stripes and a windsurfer. The girl's white-blonde hair has been cut short and styled into spiky tufts. Her only makeup is a cat flick of eye-liner, and her cream dress is made of hard linen folds, like origami. She's the coolest girl Layla has ever seen.

'Hey,' Layla says weakly. 'We made it.'

Dorian gives her a lazy grin and, in spite of the evidence, her heart flip-flops once more.

'This is my friend, TimTam.' He touches her again. 'She does projections.'

'Nice to meet you,' Layla says. Meaning, *die, bitch*.

'We have names too,' Cas says cheerfully. 'I'm Cas. This is Layla.'

'Awesome,' the girl says vaguely. 'Listen, I'm going to have a smoke before the show starts.' She kisses Dorian on the cheek, pressing her lips against his skin. Marking him, Layla thinks with an acid splash of jealousy. He watches her go.

'She seems cool,' Layla says, trying to pull him back. Lost cause.

'What the fuck is projection art?' Cas asks.

'What it sounds like,' Dorian explains. 'You set up laser projectors and you can map an animation onto 3D objects, like a hologram. She's into transformational art. Her piece runs the lifespan of a house in a really organic way, building it up from the cellular level.' It sounds like something he's repeating without understanding what it means, like a toddler using cuss words.

'Okay,' Layla says. She doesn't point out that houses aren't made of cells.

'Part of the visiting artists' residency. She's from LA.' He says it as one word, *Ellay*, like it's the magical golden land of the gods. Maybe it is.

'I love what they've done with the subsonics,' Layla says, knowing he'll know what she's talking about. 'I was trying to tell Cas about it.'

'I got it,' Cas rolls her eyes. 'Haunted houses and churches and shit.'

'That's one of the theories of Zug Island,' Dorian says, his attention finally recaptured.

'*Que?*' Cas chirps.

'That industrial place downriver, with all the factories that smell so bad. The machinery apparently creates subsonics. That's why there are so many conspiracy theories about it. Secret military operation or aliens or whatever.'

'Maybe that's why the whole city feels haunted.'

His face brightens with delight. 'That's good, Lay. That's really good.' See, Layla thinks, fiercely. This is why you belong with me, not some *Ellay* art bitch who sees you as a bit of local color. His attention shifts, and he frowns at the wall behind her. 'Did you see something move in the trees?'

Layla turns round and stares into the monochromatic forest. 'It's the contrast. Optical illusion. Unless your *girlfriend* is doing projections in here, too.' He doesn't correct her on the 'girlfriend' score. Goddammitdammitdammit.

Cas steps in. 'Are we going to check out some mother-fucking art or what?'

'I swear I saw something move,' Dorian says.

282

'Whatevs. Ciao-ciao, Dorkian.'

'Bye, Dorian. I'll—' but she can't think how to finish.

They walk back over the vibrating floor, but now it just seems dumb. Cheap shock tactics. 'Don't say anything,' she warns Cas.

'Don't know what you mean, bitch. I'm just here to take in some culture and have a good time.'

Chicken Coop

The dream parks the white truck in the street behind the house and waits patiently for The Coast To Be Clear – more words hauled from Clayton's head.

The man knows this neighborhood, this house in particular, with its disused chicken coop and the back gate that doesn't latch properly. It is a simple thing to carry the boy from the truck into the garden, light and sagging in Clayton's arms, unnoticed.

Everyone else is busy on the other side of the fence. The music starts and stops again. There is a clamor of voices, a bustling rush of activity, all the last-minute preparations. There are already people streaming through between the houses when the sound system screeches, a sonic whine, and the curator laughs nervously, and announces the Dream House project open for visitors!

The air is full of excitement, an expectant buzzing in people's heads. The dream knows what they are waiting for, even if they don't themselves.

The end of everything.

The moment when it reveals its miracle boy and all the

eyes will look and their seeing will be horror and glory and wonder and it will pierce the skin of the world, collapse dimensions, and open the doors and the work will breathe and dance in his shoes and the dream will be able to escape.

Ladybug, ladybug, fly away home.

The shadows are deepening, the fall dusk bringing the cold with it. It paces round the garden, impatient, until a young man waves at it from an upstairs window in the house. It raises a hand in acknowledgement, pulling Clayton's face into a smile that is all teeth. It waits until the figure behind the glass moves on, attention caught by something more intriguing.

It can't be seen. Not yet. It needs critical mass.

Big Bang, Clayton thinks.

It hunches in the chicken coop, crouched on its haunches above the calcified bird shit, relying on the shape of the shed to disguise its own, listening to the music and the voices getting louder and louder, competing for space.

But Clayton's wretched body gets restless. His feet start to tingle and burn and all the things the dream can sense, past the gate, inside the house…they're attractive.

It can feel the tug of the art, the currents of imagination. Maybe all the art will stir to life in the moment of reckoning. Wouldn't that be something, in Clayton's words.

It can't wait any more. It has to see for itself. It has to make things happen.

It stands up, shaking out the man's legs. It drives him up the porch stairs through a room full of frozen silver women who long to move.

Maybe it can help them.

Party People

Jonno works the crowds, getting vox pops. He makes straight for the weirdos and the hotties. He cajoles good answers from them. The artists all want to blab about their work.

'It's an improv-jam based on the hieroglyphs,' a man in overalls tells him. 'We're going to try and read them as if they were a musical score.'

He gives more airtime to the camera-friendly ones, like the gorgeous young blonde in a dress that looks like it's made out of paper, who is also eminently quotable. 'I think there's more artistic freedom in Detroit. You can do what you like here, and no-one cares. My work is intercontextual because it's about regeneration on a cellular level, using light to remake our idea of what these buildings could be. I think that's what we bring here. Light.'

They film her work, which looks like a high-school biology project projected onto the side of the building. Jonno can't resist making shadow puppets until Jen grabs his hand and pulls it away from the beam.

'That's mean,' she says, kissing his fingers in gentle reprimand.

'It's art, baby.' But he's annoyed, even though he's not the only one who can't resist interfering with the projection. He goes prowling off for other people to interview.

They run into Simon, who seems intimidated talking directly into the lens, a very different thing to hamming it up as a fake mugger, and Jonno wonders why he was ever worried about this jerk with his dumb tattoos, who can't say anything remotely intelligent for the camera.

It gets better as the crowds get thicker and the beer flows. One young woman, clinging to her friend, ponders his question. 'I think my favorite thing about Detroit is...the party stores! Whoooo!'

'Whoooo!' her friend says and they clink plastic cups, sloshing beer onto their shoes.

Sometimes they have nothing to give, so he throws in one-liners to spruce things up.

'Is that wax in your mustache, or are you happy to see me?' he says to a hipster with annoying facial hair. 'No, don't go. I have a serious question for you. Please. You ready? Are *you* personally responsible for the die-off of the bees?'

'What?'

'Because you must have plundered whole colonies of hives to keep you in mustache wax.'

'Fuck you, man.'

They're running low on good commentators when he spots his weird friend from the gallery, still in the same rumpled brown jacket, wandering dazed among the hip young people. Jonno knows how he feels. He swoops down on him, hoping he'll diss the art, say something critical and edgy. 'Hey, remember me? From the gallery? Mickey Mouse?'

The man focuses his attention on them with the unnerving zeal of a monk about to immolate himself live on TV. 'Yes,'

287

he says. 'I need a camera. I need people to see. It's ready. You have to come with me.' He turns, gesticulating for them to follow, and starts weaving his way through the crowds.

'Well, this is going to be good,' Jonno says and moves to go after him, but his camerawoman has lowered the phone and is messing around with one of her test strips.

'Now, Jen? Seriously?'

'We've been running around a lot. I have to check my levels,' she says, popping the lancet against the edge of her finger, so that a bright bead of blood wells up. Jonno shifts impatiently, trying to keep the man in sight.

'Ninety-five,' Jen says, reading off her meter. 'I'm fine.'

'Well, thank fuck for that.' The nutty old guy has vanished. Jonno sighs and segues into his brightest smile as Jen raises the camera phone once again. 'How about you, baby?' he says to a sandy-haired teenager sipping a bubble tea. 'What's your favorite thing you've seen tonight?'

'My reflection,' she says and gives him the finger, walking off.

'Let's take a break for a bit,' Jonno says, suddenly weary of all this. The scene. 'I need a drink.'

'I have to get ready for my set anyway. You'll film it, right?'

'Of course, baby.' He kisses her on the forehead, which leads him down to her mouth, which is hot and sweet. He feels a rush of tenderness for her, constantly at war with the sugar in her blood.

Unspeakable Things

Each of the six houses is curated to a theme, announced on the real-estate sign outside. They move through the buildings, peering in all the rooms: Would House, Lust House, House of Amerikana, House of Money, Luminous/Limnal, _Blank_.

Some of the art is lame, Heidelberg Project-lite. Plush toys stuck up all over exterior walls in 'Soft' and a bonfire pile of sneakers, like Tyree Guyton's high heels.

'Yawn,' Cas says. She likes the banal wall-size pop-art remixes in the Amerikana house where Marilyn Monroe has been given Kiss makeup and Osama Bin-Laden has been mashed-up with Einstein with his tongue sticking out. 'I'd wear this on a T-shirt. See, I'm an arts connoisseur.'

Layla lingers at the storm cloud of gray balloons that fills a room, set up with shifting lights that create a sense of expectancy, dawn or dusk constantly breaking in Luminous/Limnal. It's a lot more interesting than the boring porno stuff in the Lust House.

And she likes the interactive piece upstairs at _Blank_

(where presumably the floors have been reinforced), luggage tags hanging from the ceiling on red strings, where viewers have to complete the sentence prompt, 'I've lost...' The range of answers is lovely. 'My mind!' 'My grandmother.' 'My virginity.' 'All the feeling in my right leg.' 'My place in the world.' 'My dog. Reward offered!' 'My wifi password.' 'My dignity.' '$200 at the casino.' 'My sense of wonder.'

'Are you going to read every single one?' Cas complains.

'I haven't thought about what I'm going to write yet.'

'I've lost...my patience with art. I'll see you outside.'

Layla finally writes down 'my one true love' and then thinks better of it. What if Dorian recognizes her handwriting? She plucks it from its ribbon mooring and crumples it up in her fist. Then recants. When would he ever have seen her handwriting? And so what if he has? She hopes he *does* see it. She flattens it out and reties it among the others twirling gently.

In the meantime, the house has filled up. The crowd has become a salmon migration of shoving bodies. She fights her way down the stairs only to be faced with an even worse melee. It's going to take her half an hour to get to the exit. Someone barges into her and someone else steps backwards onto her toe.

'Ow!' she pushes back, but the crowd is oblivious. Screw this. She goes the other way into the kitchen, which is full of mannequins, spray-painted silver. She tries the latch on the back door and, mercifully, it opens onto a wooden porch that leads down into a dark overgrown garden. The music has become denser. She can feel it in the back of her teeth. Bass must generate its own subsonics.

She makes her way gingerly down the steps into the darkness and the long grass, hoping for a gate or an access alley down the side of the house. The grass gives way under her boots with a soft cellulose scrunch of protest. Blackjacks prick through her tights, clutching at her legs. Everything needs to propagate. She's just the vector of transmission.

She tramps past a dilapidated chicken hutch with the wire peeled back, the chickens long gone (flown the coop, ha ha), to the rickety wooden fence enclosing the yard. It's because she's watching her feet and thinking about seed cycles and aviary jokes that she doesn't see the tall figure canting forward with its malformed head and too-thin arms next to the chicken hutch, until she's right on top of it.

Layla has never been big on screaming. As a kid, she used to lie dead still, trying to keep her breathing slow so as not to tip off the monster under the bed. She goes quiet now. Blood thuds in her ears. Her mouth tastes like iron.

'Hello?' she whispers, so soft it doesn't come out. A warm flush of embarrassed relief as she realizes it's a dumb statue. Cheap thrills, like the floorboards, only this is more like a bad Halloween decoration. Shock art. A little deer with nubbin horns and a white tuft of fur on its narrow chest, its legs and hooves sticking out like arms, upright in pants and dirty sneakers. The creepiest thing about it is that its eyes are gone, so the fur around the sockets caves inwards on dark pits.

'Not funny,' she sneers at the deer-boy. It's badly done, awkwardly balanced in a wheelbarrow, propped up with rocks and cables, but it's still tilting forward. The hips are too wide for the chest, so the waist is padded with clay, which makes her wonder why the artist didn't make it all out of clay in the first place, because this thing smells fucking awful, of shit and rot. No wonder the artist dumped it out here where no-one would see it. Someone's drawn a chalk rectangle on the fence behind it, like a cheap frame.

Maybe it's the music, or heartbreak, or the cold, but she's filled with growing trepidation. Young deer are called kids, she thinks.

She takes a photograph on her phone. The sculpture doesn't look so bad on screen. The flash lights up the hollow sockets, taking away the terrible falling-away black of its eyes. It looks small and kinda stupid leaning forward like that. But she sends it to her mom anyway.

>Lay: Hi, someone just sent this to me from some art party that's happening 2nite. Remembered the Google search I helped u with. Prob nothing, right?

Just a stupid statue, but as she heads for the rickety gate in the fence, she has to clamp down on the impulse to turn around to see if it's moved. She shakes the gate, flakes of brown paint coming off in her hand. There are people right on the other side of the fence, and music and beer and good times, if she could just get through.

She could probably kick out some of the boards and squeeze through the gap. Vandalism. She can't help thinking in cop. But minor league, she reassures herself. Barely a misdemeanor. She glances back at the thing in the wheelbarrow. Its eyes bore into her. Her throat burns. She rattles the gate again and realizes her and mistake. The hinges are on the inside. Pull, not push, idiot.

She yanks it toward her and skids out onto the wet grass, disturbing a couple making out on a picnic blanket in front of the fence. They glare at her.

Her phone erupts with the ring tone she's set for her mother, which she's been meaning to change for ages. 'Mama

Said Knock You Out.'

'Where are you?' Gabi demands. 'Are you *at* the party?'

'No. Yes.'

'Layla, you lied to me!'

'No, we decided it would be cool—'

'You have to leave right now. Did you take the photograph? Where is the body?'

'In the back of the, um, Blank House.'

'The Bank House?'

'B-L-A-N-K. It's one of the houses at the art party, they're all themed.'

'Got it. I want you to leave. Now, this second. Call a cab.'

'What about Cas?'

'Take her with you. I want you both out of there right now. Do you hear me, Layla?'

'Okay, Mom! You're freaking me out.'

'I'm sorry,' her mother says in the stay-calm professional voice she's heard her use on other people, but never her. 'But it's very important that you do what I say.'

Fuck. Now she's going to be that guy. The one who brought down the cops on a party. 'Cassandra,' she yells at the top of her lungs. She can barely hear herself. She elbows her way through the crowd. Half the street has turned into a free-for-all dance floor. A drunk girl bounces off her. 'Get out of my fucking way,' Layla snarls.

She's startled by movement down the front of one of the buildings. Thick globs are running over the slats, binding them together, something happening under a microscope, made large. The light shifts and the cells thicken into layers of skin. Projection art. Someone puts their hand in the way of the laser beams, momentarily casting a giant five-fingered shadow across the entire house.

293

Cas is sitting on the steps of the house where they started, talking to some of the boys from school. Layla almost sobs with relief.

'Cas,' she calls out. There's something off about the way the guys are crowding around her. A tension in their shoulders. Her trepidation ramps up to full-blown foreboding. 'Hey, Cas,' she goes for light-hearted. 'We should bail. The art's boring, anyway.'

Travis Russo is leaning over Cas with a lazy gotcha of a smile. 'You *are* her, aren't you?'

'Bitch, please. I have no idea what you're talking about.'

'No point denying. We've all seen the video, *slut*.'

'Get out of my space, dickhead.' Cas puts her palm in the middle of his face and shoves him away. One of the other boys titters, and that pushes him over the edge.

'Hey,' he calls as she gets up to leave.

'What?' Cas whirls on him. 'What *the fuck* do you want?'

He lunges forward and grabs her breasts with both hands. He gives them two short squeezes. 'Honk-honk!' he says, like a punchline. 'Boobs.'

His sidekicks crack up. But Cas's face goes vacant. She wrenches herself free from his groping hands and flees into the crowd.

'What is wrong with you?' Layla screams at Travis. He is looking shocked and slyly pleased at his own boldness.

'Honk-honk!' one of the other boys says, miming the double-pump, folding over with laughter.

'Cas, wait!' Layla starts after her, but the keening of police sirens is cutting through the music, bringing people out of the houses, blocking her way.

'Cas!'

Curiouser and Curiouser

Jonno is wasted when the cops show up. He *is* filming Jen Q's set, but he's also filming people dancing to her set, which is important, to show how much they love her. The drunk girls have found him and are bouncing beside him, their arms around him. It feels like the whole of Detroit is alive and pumping. 'We built this city,' he shouts at the top of his lungs, jumping up and down, 'We built this city on art and te-ch-no!' Then the music dies.

It's the first thing the cops do, pull the plug on the sound system, which means he gets his camerawoman back, Jen fighting through the panic to get to him.

'We should get out of here,' she yells over the hurly-burly. Another word she would never let him say on camera.

'Are you kidding me?' he shouts back. 'We have to film this!'

He guides her against the tide, pushing against the big dumb animal the fleeing crowd has become.

He tries the police first, aiming for the feisty-pants Latina who seems to be calling the shots.

'What's the problem, officer?' He raises his voice to be heard. 'Can you tell me what's going on?'

'You're going to have to stop filming, sir.'

'Doesn't Detroit have a very high unsolved murder rate?'

'Sir. Put that phone away or I will confiscate it.'

'Fascists! Pig-dogs!' the girl from LA screams.

Obligingly, she does it again for the camera. He starts getting soundbites from other outraged partygoers.

'Jonno,' Jen says quietly. 'Why are they all round the back of that house?'

It's true. The pigs don't seem that interested in writing up tickets, even though this should be a free ride for a broke city. They're hustling people along, trying to get them to disperse as quickly and with as little fuss as possible. An ambulance pulls round the side of the building.

'Think someone fell through the floorboards?'

A young girl wrapped up in a blanket like a disaster victim is sitting on the porch steps outside. She looks wretched.

'I want to see what's on the other side of the fence. Film this,' Jonno instructs Jen. 'Keep it low key.' He plugs in the mic and beckons Jen to follow him. He counts her down, holding up his fingers. Three, two, one. 'There's something weird in the D tonight,' he says, sotto voce. 'Police bust up the party, but they're not interested in the art lovers. So what's got the cops crawling over the scene like ants on a watermelon? Is it A) A dead homeless person? B) An art-related accident? C) Something more sinister? I'm Jonno Haim, here at the heart of a crime scene.'

He hauls a deck chair over to the fence and climbs up on it, testing his weight. 'Pass me the phone,' he hisses at Jen. There are flashes going off in the garden. The police photographer circles a scrawny figure with a weird elongated head. Cops are milling around uneasily, and there are two plainclothes: a bear of a black man and the dark-haired lady detective.

'All my days,' says the fat black guy, and Jonno can't blame him. The figure is freakish.

'What's wrong with his head?' He tries to zoom in on the figure, but he thumbs the wrong part of the screen and his own flash goes off.

'Hey! Who is that?'

He scrambles down from the chair so fast it tips out from under him. It's sheer luck that he's already moving in the same direction, so he steps off as it hits the grass, like goddamn Fred Astaire. It makes him feel invincible as ball-breaker brunette storms toward him.

'What the hell do you think you're doing?'

'Concerned citizen, officer. The public have a right to know. Can you tell us what's going on? Was that a body?'

'I warned you before. Hand over that phone.'

Jen makes a little sound of dismay.

'Is that an official request?' he bluffs. You can't give up without a little resistance. Also known as misdirection. Jen asked him to keep her phone while she was playing, and now he slides it out of his pocket.

'Have you been filming all night?'

'A little.'

'Then you may have evidence that is critical to this case. Please hand it over.'

'What is the case?'

'I'm not at liberty to discuss the details.'

'Well, then I might have to ask my lawyer.'

Her mouth tightens. 'It's an investigation into the murder of a minor. I hope that's enough to guarantee your assistance?'

'Wow, of course. That's horrible. Was it someone at the party?'

'If you can leave your name and an alternate phone number with Officer Marcus over there, I'll make sure you get your property back in due course.' The cop notices the girl sitting on the steps watching them and snaps at her. 'Layla! Go wait in the car.' It's all the distraction he needs to switch the phones.

The teenager gets up and slinks over to the white Crown Vic with the lights flashing. Verrrrrry interesting. The detective sees him noticing, and that pisses her off even more.

'Sir, no shit, if you do not surrender your cell phone immediately, I'm going to confiscate it and take you in for questioning.'

'Okay, okay,' he says and gives her Jen's Galaxy.

'Thank you for your co-operation,' she snarls and heads back into the garden.

'We should leave,' Jen says.

'Not yet. We're onto something real here.'

'You tricked that cop.'

'So what?'

He raps on the car window. The girl's expression is smeary through the darkened glass. He motions for her to roll it down.

'What do you want?' she says, full of teenage suspicion.

'You okay?' he says, with all the caring concern he can muster.

'No. Leave me alone.'

'Do you know what happened? Did someone get hurt? Did you see it?'

'I don't want to talk about it.'

'That's fine. I understand. If you change your mind, give

me a call, okay?' He passes her one of the cards they've been handing out all night, with his website URL. 'Here, I'll write down my phone number as well.'

Making a Statement

It is a trainwreck with a plane crash on top. The police have to lock down three blocks. They have to hold four hundred partygoers against their will, not including the ones who have already piled into their cars and slipped away, while they search every damn inch of every damn house for anything that may or may not be related, and with some of this stuff they can't even begin to guess.

Evidence Tech are not happy. Neither are the officers, who are trying to get statements out of drunken revelers who keep insisting that they know their rights! It turns out that they do not know their rights, they're reciting lines from TV shows. But then some wise-ass does an online search for their actual rights and starts passing them around, and Gabi has to wade in and point out that there has been a murder and the DPD appreciates their co-operation.

A cluster of people become hysterical. It's catching.

She leaves the uniformed officers to handle the demands for trauma counseling, and gets on with interviewing the most useful people, starting with the curator.

There are two of them, but they've only been able to

track down the one so far. Patrick Thorpe is a slight barely-thirty with a shaved head who speaks with the low reassuring musicality of an insurance advertisement, even though he is spitting with outrage. Boyd hates him instantly on principle.

'Art fag,' he leans in to mutter in Gabi's ear, as if he is telling her something useful. Score one for the homophobes.

'Is this how the city of Detroit encourages a creative economy?' Patrick stutters. 'We have all the permits!' She realizes that he is very drunk and in shock, which she is going to use to her advantage.

'Not for open alcohol containers in the street, sir. And not for exhibiting human remains.'

'This is ridiculous. The bone gallery is made of pewter casts of animal skeletons. There are no human remains.'

'Bone gallery?' Boyd raises an eyebrow.

'Send someone to check that out too,' Gabi says. For all she knows, this place is full of corpses. 'I'm going to level with you, Patrick. You remember Daveyton Lafonte?'

'The kid who was killed?'

'He was found cut in half together with the remains of half a deer. The missing halves just turned up in your show. Now you can help me try to identify who left it here, or we can continue this downtown. Do you know what that means?'

'I'm a suspect?' His legs wobble, and Gabi grabs his arm to steady him.

'You can start by telling me if you commissioned this piece or recognize it.' She shoves her phone in front of him with the photograph of the thing Layla found in the yard.

'No. God, no.' His eyes widen. 'That's hideous. I would never...'

'You're saying this wasn't an official work?'

301

'No. No, no, no.' He shakes his head violently.

'I'm going to need you to sober the hell up, sir. In the meantime, can you give us a list of your participating artists?'

'A catalog?'

'I need names and contact details. And I need to know who had access to that yard when you were setting up. All of it.'

Honk Honk

Cas's phone goes straight to voicemail. 'Yo, bitches. Don't leave a message 'cos I can't be bothered to check. Text me like a normal human being.'

>Lay: U ok? Where r u? What WAS that? Really worried. I need 2talk 2u.

>Lay: Something bad happened @ the party. I found a body. I think it was real!!!! My mom was freaking out. Cops all over. Crazy.

>Lay: Hello?

>Lay: Cas. I'm really worried about u. Seriously. Please answer soon as u can.

>Lay: Can u just answer please? I need to know ur ok. Otherwise I'm gonna call yr mom.

>Cas: Im fine. Pls leave me alone

>Lay: R u at home? U ok?

>Lay: The body was horrible. Seriously creeped me the fuck out.

>Lay: Don't even want to hear disgusting cop stories? ;)

>Lay: Cas. Please talk to me!!!!!! What's going on? Y did

he say that? Y did u freak out so much?
>Lay: Hello?
>Lay: Fine. But remember this when u come begging to me for deets tmrrw
>Lay: Jk!
>Lay: Hey Im yr friend, remember?
>Lay: Fine. Txt me when ur ready to stop being a bitch

The cop called Marcus drives her home, because her mom is going to be up all night.

'You did the right thing,' the rookie tells her in the car. But Layla doesn't even know what that is. The whole night has been a series of stun grenades.

Back at the house, she helps him set up the sleeper couch through the shell shock. The last person to use it was her dad, over a year ago. She'd come downstairs to find him sitting on the couch in his boxers eating Frosties, the sheets balled up and shoved behind the TV cabinet, as if she was too dumb to work it out – the halfway house between the marital bed and the door. She remembers how irritated she was about it. Stay or go – don't fucking linger. But then he did go, and Layla realized that there are worse things than indecision.

'Bet you didn't think your official police duties would include babysitting.'

'I don't mind,' he says, but she can see he does. He's so earnest. He's got really long eyelashes, which make his eyes look bigger, and a small chin, like a black manga Toby McGuire. She tries to imagine her mom like this, full of eager faith. Give him a few years of department bureaucracy and see if it doesn't wear him out and break up his relationship.

'Sucks to be junior rank,' she says.

'I'll be right here if you need me,' he reassures her. 'Try to get some sleep.'

She hovers in the doorway. She can't face going upstairs and being alone with her non-responding phone and thoughts of the thing. 'Hey, do you want to watch some TV?'

'*Now?*' He looks at his watch. She likes that he has one. He checks himself. 'If you want to, sure.'

She can't stand the flit of pity that crosses his eyes. 'Probably only infomercials anyway.'

'You sure?'

'Yeah, my mom canceled our cable.'

'If it's bothering you— I mean, you could sleep here and I could sit in the kitchen. Do paperwork.'

'Do you have your paperwork here?'

'No.'

'Don't sweat it,' she says and clumps upstairs. She tries not to see the deer-boy in the darkness. But it turns out there are worse things to see.

It takes no time to find the video. It comes up in the first few results. Not on YouTube, because it doesn't meet the community standards, but there are other sites. For every takedown, for every violation of service, there are mirrors and sub-threads with links where you can stream it or download it to watch in the comfort of your home. It's right there under 'honk_honkboobsUNCUT.mp4'. They used to put people in stocks to shame them in public. Now you just need a wifi connection. On the Internet, humiliation lives forever.

Cas is beautiful, shiny California blonde. Wearing bubblegum-pink lipstick and a tank top with a skull picked out in shiny pink studs and a denim mini-skirt. She is drooping, her arm around the neck of a teenage boy Layla doesn't recognize. Fuck. She can't look. She can't.

'Oh my God, she's soooooo drunk.'

'Help me.'

'Dude, she's passed out.'

'Get her over the couch.'

'She's heavy.'

'That's why I need you to *help* me.'

'Lose some weight, lard-ass.' The sharp sound of a slap.

'Wait, wait. I want to get a picture of this.'

'Pull up her top.'

'Dumb slut.'

'Learn to handle your liquor, girlie!'

Another slap.

A boy doing a falsetto voice: 'Oh, spank me, Daddy. Harder! Harder.'

'Help me prop her up.'

'Oof.'

'Okay, that's good.'

'Take off her top.'

'And her bra.'

'How does this thing unclip? Wait, I got it.'

'Hooooooly shiiiiiit.'

A wolf whistle.

Laughter.

'Take a photo. Me and Isabella's bazoombas. We're in love.'

'I want to get in there. Take a picture of me!'

'Get out of the way, douchebags. Hey, Trent. Hey, get a picture of this. Honk-honk! Boobs!'

'Oh my God. Dude, that's hilarious. Do it again.'

306

'Oh man, what a dumb fucking bitch.'
'Honk-honk! Honk-honk!'

Layla shuts down the player. There are still eight minutes of video left. She doesn't need to see the rest. She sits very still in front of her screen. Then she shuts herself in the bathroom and kneels in front of the toilet. She spits and spits, but nothing comes up. She'd be a terrible bulimic. She turns her head and rests her cheek on the cold porcelain, wrapping her arms around the bowl. She closes her eyes and the footage starts replaying in her head. No. She forces her mind away. Something harmless. She narrates the play to herself, runs through the whole thing, everyone's lines, not just hers, and the songs, again and again, until the words all run together.

Her mom finds her like that, asleep on the bathroom floor. 'Come on, bean. You can't stay here.' She lifts her up and Layla clings to her neck. Gabi helps her into bed, still wearing her skirt and ripped tights and the stupid sequin top, and pulls the covers up around her shoulders. 'You did good,' her mom says, and kisses her on the forehead. 'I'll make a plan for Aunt Cheryl to come pick you up in the morning. I'm going to have to go back to the scene.'

'Mom!' Layla calls her back. Her mother pauses in the doorway, the light haloed behind her head. But everything is scrambled up, and she feels sick and sad and she doesn't know how to say any of the things she needs to.

'Nothing. Never mind.'

'I'm sorry you had to see that,' her mom says.

Me too, Layla thinks, and falls away into a fractured sleep.

SUNDAY, NOVEMBER 16

The Shit Show

The crime scene has become a grand spectacle ever since the sun came up, and it's getting worse by the hour. On the other side of the police tape, crowds have gathered, pulling up chairs and beers in brown paper bags, hoping to see something horrible. Gabi has commandeered a kitchen in a neighboring house for processing interviews and identifying possible witnesses, sending the most likely on down to the station. It would be nice if their man was among them, but so far they have nothing but rumor and speculation and some of the artists are screaming from the sidelines about how they're gonna sue and you think this city's bankrupt now, you wait till my lawyer is done with you! Apparently the sanctity of creative expression trumps life.

Jessica diMenna wants Gabi and Boyd to drop everything and get down to the mayor's office to discuss strategy, and that's a fair point, what with the media clamoring round the edges, trying to get shots, cameramen climbing trees, a press helicopter hanging low overhead, adding to the racket, and someone's even got a drone. Local and national out in force; hell, someone said Al Jazeera was here, somebody else heard that as al-Qaeda, and then they had to shut everything down for an hour to control the panic: no terrorists, no bomb threats. Only a sick serial killer who may or may not have hidden more body parts in other places. It's sensational enough on its own.

She's managed two hours' sleep in the last twenty-eight hours, when she raced home to check on Layla, and now she has to sit with the goddamn curator, Patrick Thorpe, who hasn't got any sleep either and is becoming increasingly hysterical, although that might also be from his hangover. Eventually, they send him to dry out down at the station, a very grumpy officer accompanying him, and continue the interview with the other curator, a woman called Darcy D'Angelo, who is ruthlessly co-operative, especially when it comes to dismantling the art for forensic testing. Gabi gets the uneasy feeling she likes watching things get taken apart.

They have to bag everything. She's sent the blogger's phone for processing. Ovella Washington is taking statements, downloading phone footage from people willing to share their videos without a warrant, taking names for those who aren't, plugging each phone into a laptop they've got for this purpose, but the card reader is playing up and they have to get a technician in to sort it out and everyone is impatient.

Some idiot decided it would be a good idea to let Daveyton's parents know, and they've come down to see for themselves, even though the body was moved hours ago. The press descend on the Lafontes – their first public appearance – like starving pigeons on a crust of bread, jostling for space, screaming questions. Mrs. Lafonte flinches with each camera flash. They cling to each other, terrified, while Boyd tries to cover them with his jacket and hustle them through the hordes.

'I'm so sorry, your son isn't here,' Gabi tells them. 'I don't know why they told you to come down.'

'I asked them to,' Jessica diMenna says, leaning in the door, dressed for television. 'Thank you for being here. We've got a media caravan where you can sit quietly and prepare. If you could just say a few words about how relieved you are that the DPD has found the rest of Daveyton, it would be such a gesture of faith and solidarity in these men and women who are working so hard to bring his killer to justice.'

'But where is he?' Mrs. Lafonte asks, confused. 'Where's our boy?' She's shrunk into herself since Gabi saw her last.

Mr. Lafonte is the opposite. The news has energized him, focused grief into rage. 'The way they're talking about it on the news, Miss Mayoral-la-di-da, I get the idea *these men and women* haven't done shit. I heard Davey was propped up on display, like a lynching.'

'This wasn't a lynching,' Gabi is quick to tell them. God, that's the last thing they need. 'We don't believe this is race-related. There was another victim on Friday. A white woman from Indian Village.'

'Another murder?' He's furious. 'And where is this killer you're bringing to justice? Is he here? I don't see nobody in handcuffs. He's still out there, probably doing this to someone else's little boy right now. Or some other nice white lady. And you want me to go on TV? Talk to the press? Oh, I can do that. I'm ready to do that right now.'

Jessica is back-pedaling furiously. 'Please, Mr. Lafonte, I think Detective Versado's right. This is a terrible shock. You should be with your boy.'

'Miss, let me tell you straight, there is nothing on God's green earth that is going to shock me again. I am disappointed that you cannot do your job, but shocked? No.'

'I'll drive you down to the morgue,' Gabi says, even though she is so tired she can barely see straight. She just prays that Dr Mackay, pulling overtime, has the body – or its constituent parts – presentable by now. 'Bob, can you get someone to supervise dismantling the collection? Not you. I need you and Sparkles to start following up on those artists' names. I'll catch up with you later.'

'No problemo,' he says, even though he's as tired as she is.

'There's a spreadsheet of participating artists – start with a criminal record search, work your way down, cross-reference with the officers who have been taking statements, if any of the names jump out. Some of them work under pseudonyms, so you're going to have to establish their real names first.'

'I know, Gabi.'

'Sorry.'

'We'll look them up in the car, get on the door-to-door soon as we can. You take care of your people.'

'Thank you.' She ushers Mr. and Mrs. Lafonte out the door, hissing at the mayor's aide as she passes: 'No more fucking surprises, okay?'

Shaggy Dog

Jonno finds that overnight celebrity suits him, even if it's Detroit-style. The brunch party at some musician's house in Hubbard Farms is an excuse to catch up on the scandal – did you hear it was made out of part of Daveyton's body? – and most of the cool culturati hanging out have been up all night, half of them crowded into the cosy kitchen, making French toast, the others smoking weed and idly shooting hoops in the tangled garden. A kid with sideburns decides they have to make it more challenging and try to score from a moving skateboard. But that's only the warm-up act, because there's no doubt that Jonno is the main attraction. They're impressed in a not-impressed way, which means very. It's the magic words 'exclusive footage'.

He and Jen stayed up all night editing it together. Well, she did – he massaged her shoulders and brought her appropriate snacks, and finally passed out and woke up at seven to find her finishing it off. It's a rough-cut, a place-holder, but Jen says they need to move with the times and put it up immediately before someone else beats them to the post.

315

Tight communities mean that word gets around. Now all he needs is for the major websites and, better yet, the TV stations to pick up on it. He keeps his phone handy, in case, but he knows he's competing with the professionals. What he needs is a scoop.

Jonno has never had a particular interest in serial killers. But he's a fast learner and a good researcher, courtesy of a million listicles: '10 Signs You Might Be A Psycho'.

Number one: Narcissism.

Oh, it's good to get close to danger. To flirt around the edges. The fascination of the terrible, just *terrible* things people do to each other. He's an ambassador from the land of monsters, and they all want to hear all about it. He plays it up, practicing lines for his piece.

Not that he has much to go on. But who needs facts when you can go with wild speculation? And there's no shortage of that. Everyone he talks to has a theory, all playing armchair detectives.

It's a gang revenge killing – all these years later, it turns out that they were targeting Daveyton all along for snitching on a drug boss he was running for.

It's the ex-mayor trying to destabilize the current administration from inside prison.

It's the result of a terrible military experiment on Zug Island.

Mutations.

It's Nain Rouge.

'Who?' he asks.

'The red dwarf,' Jen explains. 'Some cities get Olympic mascots. Detroit has a bad-luck bogeyman with his own annual parade.'

He gets as many of them as he can on camera.

Of course the most popular is the most obvious: a serial killer targeting kids. But then a jewelry designer who must be wearing half her collection in her face chirps up with something interesting: 'But what about the woman in the oven?'

'I caught a headline,' Jonno says, fishing. He pulls up the article on his phone, but it's tellingly curt, especially for a white middle-class femicide.

Woman's Remains Found In Kiln

The body of Betty Spinks, manager at the historic Miskwabic tile factory, was recovered from the pottery's kiln. Police suspect that it was a robbery gone wrong and the killer tried to cover his tracks by incinerating the body. The DPD have asked that anyone with information please call the official police tip-line.

'I hear they found her head spinning on the wheel. And she was covered in satanic symbols made out of clay.'

'Who told you that?'

'I heard it from a friend of a friend. Someone who works there. Robin Mitchell.'

Jen touches his arm. 'You remember, the guy from the dinner party.'

'There were a lot of people at that dinner party,' Jonno says. 'Can you get me in touch with him?'

'Sure.' The jewelry designer is avid, delighted to be caught up in it all. 'Let me just text Allie and see if I can get his number.'

In the meantime, the promo girl offers him a free pair

of shades. He takes great delight in turning her down.

An hour later, he and Jen have tracked Robin down and convinced him to come out to the parking lot of Miskwabic Pottery, or, as Jonno likes to think of it, 'the scene of another monstrous crime!' He does vaguely recall him – good thing the arts scene is so cosy, one of the advantages of a downsizing city.

They position him in front of the building, the yellow police tape across the door clearly visible. Robin keeps glancing over his shoulder, uncomfortable. 'The police told me not to talk about it. They were very specific.'

'You've got a responsibility to the people of Detroit,' Jonno says. 'The pigs are trying to cover this up. There's some madman killer out there and they don't want people to know.'

'Yeah, but they said it would mess up the investigation.'

'So don't talk about the case. Talk about your experience.'

'Do you have to use my face?'

'We can pixelate it out and distort your voice if you want,' Jonno promises.

The video goes up that afternoon, un-pixelated. 'A serial killer who makes Hannibal Lecter look like Woody Allen,' is how Jonno describes the murderer. That's the pull quote that gets used in all the media, that gets him calls from news outfits across the country – and that evening, one from a TV executive in New York. She has a major true-crime show, she says. A *major* show on a *major* network. *Murder48*.'

He says he's heard of it, by which he means Jesus fucking Christ.

They like his style. His insouciance. They want an exclusive documentary, following the action as it unfolds. Does he know the investigating officer? Can he get access? Will the police co-operate, does he think?

When he stalls, she cuts in. It doesn't matter if they don't. There are ways around it. But she needs to know what footage he has access to. Can he send over everything he has? She'll give him access to their upload site. They need to know they'll have enough material before they can pitch it to their commissioning board. If he can deliver 'something hot', she'll get a producer and a camera crew out to him pronto.

'What about the contract?' he manages to get in.

'I'll email you one right away. Sign it and send it straight back.'

'Shouldn't I get an entertainment lawyer to look at it?'

'It's a standard contract, giving us exclusive rights.'

Cate. Cate will know someone.

Any excuse, huh, boychick? And where are you going to get this extra material?

He'll figure it out. He always does.

He doesn't call Cate. He'd rather she switched on the television and saw him.

The contract arrives in his email inbox, and he signs the shit out of it.

319

Viral Like Ebola

'Hey, TK, there's someone who wants to see you. I've locked up already, but he ain't taking no for an answer,' Big Dennis says, poking his head into the computer room – a tiny office with two beat-up desktops that Reverend Alan believes were donated by a kind benefactor. They were, sorta. Reclaimed from an insolvent drugstore where TK happened to be the first salvager to crowbar the door open. The PCs are doing much more good here than they were there. No harm, no foul.

'Tell him to come back tomorrow. Church is closed. We got special permission to stay late and watch my man Ramón's screen debut.'

'Oh yeah?' Dennis leans over to look. 'That you, Ramón? Kneeling down on the ground?' He's impressed.

'Crazy hipsters got him talking about graffiti. You believe any of that shit you saying?'

'No, I was playing them, brother,' Ramón says. 'Look, look how pretty Diyana looks. Don't she look beautiful?'

'She really does, Papi,' TK says and then nearly falls off his chair as the creepy guy with the knife-blue eyes shoves into the room behind Dennis. He's cut his hair so that it's sticking up like white thatch, and still weirder, shaved his eyebrows.

'You! You know computers. You have to show me.' He's swallowing his vowels, which makes it hard to understand him. Further gone than he was the last time, and that's saying something. TK instinctively clicks away from the image of Ramón and Diyana. He feels like the man might taint it somehow if he sees it.

'Nice to see you too, man, but we're shut up for the evening. Why don't you come back in the morning?' TK says, putting his hand on his walking stick-machete just in case. 'You take my advice and go for a counseling session?'

'Please. I don't understand what's happening. I have to see the video. You have to show me. The one they're talking about.' He looks so broken that TK cracks.

'All right, what video? And let me say straight up that we don't tolerate pornography here.'

'The Dream House. The body.'

'Oh, that one. It's been all over the news.' TK types in the search. It comes up on the same YouTube channel as the video with Ramón. He doesn't like it. This stranger all tangled with the crazy things on the news and in his head. The video takes a while to buffer, but when it finally loads, the man shoves his face right up to the screen, watching intently. 'Play it again.'

'Ah, come on, man. We're busy here.'

'They didn't show the body.'

'Guess it's sensitive. Or maybe it's a cover-up, like the journalist guy says.'

'Who sees this?' Blue-eyes grabs hold of the screen like he might yank it right out, make a dash for it. Wouldn't be the first time someone tried that. There's a reason TK has it chain-locked to the table.

'Whole of the damn Internet. Anyone in the world. Look, this here counts the number of people who've seen it. So far it's got 158,433 views. Shit's gone viral.'

'What does that mean?' The man looks at him with what TK thinks of as gutter eyes, the expression when you're desperate for something, anything, to pull you out.

'Viral. It's spreading, catching on. Like an infection, ebola or something.'

'How do I catch it?'

'You mean how do you make something go viral? Go big, man. Dress your cat in costume. Or do something fucked-up like this.'

'The doors are going to open.' He looks alarmed. 'I...I have to go.'

'Open door round here anytime, my friend,' TK shouts after him. 'Especially for counseling, you know what I'm saying!' Good riddance, he thinks. 'Yo, Ramón, how much this filmmaker pay you to be in his video?'

'What? Uh, ten dollars each.'

'He's offering more than that here.' TK reads out the words in the 'about this video' box. '"Got leads on the Detroit Monster? $50 for your exclusive interview. No chancers." Phone number right here. Bet he gets a million calls in the first half hour. I bet I could tell him a story or two for fifty bucks.'

But Ramón isn't listening. He's staring after Mr. Crazy.

322

Disciple

Clayton's body is pacing the sidewalk outside the church, head tucked down against the wind, a cap rammed down over his hacked-off hair while the dream tries to decide what to do, where to go.

Everything it had planned is in ruins.

It watched the girl coming down the steps into the dark garden, willing her to go away, go away, go away, but she went straight to the deer-boy as if he was calling out to her. She came so close, it could have reached out to touch her. It could feel how something opened in her head as she examined its creation, the dream stirring inside her like a million butterflies.

It wanted to go after her when she fled, but then the sirens came, and it felt the man's fear of everything that meant, a thousand variations of TV shows in his memory. Trapped in a jail cell, or worse, being shot, killed. If Clayton died, his heart faltering, the blood in his veins slowing to mud, the neural stars burning out, would it be trapped within the physical flesh, watching helpless as the body started to break down?

It hid in the basement all night and all the next day, tormented by the man's fears, but it needed to know what had happened, if the Police were coming. And it still held out hope that the deer-boy had transformed, and it had missed the moment.

It found the news on Clayton's father's television, but they didn't show the boy, only dark images of the yard and the Police and a covered shape and the arrogant man, the one who was supposed to bring his camera. He kept talking about a video and how it was all over the Internet, but Clayton's memories were blank about the Internet.

Which is why it came here to the church, remembering the big black man who said he knew everything about computers. But the video it saw was no different from the dull flickers on the television screen, and now it feels more adrift than before. The man at the church talked about viruses inside the mind, and maybe that's all it has become – an infection trapped inside Clayton's head.

It has to leave here. It has to get away, back to the cool dark of the basement where it can try to make sense of things. It is so lost inside its confusion, it doesn't hear the little man approaching as Clayton slots the key into the door of the truck.

'Wait! *Por favor*, I wanna talk to you.' He reaches for Clayton's arm.

The dream pulls away, horrified at the physical contact, the fleshiness of the scruffy man's hand.

'It's you, isn't it?' says the man with red shoes, shaking with excitement. 'The doors. You're the one.' He twists a rope of beads in his hand.

'Yes,' the dream says. The man inside the body is grateful

to be recognized.

'I can tell. Things are different around you. You make them different, but only a little bit. Like looking through the heat wave from a car muffler.'

'It's leaking out,' the dream confesses. 'I don't know how to control it.'

'But you know how to open the doors, don't you? I can help you. I'm good at figuring stuff out. I used to be a mechanic. Maybe you can plug the leaks, or maybe you need to blow it all wide open? Flush the gasket.'

And all at once, it becomes clear. The art party was wrong. The scale wasn't grand enough. There were other works fighting for attention, other consciousnesses beneath the surface, like the music and the voices at the party fighting each other.

The people are the doors. It needs to bring them all together, to focus them in one place, on *its* vision and purpose. Isn't this what it has been working toward all along? Like the curator said, a solo exhibition.

But it will need – it drags the word from Clayton's head, like a dirty string – a disciple.

'What's through the doors? What's on the other side?' the man says longingly.

'Anything you want,' it says through Clayton's mouth. 'Anything you can dream.'

If it is an infection, maybe it needs to spread.

Barking up Trees

Officer Marcus Jones is trying to type names into the onboard computer of Detective Boyd's car, cross-referencing names from the spreadsheet of the participating artists they got from the curator, three pages of eight-point font. He's typing them in one by one to pull up their criminal records, if any. He wriggles his neck, still stiff from Gabi's sleeper couch, and it cricks audibly.

'Damn, son!' Boyd is impressed. 'You too young to have your bones clicking like that. You should see a chiropractor.'

'Sorry, sir.'

'I heard you stayed over at Versado's. You get in there?'

'What?' Marcus drops the file and scrambles between his legs in the footwell to retrieve it.

'Fine woman is all I'm saying. Divorced too. Bet she could use some company.'

'I slept on the couch after taking her daughter home.' Then he unbends. 'She's a good-looking woman.'

'Careful, son,' Boyd turns cold. 'That's a superior officer you're talking about.'

'But you said...' Marcus is flustered.

Boyd laughs. 'Don't worry, I'm fucking with you. She's a mess, same as the rest of us. Fine po-lice though. Take my advice, kid, don't date within the force. But don't date a civilian either. You want someone who understands the terrible hours and the drain of the job. A nice paramedic or a firefighter.'

'Lot of attractive firefighters?' he says.

'Smokin'.' Boyd snickers at his own joke. 'They'd love you, Sparkles.'

'You say so. Hey, you want to hear what I've found so far?'

'Hit me.'

'Running the names from the list, I've got a painter with a felony charge for car-jacking. A musician with a restraining order for stalking his ex-girlfriend, and the artist who made the Bone Hall.'

'Was that the one with the skulls and bones? Seems like a fit with our man's other work to me. You got an address? I think we should do that one first.'

'Yes, sir.' Marcus pulls up the details and types them into the GPS.

But the day is a wash-out. The artist who did the Bone Hall takes them through to his casting studio, his wife following them anxiously, carrying their baby on her hip. He makes his pewter models out of plaster of Paris, molded from a plastic skeleton he bought from a science shop. He shows them the pictures of the Capuchin Crypt in Rome that inspired him. 'It's about mortality – how short our lives are, how the dead are always with us. And it looks cool.' He was out of town the night Daveyton was killed, interviewing for a job as an animator at a company in

Chicago. 'Art doesn't exactly pay for diapers,' he says.

The former carjacker is a biker-type with tattoos and graying hair. 'I was nineteen and stupid. Haven't so much as run a red light since then.'

They work their way through the same list of questions with everyone: Where were you, who were you with, ever do ceramic work, do you know the Lafonte family or Elizabeth Spinks? Ever work with transglutaminase?

The man with the restraining order is living with the girlfriend who took it out. They have the ravaged bony look of dope fiends, and Marcus has no illusions about what people out of their minds on meth are capable of. Not usually given to elaborate forward planning, though. They pick their way into a room with a sagging mattress, everything littered with beer cans.

The woman climbs onto the man's lap. She's not wearing a bra under her faded black top, but not even Boyd can bring himself to look.

'I was with him all night, officers. Same as every night.' She sticks her tongue down his throat.

'Why'd you get a restraining order on him, then?'

'It's performance art,' says the man. 'We like to push the boundaries of sexuality and social norms.'

She chimes in. 'It was commentary on how you can't legislate love.'

'So you wasted the court's time and police time for your art?'

'I'm afraid so, Detective. Do you want to punish me?' She offers her wrists to be cuffed with a gruesome pout.

'You know how many women need a restraining order and don't manage to get one?' Boyd is livid.

'I'm sorry you weren't there for our performance last

night – you'd definitely have had to arrest us. Public inde-
cency.' She grinds on her boyfriend's lap by way of
demonstration.

'I see your name on a complaint form again, I will have
you arrested for obstruction of justice. C'mon, Sparkles,
I've had enough of this shit. We're done.'

'You sure you don't want a closer examination of our piece,
detectives?' the skank calls after them. Boyd drives them back
to the precinct, complaining all the way. 'You think you've
seen it all.' He shifts his weight onto one butt cheek and lets
off a massive fart. 'That's what I think of them.'

Marcus winds down the window, choking and laughing
at the audacity of it.

'Don't laugh, kid. Special privileges. Comes with getting
your detective's badge.'

'I'm supposed to go back to patrol soon,' Marcus says,
serious now. 'My partner's out of hospital. They had to
take his appendix out, but he's gonna be back at work next
week.'

'And you want to stick around.'

'I like it,' Marcus says. 'It feels like what I'm supposed
to be doing.'

'Don't sweat it. I think Detective Versado will find a way
to keep you on this until it wraps up, don't worry. And
don't let the other guys give you shit. I know we rag on
you about being her mascot, but you're doing good work,
kid. Maybe we'll see you in Homicide proper in a few
years. Now get out my car 'cos I need to fart again. And
if you thought the first one was bad, this one's going to
blow the roof off. I don't want to have to tell Versado,
yeah, sorry, I killed the rookie with poison gas.'

'You don't got to tell me twice.'

'Go home, Sparkles, get some rest.'

'Yes, sir.'

But the next morning, he sees his error – the fine print he missed on the back of the last page of the spreadsheet. It's because he's so sleep-deprived, all of them, running on empty, trying to piece this together. And hey, it's probably nothing. Another dead end, but he'll check it out on the way in to the station, so he has *something* to tell Versado.

Marcus pulls up outside the house in a quiet street of mostly abandoned homes in various states of disrepair. This one somehow looks resentful, he thinks, like a man with his shoulders hunched up.

He rings the doorbell, but there's nobody home, then tramps around to the yard past the dirty slit window of the basement, but the high blank walls block his way. He gets that same ugly feeling as when he saw Daveyton under the bridge, and he knew that it wasn't a dead dog or a trick of the light off a trash bag.

He shouldn't have come here on his own, he thinks, reaching for his phone in his top pocket, his fingers brushing against the merit ribbons.

MONDAY, NOVEMBER 17

Blogger vs Cop

'Mr. Haim,' the lady detective says, calling in via the call-forwarding number he set up for his YouTube tip-line, which means she's seen the video. Crap. 'You seem to have given me the wrong phone.'

'You know, I realized that when I got home. I'm so sorry. It was the heat of the moment. All the excitement.'

'I'd appreciate if you could bring me the correct phone, and also take down your video.'

'I would, but I'd need a court order.' He doesn't point out that she could send YouTube a simple 'inappropriate content' notice, and they'd take it down faster than a how-to-breastfeed video.

'We can discuss that when you come down to the station.'

'Do I need to bring my lawyer?'

'Do you think you *need* a lawyer?'

Uh-oh. Tough-cookie alert.

He does not take a lawyer down to the station, because he figures he has more chance of persuading her to give him access for *Murder48* on his own. She invites him for a friendly chat in one of the interrogation rooms. She leaves the door open, and offers him a coffee, which he declines, but takes as a good sign. It is not.

He shoots the phone across the table at her and she takes it, flicks through the video folder and tests some of the footage.

'Anything else you're withholding?'

'No, officer.'

'*Detective*. You know you've compromised this investigation, you shit-bag? You've set us back thirty-six hours, because what, you needed to get your little video out?'

'I'm doing my job, same as you. You wouldn't take the footage off a TV crew.'

'It's not *a job*. It's jerking off. You're like the kid in the playground yelling look at me! Look at me! Do you know what I spent the whole of my Sunday doing, while you were wanking online?'

'Working a murder scene?'

'Tagging and bagging things that might or might not be evidence. Trying to hunt down four hundred people. Showing the parents the remains of their child down in the morgue and trying to explain why someone would do this to him. Do you know what that was like? Did you think about them before you put your sensationalist crap up? How they would feel?'

'The people have a right to know,' he flusters.

'That's all you got? "The people"? Fuck you.'

He blinks. 'Isn't there supposed to be a good cop?'

'We're short-staffed.'

The jowly black detective Jonno saw on Saturday night – the guy must have bribed his way through his last physical – sticks his head in. 'Versado. You gotta phone call.'

'Take a message, Bob.'

'It's important. I think you better take it.'

'Excuse me a moment.' She pushes away from the table and leaves, taking his phone with her.

'Everything okay?' Jonno asks the fat guy with his most winning smile.

'None of your fucking business,' he says, and walks away.

'Hey,' Jonno calls after him. 'Hey! Can I change my mind about the coffee?'

It's fifteen minutes before she comes back. Long enough for Jonno to have composed several possible pieces in his head. '10 Most Outrageous Alibis.' '10 Ways To Entertain Yourself In A Police Interrogation Room' (thinking of top-ten lists is number three on the list). '10 Photos You Should Have Deleted Off Your Cell Phone Before You Handed It To The Cops'. Like the ones of your girlfriend wearing only her tattoos.

When the detective comes back, she looks even more tired and mad than before. She sits down and shoves a piece of paper at him. 'This is a list. Of times and dates.'

He examines it. 'Yeah?'

'I'm going to need you to provide proof of your whereabouts on every single one of those occasions.'

'*10 Reasons You Should Always Bring A Lawyer With You.*'

'Wait. Am I a suspect?'

'I don't know. Are you? You moved to the city three weeks ago. You needed a clean slate, according to your blog. Did something happen in New York that made you leave in a hurry?'

'I don't blog about every single little detail of my life.'

Especially not having his heart and guts wrenched out so that they drag along behind him wherever he goes. This isn't working, he thinks. He's going to have to change tack if he wants her onboard for the show. Although, hey, she's not the only detective in the pig house. 'Was that your daughter on the phone? Is everything all right?'

She ignores him. 'You'll need to provide phone numbers of witnesses who can corroborate your whereabouts.'

'I can see how you'd be worried as a mom, with what happened to that little boy last week. Abducted right out of school. Aren't you working that case?'

'Lead investigator. As you no doubt read in the *Detroit Star* this morning.'

'Is this part of the same investigation?'

'Murders happen every day in Detroit.'

'But you're saying the thing in the garden was definitely a body? I heard the boy was cut in half.'

'I can't comment on that.'

'Can I quote your "no comment"?' he asks, exasperated.

'You can fill in that list.'

'You know we're on the same side, Detective Versado.'

'No, you're interested in getting a story and I want to get the bad guy.'

'Isn't that the story?'

'It will be if you stay out of my way.'

Teeth

Layla's hands are shaking. In her head, she had imagined confronting Travis in the middle of the gymnateria in front of everyone, a public humiliation. Exactly what he deserves. She hadn't expected to find him out here on his own, sitting on a car in the parking lot, cutting class like she is, because she's too upset to sit still.

His knees are spread wide, as if he can't quite find the right position for them. Too much leg, too much boy. Baby face on a man's body.

'I've been looking for you,' she says.

'Well, girl, you found me.' He takes a drag on his cigarette, holding it between his knuckles, like something he saw in a movie.

'Stand up,' she says, kicking his sneaker with her shoe. She has been stewing about this all weekend, in church with her aunt and her cousins, listening to the choir dancing and singing, checking her phone obsessively for a message from Cas until her uncle threatened to confiscate it.

'What for?'

'Because I have something to say to you and I don't want

to talk down to you.'

'Aight,' Travis says, getting to his feet. He drops the cigarette, his limbs all loose angles. 'Is this about your friend? 'Cos we were drunk, just fooling around.' He laughs uncomfortably. 'I didn't mean anything by it. Why you being so uptight? It was a joke.'

'You sexually assaulted her! And you've been sharing that horrible video.'

'So what? We didn't make it.'

'It's disseminating child pornography, you moron.'

'Disseminating shit! It's on the Internet.' He looks scared, though. And young. *And dumb and full of come*, her brain finishes the mantra. 'Besides, they didn't do nothing except take some pictures. It's not like they *raped* her.'

Layla loses it. 'You stupid fucktard.' She swings her schoolbag at the side of his head. He ducks, laughing as she swings her bag at him again.

'Whoa! Come on now.'

'You fucking asshole. You fucking shit. You fuck.' She's whomping him with her bag with every sentence, yelling through tears.

Someone shouts 'Fight!' and the upstairs windows of the chemistry lab fill up with kids' faces, shouting encouragement.

'Get him!'

'Hit her back! You gonna let a bitch wipe the floor with you?'

'What are you doing to him?!' CeeCee screams, bursting out the main doors. She gets between them, and shoves Layla to the ground. 'Oh, baby. Are you okay?'

'Ow, shit.' Travis spits a bloody chip into his hand. 'Fuck. You knocked my tooth out!'

'You psycho bitch!' CeeCee snarls, and Layla, still down, raises her arm to fend off a blow that doesn't come. Above, kids are leaning out the windows, filming on their phones. People are streaming out of the building, forming a half-circle around them, but no-one does anything, waiting for the drama to play out. Spectators until the principal, Mr. Clarkwell, wades through, snapping at the kids to get inside, right now.

Travis spits a rope of bloody saliva.

'He was asking for it,' Layla says, gingerly getting to her feet. She's not sorry. She's not. She stoops to pick up her bag and the stuff that's fallen out of it, including a cracked ashtray. Curved glass like a seashell, rainbow colors running together. When she comes back up, Travis has a strange expression on his face. His tongue works against his cheek, and then he spits out another tooth.

'Oh my God,' CeeCee says, not without glee. 'Bitch, you are in such fucking trouble.'

'What in the wide world is happening here?' Mr. Clarkwell says, pulling Layla back, as if she was still trying to get at Travis.

'I didn't even hit him that hard.' She clutches her bag to her chest.

'Guh,' Travis says and three more teeth tumble into his hand. His eyes are wild.

'Travis?'

He retches. Vomit and blood and more teeth, yellowy-white, clatter onto the cement.

And all Layla can think is that they don't look like they do in the toothpaste commercials.

Mistakes that End Bloodily

The dream needs more disciples. Ramón is so eager, he makes everything possible. It is able to bend the world a little, enough, through his faith. It is not as rich and complex a malleability as the true dreaming, but it's a taste of what is to come.

They have already started moving.

'All of it?' Ramón looks appalled. But it is like the advertisements on TV. Everything must go!

They shuttle back and forth all through the night between the house and the place of conception, until Ramón is exhausted. The dream drops him off at the shelter, where his lady stays, anxious about letting him out of its sight, afraid she might try to wrest him back.

But it means it is alone with Clayton, moving its dreams-locked-in-form from the backyard to the truck, when it hears the car pull up outside, in a street where no-one lives, and no-one should come.

It creeps round the alley and all its human fears come swarming back when it sees the man in his blue uniform climbing out of the car with his gun, all black jagged angles

340

of impatient potential, the violence within trying to break out. The Police.

It hangs back while the Police rings the doorbell. It feels the man's panic like something caged in Clayton's chest, the heart thudding.

As the Police turns to his car, raising his phone to his ear, Clayton's body rises up behind him and rams the nail gun against the Police's head with its neat plaited cornrows, and jerks the trigger.

The Police falls, a limp nothing, the phone tumbling onto the grass. The dream seizes him under the arms and drags him to his vehicle. It clambers in and drives the car into the garage, sitting trembling behind the wheel, trying to assemble the pieces of what it should do next, Clayton's thoughts gone slippery from fear.

It's a station wagon, not a police car, Clayton notes, and the dream realizes that the species is important – that it won't have a tracking device. But it must get rid of the phone. It must smash it into a hundred thousand pieces, because they can follow the lines of communication, like threads through a maze, back to the house, and everything will come unraveled.

Unless.

Unless the Police is a gift. A centerpiece to hinge everything else on.

Principles

The principal keeps Gabi waiting, which is a classic interrogation trick, and frankly very tedious, especially when
she has a wad of messages piling up at the station that she
has to deal with. The heating is turned up too high. The
big green radiator clatters to itself and drifts of heat nag
at the ends of the blinds. She wonders if there is a state-
issued color guide for public buildings that schools and
hospitals have to conform to.

Mr. Clarkwell, the engraved brass paperweight declares.
She has only spoken to him once before this, during Layla's
entrance interview. He seemed friendly, she remembers, and,
as Layla pointed out afterwards, he had a pointy head.
Bald and pointy. They laughed about it in the car. She
cannot summon up anything else. Except that she had made
a vague promise to come in and give a talk about her job
to the eighth graders during careers week. Boy, she wishes
she had done that talk now.

Layla's bag is sitting on the desk, the contents spread
out like evidence. Her books are arranged in a neat stack.
An algebra textbook. Three spiral-bound notebooks she

bought her at the beginning of the year, purple print with a reclining leopard on the front. She remembers what a pain in the ass it was going store to store until Layla found ones with a cover she liked.

A heavy glass ashtray, cracked down the middle. Hers, from the basement.

She flips through one of the notebooks. Her daughter's handwriting is loose but neat, the letters all separated out, given individual weight and merit, beautifully formed. Not the handwriting of someone who would club a fellow student in the head until all his teeth fell out. And yet there are bloodstains. And witnesses and videos. And the cracked ashtray. Prop turned evidence.

She remembers when her own world was regulated and finite. Before Layla came along. It was an emergency C-section, the doctor pulled her out from behind the screen like a magic trick, full of howling outrage at being ripped from the certainty of everything she had known and into the bright lights of the hospital delivery room. Gabi had felt the same way. As if the universe had abruptly expanded, like opening up a map, in a way she wouldn't have believed was possible. Love. The real thing. Huge and hungry and savage. She has never felt the animal inside humanity so clearly as on that day, with the shock of the naked creature on her chest, rooting for her nipple. She would rip out someone's throat with her teeth if they even thought of hurting her, this tiny stranger with the bloody cord still joining them together. The raw violence of it was shocking. Love has claws.

Maybe it would have been different if they'd had another child. Maybe the intensity would have been diluted. You could dish out the love between two kids, like creamed potatoes at dinner. Maybe.

343

Gabi stands up as the principal ushers her daughter into the office.

Layla is trembling with shock, her hands clamped on her elbows as if to prevent them flying away. No, not shock. Indignation. The same righteousness with which she'd marched downstairs at midnight to confront her parents during one of their fights. She was holding her arms the identical way. She stood at the bottom of the stairs, shaking, until they were forced to shut up.

William asked her if she was all right and she demanded, over-enunciating her words to cover the way her voice was trembling, that they 'stop acting like fucking toddler beauty queens throwing a shit fit'. She must have been thinking about the insult all the way down the stairs, crafting it in her head. Gabi had laughed. She couldn't help it. Her clever thirteen-year-old daughter with her HBO vocabulary, and a child's unshakeable belief in justice and the importance of people being nice to each other.

She wants to open her arms for Layla to fly into them, the way she used to when she was little and she bumped her head, or that night on the stairs, when they pulled her into a hug, laughing at her, even as she protested, outraged, that it wasn't funny. It wasn't the last time they had a group hug, but it was the last time it felt uncontaminated.

'Mom! I didn't do it,' Layla bursts out. 'Not like they're saying. I forgot it was in there.'

'I think it's more appropriate to talk about why you did it, Layla,' the principal says. Gabi's intention is to steer the conversation away from talking about it at all until she has had a chance to grill Layla on her own.

'Thank you for coming in so quickly, Mrs. Versado.' This is not the time to point out that her title is Detective. 'I hope you weren't in the middle of something.'

'How is the other teenager?' She is careful not to use the word 'child'.

'We don't know yet. He's been taken to Wayne County hospital. I was hoping you would be able to talk to his parents, but they've gone with him.'

'Was he conscious? Talking? Making sense?' She has seen enough head injuries to be able to guess at the severity of the diagnosis.

'He was awake and in shock. I'm sure we'll get a full medical report soon. You need to know, Mrs. Versado, that if the parents want to press charges, they'll have our full support. We take bullying very seriously at this school.'

Only this isn't bullying. It's assault.

'Does the family have insurance?' She'd rather try to calculate the costs of dental reconstructive surgery than the possible criminal charges.

'I'm really not sure.'

'Can we set up a meeting with the other parents? I'd like to resolve this as soon as we can.' She avoids the word 'settle'.

'I'm sure they'll agree, once Travis is stable and there's been a police report. In the meantime, I have to suspend Layla.'

'Until when?' Layla is furious.

'Until we've settled this.' He has no problems using the word, she notices.

'What about the play?'

'Layla!'

'You should have thought about that before you knocked all the teeth out of a boy's skull.' The principal peers at her, baffled. 'You know, you've always been a good kid, Layla. I just can't understand why you would do this.'

The echo of the words 'good kid', heard so recently about a dead boy, is like a needle in Gabi's kidneys. But she can't let Layla answer. Not here, not on the record. She summons all her cop-smarts. 'Obviously whatever course of action we take has the potential to seriously affect the lives of two minors going forward. And there's the school's reputation to consider, Mr. Clarkwell.'

'That goes without saying. But we still need to do this right. The school has procedures. We need to do an investigation into how this happened.'

'Why don't you ask Travis?' Layla interrupts. 'Ask him what he did to Cas!'

'Yes, Cassandra's history is very sensitive. And confidential.' Sweat is gathering on Mr. Clarkwell's forehead. 'You'd have to discuss it with her parents. This is a very difficult situation all round.'

Layla opens her mouth to speak, but Gabi interrupts her. 'I'll talk to them. Layla, could you wait outside, please.'

Her daughter snaps her trap shut and makes her exit, glaring at the floor, burning holes in it. Gabi's phone rings.

'Do you need to get that?' the principal offers.

'No.' She hits 'reject call' on Sparkles. Whatever it is can wait.

Gabi turns it on for Mr. Clarkwell. She is authoritative, objective, soothing. The voice of cool reason. 'It seems like there are a lot of sensitivities here. You should know that Layla had a terrible shock on Saturday night. I'm not saying it explains her behavior, but it's certainly a mitigating factor. I should have sent her for counseling. She shouldn't even have been in school today.'

He tries to reply, but she cuts him off. 'Let me speak to the boy's parents. I know we'll resolve everything in the way that's least damaging to these kids' futures *and* the school. Thank you for your time, Mr. Clarkwell. And for taking care of Layla.'

She stands up and puts out her hand to shake and he responds automatically. This is something you learn as a cop – that we're programmed by social conventions.

'We'll sort this out, Mr. Clarkwell,' Gabi says, looking him in the eye as she scoops Layla's stuff back into her schoolbag, including the cracked ashtray. She, of all people, knows how easily evidence can get lost.

Exile

In the car, her mom is as quiet as the moment before the tornado hits.

'I'm sorry. I forgot it was there!' Layla protests. 'I put the ashtray in my schoolbag on Friday and forgot about it.' The details seem far away. Like a dream. 'I didn't mean for it to happen like that.' Didn't she? She remembers being full of rage so clear and hot, it was like the light blowing out on an old film camera and she was just a shape moving through the white. 'Anyway, he deserved it, and I'm not sorry.'

Her mom hits the brakes. So hard, the car behind them erupts into hooting as it screeches around them, the driver yelling unheard. Her mother is gripping the steering wheel as if she is strangling it.

'Don't you ever say that, Layla. *Ever*. Not to me, not to anyone.'

'But what he did to Cas!' She means Isabella. It's all getting mixed up in her head. The video and the party and the secret identity of the girl she thought she knew. Like a game on her phone, when the blocks are coming faster and faster and you can't slot them into the right places in time.

'Layla, you need to understand that you're in serious trouble. This could ruin your life.'

'We could move to another city, change our names.' Lie to our best friends.

'Listen to me. It's very likely that as soon as that kid's parents come to their senses around that hospital bed, they are going to press charges. There will be an investigation – a criminal one, not just at the school. And there may be a court case.'

'Am I going to go to jail?'

'I'm going to do everything I can to make sure that doesn't happen. But you need to help me. And saying stupid shit like you just said is going to mean the difference between a suspended sentence and juvenile detention. Do you hear me?'

'Yes.'

'So why did you do it?'

'Because of Cas.' Layla realizes she is crying and is furious with herself. 'Because of what they did to her.'

'Okay, beanie. You have to calm down. You have to tell me exactly what happened.'

'At the art party. Travis and his friends. There's a video of Cas. On the Internet—' She doesn't know how to explain, but Gabi gives a small, tight nod.

The rest comes out in a rush of tears. 'Travis grabbed her boobs, just like in the video. And he put it up on Facebook. Like it was *funny*.'

'Can you show it to me later? Do Cas's parents know?'

'Yes.' Layla wipes her nose. 'About the video – that's why they moved here. I don't think they know about Travis.'

'All right. I need to talk to them, later. Right now, I have to go back to work. Will you be okay to come hang out with me for a couple of hours in the office?'

'Like the old days.'

'Exactly. And tomorrow I'm going to get you some counseling, and then I'm sending you to stay with your father for a few weeks.'

'No!'

'You'll be there for Thanksgiving, Lay, it'll be nice. I should have sent you to Atlanta anyway. The crazy hours I'm working. It's not fair on you.'

'Wait, like this is somehow your fault? Because you're not there enough for me?' She is incredulous.

'Maybe. The divorce and then this insane case. You finding that body. You've been through a lot. I'm sorry, I've been so wrapped up in everything.' The PD lines around Gabi's mouth tug down her whole face.

She suddenly looks older. Older than the image Layla carries in her head, of her mom back when she still wore a uniform, her dark hair in a high ballerina bun, gun at her waist, like the cops on TV. If safe was a person, her mom was it. But nothing is safe any more, and that makes her hate them even worse. The boys who did this.

'Whatever, Mom.' It's *their* fault.

Get Your Hat

'New recruit?' Croff says, indicating the heap of abject unhappiness that is her daughter, slumped in Gabi's chair with her sneakers on the desk, tapping and swiping at her phone. 'This isn't daycare, you know.'

'Lay off, Mike. I know you have the perfect family, but I don't have *a wife* to stay home and take care of things. It's for a couple of hours, all right?'

'Touchy, touchy!' He throws up his hands.

'Where's Marcus?'

'Haven't seen him yet today.'

'And Bob?'

'In the briefing room with Washington. Going through the footage on your citizen journalist friend's phone.'

'What are *you* doing?'

'About to go relieve Stricker, who's cleaning up your mess. You know it's going to take them five days to process that scene?'

'I'm sorry it's such an inconvenience for you. Or were you angling for overtime?'

'Your kid shouldn't be here,' he snipes, stalking away.

She finds Boyd with Ovella Washington, scrolling through the videos, marking the ones that are potentially interesting, getting screengrabs, printing them out and pasting them up.

'How'd the interviews go?'

Boyd groans. 'We got nothing. Crazy artists. You get more sense out of junkies. It's all in the file for you. Only the first round, though. Those were the most obvious ones. I'm going through the list again. We've got the curator guy coming in first thing tomorrow to look at the names again.'

'I thought we were holding him?'

'He got a lawyer, who got him a doctor, who wrote him a note. Shock and alcohol poisoning. He's home with some happy pills and assures us he will be here tomorrow to facilitate us with our enquiries.'

Gabi sighs in disgust. 'Thanks anyway, Bob. Ovella, you're cross-referencing the artists' names against the ceramics place?'

'Yup. So far I've got over thirty people whose names have come up as participating artists and people who have used the pottery at one time or another. Slow going. I haven't even got to your slaughterhouses yet.'

'Can't Sparkles do that?'

'I think he's helping out on scene. Stricker's down there.'

'I know, I ran into Mikey, who is being a gigantic a-hole.'

Boyd shrugs. 'Earth goes round the sun, bears shit in the woods.'

'Well, get someone else to make the calls until Sparkles shows up. What do you have on that graffiti?'

'Your blogger friend, Jonno Haim, did a video report on it. See for yourself. Problem is that he's made it a thing – whatchoocallit?'

'A meme,' Washington supplies.

'Exactly. You got copycat artists in other cities doing their own doors. Plenty here in Detroit, too. They've posted pictures to the comments.'

'So how do we tell our man's from the others?'

'Our killer uses chalk. Some of these others are spray-painted. Some people are doing really elaborate ones, sticking actual wooden doors up, or painting them all realistic.'

'Dammit. We're going to have to check each one.'

'Guess I'll get my hat,' Boyd says.

'Want to grab coffee first?'

'Nah, I just had one,' he says, but then he catches on. 'Oh, right. Okay, caffeinate me.'

In the kitchenette, Gabriella speaks softly. 'Layla's got herself into a sewage plant's worth of the brown stuff. I need to sort it out. Two sets of parents and a hospital, can you believe. Do you think you can handle this for a few hours?'

'Now?!' He is incredulous. 'Your daughter sure has timing.'

'Tell me about it.'

'Don't worry. It's all good. We're chasing what we got. We don't need you right this minute. I can do the door sites on my own.'

'Thanks, Bob,' Gabi says, 'I'll get back to you as soon as I can.'

'No problem. But don't forget your homework,' he says, and dumps a pile of files on her.

Anti-social

You have been tagged in a video: Detroit School Fight – Dis Shit CRZY

Uploaded by Tellyban
4174 views
This video was uploaded from an Android phone.
Description: Bitch goes crzy whomping on his ass. Those r his teeth spititng out!

All Comments:

Bazzguy2012: take the camera away from this fuckin idiot forever.

Niesha Grange: omg i want to kill the camera man, why do you have the camera sideways ? Zoom in. Cant see shit.

Mikal_: Dammm girl! U can whale on me anytym 8==D- – -

Froofoot: niggas always fighting I love my city but damn

354

I cant live in detroit just so ignorant no wonder were the laughing stock of america

CeeCeeCee777: This happened @ my school!!!!!! She went postal!!!!! Nobody even knows why!!!! Travis, your in my prayers, baby boi. Hope you get out of hospital soon. Mwah xxx

Jacks0nN@sh: Tooth fairy: 'Jackpot!'

GawdamBatman: this is why prisons exist, zoo's for animals.

Tybabi: LMAO

Anna_Sussman: wowwww, this girl has no class or respect for herself or the kids aroudn her.

90000560000: shut the fuck up ya stupid homo ass that's why we kill people like you stop hating on us black people you know damn well white people can't fight if it saved there live y'all be some dead cracker fuckers.

GawdamBatman: Maybe if you got an education you could string a sentence together. Oh, I'm sorry. You're too busy being ratchet to go to class.

90000560000: dont it jus kill u? Ya feelings must be real hurt.

HufnaMcKnighty: Hmm. Phys eds changed some since I was in high school O_O

Report this video:
What is the issue?

O Sexual content
O Violent or repulsive content
O Hateful or abusive content
O Harmful dangerous acts
O Criminal activity
O Child abuse
O Spam or misleading
O Copyright infringement
O Infringes my rights
O Captions report (CVAA)

Flagged videos are reviewed by our staff 24/7 to determine whether they violate our community guidelines. Serious or repeat violations can lead to accounts being terminated.

You have 153 new comments on your timeline.

Woah! Insane. What did he DO to you? I'm sure he had it coming.

Did he hit you first? What's going on? This video is so unclear.

Male abuse!

That's so dumb. Like domestic violence isn't perpetrated by MEN against WOMEN every day. There's no such thing as male abuse. Men are in power.

Tell that to the guy who got his teeth knocked out.

Travis's an angel. He didn't do anything to deserve this! He's in hospital! How can you even say that?

You're sick, <u>Layla Stirling-Versado.</u> I hope you get expelled and I hope you go to jail for what you did to our boy.

And I hope you get raped in there by some hardcore dyke with a strap-on made from a toothbrush shank.

Come on, that's seriously fucked up.

Jk! Why can't anyone take a joke!?

Both sides of the story will come out. Everyone just chill out until we know.

We know she did it, there's video evidence! We just don't know why she went whaling on his ass. Why did you, <u>Layla Stirling-Versado</u>?

Inbox: You have 23 unanswered messages.

Jade Cox: There's mad shit being said about you. Is it true?!!! Really worried! Call me, babe.

Dorian Lloyd: Hey Big L. Heard what happened. Hope you're ok? Let me know if there's anything I can do. Me and TimTam are sending you good thoughts.

Amanda Feldman: You don't know me, but I know what

you're going through and your experience has really touched me. I had a boyfriend who abused me for years in ways no-one ever saw. He isolated me from my friends, and he broke me down bit by bit, until I felt so worthless, until it still hurts when someone compliments me. I eventually found the strength to walk away, but I understand why you would snap like that. That might have been me. You might have been me. If you ever want to talk, please message me.

Shawnia Durrell: Everyone at the Masque's thinking about you. Hope you're okay. xxx

Jonno Haim: Dear Layla, I hope you don't mind me messaging you. I see your profile is set to private, so I hope I got the right person! We met after the Dream House party. That must have been a terrible experience for you. I'm trying to put together an honest portrayal of what all this means for the people of Detroit. If you'd be willing to share your story, let me know. I have a generous budget to compensate people for their valuable time, especially if they're willing to be filmed, or if they're able to provide additional images or exclusive footage. Hope to hear from you. All best.

You have 324 new texts.

>Keith: Is it true? You okay?

>Unknown number: You ratchet skank! wtf is wrong with you?

>Bigsie: Shit, you wanted to go all Chris Brown on boys, Layla, you coulda asked me. I'd take it from you anytime! Long as you take as good as you give, know what I'm saying?

>Unknown number: u so ghetto u were born in a bucket of KFC

>Cas: Call me xCas

You have 32 new questions on ASKME.

'Why you such a psycho biatch lol?'

'What did T ever do to you?'

'Does violence run in your family or are you special?'
Answer / Record video answer

You have 67 new voice messages. Press one to play messages.

You have 110 new followers. Win!

If you do not think you will use Facebook again and would like your account deleted, we can take care of this for you. Keep in mind that you will not be able to reactivate your account or retrieve any of the content or information you have added. If you would still like your account deleted, click 'Delete My Account'.

We hate to see you go! Was it something we said? We'll

park your profile for 30 days in case you change your mind.

Are you sure you want to delete your *entire* account? This will delete your blog and all of its content.

Nobody will be able to find or visit your page. You can activate your page by entering your username and password at log-in.

Press seven to delete this message.

Press seven to delete this message.

Press seven to delete this message.

Press seven to delete this message.

Press seven to delete this message.

Press seven to delete this message.

Press seven to delete this message.

Press seven to delete this message.

Press seven to delete this message.

Call Me Maybe

'Hey, this is Jonno,' he says, the phone wedged between his chin and his shoulder. One of '10 Bad Workplace Habits That Cause Back Pain', he knows, but he's clicking through Instagram and Tumblr accounts tagged with #Detroit and #artparty and #dreamhouse.

His phone has been going nuts, so it's infuriating to get that bubble of silence that indicates he's about to be connected to a chipper telesales recording offering him better mobile rates.

'He-llo? Anyone there?' It's the last tag that's screwing up his search, he realizes, pulling up lots of ironic pictures of ruin porn. He refines it to #dreamhouseparty.

'Hi,' a girl says, her voice calm. 'This is Layla. Layla Stirling-Versado. You messaged me.' She sounds older on the phone.

His hand goes up to the phone automatically, as if to keep her from getting away. 'Sure, Layla. I was so hoping you'd call.' He's trying for casual. 'How are you?'

'Not so good, actually.' He can hear traffic in the background, like maybe she's calling from a parking lot. The single whoop of a police siren in the background.

'Yeah. I'm sorry. It must have been terrible. I mean, you found the body, right?'

There's a long stretch of silence.

'Layla? You there?'

'Yeah. Yeah, I did.' Her voice is strangled. He's got to take it easy, get her to save the tears for when there's a camera pointed at her.

'I was serious about the offer. I want to tell the story right, you know? So many people just parachute into Detroit, make all these proclamations of what it is or isn't, and that's not the place we live, am I right?'

'Right.' She doesn't sound so sure, but that's okay. As long as she's agreeing with him.

'This isn't one of those exploitative pieces. I want to show how this affects people, what we have to live with, what this is doing to us.'

'You said there was a budget.'

'Yes, for sure. This is an important film.'

'How much?'

'I'm paying fifty dollars an interview, but because you're an eyewitness, it's a hundred dollars. That's a hundred smackeroos for half an hour of your time.' More like three hours, but who's counting. *Smackeroos?* His troll shudders.

'A hundred bucks?' She's incredulous, but not in the damn-that's-a-good-deal way he was hoping for.

'I'll make it two hundred.'

'This was such a mistake.'

'Hey,' he says. 'Hey, hey, Layla. Listen. Don't hang up. You're the detective's daughter, right? Gabriella Versado?'

'You worked that out from our last names, genius?' *Teen sarcasm. Gotta love it.*

'Which means you know how much pressure your mom

362

is under. The mayor's office is going mental about this case. You know that they're putting Detroit's reputation ahead of solving the crime? They're so worried about bad PR they're willing to compromise your mom's investigation. They're letting this murderer get away with it.'

'What are you even talking about?'

'Why haven't they released any photographs, Layla?'

'Because they always keep some details back, so if a tip-off comes in, they know whether it's real or some crank.'

'You got it,' he scrambles. 'But there's a point where holding back does more harm than good, because the rumor mill is going crazy. I mean dead kids and animal parts and clay ovens and art parties? Have you seen the speculation online? Reddit's got more posts trying to solve the mystery of the Detroit Monster than they ever did on the Boston Bombers. There's like a thousand conspiracy theories, and it's getting in the way of your mom's investigation. She needs to get some intel out there. But she's not allowed to.'

'Because of the mayor's office.'

'Exactly.'

'But you do.'

'And so does your mom. She would never say it. The mayor's office has her practically handcuffed.'

Oh, nice one.

'I can help. It won't be exploitative, I promise. But if I can put some images out there, it might spark off something in someone's head. Remind them they saw something suspicious. You would be helping your mom and the victims and maybe even saving someone's life, Layla. This guy is still out there. Right now.'

'Oh, fuck,' she says, back on the edge of tears. One more nudge and he'll have her.

'You're in some kind of trouble, right? Don't worry, Layla. I don't want to know. I'm not going to ask. Look. You get me photographs, some video footage. I'll pay you for it, you can sort your shit out. That's what it's going to take, right? Money?'

'Yeah. It's magic like that,' she says.

'You're a cool girl, Layla. We can help each other out, and we can help your mom nail this creep. I'm not going to ask any questions about where you get the images. If it's from your mom's cell phone or her computer, that's none of my business. You can make up an email account and Dropbox them to me.'

'How much?'

He takes a stab in the dark. 'Two thousand dollars for exclusive crime-scene photographs.'

'I need ten.'

He leaves her hanging while he does frantic math. 'That's a lot of money, Layla. I'd need everything for that. Video footage of the scene, shots of the bodies, close-ups.'

'And I don't have to do the interview.'

'Not if you don't want to.'

'Will my mom get in trouble?'

'There'll be a fuss. But ultimately it's going to make the difference between catching the killer and trying to bury the whole mess under the rug.'

'And she won't ever find out it was me?'

'Journalists have a moral obligation to protect their sources.'

Journalist? Moral? Ha.

'It's a big department. This isn't just the DPD, remember, but the medical examiner's people, the mayor's office, I reckon even the FBI are looking at this. Anyone could leak it.'

'Okay.'

'Okay, okay? As in deal?'

'But if I send you the files, you send me the money straight away. Same-day clearance. I don't care if your bank charges extra.'

'Me neither! If it's what we've agreed on, I'll be happy to give it to you in hundred-dollar bills in a glowing brief-case hand-delivered by Samuel L. Jackson.'

'Huh?'

'Never mind. Thank you, Layla. This is important. This is going to be a game changer.'

'I hope so. I really hope so.'

BFF

Layla's phone rings the second she hangs up on Jonno. Her mom. Like she's freaking psychic.

'Hi?' she says, going for annoyed to cover her panic.

'Where are you?' Gabi snaps.

'In the parking lot.'

'Where the news crews are?'

'No! Give me some credit, Mom. Round back, where you park your car.'

'Good, stay there. We're going to visit your friend Cas.' It's an indication of how stressed out Gabi is that she doesn't ask Layla what she's doing in the parkade.

She doesn't talk to her on the drive, which Layla is grateful for, because she's terrified that if she opens Gabi's all her secrets will come flying out – VelvetBoy and now Jonno Haim. She studiously avoids looking at Gabi's laptop bag and the camera on the back seat. It's weird to see her mom so caught up in this case that it's almost a physical thing riding on her back, like the ghost in a Japanese horror movie she saw once.

The doorman at Cas's apartment block starts to say a

366

flirty hello, but then he registers their air of bleakness and he bites it off. 'Afternoon, miss, ma'am,' he says, giving a little salute.

'You okay, Lay?' her mom asks as they ride up in the elevator.

'It's all fucked up, you know?'

'Oh, beanie, I know,' Gabi sighs. 'I know. It's not your fault.'

Layla clenches her jaw. It takes everything she has not to spill it all.

But then Cas throws opens the door of the apartment and flings her arms around Layla, almost knocking her off her feet. 'You crazy, crazy bitch. What did you do?'

Layla hugs her back, holding onto her to stop the ground falling out from under her.

'Take it inside, girls,' Gabi says, grim.

Cas's dad is in the kitchen, pouring a double scotch. 'You want one, Gabriella?' he says, also wearing his serious parent face.

'Seems so.'

'I'm afraid Helen is out of town. But I can tell you everything you need to know. Cas, why don't you and Layla go to your bedroom?'

'But you're talking about *us*,' Cas protests.

'That's exactly why you shouldn't be here,' Gabi says.

Cas slams the door of her room. Her bed is unmade. She's ripped all the pictures off the wall, leaving them bare with traces of blue tack. She sits down on the floor with her back against the wall and hugs a pillow to her knees. Layla finally sits down next to her. It's not like it was before. They're quiet, trying to find a way back to each other.

'I can't turn my phone on,' Layla says. 'Every time I do,

367

thousands of messages come in. It's just beep-beep-beep-beep-beep-bitch-bitch-bitch-bitch. At least they could be more original.'

'It's text-bombing,' Cas says. 'You can get an automated program for it. I had the same thing. Only I think I got more like thirty thousand.'

'Always with the one-upmanship,' Layla complains.

Cas snorts. 'Hey, I didn't do what you did. You were pretty fucking bad-ass, Miss Avenger.'

Layla puts her head in her hands. 'Shit, Cas. I'm in so much trouble, and the thing is I barely remember doing it. It was like a dream. You know when you wake up and you can't really remember? I blanked the whole thing.'

'It's the brain's way of protecting itself. Like, I don't remember anything about that night.' Cas laughs, but it's full of glass. 'I found out about it the same way everyone else did. Online. I was in trig and these kids were watching it. I thought it was some stupid porno parody. Then this boy I've never said a word to before comes up to me and grabs my breasts in the middle of the cafeteria, and suddenly everyone is laughing.'

'Is that why you don't drink?'

'Not after that. My dad had me go to the hospital for all these blood tests. He wanted to prove that they roofied me. But it only stays in your bloodstream for like one day, so it was already too late.'

'Did they…?' Layla can't say it. Rape. Happens to nice girls every day. But the word sticks in her mouth, like taffy to her palate.

'Oh, I got the gynecological works. That was the first thing they were worried about. But turns out I'm still a virgin. Oh, please. Don't look so shocked. Like you're not.'

'Actually...'

'What? No way. With Dorian?'

'No. The boy next door in my old 'hood. Tim Schosswald. I used to walk past his front yard every day. It was full of flowers. His mom was this big gardener. It was warm out, and he sprayed me with the hose as I went by. I was so angry, I chased him and he dropped it and ran for the back, and then when I caught him and told him he was an asshole, he kissed me. We just kissed for a long time. Do you ever wonder about that in the movies? Why they don't kiss more? It's like kissing-to-fucking without changing gear. Why do they do that?'

'They're movies. They also have serial killers with social consciences and teenagers accidentally hacking in to the FBI database with their cell phones. Oh my God, I can't believe you never told me this.'

'Yeah, well, turns out there's stuff we didn't tell each other.'

'I'm sorry.'

'Me too.'

'Are you going to tell me what happened with Tim?'

'It went on for a week. We never talked about it, but I'd go out every day at five, in my shorts, and walk past his yard, and he'd be watering the flowers and he'd spray me, and I'd chase him and we'd end up kissing on the grass.'

'No texts, no emails?'

'That was what was beautiful about it. I don't think we said more than ten sentences to each other.'

'And?'

'It got heavier.' And more intense. Her desire came as a surprise to her. 'We kissed a lot and we got naked.' *She* got naked. Shedding her wet clothes. Her T-shirt with the Flying

369

Spaghetti Monster, her pastel-yellow shorts, wriggling out of them, pulling them down over her sneakers. He helped, kissing her hands, kissing her stomach, the hard points of her hips, moving down lower so that she gasped and tilted her hips up to his mouth. He kissed her between her legs and she felt everything realign around that part of her body. The earth revolves around the sun. The grass was itchy under her back and it wasn't fair that he was still wearing his clothes. She fought with his belt and he pushed her hands away and unbuckled it himself and yanked his jeans to his knees. He said, 'Oh God,' and then he was inside her and it was excruciating and sweet and the smell of blossoms was overwhelming, like walking into the perfume aisle, and she had thought *this*, this is it.

'And he came in like three seconds. Does that count?'

'Was there penetration?'

'Three seconds' worth.'

'Then it counts. Oh my God, Layla, you slut.'

'I didn't really know what had happened. He was so embarrassed, he pulled up his pants and walked into the house and never spoke to me again. That was like the one good thing about the divorce and moving away, that I didn't have to see him every day, specifically avoiding me. It was so sad and stupid. I mean, I thought I was in love with him. I sent him like a hundred text messages. And selfies. "Look what you're missing out on." How pathetic is that?'

'I think my mom thinks I was asking for it,' Cas says, quietly. 'She looks at me sometimes, like she knows how it is to be a girl. In a room full of boys.'

And have them want you, Layla thinks. That was what was so intoxicating with Tim. Her own desire amplified by the urgency of his desire. Not like touching herself, where

370

it's just your need to contend with, your sexual imagination. It's better when the craving is mutual, a feedback loop. She felt like a goddess. She felt worshiped.

'Like maybe she's done something just as stupid.'

'There's no copyright on stupid. And you were drunk.'

'I wish…' Cas cracks. 'I wish she'd tell me. Because all the time I feel like she's judging me, and I feel like she's disappointed in me. That's the worst. Worse than the stupid text messages from crazy bitches calling me a whore, or the looks I got in the hallway, or knowing that everyone had seen it. That's why I took the pills. I had this whole plan. It wasn't a cry for help. It was real. I was going to swallow pills, then throw myself off the garage roof into the pool, with a plastic bag over my head so I'd suffocate and drown. But I passed out before I could even get out the front door. My dad found me in the kitchen, covered in puke. He's the one who got crazy about it. Lawsuits and take-downs and all that shit. My mom talked him out of it. Said I had enough to deal with. So we moved. Changed our names. I mean, they're still all Amis-Holt, but I'm just plain Holt. And I'm not Isabella any more. That's why Ben and I go to different schools, to try and protect him. Every single time he gets a message on his phone, I worry that it'll be a link to the video. And my dad still gets Google alerts on it. I just want to say to him, Dad, it's done. Enough already. This proves it, right? You can't outrun your past.'

'Not even in Detroit.'

'Those guys were just stupid kids. I've forgotten their names already.'

'Screw them. And Travis and his crew.'

'You mean Gummy Russo?' Cas cracks a grin. 'The tooth fairy must owe him like a thousand dollars.'

'Wish she'd pay up. My mom reckons we might be liable for his medical bills, that maybe if we pay for them, they won't lay an assault charge. I don't want to go to juvenile detention, Cas.'

'How much are we talking?'

'Ten thousand dollars, maybe more. She can't afford it, Cas. I don't think we've got that much in my college fund. And I can't ask my dad. He's got little kids to look after now. This is my fuck-up. I need to sort it out.'

'What are you going to do?'

'You know the guy who put the video up about the art party? He says he'll pay me for exclusive images.'

'And if you read between the lines with the secret decoder ring?'

'He said I'd be helping the investigation, that my mom's hands are tied...'

'Gross. Bondage.'

'Can you be serious for one second?'

'No. It's how I live with myself.'

'Well, he offered me two grand to steal crime-scene footage from my mom. I told him to make it ten.'

'If you think about it, it's not *really* stealing. It's more like piracy or, I dunno, WikiLeaks, because you're copying them rather than taking them away.'

'You're a terrible moral compass.'

'But I'm a great GPS for dollar bills.'

They both jump at the knock on the door.

Gabi looks drawn, and Layla realizes she's carrying two Japanese ghosts on her back – her responsibility for the case and her responsibility for her daughter – and that she's the one really weighing her down.

'Come on, Layla,' Gabi says. 'We have to go. It's late.'

'You're not going to fill us in?'

'We'll talk about it tomorrow. I have to go see Travis's parents.'

'Can I come?' She wants to take that load off her mother's back. 'I can grovel, Mom. I can be the sorriest girl in the world.'

'They don't want you there right now. He's just out of hospital. But I promise, tomorrow we'll sit down and figure out what to do together, all right?'

'Can I sleep here, then? Please? I don't want to be at home by myself right now.'

Gabi is surprised. 'If that's all right with you?' She looks at Cas's dad.

Andy nods. 'It'll be good for them. You girls can cut class tomorrow. Go see a movie at the Renaissance Center. Use your mom's taxi account. Take it easy. Heck, if you like, Layla can stay over tomorrow night too.'

'Are you sure? That would be a huge relief,' says Gabi, pulling Layla into a hug. 'I love you, sugarbean.'

'I know, Mom,' Layla says. 'You too.' The guilt chews on her. 'Don't send me away, okay?'

'We'll see,' Gabi says. 'Let's start with you phoning your father to explain all this to him.'

Parlay

Detroit's roads are built like spokes, radiating outwards, with the miles marked off. You can follow Woodward Avenue all the way up past Eight Mile, which is the hard border of the city, and watch the urban blight transform into suburbs with rolling lawns out front and SUVs and Priuses parked in the driveways, occasionally together.

On the way to Grosse Pointe, Gabi tries to call Sparkles back, but his phone goes straight to voicemail. She leaves a message as she pulls into the driveway, fringed with rose bushes. 'Hey, rookie, call me. Where are you?'

Edward and Donna Russo's house is done up in rustic country style, with the wood showing through the paint. Like ripped designer jeans; you pay more for a touch of shabbiness. Maybe it's like a magic ward, Gabi thinks, to help keep *poor* at bay.

Travis is somewhere upstairs, in his room. When Gabi called earlier, Donna Russo had explained that it would be a very bad idea to bring Layla. 'He practically has PTSD, the psychologist says. He's on anti-anxiety medication. And painkillers, of course. I don't know what seeing her would do to him. It might be a trigger.'

'She wants to apologize.'

'She should have thought of that before she beat him within an inch of his life,' the woman gasped before hanging up. Frankly, it makes it easier that Layla stayed with Cas. It means Gabi only has to play nice up to a point.

She has managed to get hold of the doctor's report. It helps to be on first-name terms with half the city's ER nurses from her days on patrol, walking in wounded thugs and civilians caught in the crossfire.

There is no doubt Travis is badly hurt. He has a mild concussion that needs monitoring. His jaw is fractured. A hairline crack that runs from his mandible joint, halfway to his chin, although no-one can explain how that caused all his teeth to fall out. 'Possible early-onset osteoperosis??' one doctor has scrawled in almost illegible blue pen. It doesn't make sense. It gives her the same queasy feeling she has about the case.

There is an enormous lamp looming over the dining-room table, a red sphere of unraveling wires that has her wanting to duck. It's incredibly warm in here. Underfloor heating, Gabi reckons, because the fireplace is one of those fake gas numbers with glowing coals.

On the shelf above it are a series of black-and-white professional photographs, in frames made from reclaimed wood. Here they are laughing, smiling, goofing around, Travis jumping on his dad's back, his mom holding her hand to her mouth, the smile peeking through her fingers. Here they look terribly serious, all in plain white T-shirts and jeans, their arms tangled round each other's waists or thrown over a shoulder, staring unflinchingly into the camera. This is love, the photograph says. This is family. What you got?

When Gabi was picking out a new school for Layla, she liked that Hines High had a mix of students from different backgrounds and classes. But now, sitting here, at this table, under a wire sun with the Russos, she's not so sure there should be any mixing. Hell isn't other people, it's other parents. And parents with money are another species, even though on the surface they have so much in common. Only child. Mixed race.

She wonders how their son ended up at a charter school in the city – maybe he has a track record of expulsion or sexual harassment, something she can use as ammunition.

The Russos sit opposite her: Edward with his thick dark hair and Italian nose in business casual, and Donna with her straightened hair pulled back into a loose ponytail, resting her hand on his on the table, as if to remind him to stay calm. They want her to beg for clemency. Which they have already intended to deny, she knows. Because the prosecutor phoned her this afternoon. The family have political connections – in Lansing, not Detroit, but enough to force him to go all out with the charges.

'I want to start by saying I'm very sorry for what happened. We want to make this right with you and your family. Layla has never done anything like this before.'

The mother opens her perfect mouth, and any guilt Gabi is feeling is allayed by the incredible stupid that comes out of it. 'I hope not. I really hope not. You being a single mother and all.' It's worse than patronizing. It's *matronizing*. 'I admire your courage, trying to do it on your own. But it means... I'm sorry, this is probably hard to hear. But it means you can't be there all the time. You don't know what she's doing. Where she's going. What she's taking.'

'Layla wasn't on any drugs.'

'We've asked for blood tests.'

'Not without parental consent.' She'd give it, of course, but she wants to remind them that there are procedures, that the law is democratic and justice is blind – or that it's supposed to be.

'The school is going to search her locker. We're going to prosecute. And take it as far as we can.'

'I understand you want her to be punished—'

Donna smacks the table with her open palm. 'She *ruined* his face!'

'It's going to cost nineteen hundred dollars per tooth,' Edward says with awe, as if this is something to be proud of.

'I'm absolutely willing to cover whatever your insurance doesn't pay. It'll come out of Layla's college fund.'

'College?' Donna laughs bitterly. 'She shouldn't be going to *college*. She should be admitted to a mental hospital! She needs serious help. And it's not just the reconstructive surgery. What about the humiliation? In front of the whole school. Do you know what kind of damage that does to a young person's confidence?'

'Please listen to what I'm about to say to you. You're well within your rights to press charges—' Gabi is holding on to her patience with a death grip.

'Yes, we are.'

'But even with the most severe judge on earth, I can tell you that Layla is not going to serve any time in juvenile detention or prison. She will do community service. It will go on her record, but because she is fifteen, it will be expunged when she turns eighteen. The judge will take into consideration that she has no priors, that she is the daughter of two upstanding long-serving police officers, and that she experienced a traumatic event two days earlier that affected her emotional state—'

'This is *corruption*!' Donna shrieks. 'This is exactly what people are talking about when they complain about the system. You people look after your own.'

'It's the way the law works. For any teenager with no prior record.'

Edward puts his arm around his wife. 'Your daughter is *not* going to *walk* after assaulting our son with a deadly weapon.'

'The charge would be "serious assault with intent to do great bodily harm less than murder".'

'That's for the judge to decide. Whether she was trying to kill him. Totally unprovoked.'

Gabi finds her death grip is slipping. 'Let's talk about that,' she says. 'About provocation. About what is going to come up in the case, and parents who don't know what their kids are up to. Let's talk about Travis distributing child pornography.'

'Honey?' Mrs. Russo looks across at her husband, but it's more of an appeal for him to put Gabi in her place than any real concern.

'Do I need to call my attorney?' He's bored with all this. Money buys you a nice house in the suburbs, along with expensive lawyers who can make problems disappear.

'Travis posted a video to his Facebook page of an underage girl being sexually assaulted at a party.'

'That's not child pornography.' Still bored. Still the upper-class hand.

'Technically, it's exactly child pornography. If convicted, Travis will get a place on the Sex Offender's Registry. Which does *not* get expunged from your record when you turn eighteen.'

'You've got to be kidding me,' the father says, half-standing up. She worries that he is going to bump his head on that ridiculous lamp. 'Your daughter viciously assaults our son, probably hopped up out of her mind on drugs, and you dare to try to turn this around on him?'

'This is America. Sex is worse than violence.'

'You think he made some video? You think *our* son would do that?'

'That would be a much more serious charge. It's from Oakland, made a year ago. It's of a fourteen-year-old girl called Isabella Amis being sexually assaulted at a party. Travis was just being a dumb kid and sharing it around without thinking about the consequences. He made a stupid mistake.'

'And your daughter did the same?' Donna sneers. Gabi admires the way she loads up her sarcasm with extra syrup.

'*Your son* also grabbed Isabella Amis's breasts at a party, in front of her peers, if you want to talk about public humiliation. So, add sexual assault plus a cyber-bullying charge, although Michigan lawmakers are still figuring out the protocols on that. This could be a landmark case. None of this excuses what Layla did – but her defense would definitely raise this as extenuating circumstances. It would all come up in the trial, if you did decide to prosecute.'

'You've got proof?'

'I have screengrabs of his timeline. Comments by his friends. I'm sure he's deleted everything he can by now, but social media leaves ghosts. The corporations back up everything: Facebook posts, text messages, Snapchats. All on a central server somewhere, and they can be requisitioned by a court of law. Deleted is a terrible misnomer.' Only half of this is true, but Mr. Holt gave her all the jargon to dazzle them with. They sat and went through the kids' profiles together, grabbed what they could. He did it with the grim satisfaction of a survivor.

'Show us this video,' Donna Russo challenges.

'I'm afraid I can't do that. It would constitute a criminal offense. You'll have to ask your son about it.'

TUESDAY, NOVEMBER 18

Turning Over

Gabi wakes up from an uneasy sleep, too early, five a.m., to a house that's unnaturally quiet. Layla's absence is a physical thing in the darkness. Is this what it will feel like when she goes to college? There's a warm weight on her legs. NyanCat, who hunkers down in protest and tries to make herself heavier when she moves.

'I'm bigger than you, cat,' Gabi says, tipping the animal off the bed. She stalks away, tail quivering in outrage.

She never understood the name. Some video game? Layla showed her a clumsy animation of a piece of toast with a cat's head trailing a rainbow, so she took to calling the kitty-litter box the 'rainbow dropzone' just to annoy her. Layla makes it too easy. Gabi mangles pop culture on purpose to get under her skin. Somehow this has become an acceptable shorthand for 'I love you'.

Gabi gets up and starts flipping through the reports. Boyd dropped off a bunch more last night, after she got back from dealing with the asshole parents, looking as exhausted as she felt. She was so wiped she forgot to ask him if he'd heard from Sparkles.

She flips open the files.

'What the fuck do you want? What are you trying to do?' She flips through the photographs of the doors. The monstrosity of Daveyton's remains in the garden, the deer's hollow eyes.

NyanCat meows plaintively from the floor, and she rubs her with her foot, idly. It's all the encouragement the cat needs. She jumps into Gabi's lap, tipping all the files onto the floor.

'You ridiculous animal!' She pushes the cat away and starts sorting the reports back into the right folders. She examines the names of the participating artists on the spreadsheet. Fifty people. She turns the page over, not for any good reason. Cop instinct.

There are three more names, printed in red, in an eight-point font, and struck out. Two men, one woman.

~~Vincent Nadel~~
~~Clayton Broom~~
~~Alette von Randow~~

She gets onto her knees on the floor and starts digging for the student registry at Miskwabic Pottery, running her fingers down the names from the last three years, looking for a Vincent or a Clayton.

Nothing.

But maybe he was there before that. There's an accounts book in the evidence box at the precinct. She pulls on a sweater and a pair of jeans, gathers up all the files, and drives down to the station.

She phones Boyd from the road.

His voice is thick with sleep. 'Another one?'

'No. But I think I have something. Can you come down?'

He finds her flipping through the hardcover book where Betty Spinks tallied her income and expenses.

'Here. 19 April 2010. "$50. General assistance. C. Broom." 30 April "$35 Custodial work. C. Broom." 11 May "$50 minus clay purchased = $35." And look at the list of participating artists. Clayton Broom. Crossed out on the back pages. What do you think that means? He dropped out? They dropped him? Why?'

'Because he's a psycho killer? I'll run his name through the system.'

'Can you get me the curator on the line?'

'You know it's six in the morning, Versado.'

'I give a fuck.'

Patrick Thorpe materializes half an hour later with Darcy D'Angelo, both of them effervescent with nerves.

'Of course it's him. Of course!' Patrick says. 'I should have put this together! He's always been peculiar, but lately he's been…'

'More insane than usual,' Darcy offers.

'His work developed very suddenly, almost overnight. This amazing vision, but a very disturbing direction. Do you think it's because he was killing people? Do you think that opened him up creatively?'

'Can you slow down please, Mr. Thorpe.'

'He was supposed to deliver this wonderful waxy fat man for the show, but he bailed. Oh God, do you think there was a body in there, too? But the picture you showed me of the thing in the garden, it was so crude. Not like his other work at all. Slapped together. But that makes sense, doesn't it, because don't serial killers start unraveling, getting sloppier? And he's got a history, hasn't he Darcy? That blood-stained hospital sheet he once put up as an artwork.'

'Don't you remember what he did to Marcelle?' Darcy chimes in. 'You all tried to play it down as a prank, but let me tell you the girls in the house knew he was off from that moment.'

'What prank? When was this?' Gabi snaps.

'It must have been seven or eight years ago,' Darcy says. 'There were a group of artists sharing a communal studio squat. It was a scene, lots of parties, and Clayton was couch-surfing there for a while. No-one really liked him – he was very intense – but they couldn't figure out how to ask him to leave. Anyway, there was a girl he liked, Marcelle. Clayton painted her portrait and when she said it was ugly—'

'He said, "I'll show you ugly!", Patrick interrupts.

'He went and got dried-up sheeps' intestines from the abattoir next door and glued them onto the painting, over her hair. Marcelle was very upset and there was a huge fight. They threw him out over it.'

'I'm going to need you to go on the record with this.'

Patrick gasps. 'Darcy! What if it wasn't sheeps' intestines?'

'I don't think speculation is useful. Rather let us investigate. You've been very helpful,' Gabi hustles them out. 'We'll follow up with you, but in the meantime, please don't talk to anyone about this, especially not the media.' She shuts the door on the pair and leans against the wall.

'Jesus,' she breathes.

He's been right here, in front of them, this whole time. They've even got him on tape at the party, just for a second, before the camera dips down. 'I need a camera,' he says, chillingly. 'I need people to see.'

Clayton Elias Broom. Fifty-three years old. Arrested several times. But never for a felony crime that would have required fingerprints. Loitering. Disturbing the peace, traffic obstruction.

He's on the personnel list from the meat-packing plant. Worked there for three months in 2010, and again more recently, before they ran into trouble with the unions. He definitely would have had access to the meat glue.

He is in Betty Spinks's accounting registry.

He's in the fucking phone book, address and all. Daveyton's bus route goes right past his house.

'We've got him,' Boyd says.

'Not until he's in custody,' Gabi says. She is strapping on her bulletproof vest. Everyone has rallied. Everyone is ready.

'Shit,' Boyd says, shaking his head. 'Can't believe me and Sparkles missed this.'

Gabriella freezes. 'Have you seen him?'

'Not this morning, no.'

'When did you last see him?'

'Dropped him off on Sunday after we did the door-to-doors.'

'And yesterday?'

'No. But I was busy. We all were.'

'Has anyone seen Officer Jones?' Gabi yells out. She thinks about the missed call from yesterday. She never checked to see if he left a message. She dials voicemail. 'Hi, Detective Versado,' Marcus's voice says, 'I found some more names on the list, I'm going to—'

It cuts out there. She plays it again. Fuck.

Fuck.

'Did Marcus have this list?'

'We had a couple of copies. He was working from one on Sunday.'

She punches in a different number. 'Hello, 4th Precinct? This is Detective Versado from Homicide. Is your supervisor there? Can you tell me if Officer Marcus Jones reported for duty yesterday? Yes, I know he's on special dispensation. He didn't call in sick with you? I know he's supposed to be with me. He's not.'

Finders Keepers

'Damn, it's cold,' Cas complains, perched on the edge of the merry-go-round turning in lazy circles. Every so often, she kicks off with her sneaker to maintain the momentum, leaving tracks in the icy sludge from last night's snow. 'You think he's going to show?'

'He has to.' Layla sits on the fence, freshly painted, low enough to jump over and run, if necessary. There are houses and shops nearby. There's a gas station across the road. This is not her mom's advice. It's an adolescence of watching bad horror movies and yelling at the dumb-ass characters.

Ten thousand dollars. That has to be enough to pay for Travis's dental work, surely?

VelvetBoy didn't want to pay that much, of course. But she told him he had to match her other offer. Call it a finder's fee for his wallet. Which also includes deleting all the screengrabs of their chats and texts and the video footage from the diner, which she doesn't have, but hey, he doesn't know that. She didn't tell him that the 'other bidder' wanted crime-scene photos off her mom's laptop, not proof of a pedophile chat.

'Can I see the gun?' Cas asks, swirling past her.

'No! God.' The .38 in the pocket of her hoodie has its own black-hole density. They made the cab driver wait outside Layla's house while she fetched it out the safe, before he brought them here. All courtesy of Cas's mom's taxi account. 'What if he comes round the corner right now? We'll scare him off.'

'Or scare him into paying up, no questions asked.'

'Is that the same car?'

'What?'

'The green Pontiac. I'm sure it went past earlier.'

'Girl, I can't tell the difference between a Porsche and Pontiac.'

'There it goes again. Same license plate. Don't bail on me again, okay?' she warns.

Layla pulls her cat mask down and steps forward, waving. The other hand is in the pocket of her hoodie. Cas sits up, digging her heels into the gravel to bring the roundabout to a squeaking stop.

'What are you doing?'

The Pontiac slows and she sees Philip's pink, frightened face behind the wheel. She beckons. The car leaps forward, tires squealing, and speeds away.

'Was it him?'

'Yeah.'

'Where's he going?'

'To have a panic attack. He'll be back.'

'How do you know?'

'Because he's been past twice already. He's already invested.'

Cas comes to sit beside her on the fence, pulling down her own mask. Sure enough, five minutes later, the Pontiac creeps round the corner and pulls to a stop, engine still running, exhaust pluming from the back. Phil leans over to lower the window: 'Hey! Why don't you get over here?'

'You come here,' Layla calls back. He has red leather seats in his car. How lame is that?

'I don't want to talk about this in the open. We can go for a drive.'

'We're not getting in your car. You come here, or the deal's off.'

'No.'

'Okay. Hope your boss at the electrical place is really understanding when I email him our chat sessions.'

'All right! Just wait.' The window slides up. He turns the key and the car shuts off. He sits in the driver's seat for a moment, gripping the steering wheel.

'What's he doing?' Cas is tense as a guitar string.

He's banging on the steering wheel, his mouth open, yelling silently. Layla tightens her hold on the gun in her pocket. It feels even heavier.

He stops yelling and banging and closes his eyes. He takes a deep breath and turns to open the door. He comes round the side of the car, smiling. It's not a real smile.

'Snowing already, huh? Who would have thought.' He's rubbing his hands together, because maybe that way he can stop himself from lunging forward and choking them.

'Stay there,' Layla warns him.

'Make up your mind,' he snaps, the smile gone.

'Where's the money?' Cas says.

'In the car.'

'Get it, please.'

'Why should I? How can I trust you? You've been lying to me this whole time.'

391

'Because you know the consequences,' Layla says. This sounds bad-ass. She thinks about what it looks like, two girls in cat masks in a playground facing off against a lanky white guy in a Lions beanie. Probably pretty damn cool. It has the displaced feeling of a movie. She's watching it happen. 'Don't fuck with me,' she says, because it seems like the sort of thing she should say.

'Bitches.'

'Go on,' Cas goads.

'I don't have it.'

'What?' Layla is stunned.

'Where'm I s'posed to get ten gees?'

'You said you would.'

'Look at me. Look at my car. I pull in two grand a month. My rent is seven hundred dollars. I spend four hundred dollars on groceries. I got debts. I got a real sick father. He's got Parkinson's. It makes your whole body claw up like a dead crab. He sits in a wheelchair all day. His insurance wouldn't pay for a colostomy. So he shits himself and I have to get him out of the wheelchair and change his diapers. My father.'

'You got enough money to buy online vouchers for little girls,' Cas says.

'It's a fantasy. I never acted on it. I'm lonely. You don't have fantasies?'

'You asked for photos!' Layla objects. 'You wanted her to send you videos. You wanted to meet her!'

'Who's her? There's no *her*. SusieLee doesn't exist. There's you. You two playing some crazy headgame. Leading on innocent people. I didn't want to meet. *You* did. I thought...'

'What? You thought what?'

'I don't know! I thought maybe you were lying. That you were older. You seemed older. But not so old that you were

392

already screwed-up and bitter, like the women I've dated.'

'You're pathetic.'

His face tightens. 'You want your money, girly? How about I pay you and your fat friend twenty bucks to suck my dick.'

Cas loses it. 'You pig! You're a disgusting pervert. You're just like them.' She barges into Layla with her shoulder. The hand holding the gun comes out of her pocket and Cas wrenches it away from her.

'No, Cas!' Layla shouts.

'Fucking liar. Fucking pervert!' She screams. She shoves the revolver into Phil's crotch. He yelps, a high-pitched sound, backing up against the car.

'Where's the money, pervert?'

'I don't have it! I told you.'

'Cas, stop it,' Layla begs.

'Of course you don't. Because you're a loser. You want a blow job? How about I blow off your fucking balls? How does that sound, Phil? Hope you got a spare pair of your daddy's diapers in the car. You're going to need them, motherfucker.' Tears are streaming down her face.

'I'm sorry! It was a joke.'

'Stop it!' Layla grabs Cas's arm, but she's stronger and she's not letting go.

'Yeah, that's what *they* said. A joke. I'm so sick of you all!' Cas screams into his face. 'You're all the same.'

'I'll get you the money!' Phil shrieks, cringing away.

'He's not them, Cas!'

'Please! I'll get a loan!' he squeals. 'Don't shoot me.'

'He's not the same. He's not the guys who did this to you.' Layla gets hold of Cas's thumb and wrenches it down, forcing her hand to twist sideways, her whole body following.

The gun goes off, louder than Layla could have imagined.

They all jump and Phil screams. It's muted, like it's coming through a tin-can telephone on a string. For a moment the whole world turns to pearlescent glass, an art-deco ashtray. And then it snaps back to normal.

Her head is ringing. Cas is crouched down, her hands over her ears, shoulders jerking. Phil is screaming and gasping and screaming, his eyes scrunched shut, palms flat against the car.

Layla looks down at the gun in her hand. She raises it and taps Phil on the forehead with the butt. 'Hey, dummy. It didn't hit you.'

He opens his eyes and flinches, his eyes darting to the gun. She's never had someone be afraid of her before.

'You're okay, Phil.' Her own voice sounds dulled.

'Oh sweet Jesus. God in heaven. Thank you, God.'

'Get in your car, Phil. Drive away. Don't come back. Don't ever try this shit again. We'll be watching you. Next time, I'll let her shoot you.'

'Yes, yes. I will. I mean, I won't. Whatever you want.'

'Get in the car.'

He scrambles round to the driver's side, and drops his keys in the street. He fumbles around for them, his breath coming in shallow grunts. He peers under the car, reaching in, then peeks over the hood to see what she's doing. 'I can't,' he implores.

'Take your time. I'm not going to shoot you. See, I'm putting the gun away.'

He nods, his eyes wet, and lies down in the icy sludge, reaching under the car.

Layla reaches into her pocket for a Sharpie. She writes 'SusieLee' in giant letters across his back windscreen. From this angle, the red leather in the back of the car looks almost vaginal – warm and fleshy. She imagines him being swallowed by his car. She's losing her mind.

'What's that?' he says, standing up, keys in hand. His hands are shaking. But then so are hers.

'In case you forget. If you even think of following us, if you try to find us, I'll let her shoot you in the balls. We know where you live. C'mon, Cas.' She pulls her sobbing friend to her feet and walks away, fast, across the street to the gas station and the neon safety of the gas pumps and the aisles filled with produce. She doesn't look back.

The Footage

It's Jen's idea to release the footage with different cuts. Twenty-eight minutes for the aficionados, twelve minutes for the curious new converts, three minutes for the casual YouTuber, ten-and thirty-second chunks for the news channels, always with Jonno in frame or their captions over the images. Brand recognition. He can't wait to have a professional cameraman, a real producer, an editor.

Jonno looks straight-to-camera, his delivery super-serious. 'This is what the City of Detroit doesn't want you to see.' He pauses for emphasis, grim. 'I can't blame them. The images we're about to show you are graphic and disturbing.' Guaranteeing that no-one is going to click away. But they let them wait.

Cue photograph of Daveyton grinning goofily in an oversized football helmet. Zoom out to reveal it's one of many photographs pinned up among flowers and balloons and cards and stuffed toys at the bus stop where he was killed. The camera lingers on a piece of cardboard that reads, 'We miss you Davey,' in childish script, with handprints from his classmates.

'Daveyton Lafonte. Eleven years old. When he was six, he survived being shot in a gang fight. But death came back to claim him. He was abducted from this bus stop on his way home from school.'

A shaky driving shot of the tunnel at night. Jen reassured him that it would make it look more real.

'Someone killed him and left his body here, like trash.'

Cue the crime-scene photographs, and a photo click sound effect, which Jonno thinks is cheesy as hell, but every click gets them closer to the scene. The cop cars blocking off the road, the graffiti on the tunnel wall, the shape of a child curled up on his side, indistinct. 'The police reported that the body was found with animal remains. Whatever that means. Roadkill? A dead cat found in the vicinity?'

Cue panning shot of a newspaper headline that says 'animal remains'.

'We didn't know what that meant. We didn't know the truth of how his body had been desecrated. Until *these* disturbing photographs were leaked by someone close to the investigation.' He uses all the right lingo that suggests concerned citizens, government cover-ups, the people's right to know.

Cut back to a close-up of Daveyton's face, eyes closed, serene. Slow zoom out to reveal his naked chest. Zoom out further to reveal the seam of fur creeping over his stomach, the length of the deer haunches. Full reveal: lingering on the unspeakable.

He speaks it anyway: 'Daveyton was killed by a sick and twisted murderer. But merely killing a little boy wasn't enough for the Detroit Monster. No. He cut Daveyton Lafonte in half, and attached him to a fawn.

'The rest of Daveyton's remains were discovered at the

now infamous Dream House party, hidden among the art installations.'

Cut to the footage, re-cut so it looks more dramatic. They've included some of the weirder art, but they've also re-contextualized the girl screaming in delight on the dance floor, among the images of people leaving the party. Quick cuts, tense close-ups, like the scene in *Jaws* when everyone is fleeing the beach.

'The police don't want you to know how bad this is. How deep it goes.'

Cut to the Tudor exterior of Miskwabic Pottery. A photograph of a group of students throwing pots on the wheels. The photograph turns to monochrome on everyone except for a cheerful middle-aged lady in an orange apron, who is holding up her hands to demonstrate the curve of a bowl.

'Pottery teacher, Betty Spinks, was covered in clay and baked to ash in the Miskwabic kiln, after the killer cut off her feet.'

Photographs of the kiln, looking creepy as hell, with singed bricks and a gaping interior. Generic ones he found online, because they wouldn't let them in to film, and his source wasn't able to get at those particular photographs.

'This is a twisted killer who is on the loose in Detroit right now... And the police don't want you to know about it.'

Shaky footage from the party. Detective Versado yelling at him. 'What the hell do you think you're doing? Hand over that phone.'

'Why are they trying to cover it up? Why don't they want us to know what's happening in our own city? I'm Jonno Haim and I'll keep you up to date on the Detroit Monster as events unfold.'

SUBREDDIT / Detroit Monster

If you're new here, please read the FAQ before posting. Please post in the appropriate sub-threads and check to see if there isn't an existing conversation topic before you post. Please note that these theories and discussions are for entertainment purposes only and are not intended to compete with or undermine proper judicial processes.*

(*Yeah, yeah, we're putting this here to keep the nanny brigade off our backs, but seriously, you guys, we don't want another Boston Bomber or Sandy Hook situation. No false accusations, no finger-pointing, no DOXing without good cause.)

> Start here: Welcome newbies and FAQ
> New Video! Holy shit!
> Jonno Haim
>> Who is this guy?
>> 15 minutes of fame.
>> Ruh-roh! Anyone think he's the killer?
> Everything we know about the victims:
>> Daveyton Lafonte

> Betty Spinks
> The crime scenes
    > Bus stop: Daveyton Part 1
    > Miskwabic Pottery: Betty Spinks
    > Dream House party: Daveyton Part 2
> Dream House on social media
    > Links to videos, pictures
    > Suspicious status updates
> Interesting tweets
> Dream House attendees
> Similar cases
    > The Craigslist Ripper (New York)
    > Amputated feet washing up on Salish Shore (British Columbia)
    > Cattle Mutilations (Montana)
    > Alien corpse is really a mummified baboon (Nature's Valley, South Africa)
> Other serial killers who mutilated their victims:
    > Edward Theodore Gein
    > Richard Trenton Chase
    > Joachim Dressler
    > Robin Gecht
    > Mary Bell
    > Charles Albright
> Other serial killers who left signs:
    > Roger Kibbe
    > Harvey Murray Glatman
    > John Allen Muhammad & Lee Boyd Malvo
    > Richard Ramirez
> Animal theories
> Hate crime theories
> Rogue taxidermy links

> Mythology: animal hybrids
    > Daveyton: Satyrs
            > Pan
            > Puck
            > Dionysus
            > Pan's Labyrinth
            > Disney's Fantasia
    > Betty
            > Gorgons/Medusa
            > Hydra
            > Kali
            > Kraken
            > Sphinx
            > Ursula the sea-witch
> Graffiti
    > Doors
    > Fake doors
    > Quit doing fake doors!
> Better names for 'The Detroit Monster'
    > Yo Momma
    > The Mangler
    > Monstermaker
    > The Mythmaker
            > The Killer Mythtake
                > The Killer Milkshake
                    > My milkshake brings all the
                        serial killers to the yard
                            > ZOMG. STFU.

Breakdown

This should be the end of the story. Cops with guns and flak jackets, squad cars surrounding the house, the blue and red lights strobing the street.

They have checked the satellite photos and the street view, calculating the entrances and exits, every possible escape route out of the neighborhood. They have them all covered. Snipers have guns trained on the windows. Two police helicopters are circling overhead along with three news choppers, who got wind of something, hovering close by.

The excitable curator, Patrick Thorpe, is with them, standing back out of harm's way, briefing the entry teams. He's wearing a bulletproof vest and a helmet even though he's not going anywhere near the scene. They wouldn't have brought him, but they needed to move fast, and he was the only person who could brief them on the interior of the house. They need all the intel they can get, and he's already told them that Broom is a hoarder, that the inside is an obstacle course of newspaper stacks and heavy old furniture.

One of the news crews has a drone. Gabi's commandeered it to get a look in the windows upstairs, the quadrocopter buzzing round the house with its camera, but the technology is stymied by an older one: curtains.

Captain Miranda is standing out front with the megaphone, issuing the scripted demands. Come out, come out, wherever you are, Gabi thinks. Please make it easy. They're all wired into the same circuitboard of tension.

There's no response. The front door, which has a dozen guns trained on it, does *not* crack open so that Broom can release Officer Jones and come out slowly, his hands on his head, as instructed. But he also doesn't burst out of the house with a semi-automatic blazing. And that's something. But her heart is a wild animal in her chest. All she can think about is Marcus Jones and how she's let him down.

'Going in,' Miranda confirms. Boyd stays with the team in front. Gabi goes through to the yard, because the back door will yield more easily, which means she can get in faster. The grass is dead, frosted with concrete dust and yellow patches marking where things used to stand. The curator said it was full of statues. She wonders where the hell they are now, how many of them are human. What are they even dealing with?

Gabi takes her place behind the huge officer with the battering ram. The worst job. The most vulnerable. No cop wants to be in a situation where you can't get your hands on your gun.

The instruction comes through clear on the radio and simultaneously, front and back, the teams swing the battering rams into the heavy doors. The wood resists the siege. It's old and sturdy, from the days when they built houses to last. But even history has to yield to force, especially when you know the weak points: the lock, the hinges. The wood splinters. Another officer wedges a crowbar under the lock and pops it out.

They drop the ram, draw their guns and swoop in, avenging angels. For Daveyton Lafonte and Betty Spinks and Sparkles and for themselves, so they never have to get that call about someone they love.

The kitchen to the right, the refrigerator yawning open, the living room to the left, heavy curtains pulled shut. Stairs leading up to the second floor.

The place stinks of damp and old paper. Sweaty feet in an old library. And blood. Splattered over the kitchen. In the basement, over a work table. A slaughterhouse. The carpets are discolored, like the yard, marked by things that have stood here long enough to leave their ghosts. Stains creep up the walls, damp and black mold. There are rat droppings. Silverfish and cockroaches scatter into the darkest corners. And hundreds of chalk doorways drawn everywhere, overlapping each other.

'We got a car,' a voice crackles over the radio. 'In the garage. Blue station wagon. We're running plates on it.'

'Check if it's registered to Officer Marcus Jones,' Gabi says. 'It might be his private vehicle.'

'Affirmative,' the voice comes back a moment later.

Gabi bites her tongue until she tastes blood. Her fault. She should have answered the phone. All this time, they were so damn close, all this time.

They fan out, cops spreading into every room. Pounding up the stairs. They call out the prescription warnings, about coming in, coming up, last chance, with your hands visible. Using Clayton's name like an invocation to summon him.

But every room is the same. Empty. No piles of newspaper, no furniture. Everything has been cleared out. Another vacant house, another day. It's all gone.

Including Clayton Broom. And Marcus Jones.

Call of Duty

The aftermath is a clusterfuck. The media has gone ballistic. They let the Detroit Monster get away, and a cop is missing, presumed dead. One of their own. Clayton Broom has disappeared and they have no idea where. They had to release his name and photograph officially, before the press did, so the department looks slightly less ragingly incompetent, and somehow the video blogger has gotten hold of crime-scene footage off *their* computers, and she's got what feels like the whole of the Internet trying to solve the case.

She knows it's over the moment she is summoned into Miranda's office and finds it full of important people. Honey-blonde Jessica diMenna, someone from Internal Affairs, the Chief of Fucking Police. Boyd's there, too, sitting in a corner, staring down at his hands as if his chewed-up fingernails might reveal great truths.

'You must know why you're here,' Jessica says.

'Sure. Can we skip to the punchline so I can get back out there and find Officer Jones, who might still be alive?'

'We appreciate your dedication, Versado, but this has to be done by the book.' Joe Miranda picks up a sheet of paper. He reads it in a monotone without meeting her eyes. There's a lot of legal jargon. But the summary of it is that she's done here. She tunes out the reasons listed: the only one that matters to her is that she put an unqualified officer in danger, and now he's missing, probably dead.

Miranda finally gets to the end of the spiel. He takes a swig from the bottle of water on his desk and meets her eyes, ignoring their audience. 'I'm sorry, Versado. Someone has to take the fall. We have to save face. You can still work it, we need everyone. But you're no longer in charge. We're putting Detectives Croff and Stricker on it, and we're bringing in the feds. There's an agent flying in tomorrow morning.'

'Permission to speak, sir.'

'You don't have to explain anything. This isn't a tribunal. You're a fine officer, you were in over your head.'

'I don't want to explain. I want to say that I'm not coming off this case. Not until I find Officer Jones.'

She walks out of his office to find Stricker and Croff already waiting outside, as if they've already been briefed. Luke reaches for her hand and then thinks better of it. 'Gabi. You did everything right. It just wasn't fast enough. I'm sorry.'

Croff shrugs. 'Hey, cheer up, Versado. They'll make it up to you down the line. And you got your kid to worry about. You can't be a good mom *and* a good cop.'

She gives him the finger, but as if to prove his point, she gets a text from Layla before she even gets back to her desk.

>Lay: Can you come pick me up? Pls mom, it's urgent. I wouldn't ask.

She phones her immediately. 'Are you all right?'

'I'm fine. It's just—' She's crying.

'Are you in danger, right now? This very second?'

'No.'

'Because someone else is. They might be dead. Because of me.' Because of you and your amazing timing with your teenage drama, she's tempted to lash out, but that's not true. It's all on Gabi.

Words Like Wounds

Layla wakes from muddy dreams at the sound of the front door opening. She thought she was too wound up to sleep, but somehow she drifted off. She moves to check her phone and remembers she can't risk turning it on. NyanCat is curled up tight next to her, a warm furry ball of reassurance. She sits up and turns on the light, wiping the sleep from her eyes.

'You're not supposed to be here,' her mother says, stopping in the doorway. There's something wrong with her. 'I thought you were going to stay over at Cas's house again.'

'I needed to talk to you,' Layla says, sick with terror. It makes her feel hyper-attuned to everything. The sound of Gabi throwing her keys onto the desk by the front door, the bug pattering softly against the lightbulb, the glassy brightness of Gabi's eyes. 'Have you been *crying*, Mom? Are you drunk?'

'I've had *a* drink. Grown-up's prerogative. It's been a bad day.' She walks into the kitchen with particular deliberation. The soft pop of a cork, the clatter of ice: the good whiskey she keeps in the cupboard above the sink for special occasions or especially shitty days.

She comes out holding a coffee mug, drops onto the couch next to her daughter and rubs NyanCat behind the ears. The cat opens one eye and nudges its head up into her hand, purring.

'Least someone still likes me.'

'I saw the news,' Layla says, carefully. She's never seen Gabi this shattered.

'Yeah, well.' She takes a sip from the mug, which is three-quarters full, Layla notices with alarm. 'I got demoted and Travis's parents are dropping the charges. So, you and me, beanie, we got a load off. Although I spoke to your dad earlier, and he's riled. He said you had *not* called, as instructed—' She notices the revolver on the table and stops mid-sentence. 'Why is my gun out of the safe? *Jesus*, Layla.' She puts down the mug with a sharp clang and picks up the gun, flicking open the barrel to reveal that one bullet is missing. 'What did you *do*?' Totally alert now.

'Did someone hurt you? Shit, did you kill someone?' There's a sharpness in the way she says it that Layla hears as: 'Am I going to have to get a shovel and a carpet to wrap him in?'

'I was— oh God, Mom.' Layla grabs the mug and takes a big gulp of the whiskey. Gabi doesn't stop her. It tastes like gasoline, burning down her throat into her chest. But there's a soft blob in her mouth. She sets the mug down and spits into her hand, jerking her head like a cat, until she gets it out: the moth that was pattering against the light, half-drowned, still moving limply. 'Oh God,' she says again, in revulsion, but it's like the bug has made way for the words to come spilling out. All of it, in between racking sobs. The dumb shit they were doing online, trolling pervy boys on SpinChat, VelvetBoy and the diner and all the

409

awful messages she's been getting, and Jonno's offer and the money and their stupid, stupid blackmail ploy and the tussle over the gun.

Gabriella listens attentively and doesn't say anything until Layla runs out.

'Why didn't you tell me about this?' she says in a very soft, very dangerous voice. It's worse that she's not rampaging round the room breaking stuff. She once saw her mom throw an apple at her father's head in the middle of a particularly bad argument. It smashed in a splatter of pulp against the doorjamb.

'I was trying to sort it out. It was my fault. I didn't want you to have to deal with it.'

'You're fifteen years old! You can't sort out *shit*.' Gabi closes her eyes. 'Give me your phone.'

Layla hands it over, contrite. 'The messages are horrible, you shouldn't look. I can't even face turning it on.'

'And get your jacket.'

'Where are we going?'

'Tomorrow, you're getting on the first plane to Atlanta.'

'What? No!'

Gabi drops Layla's phone in the mug of whiskey.

'Are you crazy? Mom!'

'But right now, we're going to go dig a bullet out of a playground, so it doesn't mess up some future case if someone gets shot nearby. I've already screwed up one case. I'm not having this on my damn conscience too.'

'I'm sorry.' Layla trails after her, desperate. 'Please don't send me away.'

'Do you know where my toolbox is? We're going to need pliers, maybe a screwdriver to pry the slug out. Did you see where it went?'

'I said I'm sorry!'

'That doesn't cut it, Lay.' Gabriella turns on her. 'That's not enough. Sorry means that you *stop* doing stupid shit.'

Hotline Transcripts

Time: 14:07
(773)-936-[Redacted]
Caller #0054
Hi there, this is Amber Parkwood. The psychic. I helped your department with the train-track murders a few years ago?

Yes. Please could you ask the detective who found the body to call me. I have critical information from Daveyton Lafonte.

Yes, he has my number.

She.

Of course. Excuse me.

Her energy is very male.

Please ask her to call me. It really is critically important. Daveyton says the next body is going to be found in the river.

Time: 20:39
(412)-873-[Redacted]
Caller #0106
Hi, yes. Um. I have information about the man you're looking for.

Clayton Broom.

My name? Louanne.

You need my last name too?

All right. It's Becker.

No, Bee not Dee. That's B-E-C-K-E-R.

I dated him a few years ago, well, we went on *a* date. It was a mistake, I was drunk. I never would have... But never mind that.

The last time I saw him? I'm getting there, I'm getting there. Coupla weeks ago, before Halloween, he comes and finds me. Middle of the night, he hunts me down to a parking lot in Traverse City, can you believe that? And knocks on my car window.

Yes, I was in the vehicle at the time. I was sleeping in my car, all right? You never had a rough patch?

Fine, establishing the facts, whatever. Think I don't hear you judging me?

I'm trying to tell you what happened. Be patient, jeez! First you want every little detail, now you want me to rush?

Clayton knocks on my car window, wakes us up, me and Charlie.

He's my kid.

No, he can't corroborate.

He's two years old, ma'am! He can just about say mama and bottle and Buzz Lightyear.

Okay, Clay knocks on my window, scares the bejesus out of me. He's all talking crazy. About how he misses me and we can be a family. Then he starts in on his usual crazy shit. About this other dimension and I don't know. Like God gave him magic 3D glasses so he could see angels and devils.

No, not actual glasses. He always used to talk like that. Ever since I've known him. The waitresses at the diner used to rib

413

him about it. I guess I encouraged it. I'm not proud of that.

Oh, yeah. Yeah, I reckon he's definitely capable of all those things they say he's done. Stalked me halfway across the state, didn't he? Nearly ran me and my boy off the road when I took off. Serves him right he crashed his truck. Scared the bejesus outta me. But shit, if I think…

No, I don't know where he is now. He has a house in Detroit, don't he? You checked there?

No, that was the last time I saw him, smashing his car through the trees. I didn't stop to check.

No. I didn't call 9-1-1.

I just didn't.

I was scared. I didn't want to get involved.

I wasn't leaving the scene of an accident! I didn't cause it! He did. Going crazy like that.

Oh God, he's proper crazy. I never thought. I never would have—

No, I didn't hear anything from him after that. I guess I hoped he was dead. Not dead. That he'd learned his lesson. I took off anyway.

Pittsburgh, yeah that's where I'm calling from. It's nice enough. That's a lie. You try to get away, but every place is the same, you know? You're still right there in it.

I didn't want to report it. I wanted to forget the whole thing. I tried to put it outta my mind. Didn't even think about it again till I saw him on the TV. Hey, is it true what they're saying on the Internet?

Even though I was nearly one of his victims!? And you can't say? Don't I got a right to know?

I will take it up with the detective. You bet. You tell him to call me.

Yeah, I'll be willing to testify 'bout what happened. If it

414

helps you put him away.

This is the best number to get me on.

I don't have a permanent address right now. I'll give you my mom's in Burton.

Hey, you think I got a legal claim against the state?

For, I dunno, undue distress from being stalked by a madman who should have been locked away?

Well, can I get a restraining order?

Yeah, yeah, fine, I'll get a lawyer. Somewhere. No harm in asking. Not like the law is part of your job.

No, that's all.

Hey, hey wait. You still there? What do you think he was going to do to us? To Charlie and me?'

Time: 22:25
(313)-402-[Redacted]
Caller #0114

Yes. Police. The killer is outside my house! He's outside my house right now!

What? No.

No, he's black.

I don't know. Maybe early twenties? Thirties. It's hard to tell. He's got a black hoodie and a backpack.

What is he *doing*? What do you think he's doing! Figuring a way to get in and chop me up and stuff me like a turkey for Thanksgiving! Just like all those other murders on the news.

Excuse me? What kind of question is that? Have I been drinking? You should be asking where the killer is. You should be asking what *he's* drinking.

You mean right now? He's walking. Like he doesn't have a care in the whole world. Yeah, right past my house.

Don't tell me to calm down! He's outside my house! He's

going to break in here and kill me in my bed and the police don't give a flying fuck. I know my rights! I can stand my ground. That murdering son-of-a-bitch comes near my front porch and I'm gonna blow him away!

Hell yeah, I think you *should* dispatch someone. Right away. Damn straight.

For my own safety? I got a shotgun, lady. But all right, I'll stay on the line. But you tell your boys they better get here fast, because otherwise I'm going to shoot the shit out of the murdering nigger before he tries to do the same to me.

Time: 06:28
(313)-690-[Redacted]
Caller #0132
<Unintelligible sobbing>
He got…he got Ramón. You gotta come. He killed him. I can tell it's him by the shoes. Them red shoes. I gave him those damn shoes. But he's stuck. <Sobbing>

You gotta come…<sobbing> cut him down <unintelligible>

It's right here.

Where I'm standing! Here. It's corner of, let's see… I'm looking. Jefferson and, I, I don't know. The street sign has fallen down. Where that big mural of the eagle is. By the bus stop. Where the kid was killed. You know the one? Please come. Right away. Please.

Time 06:42
(313)-690-[Redacted]
Caller #0132
It's me, again, I'm sorry. 'Bout earlier. I— he's my friend. <Unintelligible>

Are you on your way? Please, you gotta come cut him down. He's stuck here with the bears and the balloons and <sobbing> his shoes sticking out. Please come.

I got the other street name. It's Clare. Corner of Jefferson and Clare. You got it? His name's Ramón Flores. I got to go. I know where he is.

Not Ramón. Ramón's right here. Aren't you listening? The man who *did* this to him. He's covered with, oh God, all kinds of stuff. I can't—

It's some kind of pattern. I don't understand it. Like the chairs.

What do you mean, what do I mean? The chairs. The fucking chairs! The patterns. He infects you. He brings things out!

No, I can't wait here. You just come get Ramón down. You phone Diyana. No, wait. Don't phone her. She can't see him like this. Phone Reverend Alan. Get him to keep her at the church. She mustn't come down here. Under no circumstances, you hear! She can't see this. Oh, Ramón, I'm sorry, man. I'm so sorry. Jesus.

No, I can't wait, I told you. I have to go find him. I know where he is. The chair told me. I have to go.

Time 06:45
(212)-495-[Redacted]
Caller #0133
Hey! Is that the hotline?

Oh man, this is so cool.

No, I'm phoning from Fort Green, in Brooklyn. We've got a theory about the killer. We know who she is. Well, me and Martin. Some of the others on the board think it's unlikely, you know, being a woman, but if you look at the footage from the party, there's this one woman who is acting incredibly suspicio—

What? The Detroit Monster board. On Reddit.

No.

Time 07:11
(606)-553-[Redacted]
Caller #0146
Yes, hello, Detroit PD.

Because I'm using a voice distorter.

Because I want to be anonymous.

This is not a waste of police time! We are doing your job for you. You should be grateful.

Time 08:17
(919)-167-[Redacted]
Caller #0398
We've figured out who the killer is. It's Clayton Broom!

No. I didn't see it on the news. We worked it out from the evidence.

Wait, it was on the news? Shit, I haven't checked the board this morning. Yep. You're right. There it is. My bad. Well, hope you find him!

Time 08:22
(313)-690-[Redacted]
Caller #0132
I know where he is. I found him. There's a truck—

No! Don't hang—

WEDNESDAY,
NOVEMBER 19

Come One, Come All

Ramón was a good disciple. He worked so hard to help Clayton move all the furniture and the newspapers and the sculptures to the place they had chosen. He helped arrange them, even though he didn't understand and he got scared when he saw how the dream was alive in them, how things stirred and rustled and turned their heads to look.

But it was able to reassure him that this was as it should be, that they were bringing everything together like storm clouds. The dream could feel it. The possibilities catching in people's minds. But it still had to show them what could be.

Ramón wanted to bring Diyana to show her that the work he was doing was important, and his friend, TK, because he didn't believe in this stuff, and he wanted to show him what could be possible. But the dream said he had to wait, there was one more thing it needed him for.

But he was upset when Clayton pulled the Police out of the car in the garage and told him they were going to do something special.

Ramón started crying then. Louder when he saw what the dream had made for him, his new head. He called out for Diyana and he fought. He hurt Clayton. He cut his arm with a chisel he picked up from the tool rack, tried to stab him in the neck. But it was only a chisel, not a knife, and Clayton was bigger and stronger and although the physical pain was alarming, the sharp burn of it firing through his nerves, the dream could push through it.

'This is what you wanted,' it told Ramón over and over, until he stopped struggling. 'This is what you wanted.'

It tucked the envelope into Ramón's mouth, his real mouth, underneath the big papa-bear head, like he was a mailbox. (Don't Kill The Messenger.) The card inside was hand-lettered.

> *Come One! Come All!*
> *Everyone is invited!*
> *Clayton Broom First Time Ever Solo Exhibition!*
> *The Fleischer Body Plant*
> *One Day Only! Don't Miss Out!*

They will find it and they will come, like disciples, and so will the reporters with their television cameras and their helicopters and the arrogant young man with his Internet, and everyone will see what they are supposed to see.

They will bring all their eyeballs, and all their minds will open like doors, and then maybe they will all be free too.

Head Like a Hole

TK sits on the bench, a new one, underneath what's left of Ramón and waits for the police to come. He has tried to be patient. He's already read all the cards for the kid, the tributes and prayers and outpourings of love and the police notice with the hotline number, squinting to make out the fine print under the sodium glare of streetlights.

He stares at his shoes, the scuffed black ones that keep blurring through his tears. It has taken all his willpower not to rip down the shit attached to Ramón's body and lower him to the ground. He doesn't have the heart to call Diyana, who called him late yesterday, worried, begging him to go out looking. Not yet. He can't face it.

Please, Jesus, I know we ain't had much truck of late, even at St. Raphael's. I know I've used your name in vain a shit-ton, and called you out as a phony for people who need comfort when the world don't got any. Like the huggie pillow they give little kids in kindergarten when they crying for their mommas. I never asked you for anything before. Not lately anyhow. Not since my momma. But I need you now. I need you to show me the way. I need a burning bush or maybe a giant flashing neon arrow. That would be good. Help me find the bastard, excuse me, Jesus, the sinner who did this to Ramón. The man Ramón's been working for, the crazy one. I won't shoot him. I don't even have a gun. Not this time. You can judge him, Lord. I'll let you handle that. You and the justice system. But help me find him. Show me the way.

He looks up, hoping for, he doesn't know, an archangel floating in a golden sunbeam, but the scenery hasn't changed; just shabby buildings, and the sky fading up to dawn and a gimmicky billboard for Debbie's Diamonds Dealers, a woman with take-me-to-bed-daddy eyes and tits popping out of a shiny gold dress, holding up her hand to show off the giant fake bling that flashes like Christmas lights.

It would be easy to overlook the faded sign behind it. OfficePlus: for all your office furniture needs. It has a woman joyously spinning across the room on a bright red office chair, having *so* much fun at work. Her arms are outstretched, as if reaching for something. To the west.

'If that's the best you got, I guess that's the best you got,' TK sighs. He gets up from the bench and turns to face Ramón, somewhere under that grotesque mask, like a bobble-head toy or a piñata. He hasn't been able to bring himself to try to pull it off. He's too afraid of what might be underneath. He forces himself to put his hand on Ramón's shoulder. 'I'll find him, buddy. You hold the fort 'til the cops come, okay?' He bites back a sob.

He phones the police hotline to try to explain, calmer now, but the woman on the other end of the line is as useless as she was the first time, so he walks down the road Happy Secretary on her red chair was pointing to – and walks and walks.

Past a shuttered RiteAid, a small church, an apartment block with the jabber of morning radio shows leaking faintly through the double glazing as the yellow light sneaks up the edge of the horizon.

He walks until the sun is fully up, bringing the first morning traffic with it, sullen metal animals migrating toward the highways, and walks and walks, until he sees the second sign.

An old chair, set out as if awaiting an occupant. Battered, but well made, the wood dark and heavy.

It is at the entrance of a dusty parking area. No entry, the signs say. Condemned. Set back between the trees is a blocky building with broken windows and barbed wire.

TK looks askance at the chair. The brown leather of the seat is cracked from years of use. 'Here? For real?' The chair doesn't answer.

He clambers over the chain and walks up the driveway toward the building, glancing back at the street. The traffic has thinned again. There's no-one to see him go in.

He tries the police hotline again. Five times. It's engaged over and over. Motherfuckers. Fine. He's been through worse, on his own. This is God's plan, right? If only he believed in God.

He walks right to the entrance. Someone has cut open the padlock, but kept the chain looped around the gate, so it still looks locked to a casual observer. TK knows this place; he knows men who used to work here in the nineties, back when they were installing all those fancy new robots. The Fleischer Body Plant. There are trees and thick bunches of ivy clinging to the sides, like the hanging gardens of Babylon. Nature finds a way back. He is thinking about this as a way of distracting himself from what he's doing, which is slipping through the gate, leaving it wide open behind him in the hope someone notices, strolling down the driveway like he is not forcing himself to take every step.

The entrance is boarded over. He saw that already from the outside. He knows from personal experience that when someone is squatting in a place, they'll prop it up loosely, make it look like it's still sealed up. But this one actually is. He yanks at the chipboard, but the nails are immovable. Job for a crowbar. He pulls at it again, for luck, but it doesn't give.

He walks round the back and spots a white pick-up truck half-hidden behind a collapsed wall. The windscreen is cracked and the canopy has a heavy dent in it, as if someone went over the top. Shit. He can't do this alone. He ducks down and hits redial on his phone and halle-fuckin-lujah, the call goes through.

'Detroit PD hotline,' the operator says. 'This better not be another crank.'

TK turns away, hunching over the phone, whispering. 'I know where he is. I found him. There's a truck— No! Don't hang up on me. Don't you dare! Godfuckingdammit!' He stares at the phone in disbelief and resists the urge to hurl it to the ground. 'Sorry, Jesus,' he says.

He phones St. Raphael's, but Reverend Alan's line rings and rings and rings and finally goes to voicemail. His service informs him he has one minute of call-time left.

He could call 9-1-1, but the answer is right there in his contacts list: he saved the number after they watched the video together, him and Ramón and Dennis. 'YouTube Guy $$$.'

'This is Jonno Haim,' the voice answers immediately.

'The cops won't listen to me.' He is on the verge of tears again.

'I'll listen. What's your name?'

'TK. He killed Ramón. Just as bad as the others. Maybe worse. But I followed him here. He's inside. I know he is.'

'Okay, TK, I believe you. Where are you now? Who is Ramón? Where is he?' His voice is calm, in control.

'Some place called the Fleischer Body Plant. Ramón's at the bus stop. Where the little boy was killed.'

'Can you wait for me? I need to check this out.'

'This place makes me feel sick,' TK says. And yet he's stepping under the avenue of trees that runs down the side of the building. Drawn in. The bare branches are knitted over his head, like a tunnel. He can see the windows upstairs, also bare. There are people watching him through the dirty glass. Hundreds of them.

'I found it,' Jonno says on the other end of the phone. TK had almost forgotten he was there at all. 'Big abandoned factory, near the freeway.'

'That's the one. Hey, Mr. Haim, I can hear someone inside.' Or something. Tik-takking. Skittish chairs, cantering across rotten wooden floors. He can't think like that. 'I think there are people upstairs. Children maybe.' They're so slight. Bony, he thinks. With malformed heads. Balloon heads. Like Ramón's head. TK tastes bile in his throat.

'I'll be there in twenty minutes. Just wait for me. Can you do that?'

'I don't know, man. I think we need the police.'

'Twenty minutes max. I'll call the cops. I promise. I'll see you soon. We'll be in a blue Hyundai. Watch out for us. Hang tight, TK.'

He wants to. He really does. He could go back out the front, past the chain and the lounger and wait for Jonno to come to the rescue in his blue car, the police behind him.

427

But he's drawn into the tunnel of trees. Deeper.

The children watch. Leaning over at crazy angles.

I'm coming to get you, he thinks. There's a door at the end of the tunnel. It's drawn on the wall. Just an outline in chalk, but it's glowing, and he knows it will open for him.

The Red Shoes

It's like a puzzle. Where's Waldo. You have to look really closely to see the man hidden in the debris of affection. It doesn't help that his head is gone, replaced with a remarkable approximation of a teddy bear, an oversized bobble-head made out of papier-mâché and painted baby blue, peeking out among the forlorn stuffed toys bunched up around him, as if he's trying to fit in. The head has big round ears and a soft blue fuzz growing on it, like bread mold. The sockets are hollowed out and painted over with dollar signs. The mouth is a red painted X.

You have to look carefully to see that the head is resting on human shoulders in a puffy black jacket, which has other toys stapled to it. The hands, like the head, are missing, and have been replaced with fat balloon fingers, like Mickey Mouse gloves. Two of the fingers have popped already. The real clue is the feet, red sneakers with an oil stain on one toe, sticking out the bottom, brushing the chalk rectangle drawn on the sidewalk, like a hangman's trapdoor.

Mainly, she's relieved that it's not Marcus. But that means he's still out there. Still alive. Maybe. Boyd fills her in. The victim's name is Ramón Flores, if their anonymous informant is to be believed. They have people working to confirm that, on the information they've been given, starting with phoning all the local churches to track down 'Reverend Alan'.

The man who called it in is long gone, just as he said he would be – and he is not answering his phone.

'You should have heard Stricker crapping out the operator. He's plenty mad,' Boyd says.

'He should be.' She feels restless, not sure where she stands now. Luke is crouched down with Evidence Tech, examining the sidewalk. She wants to remind them that the blood spatter might be old, might be Daveyton's, but it's not her case now. Croff is pacing up and down in agitation, talking into his mobile.

They've cordoned off the street. Again. But this isn't a tunnel. There isn't a way to control the news vans with their telephoto lenses or the people crowded outside the police tape, craning their necks to see. She goes over to the paramedics who are standing by, smoking, and asks if she can borrow a medical screen to shield some of the scene, at least.

'Fuuuuuuck!' Croff yells. 'That motherfucking blogger!'

'What's that about?' Gabi asks.

'It's out,' Boyd says. 'On the Internet.'

'*This*? Already?'

'Your boy – Jonno. Mikey's taking it very personally.'

'How the hell did he get it so fast? Is he here?'

'I'm not sure. The post went up half an hour ago. Before we got here. You ever think he's the one doing it?'

'That idiot? No. No way in hell.' But isn't that what policing is about? The uncomfortable truth that anyone is capable of anything. Croff is now screaming at the Fox News Detroit journo to back the fuck off, so Gabi takes the initiative and looks up the blogger's number on her phone – and his little girlfriend's.

Infuriatingly, neither of them is answering.

'Mr. Haim. This is Detective Versado. Gabriella. Call me back please. You're not in trouble. But I need to know where you are, if you're with the man who called in this new murder, it's—' The service cuts her off.

She phones again, it rings and rings and finally goes to voicemail. 'Jonno. I need to know where you are. You might have the information we need to take us to the killer. We have a missing officer. We need to find him. Please call me back immediately.'

She hangs up before the infernal message system has a chance to interrupt her again.

'Detective? Can you help me out here?' A female uniform approaches her. 'This is Reverend Alan from St. Raphael's.' She introduces a wiry man with a white collar under his black shirt and the deep calm of the true believer.

'Hello,' he says, shaking her hand. 'I'm so sorry about this.'

'Me too, Reverend. Believe me. But I think our lead investigator should probably be interviewing you.'

'Can you handle it?' Luke calls. 'We're a little busy here.' The team is trying to get under the body to see how it's attached to the bus stop without disturbing any evidence.

'Yes, Detective.' She walks the priest over to the bus stop, close enough to see without getting in anyone's way. She indicates the body. 'Can you identify this man?'

He is appalled. 'No. I don't… How could anyone? My God.'

'How about the shoes. Do they look familiar?'

'I…I don't know. I don't really pay attention to shoes.'

'Someone in your congregation?' She leads him away again.

'I'm sorry.'

'Do you know a Diyana?'

'Diyana? Yes. Diyana Green, she's a regular at the soup kitchen. But *this* isn't Diyana. This isn't a woman, is it?' It sinks in. 'Oh, no. Is that Ramón?'

'Do you know how to get hold of Ms. Green?'

'The office might. Can I call my office? TK would know.'

'Who is TK?'

'Thomas Keen. He works as our community liaison. He does several hours a week with us. Computers, job advice, general dogsbody. He knows everyone. He's close to Ramón. He could probably identify him.'

'Does he have a cell phone?'

'Yes. One of those subsidized phones.'

'Do you happen to know the number?'

'Hold on.' He takes out his phone and scrolls through the address book, his hands shaking. He reads out the number that the hotline logged.

Gabriella writes it down as if it is new information.

'Do you know where he lives? Do you know any other way to get hold of him?'

'What is this about?' he says, as if he's not standing in front of a dead man bound to a pole with a hundred teddy bears stapled to his body.

'We believe he's an eyewitness. But it's also possible he may have been involved.'

'Not TK.'

'Thomas Michael Keen,' Boyd calls out from the squad car, reading from his file on the computer. 'Served ten years for murdering a man when he was fourteen. Since then,

432

breaking-and-entering, drugs, assault. Most recent charge was a year ago, fist-fight at St. Raphael's, but the charges were dropped.'

'It was a misunderstanding.'

'This guy works for you?'

'Everyone deserves a second chance. Or a third one or a fourth, or however many it takes. God doesn't have a three-strikes law.'

'He's a convicted killer and you have him working in your church?'

'No-one else would take him. Would you?'

'You think he's capable of this?'

'Absolutely not. Under no circumstances. He was a kid when he shot the man who murdered his mother, but he called it in right away. He gave himself up. And after that, the system failed him. He could never do this. Ramón was his friend.'

'How close was he to Diyana?'

'No. I know that's your job. To imagine the worst things you can. But there was no...romantic rivalry or whatever it is you're trying to suggest. TK didn't do this.'

'Well, he called it in, and he's not answering his phone. Maybe he was trying to give himself up again.'

'Isn't this the work of your serial killer? The Detroit Monster? And you're trying to pin TK as an accomplice? That's absurd. I won't help you do this.'

'We don't know anything until we do. If you can help us find Thomas, we can exonerate him. But we need to know what he's seen, if he saw the killer. And we need to identify this body. Can you help us with that?'

His shoulders sink in resignation. 'Let me phone the office.'

'I'm going to have to leave you with my colleague,

Reverend.' She checks the time on her phone. 'Bob, can you take over? I have to take Layla to the airport.'

'Want to pick up the FBI agent while you're there?' Boyd says.

'Not particularly.'

'Kidding. He's only flying in this afternoon.'

'Detective Stricker? May I be excused?' She can't keep the gall out of her voice.

'Of course.' And he can't keep the awful sympathy out of his.

Leaving on a Jet Plane

Layla has packed and repacked twice. She's hauled out the box of old books and toys her dad left behind to give to her step-brother and step-sister. NyanCat has found the pet-carrier and is nesting in it on an old towel, padding and purring in delight at this new hidey-hole. Wait until the cage door closes.

Her mom is late, which makes her think maybe she's got a reprieve. She had a stilted call with her father this morning – she's dreading the big fat lecture awaiting her the moment she touches down in Atlanta – and then a call to Cas to say goodbye, both under Gabi's watchful eye. Then her mom unplugged the landline and took the phone away with her, along with the computer power cord. To keep her out of trouble, she said. It could be worse. She could be going to Aunt Cheryl for some Jesus therapy or, worse, to Miami to stay with her grandparents, who would be insufferable told-you-sos about how many times they'd warned Gabi about raising a child in Detroit.

She's tried to dry out her mobile by putting it in a bag of uncooked rice, which supposedly sucks out the moisture, but maybe that doesn't apply to twelve-year-old scotch, because her phone is deader than her reputation.

She thought about running away. Moving in with Cas. Maybe they could build a secret room for her in the closet, and her parents wouldn't even have to know.

That's the most fucked-up thing about being sent to Atlanta – that the only person who has any idea what she's going through is here, in Detroit.

Her mom hoots from outside, two short, sharp notes.

'C'mon, Nyan,' Layla says, closing the door on the carrier and hoisting it up along with her suitcase. The cat immediately starts howling.

'That's how I feel too,' she says, swinging the suitcase into the open trunk. She sets the carrier down on the back seat and moves to climb in beside it.

'No, I need you up front. I have to make calls and I want you to help me.' Gabi is already tapping at her phone, her hair escaping her hastily pulled-up ponytail. At least they won't have to continue The Talk, Layla thinks, sliding in next to her. It's a reprieve; her mom consumed by the job, her focus tugged away from her.

Butterflies in Your Stomach

'What do you want me to do, Jen?' Jonno is pacing outside the chain gate.

'Quit shouting at me!' She looks desperately unhappy, leaning on the chair someone (a security guard?) has placed outside.

Maybe that's your special talent. Making women unhappy.

'I'm not shouting,' he says, lowering his voice.

'We should call the police.'

'I will. As soon as we've got the footage we need. Just the outside. We film the call. It'll be great.'

'This is so stupid. This is the all-time stupidest thing I have ever done. There might be a madman in there.'

'It's probably a false alarm. He's not even here. No-one's here. Not even the guy who called me.'

'How do you *know* the Detroit Monster isn't in there right now? With a gun pointed at our heads?'

'This guy doesn't use a gun. Be logical, baby.'

'Fuck logic. I'm scared.'

'Of course you're scared! You've spent your whole life being scared! That's why you're a DJ living with your dad!

Cowboy up, Jen.'

She recoils and he knows he's pushed it too far, but they're *already* too far, and there's no going back. He softens, in case she decides to climb into her car and drive away. He needs her to film.

'C'mon. It's history. Imagine someone had been there when the cops came for Jeffrey Dahmer, filming it? Or that horror house in Cleveland? Got it on camera as it happened. Not after-the-fact, follow-up interviews, no cheesy re-enactments. The real deal. This is JFK-bullet-in-the-head stuff. OJ on the highway. This is the Zapruder film of serial killers.'

'That's great,' she says, sarcastically.

'It will be iconic. Every news channel in the world will be showing this. *Our* footage. We'll be famous forever. Don't you want that? Think of the doors it will open for us. We can do anything we want after this. Anything.'

'Just outside?' she wavers.

'One set-up for an intro, then we call the cops, on camera, and wait across the street until they get here, then we can follow them in. Tell you what, we'll even live-stream it. That way we got half the Internet watching our backs.' And the hits coming in, so that CNN and Fox and BBC World will be calling *him* before the hour is up. He updated the contact details on his YouTube channel while Jen was driving over here. He's already getting text messages from numbers he doesn't know. 'Yo is this shit 4real?' 'Yay! Creepypasta!' whatever the fuck that means. No phone call from Rupert Murdoch. Yet. Although he does have eight missed calls from 'Bitch Detective'.

Jen looks up at the building apprehensively. 'I still think this is a bad, bad, terrible idea.'

438

'I won't let anything happen to you. I promise. You ready to roll?'

Jen nods, and raises the camera phone.

'The Fleischer Body Plant,' Jonno says. 'Just another blight highlight in a city over-run with abandoned buildings. Except that twisted serial killer, Clayton Broom, nicknamed the Detroit Monster, is rumored to be holed up inside.'

He starts crossing the parking lot, to the back of the building.

Jen hisses at him. 'What are you doing?'

'Come on. We need to change up the shot.'

Jen follows him reluctantly, picking her way over the rubble. There's discarded furniture everywhere. Not junk, either. Nice stuff. Worn, antique even, as if someone was starting to haul it inside and got tired.

'I don't feel good, Jonno. I need to check my numbers.'

'Can you hold out one minute for me, please, baby? Are you having a low? Oh shit! Do you think this is his truck? Film the license plate. Zoom right in on it.'

But Jen isn't paying attention. She's standing swaying slightly. 'I don't think so. It doesn't feel like a high either. It's different. Butterflies in your stomach? You know that feeling?' She wrinkles up her nose. 'Something fluttering inside me.'

'Are you filming?' He takes up a position next to the truck and puts on his camera voice. 'Is this the car Clayton Broom used to transport little Daveyton Lafonte's body before he mutilated him? Is this where he brought him to do it?' He points at the factory: 'Pan up to the windows. Low angle.'

'Are we calling the police now?'

'One more shot and then we'll do it. And then you can shoot up or have a snack or whatever you need to do. Up against the wall so you get an extreme angle on the building. Hey, neat, there's one of those chalk doors behind you,' he says. 'Maybe I should stand there. That would be a great framing device, right?' But she's not paying attention, rubbing at her chest with one hand and he can see that it's jiggling the camera.

'Baby doll, can you focus?'

'It is in focus!' she snaps, still rubbing at her chest.

'I mean cut that out, you're making the camera shake.'

'It hurts,' she says, looking down her jacket. 'Ow!' She jerks violently and drops the phone. She grabs at her zip, yanking it down. 'Something's biting me!'

'What are you doing?' Jonno picks up the camera phone and examines the fine line zagging across the screen. 'You've cracked it, Jen, goddammit.'

'I'm bleeding,' Jen says, showing him the red seeping through her cream sweater. There's something hard and dark nudging up under it. She pulls off her sweater. 'Don't film this!' she cries as he raises the phone automatically.

She's standing there in the freezing cold in only her bra. The pale green one with polka dots. He wishes she would wear sexier lingerie. There's something wrong with her tattoo, the birds spiraling up her collar bone onto her neck. There are sharp objects, arrowheads, pushing through the ink, and he realizes that this is all wrong. Badly wrong. 'Forget this. You're right. Come on, we're going back to the car. We're calling the police.'

'It's coming out,' Jen says, detached, watching the pointy tips poking through, the blood running down her chest, soaking into her bra. 'I'm falling, Jonno.'

'No. No, you're not. I've got you.' He grabs at her arm. But she *is* falling, backwards through the outline of the door that is suddenly a gaping hole behind her, and the things poking out of her chest are not arrowheads, they're beaks attached to dark feathered heads, slick with blood, with bright black eyes. She's falling, and he's falling with her and there are birds squirming out of her chest and he lets go of her hand.

To save himself.

He cowers and uses his arms to shelter his face from the torrent of crows with their slashing beaks and battering wings bursting out of his girlfriend.

Like Meat

It's excruciating. This is Layla's last chance to beg for another chance, but her mother is preoccupied, on the phone.

'Well, can you trace a trackerphone? Do we need a warrant to triangulate it?' A truck blasts past, the Crown Vic rocking in its wake.

'Hang on, I've got another call. It's him, the blogger. I'll phone you back. Hello?' Gabi jerks her head back from the phone in reaction to the static-squeal coming through the speaker. It sounds like a buzzsaw in a wind tunnel. There's someone screaming.

'Hello? Mr. Haim?'

'Help! Fuck. Help. Oh God, Jen. The birds. This place, it's— Jesus. Fuck! What was that? What *was* that? Jen. She's really hurt. And shit, oh shit. I don't know what's going on.'

'Jonno, where are you?'

Gabi yanks the car over to the side of the road and stops abruptly, flicking on the blue and red police lights.

'An old factory,' the man on the other end of the phone is hysterical, shouting loud enough that Layla can hear him.

442

'An auto plant. Fleischer something.'

'Not Fischer? You're sure? I'm calling it in. Stay on the line with me.'

'Fleischer like meat. Fuck. She's hurt. She's bleeding. I think I can see her heart. Oh God, I'm going to puke.' His voice crackles and disappears into the screeching wind.

Gabi flicks on the radio, 'Dispatch. 10-35. Possible 0900 at the Fleischer Body Plant. Priority Code Faline. I repeat: Faline. All cars.' She starts typing the address into the computer, the phone wedged under her chin. 'Jonno. Keep talking to me.'

'Mom?' Layla says. Gabi looks at her like she's forgotten she's there. In full cop mode.

'Here, take the phone. Keep talking to him. Even if he doesn't answer.' She shoves the phone at Layla and gestures impatiently. 'Hello. Jonno? Um. This is Layla. Layla Stirling-Versado. I'm going to keep talking to you.'

'Dispatch, can you confirm the address for the Fleischer Body Plant? Yeah, I'm putting it into the GPS.' She nods at Layla, 'Ask him what he can see.'

'What can you see?' Layla repeats. 'Um. Are there any windows? Doors? Is there someone threatening you right now? Can you get to a safe place?'

She looks askance at her mother, but Gabi is preoccupied with the GPS. The robot voice says, 'Your destination is twenty-four minutes away. Drive straight for six miles, then turn right.'

'Fuck that,' Gabi says. She twists round in her seat, putting her arm over the backrest. 'Keep talking, Layla. Are you buckled up?'

Gabi flips on the siren and Layla flinches at the aural assault. She concentrates on trying to find useful things to say. 'Can you see any landmarks? Is there anyone near you? Uh. Do you know CPR? You should probably do that, if she's bleeding. Try and stop the bleeding. Pressure is important.'

Gabi throws the Crown Vic into reverse, heedless of the oncoming cars swerving around them, hooting their outrage. It all merges with the howling from the phone and the blaring siren and the yowling cat, so that Layla wants to cover her ears, but she tries to stay calm, keep talking, even though there's nothing but noise on the other side. She sticks her fingers through the holes in the pet carrier to touch Nyan's fur, as much to reassure herself as the cat.

'Are you still there? We spoke on the phone. Before. Remember? I'm Detective Versado's daughter. Oh shit, Mom, watch out!'

A silver Taurus misses them by a whisker. The driver is screaming and waving his hands as he zooms past, underneath the sign for the off ramp. And suddenly it all makes sense, this crazy reversing down the highway. The GPS has changed its tune.

'Take the off-ramp,' the calm robot voice declares. 'Your destination is two minutes away.'

Gabi hits the brakes, hard, shifts the car into drive, and roars up the exit.

Brain Stew

Jonno is standing in a huge warehouse space, with pillars and windows that have been painted over. The light leaking through is greenish. Poisonous, he thinks. The room is trashed. Broken bricks and black plastic garbage bags and piles of newspapers with a narrow passageway between them. The cicada sound is still ongoing, a deep buzzing that sets his teeth on edge.

Dark feathers drift down like snowflakes, carpeting the floor. Jen is lying on the ground in front of him, her chest and neck ripped apart, exposing the bloody tendons. Like an anatomical drawing. He knew someone who had a tattoo like that, the musculature finely detailed on the outside of his calf. It was vile.

He fumbles for his phone and his thumb flicks automatically to the camera icon.

Phone. It's a phone, you dumb fuck. Phone someone for help.

He taps the green phone icon and hits return call on the most recent missed call, the name he saved as 'Bitch Detective'. Then he deliberately selects speaker phone and swipes back to the camera while he listens to it ring. It's not just a phone. There's no reason he can't call and keep filming. He's calm. This is a hallucination. What did Jen say about the chemicals and asbestos in old buildings like this?

The phone on the other side rings and rings. Pick up, come on. He's looking at the screen, still on camera mode, and the muscle around Jen's chest peels back, revealing a black cavity inside her, total darkness beneath the slim white arches of her ribs. Something moves underneath them.

She's dead. You know that, right? She's dead. And you're not hallucinating. And you're pretty much fucked now, boychick.

The thrumming is louder. The trash bags are scuffling. Rats. Pigeons.

It's not rats.

The phone rings. Pick up!

The lady detective answers and the sound of her voice cracks through his calm like a hoof through a windshield.

'Help!' He says it weakly, because the words have fled. Fluttered away. 'Fuck. Help. Oh God, Jen. The birds. This place. It's…'

A rush of white brushes past his face, brittle and papery against his skin. He whirls. 'Jesus. Fuck! What was that? What *was* that?'

'Jen. She's really hurt. She's diabetic. I think she might be— And shit, oh shit. I don't know what's going on.'

He hears the detective's voice from far away. An old gramophone transmitted through a seashell. He manages to decipher the question. 'Fleischer. The Fleischer Plant,' he says and turns the camera back on Jen. Her eyes are wide open with a look of wonder. That sweet curiosity. All her delight in the world, ripped right out of her.

'She's hurt. She's bleeding. I think I can see her heart. Oh God. I'm going to puke.'

He gags, his hands flying to his face and for a moment everything is normal again. Or as normal as it can be. The room is just a room. Jen is just dead, and there is nothing stirring in the black hole of her chest.

There is a girl's voice coming from the phone speaker, familiar, conspiratorial. It's the detective's daughter. Talking about CPR as if he could breathe life back into Jen's ruined chest. The deep buzzing sound is getting louder. Not cicadas any more, but a jet engine gearing up.

Abandonment Issues

The red dot on the GPS is three blocks away. Close enough, Gabi thinks. Layla is still talking into her cell phone, meaningless gabble, because Jonno still isn't responding and she's run out of medical advice. She's proud of her for holding it together. She's even secretly proud of her insane adventure. Impressed, too, that she got away with impersonating a police officer. Not that she would ever tell her. They were up until dawn, trying to find the damn slug, buried in the splintered wood of the merry-go-round.

When all this is done, when Layla is on a plane and safely away from here, she intends to look up this pedophile and shoot him in the head. She knows which abandoned building she'll dump his body in, how to set a fire to make it look like dumb kid arsonists. Then maybe she'll quit this whole gig. Go private like William. Special prosecutions investigator, maybe. Somewhere nice where they only have rich-people problems. Ann Arbor, you say?

'Just stay calm,' Layla says into the phone. 'We're on our way. The police are nearby. How is your friend? Hey, did you know I'm in a play? It's pretty cool. You should come.

I'll get you a ticket. Unless you don't like musicals.' Increasingly desperate. 'Are you still there? I'm here. I'll stay on the line talking to you until the police arrive.'

Gabi pulls over and leaves the engine running. She gets out.

'Mom! Where are you going?'

'I *am* the police, sugarbean.' You do what you have to.

'No, wait,' Layla clambers out after her, still holding the phone. 'You can't go in alone. I can't drive a police car!'

Gabi ignores her. They are way past worrying about regulations now. She pops the trunk and yanks her bullet-proof vest out from under Layla's suitcase and starts pulling it on. Because you never know. You could be getting takeout and someone hits the ATM next door. You could find yourself at the serial killer's hideout in some godforsaken part of abandoned industria near the airport, with back-up still ten, maybe twenty minutes away. And maybe Sparkles is still alive in there.

She glances at the building through the trees. It's squat and low, like an oversized Lego block. 'Give me the phone, Layla. Jonno. If you're listening, I'm here. Can you tell me anything about where you are?' There's nothing but crack-ling for a while, and then a man's voice, sobbing.

'Oh God. Oh God. Don't kill me.'

And that decides it. Like she had another choice. Gabi slides out the clip of her Smith & Wesson. Shit, she wishes she had more rounds with her. Next time.

'Don't you have to wait for back-up? Mom!'

'They'll be here any minute.'

'So wait for them!' Layla screams at her.

Gabi takes her daughter by the shoulders and guides her toward the driver's side, where the door is still open. 'Marcus

449

Jones might be in there. He might be alive. And someone else is hurt. Badly. I can't wait. Do you understand? I need you to get back in the car and drive yourself somewhere safe. Home or Cas's house or the nearest police station.'

'Drive myself?' Layla starts to cry.

'You've got it down, Lay. Except for parallel parking, but you don't have to do that today. Just get yourself home. You can do this.'

'I don't have a phone. You drowned it.'

'You don't need it. Drive somewhere safe.'

'I can't. I can't. Please don't make me,' Layla sobs. Gabi pushes her down into the seat and puts her hands on the wheel.

'You have to. I need you to get out of here right now. Put it in drive.'

'Mom...' she pleads, even while she's doing what she's told.

'It's not you I'm worried about. It's Nyan. You want your cat to be safe, don't you?'

Layla glances into the back where NyanCat is crouched low in the cage, a miserable bundle of fur with big eyes, quiet for once. 'Yes?' she says, uncertainly.

'So drive, Layla. I love you.' It's a heavy load for those three words. Because what she means is I'm sorry. I'm sorry I was busy and I'm sorry I have to go inside and I might not see you again and I didn't tell you enough that I'm proud of you, even though you do stupid shit, because it comes from the right place and that's rare and precious, and you'll grow up to be a good woman, and you won't make the same dumb mistakes I did, you'll make your own, but hopefully only to get you on course, and the world is greater and richer with you in it, sugarbean.

She shuts the door and slaps the top of the car, hard, as you might a horse's rump. Layla gets such a fright that she puts her foot down, and the car leaps forward and swerves across the street. She pulls it back on course.

'Carefully!' Gabi shouts after her, watching her long enough to see Layla take a wide turn on the corner, tears streaming down her face as she glances back fearfully at her mother. She waves her on until she's out of sight.

Safe.

The Inside Scoop

One of the trash bags in the darkness moves. Not a bag. A man, crouching there all this time, watching him. He stands. His face is blank or peeling, and there is clotted blood on his neck, spattered down his shirt. 'You came,' he says.

'Shit!' Jonno scrambles back against the wall, waving the phone like it's a magic wand that can keep the thing at bay. 'No. Nonononono. Detective!' he screams into the phone.

Realization sinks in. 'It's you. The gallery guy. They had your picture on the news. But it didn't look like you, your hair was shorter, you had a beard. Oh God, you were trying to show me something at the party....'

The man keeps drifting toward him. *Drifting*, not walking. 'You're part of the infection,' he says. 'You're the messenger. You're going to help me.'

'Fuck off, leave me alone. I don't know what you're talking about. What's wrong with your face?'

'Sorry. I forget. It's easy to forget. I have to hold on to things so tightly.' It shoves its hands up over its cheeks and his face takes shape. A half-remembered semblance of Clayton Broom. The eyes too deep, too small, too far apart, the nose a malformed lump. The scab on his neck is weeping blood. When he speaks, his jaw opens up too wide. Kermit the Frog, Jonno thinks. Like someone has his hand stuck up inside him.

'Christ,' Jonno screams. 'Jesus fucking Christ, don't kill me.'

'No,' Clayton says. The face looks amused. A semblance of what it thinks amused might be. 'I won't. I need you. You and your Internet to set it all loose.'

Nowhere but Up

Gabi circles round the building. The front door is sealed. So are all the windows, on the ground floor at least. But there must be a way in. No sign of Jonno and his friend. Jennifer, she thinks. No, Jen. Whose heart might be visible – an injury that sounds fatal, in her professional opinion.

White pick-up truck parked out of sight. He's here. Or was. She edges down along the wall, through an alleyway of trees with black squirrels skittering between them. There is one of those damn painted doorways on the wall, and she wonders if a simple rectangle has ever inspired so much dread. Coffins maybe.

And there. A rusty fire-escape running up the side of the building. A door hanging off its hinges at the top. Somewhere she can get inside. She tries to radio it in, but gets only a burst of static. Her cell phone has no signal.

She doesn't think Clayton is sophisticated enough to have blockers in place. It could be the building, all the metal inside messing up the electronics.

Someone screams inside. A man. Pure terror. Marcus, she thinks, although the rational part of her knows he's dead.

Has been dead since Monday morning when she rejected his phone call in the principal's office. She knows this is true. Which means it's Jonno. Or Thomas Keen. Or someone she might be able to save.

Dammit. She has been hoping for sirens, for good men and women in uniform storming over the rubble with guns.

'Dispatch, I'm going in,' she tells the useless radio and starts running up the stairs.

Nothing's Accidental

Layla is trying to concentrate. But she keeps looking back in the mirror, hoping to see her mom, who has gone now, disappeared into the terrible building with its blacked-out windows and broken glass. She can't pull her eyes away from it. Her mom is going to die in there – they both know it. Isn't that what she was saying? She's sobbing so hard, she can barely see the road through the tears, but she has to get home. She has to get somewhere safe. She promised.

She steers the car round the corner, not even knowing where she's going. Back toward the highway, but that's terrifying. She doesn't know if she can handle it on her own. She should take the back streets. She presses the GPS. Home.

'Turn left,' the calm woman's voice says, with mechanical confidence.

But when she does, it's to see the blunt ugly factory directly in front of her again. No. She glances fearfully in the rear-view mirror and sees that it is *also* behind her. Like an Escher loop.

She panics and slams on the brakes, stabbing at the GPS screen with a frantic finger. 'Home, goddammit!'

When she was a little kid, her mom told her that the GPS was a robot lady in the sky who watched down on them from her space station.

'Like God?' Layla said, innocently, which made both her parents laugh.

But now no-one's watching. Not the robot lady in the sky, not God. She's on her own. With a hysterical cat mewling in the back. Calm down. Deep breaths. Cas's mom took them to a yoga class once. She closes her eyes. Find your center. Feel the roots going deep down, anchoring you to the earth.

It's two similar but different buildings. Probably a bunch of them in this broke-down industrial hell. She opens her eyes and keeps her attention on the chunky little screen that will get her home, specifically avoiding looking up or behind her. She doesn't know what she'll do if she's wrong. If they're the same place, and she's caught in between.

'Turn around,' the computer voice says with implacable calm and authority. 'Turn around.' No shit. She guides the car into a U-turn. NyanCat raises her voice to a howl. Like a siren or a blaring horn. But it *is* a blaring horn, an eighteen-wheeler MACK truck bearing down on her and she's stuck in the middle of the road. Layla screams and hits the gas, yanking the steering wheel to the side as hard as she can, but the truck still clips her.

There is a brittle crunch, the same sound NyanCat makes when she's eating a grasshopper. The window shatters, a bright rain of glitter falling in on her. The Crown Vic spins across the road. She can't control it. The car is full of moths suddenly. The steering wheel snaps off in her hand.

The car turns, weightless. It hits the curb, and gravity reasserts itself and just before the airbag leaps up into her face, she sees a tunnel of trees opening up in front of her, the branches folding back with balletic grace, to grant her entry.

But she knows it's a trap, that they will close up behind her, like a fairytale, and no-one will ever see her again, and there will be no sign that she was ever here.

And then she cracks her head on the side window and a womb-red darkness roars up around her.

Mechanical Animals

It's too dark to see, so TK feels his way into the tunnel of trees that has turned into a corridor that clangs metallically under every step. He has to crouch so he doesn't hit his head on the ceiling, waddling forward, bandy-legged like a cowboy. His shoulders are cramped, his knees aching, but there are tinny voices reverberating from somewhere ahead, and warmth and light.

He emerges into a bright room with floral curtains and a fire in the fireplace and a dining table piled with food for Thanksgiving – turkey and barbecue ribs and sweet-potato mash and grits and plastic cups of Kool-Aid – and all his friends are here, waiting for him. Ramón, with his big teddy-bear head, leaning jauntily with one elbow propped on the fireplace, and Diyana, braiding her hair, which is so long it trails on the floor. Even Lanny is there, wearing an apron that says 'World's Best Cook'. And there's his sister Florence, perched on the edge of the table, reading a book, her fingers scrabbling over the raised bumps of the words like spiders.

They're all so happy to see him.

459

'Welcome *home*,' Lanny says and slaps him on the shoulder.

'Do you like it, Thomas?' Diyana says, smiling a blazing smile of white teeth, while her hands knot and twist, braiding, braiding, braiding.

'Happy Thanksgiving!' Ramón says, his voice distorted by his big piñata head.

'There are no chairs,' TK laughs. 'Where's a man gonna sit down?'

'Who has time to sit?' Lanny complains. 'We've been getting everything ready for you.'

'We've got a surprise for you,' Florrie says, looking up from her Braille.

The doorbell rings, a somber church-bell tune, like a wedding or a funeral.

Ding-dong-ding-dong. Ding-dong-ding-dong.

'You won't even believe it,' Florence says. She has coins on her eyes. Old pennies, not even one-dollar coins. His sister deserves one-dollar coins, you can't tell him otherwise.

'This like some reality show?' TK says, smiling as they surround him, tugging him toward the front door. He can't remember why he didn't come in that way. Diyana puts a playful hand over his eyes.

'No peeking!' she says.

Ding-dong-dong-ding. Ding-dong-dong-ding

But he knows with sudden dread what's going to be on the other side, just like he did that Halloween night, with the door slightly ajar and the light coming out into the street.

'No,' he says, pushing back against them, 'I don't want to.' Fourteen again, and the dry burn of fear in his throat and the pitcher of ice water running down his spine. He

460

can smell the blood. The rich iron of it.

Ding-dong-dong-ding.

'Don't spoil it,' Diyana pouts. 'We all came specially for this.'

'Come on, you big baby,' Ramón urges. 'You should see what *I* been through!'

'Open the door, Thomas,' Florrie says.

Dig-god-dog-dig.

But he doesn't want to see his momma. He buried that woman, and he ain't gonna do it again.

'Get off me,' he says, wrenching himself free from their grabbing hands, and he pushes too hard, because he knocks his sister to the ground and she lands like a trash bag of old clothes thrown out the window.

She lies crumpled, making a shrieking wounded animal sound that makes him think she's broken something.

'Florrie, I'm sorry.' TK is appalled, falling to his knees beside her. 'I didn't mean to. It was an accident. Are you all right? Let me see.' In all his life, he's never hit a woman.

He realizes the sobbing is familiar. Not a woman's crying at all, but a teenage boy's. His voice. The sound that came up out of his throat, standing over the body of Ricky Furman shot to death and the gun dangling from his hand. A keening moan that didn't belong in anyone's mouth, a sound straight out of hell. The devil's own. Which is all he's ever been. *Whoreson. Murderer.*

He takes his sister's shoulder, 'Please, Florrie.' Her bones twist under her dress and she turns to snap her teeth at him, dirty yellow canines in a long snout. The keening is now a growling whine. She is crawling out of her skin, emerging from an amniotic sac, her paws scrabbling on the floorboards, her coat matted red. She stands on spindly mongrel legs and shakes out her fur, spattering the room with blood.

461

TK screams and scrambles away from her, getting tangled in the braids coiled round and round the room. Cockroaches skitter into the depths of the hair.

'Don't go yet, you haven't opened the door,' Ramón says, his voice plaintive through the giant paper head. He is the only one who is not changing. The rest of his friends are spasming, falling onto all fours, pushing their haunches up into the air. Their bones crack and their skulls stretch out as they give birth to the wild dogs that have always lived inside them, wriggling out of their humanity.

The bloody yellow dog that was his sister stands her ground, hackles up, her lips peeled back to reveal black gums and thick gray slobber dripping from sharp teeth.

TK gets to his feet, slowly, one hand out to stop her, the other fishing in his pocket for the pepper spray. The other newborn dogs are up on their feet, snarling and yipping. Florrie lunges for his ankle, a pre-emptive nip, and TK turns and runs.

'You have to open the door,' Ramón says sadly.

He runs faster than his heart can take. His chest hurts, like someone has driven a spike into it, but he keeps going, because the dogs are after him on their skinny legs, baying and howling and tearing at his pants, driving him toward a dark lake that stretches out ahead.

He trips in the coils of hair and falls into the implacable black water. He smacks his knee into something under the surface, and bursts up, flailing and gasping from the shock of the cold. It's like a baptism, and for one instant he sees clearly. It is not hair that has tangled his feet, but coils of electrical cable. He is waist-deep in filthy rainwater clogged with trash on a flooded factory floor in a basement. Shafts of sunlight from broken windows play on the water, casting ripples across the walls – and a metal stairwell on the far side.

But then he turns back and sees the dogs pacing the water's edge, whining and working themselves up to plunge in after him, and high above them, mounted on the crossbeams above, Jesus is looking down from above – and urging them on.

Assembling You

Layla clutches the pet carrier to her chest. It's dark and she trips on the uneven floor. Blood pours down the side of her face. She has tried to feel the wound on her temple, but even brushing her fingers against it threatens to bring the darkness swarming up again.

If she stands still, the blood runs down her arm and drip-drip-drips on the floor. It freaks her out, so she keeps moving, even though she doesn't know where she's going. Story of her life, she thinks and chokes down a sob. If she starts crying again, she won't be able to stop, and it will knock her to the ground and she won't be able to get up.

She doesn't remember how she got here or even where here is, but the pet carrier is something she can hold on to, a prop to prop her up. She is a fierce young woman protecting her cat. Never mind that the wire door is open and NyanCat is not inside. She is on a quest to *find* her cat, then. And her mother.

Like a video game.

There is a sign on the wall, but the words keep moving when she tries to read them. They're naughty words. They're not even trying to look like words any more. They have ambitions beyond their abilities. This is definitely going to be in the exam. The words rearrange themselves. EMBSLSYA. BEMSALYS. MBYSSAEL. SESYLAMB. LESSYBAM. YSLASBEM.

Inside, someone is waiting for her, a huge lumpen man, sitting in front of a massive control panel, complete with screens, jabbing at dials and gauges. It's VelvetBoy, she realizes, swollen into morbid obesity, his skin yellow and waxy, but she recognizes his features under the fat, the nice-guy face he doesn't deserve. He squints at her and then looks pointedly at the cage.

'You want to lock someone up?' he says, turning back to his panel. 'Or you want to play games?'

'It's for my cat,' Layla says. 'Have you seen her?'

VelvetBoy cackles. 'Oh I've seen a shit-ton of pussy. All the pussy you can gobble. Pussy buffet.' The screens are all playing videos of little girls. Little girls jumping rope, trying to walk in Mommy's oversized shoes, running with a kite, sitting on a fence, playing guitar, blowing a dandelion, licking an ice cream, licking other things. Layla looks away.

'What are you doing here?' she says, angry with him.

'What are you doing here?' he echoes in a sing-song voice.

'I was driving,' she remembers.

'Lost your car. Lost your pussy cat. Lost your marbles. At least I only lost my wallet. And my heart. Have you seen it?' He pats himself down, as if looking for his keys in a forgotten pocket. 'Oh there it is.' He points at the screens, which are now showing penises, an infinite variety of penises, except for one screen where a teenage girl is lying on damp grass kissing a boy who has his hand under her dress.

'Slut,' he says. 'Dirty little whore. You wanted it. You all want it. Taking sexy little pictures in your sexy little panties on your phones, putting yourselves out there. On the Internet for all of us to enjoy. We've got the whole private world in here.' He rubs his distended stomach. 'I may have overindulged myself,' he smirks and she realizes he's rubbing somewhere below his stomach, and looks away.

The screens start displaying selfies. Bathroom mirrors and bedrooms, girls pouting and posing, in their underwear or naked, laughing, serious, scared-looking, all of them trying it on for size.

'No,' Layla says. 'It's not for you.'

'Of course it is. It's what we've taught you. Come here. Sit on my lap. I'll give you a ride.' He reaches for her with his fat arms and she shoves him as hard as she can in the chest. It sends the roller chair shooting across the room until it catches on an uneven bit of flooring and tips over, spilling him onto the ground. He lies there, drowning in fat, laughing. 'We can play rough, sweetheart. I can teach you to think *that* was your idea too.'

'Fuck you!' She throws the cage at him, and turns and runs. 'Mom! Mom, where are you?'

'Dead whore!' he shouts after her. 'You're all dead whores inside!'

She clatters down a flight of stairs into a narrow corridor with a trench running down the middle and robotic manufacturing arms bending over it at uneven angles. She steps into the channel – there's light on the other side, if she can make her way through.

'Mom! Where are you? I need you!' Layla yells. Her voice echoes through the cavernous space, bounces back to her so she can hear just how small and frightened she sounds.

At the sound, the robot arms twitch and all around her, they start jerking to life, shifting on their swivel bases, turning their heads in her direction, curious.

'Leave me alone,' she says, angrily, ducking as one of the arms reaches out for her, a pincer claw grasping blindly. But then another swivels out and grabs at her chest, the metal tips raking over her jacket.

VelvetBoy's voice crackles through the intercom as the robot arms dip and lunge at her, tipped with pincers and whining drill bits and fizzing, sparking welding torches. 'Honk-honk!' he giggles. 'Honk-honk!'

'Mom!' Layla screams. She drops flat in the trench and puts her hands over her head, waiting to die, for a drill bit to bite through her skull. It doesn't come and she peers over her shoulder to see that the bottom of the channel is just out of the range of the mechanical arms' articulation.

She crawls along on her stomach, agonizingly slowly, with the arms plunging up and down, up and down, whirring and screaming and sizzling only inches above her. But then she reaches the end of the trench and there is nowhere to go and the robotic arms seem to know it, pecking down relentlessly. She lies there trying to work out how many seconds she has between the mechanisms rearing up like cobras, and striking down again.

She launches herself up and out, tumbling across the floor, but one of the welding torches catches her shoulder. She howls in agony. The smell of her blistered skin is exactly like bacon and she knows, sacred food group or not, that she's never going to be able to eat it again.

Layla stands up, unsteadily, watching the arms fall silent in a ripple down the assembly line. Her arm is on fire. Don't touch it, she thinks. Third-degree burns and infections. She has to get help. She has to get out of here.

'Oh please don't go, we hate you so,' VelvetBoy mocks from up in his control room. She can see his fat face staring down at her through the greasy window.

Layla turns her back on him and stumbles deeper into the factory, toward the sound of water splashing.

Labyrinth

Gabi emerges through the door onto a walkway above the sprawling factory floor. The narrow band of windows that run just under the ceiling are crusted with gunk, creating a grubby fuzz of light that fails to penetrate the gloom below.

She takes shuffling steps, testing the walkway for rot, feeling her way through the half-dusk, wary of walking into something with sharp edges, one hand on her gun, the radio on her belt humming with useless static. She's turned the volume down, low enough so she can hear it, but not so much that it will give away her position.

Her eyes are starting to adjust, so that she can make out the armatures of the assembly pit, gap-toothed, because the scrappers have taken everything they can, and destroyed what they couldn't. The remaining robot arms are canted at crazy angles on their heavy stands, wiring dangling like guts, leaning over the rails that run down the center of the pit, waiting in vain for the husks of cars that will never come through here again.

A trick of the light makes it look as if the remaining robot arms are moving; the heads swiveling to watch her.

Clayton could be anywhere in here – eight stories of automotive ruin. Not quite the thirty-five acres of the Packard Plant, but it's still going to be a bitch. But hey, when you don't have a yellow brick road, Gabi reckons, you can probably follow the disturbing art.

The factory would be creepy as fuck on a good day, weirder still with all the old furniture that doesn't belong, as if he's playing house. But it's worse, much worse, with the horrible artwork everywhere. Like Luke's basement full of dead baby dolls. Except there may really be a corpse in one of these, with their distorted faces and corkscrew necks. Like the woman with the melting features or the effigy of Jesus strung up on the railing, looking down, his clockwork mouth opening and closing like he's muttering a prayer. Evidence Tech is going to have a field day.

She takes a rusty staircase up to the mezzanine level. The metal steps ring out under her boots, echoing across the floor, as if the whole damn building wants to give her away. She cringes, but hey, reciprocity. If every sound travels and she can't hear the bad guys, it means they're not on this floor.

She moves cautiously deeper into the building, up a set of stairs and past a control room where a fat figure made of discolored beeswax lies on the floor, wedged into a swivel office chair facing a wall of screens and buttons, graffitied and smashed-up. The wax has set badly, in drips that ooze over the edge of the seat. Or maybe it's intentional. The fat effigy has exaggerated hollows for eyes, like someone gouged out the wax with their fingers, and old toys embedded in its yellow flesh. He's reaching for the controls with one flabby arm, joined to the body with webbing, like a frog's foot. It's disgusting.

She passes offices with filing cabinets overturned and

trashed computers, the floor buried under cardboard boxes, vomiting files and paper. A scattering of neon highlighter markers stand out, like pink and green and blue plastic cockroaches among the junk. There's so much trash, it doesn't seem possible that it could all be indigenous to the plant.

Someone has taken the time to systematically kick down the urinals in the men's bathroom and smash the porcelain to bits. When everything else is fucked up, mere destruction isn't enough. You gotta step up your game to total obliteration, she thinks.

She backtracks, and ends up in an office overlooking the factory floor. But across on the other side of the factory, she can make out the familiar sweep of blue and red police lights, visible through an open loading door.

Always late to the damn party, she mutters in her head, but she can't help grinning. She's already strategizing routes. She'll take a team upstairs. It makes sense that he'd go up. She hopes Boyd's been able to get hold of the building blueprints.

'Hey assholes,' she calls down, as she bounds down the stairs toward the car. 'Don't shoot, it's me.'

But there's something terribly wrong here. It's not the cavalry and it's not a loading door that's letting in the white glaze of daylight.

It's her Crown Vic, smashed straight through the wall. The bonnet is crumpled, the windscreen a blue splintered map. The driver's door is hanging open, a nasty crack running down the window. A smear of red across the glass. Her heart freefalls.

'Layla!' Gabi holsters her gun and sprints to the car, twisting her ankle on one of the fragments of bricks from the ruined wall. Inanimate revenge.

She shoves down the obese airbag in the front seat, fighting the deflating fabric in the hope of finding her daughter underneath. But she's forced to concede that there's no-one there. The cat in her cage is gone, too.

An incessant low humming breaks through her panic. Her phone, in her pocket, set to vibrate. There's no possible way it could be her daughter. But she can hope. That's what parents do. Hope.

'Layla?' she says, frantic.

Fragments of noise come through, garbled. '-ersado? Weh—'

'Where the fuck are *you*, Bob? Why aren't you here yet? Fucking get here!' She disconnects and starts running back upstairs. He would go higher. For his grand exhibition. Isn't that what this is about? Why he hauled all his awful statues and this shitty old furniture over here?

Layla, she thinks. Layla, Layla, Layla.

Summonings

Layla steps out onto the catwalk above a flooded basement, with unidentifiable bits of old machinery protruding like shipwrecks, and slashes of sunlight from the broken windows like tiger stripes on the dark water. The splashing is coming from a big black man, his face drawn in terror, running from a pack of mad dogs that are bounding through the water behind him, baying and howling.

'Here!' she yells. And he looks up, startled, and trips, landing hard on his knee. It's her fault, she thinks. He turns, fast, yanking pepper spray out of his pocket, but the dogs are on him, knocking him down onto his back, in the water.

He comes up, gasping. 'Get off!' he yells, kicking at one of the dogs. He maces the second dog at the same time and it jolts back, as if electrocuted, whining and plunging its nose into the water.

But three dogs is too many, even for a big guy like him. The third sinks its teeth into his wrist and, with a shout of pain, he drops the canister into the water. The dog worries at him, teeth ripping through muscle, its head distends with the movement, stretching like putty, a blur of muzzle and teeth.

This is not real, she thinks, and then: real enough, the agony in her shoulder reminds her. But it is *also* a dream, she thinks. A simulation is running in your brain, and you can control dreams if you try, if you're aware you're dreaming. Exactly like a video game. If only she had a power-up, a cluster bomb or a special move. What the hell. She has failed to summon her mother, but she remembers the cage and her cat, who might be in here somewhere, wandering lost.

She leans over the railing and shouts for NyanCat. The sound echoes and the dogs raise their heads as one to look at her, mechanical, like the robot arms.

But on the surface of the water, the sun slashes swirl and rearrange themselves into new symmetries, and then something explodes from the dark. A tiger. No, a cat, lithe and enormous. The dreamcat lashes out, burning bright, claws and teeth and fury. No toying with grasshoppers now. This is savage, ancient war.

'Run!' Layla yells down to the man and he does, not looking back at the howling, shrieking, ripping behind him. She climbs down the steps to where they have broken off, a yard above his head and hooks her arm around the railing, ignoring the hot white pain in her shoulder, reaching her hand out. 'Climb up!'

Behind him, the dreamcat shreds two of the dogs like paper, leaving red ribbons drifting on the water. The final animal turns and bolts, tail between its legs, but not fast enough. The cat pounces on its back, claws gouging into its yellow flank for purchase. The dog struggles on for a few more steps and then collapses, plunging both of them into the dark water that closes over their heads.

The man grasps her hand, his palm clammy and ice-cold.

He's careful to only use her for leverage, grabbing on to the edge of the step with his other hand, his legs kicking, until he gets one knee up, and hauls himself onto the stair alongside her.

The water thrashes for a while and finally stills into uneasy ripples. A red ribbon drifts up and starts spreading across the surface.

The man sits with his back up against the railing, panting and soaked through and bleeding. 'Jesus,' he huffs. 'Jesus Christ.'

'Did you see that?' Layla asks him. The ribbons on the dark water are fraying, hard to see now.

'I didn't see nothing,' he says, not looking back. 'Not one thing. Are you real?'

'Are you?' she challenges.

'I think so. Bleeding enough to be. You're not in such great shape yourself.' His teeth are chattering like the clacker you give the kid in music class who can't play a real instrument.

'We have to get out of here. You have to get warm. You're going to get hypothermia.'

'Nah. I got to find the man who did this. He killed my friend. He does something to you, maybe when he touches you. It makes you sick in the head. Makes you see shit.'

'The Detroit Monster?'

'That's what they call him. I'm TK.'

'Layla.' It's weird to be shaking hands, but hey, maybe it means they don't have to talk about dogs and dreamcats. 'Is this the Fleischer Plant?'

'Yeah.'

'Then my mom's here. We have to find her. She's a homicide detective.'

'That so? 'Bout fucking time. Excuse my French.'

'I'm fluent in French.'

'Detective brought her little girl along?'

'No, she sent me away. But I found one of the bodies, before. So…maybe, proximity? That's how he drugs you? Like a gas.'

'Maybe.' He makes a decision. 'We have to get you out. Find your mom and the other cops. Then I'll come back and rip his head off myself.' But Layla can see it's only bluster. He's as shit-scared as she is.

All that Sparkles

Gabi dismisses the second floor at a glance. Another sprawling space filled with garbage and bricks, but no indication of people. The third floor is a maze of offices, the windows smashed in between, stains across the floor. But when she emerges onto the fourth floor, she's confronted with a wall of newspapers piled high to the ceiling, hardened with damp, like papier-mâché. She's seen rat's nests like this. There is a narrow track between the walls of paper, just wide enough to walk through. It turns sharply to the left. This is madness. How long has he been doing this? How many bodies *are* there? Somewhere ahead, she can make out muffled voices. Male. Not her daughter. Maybe Marcus. There *might* be another entrance. She's seen enough of the factory to establish that there's a (non-functioning) elevator on the other side of the building, and there may be another stairwell close to it. But there's no time for that, and there is no sign of Layla.

She tries the radio again because routine is all she has right now. 'Dispatch. I'm on the fourth floor. Could be fifth, depending where you start from. There's a wall of newspapers like a maze. Suspect is somewhere beyond it. I'm going in. Suspect may have my daughter hostage, or she may be hiding somewhere in the building.' Please let her be hiding. Let her be safe.

The radio crackles back uselessly.

She wipes her hand on her pants, sweaty, even in the cold, readjusts her grip on the gun and moves along the tunnel of congealed paper, working her way through as it branches, forcing her to choose a path. She tries to follow the voices, but the paper swallows up the sound. It smells terrible, acrid and wet rot. The walls rustle and sometimes bulge out as if there are things scuttling between them, or trying to dig their way through. Rats and cockroaches. She keeps right. Right, right, right, please get it right.

Something swoops over her head, a flash of white, dry and rustling. She ducks instinctively and it takes everything she has not to open fire on the pages fluttering past. Loose pages in the wind. That's all. Get a hold of yourself, she thinks angrily, pushing away the thought that there's no wind.

She turns left again and comes to the center of the maze – and finds Marcus.

She only knows him by his nametag.

He is wired to one of the big industrial pillars, his arms outstretched in benediction, wearing a spiky halo of beams as if in a medieval painting, gold wires stuck into his scalp. One palm has been painted with a sheaf of barley. The other has a sun. Religious symbols, she remembers from one of Layla's school projects. Life and death and rebirth. There are wooden angel wings attached to his back, painted to look like flames, red and yellow, and a giant clay egg split open at his feet as if he has hatched out of it, amidst a messy nest of kindling.

She focuses on these details because she can't bear to look at his face. Where his face should be. Her chest is so tight she can hardly breathe.

Oh, Sparkles.

His face is gone, sheared clean off, and in the center, where his nose and mouth and eyes should be, is an ornately carved wooden door embedded in his skull, with tiny gold hinges. She can't open it. She won't.

She doesn't want to know what might be inside.

She nearly succumbs to the guilt that takes her down at the knees. But she has to find Layla. Her terror for her daughter is a dark engine propelling her forward, even past this.

I'll come back for you, Marcus, she promises, and reels back into the labyrinth.

Baby it's You

Jonno has his back against the wall, holding his phone out in front of him like it's a weapon. Maybe it is.

'I'm filming this! You can't hurt me because the whole fucking world will see it. It'll be evidence. It's live, do you understand? It's streaming. People can see this right now, and they're phoning the police *right now*.' Assuming this is even getting out of the building. He glances at his signal. Yep. 4G. Two bars. Going out live – and he's alive. So far.

'I didn't understand. I thought it would be enough. I thought I could do it on my own.' The man looks down at his calloused palms, the thick fingers. 'With these hands, with the tools Clayton had, the things he knew. It didn't work.'

'What the actual fuck are you talking about? You killed people and turned them into freak shows.' Easy, Jonno thinks, don't get him riled. Next thing you know, he turns you into a freak show too.

The Amazing Heartless Man. Did you forget your dead girlfriend? How her tattoo came to life and ripped her to pieces? Hope you got that *on camera.*

He can't think about that now. He can't even look at

her. He can't, or he will lose his shit, and he is hanging on by a very fine thread as it is. Calm down. Think veteran war reporter. This is Charlie Manson right here, and he has the exclusive, and he just needs to hold it together until the cops come.

Clayton looks terribly sad. 'They weren't supposed to die. Nothing should die. They were supposed to *change*.'

'So the kid you cut in half was supposed to become a happy little deer and go skipping around the forest?'

'Yes,' Clayton says with the simple conviction of the believer. Jonno laughs, a high-pitched sound he cuts off in his throat because it's such a giveaway of how fucking terrified he is. He's dealing with a madman. An actual madman. Which means he has to keep him talking, because he is totally unpredictable. Jesus. Put that on your CV. Career highlights: playing Scheherazade to a serial killer.

Jonno takes a breath, clutching his own wrist to stop his hand from shaking. He goes for smooth, gets choked instead. 'Please explain it to me. I want to understand.' He can't stop himself from adding, 'Just don't hurt me.'

'I opened them up to let the dreams out, and then I made them into the dreams they wanted. That should have been enough.'

'But it wasn't.'

'Everything is so *physical*. I wanted to get at the meaning. You can feel it, can't you? Underneath.'

'Yes. Of course.' He's hardly going to disagree.

'There are places that are borders. Where something was but isn't any more, and other things can surface.'

Jonno keeps his eyes on the screen so that he is not tempted to let his gaze slide away to Jen. It's easier. The distance through the lens. One step removed.

'It's all coming through. It's because of you.'

'What?' Jonno rubs his chest, suddenly afraid his own ribcage is about to burst open. He doesn't even have any tattoos, he thinks wildly.

'Art needs an audience,' the killer says, as if he's the first guy to ever think of this. 'It's like a fire. It needs to catch in the imagination if it wants to live.' He looks almost happy. 'Can't you see?'

'Why don't you tell me about it?' Jonno manages, not seeing at all. Trying, in fact, not to see anything outside that glowing square in his hand.

Oh but you have an inkling, don't you, boychick? About giving him exactly what he wants.

Clayton points to the camera phone. '*They* see.'

Jonno staggers. Who would have thought two little words could have such weight?

'The police hid the bodies,' Clayton continues. 'They knew what would happen if they let people see.'

'What would happen?'

'It would spread. The world would break. It would be re-made. But no-one saw.'

'Until I put the videos online.' He should turn the camera off. Right now. Cut him off cold. But won't that make him mad, and even more likely to chop him up and turn him into a chandelier? Serial killers like attention. Just keep giving him attention. Even if that makes you an accomplice to his fucked-up fantasies. Isn't that just what mainstream media does? At least he's also getting a confession. He's helping. Plus he's keeping himself alive.

'I've seen other doors around the city. I didn't draw them,' Clayton marvels. 'But they're there.'

'I did a report on it. It's become a thing. You're a global

482

trendsetter. You're like the Banksy of serial killers!' Keep it together. 'So is something going to come through all those doors?'

'You did. And so did she. But they're just cracks in the surface.' He smiles at him, with love, Jonno thinks, horrified. 'I know what you dream.'

'Is that so?' he squeaks.

This is the part where he cuts off your head and makes it into a lovely hat.

'It's all exposed, the currents that run through the world.' Clayton kneels down next to Jen, forcing Jonno to bring her into frame. He can't look away. Staring into the abyss.

'If you kill me, I can't film it,' he says, weakly.

'I'm going to give you what you want.' Clayton reaches into his pocket, then stretches out a hand to Jonno. There's something in it. Oh no. No.

'What *is* that?' Jonno screams. 'I don't *want* that.'

'It's what you dream. Clayton dreamed it, too,' the killer says, offering it to him.

It's a baby's shoe. A little red sneaker, with a Spiderman decal. The size of a lime. 'A legacy.'

Shoot to Kill

Gabriella can hear voices through the newspaper maze, as she twists away from Marcus toward the other side.

'Get it away from me!' she hears Jonno yell. Close. Very close. 'Please. I don't want it.'

'I know you do,' Clayton says. She recognizes his voice from the brief video clip.

She pokes her head out, just enough to get a glance at the room. The labyrinth opens onto a pillared space, fractured light leaking around the edges of blackened windows. She takes in three figures. The killer, the blogger, a woman with braids prone on the ground – the pretty DJ who is never going to bring the house down again, by the way her chest is ripped open. Bags of garbage, newspaper stacks, like columns. They're looking the other way from her, which gives her another second to take it in. Entrances, exits, anyone else in the room. Where the hell is Layla?

Jonno Haim is hunched over himself, wielding his cell phone at Clayton Broom like it's a cross against a vampire.

Gabi steps out, her gun steady in both hands. 'Detroit Police!' she says in a voice that brooks no argument. 'Stay where you are. Where is my daughter?'

Clayton turns to her and for a moment, just a moment, his whole face distorts. When she was ten years old, her father, the big fisherman, showed her the quickest way to kill an octopus. You reach in and you turn it inside out, just like that. Clayton's face does that – inverts itself.

'All the dreamers are here,' he says.

She shoots him.

The bullet rips through his shoulder and spins Clayton into one of the pillars of newspaper. He sags against it, blood soaking into the paper.

'I'm going to ask you again. Where the fuck is my daughter?'

Jonno scrambles to his feet, closing his hand tight on whatever it is he's holding. He swings the phone in her direction. 'You're here. Thank God, you're here.'

'Are you *filming* this?' Gabi yells at him, keeping her gun trained on Clayton, who has his head down, gripping his arm, still facing the other direction. 'What is wrong with you?'

'I have to,' he whines. 'He made me. The eyeballs.'

'Don't get in my way and stop filming,' she snaps at the idiot blogger. 'Clayton! Where is my daughter? I'll shoot you again. I'll keep shooting you until I run out of ammo. But not one wound will be fatal. You will be in agony, but you won't die. I'll keep you here until you tell me.'

Something flickers in his eyes. Fear. Finally. 'I don't know,' he says, teeth gritted against the pain. 'I think she might be here. She's one of the open ones. I can't control what they've brought with them.'

'Not good enough.' She is not thinking about the words, about *opening*, about what that might mean.

Jonno steps back to get both of them in the frame, she

realizes. 'Cut it out!' she screams at him, and it takes everything in her not to shoot him in the shoulder too, if only to make him stop filming.

Clayton turns slowly from the pillar, his injured arm dangling. His face is back to normal. If it was ever otherwise. His skin is gray and saggy, his shorn white hair sticking up, but he looks at her with hope. 'Shoot me. Let it out. I've tried to hold it in so long, but it doesn't belong to me. Nothing belongs to any of us.'

'Mom, watch out!' Layla yelps and Gabi turns to see her daughter and a big man, shivering and bleeding, emerging from the newspaper maze, clinging to each other. The relief knocks the breath out of her. Alive.

And then she feels someone – Clayton – grab her ankle. Somehow, in that split second, he has crossed the room and caught hold of her. She fires, but the bullet goes wide, skimming one of the pillars and punching through the blacked-out window. It explodes in a spray of glass, which isn't right, she thinks with odd detachment, a bullet should punch through the glass, leave a perfect splintered hole. But then he yanks her right off her feet. The back of her head hits the concrete with the bright smack of a score at the coconut shy. She gasps with pain, black stars behind her eyes.

All her bones go limp and she realizes she's let go of the gun. She twists to grab at it as he drags her across the floor and manages to snag it with a fingertip. She sees her daughter moving. 'No, Layla! Run. Run as fast as you can. Get out!' Maybe she only thinks the words because her daughter is not running.

'You can feel it,' Clayton says, not to her, but to Layla. 'It's open in you.'

486

Gabi fumbles at her Smith & Wesson, gets a grip on the barrel and turns it round so she's got the handle. She flips onto her back and braces her elbows against her ribs, and as he hauls her in, like the goddamn catch of the day, she levels the gun and blows his fucking brains out. Which is when everything *really* goes to hell.

All Your Fears

The gunshots hurt. Searing pain. The body is alight with it. The shreds of Clayton that still live are moaning and gibbering. *He* wants to run. The dream can't let him, not yet.

The Police is ruining everything. It needs to complete its design, it needs everyone to see the phoenix, its most perfect piece. It needs to be alive for the door to open.

The time is now. Dream is wild in the factory, the Wanderer and the Daughter brought it in with them, and the Messenger has unleashed the seeds, spreading it across the Internet, a thousand screens, a hundred thousand, and the dream will grow and it will live on, it's legacy, even if it dies now.

But it doesn't want to die. It's afraid of the darkness. Which is why it twists its arm out, lashing across the floor, so easy to reshape reality now that people have seen and believed. It grabs the Police and pulls her down. It only wants to make her stop hurting it, to get the gun away. It only wants to live.

She fires and dreams explode across the room, birds of dark glass and whirling papers, possessed, all their imaginings set free, and it wants to laugh and scream in delight. Finally!

The next bullet tears into Clayton's head. Too fast. It should have been able to stop it cold, transmogrify it into a bud exploding open into a flower or a dragonfly or a fish. But it wasn't paying attention, and now it is too late.

Clayton's head jerks back as the hot metal drives through his forehead, shredding its way through the gray pink tissue with its secret folds and the thoughts that spark in the meat, and bursting out the back, pulling the flesh and blood and bits of bone with it – and all of Clayton.

The man's thoughts that have haunted it are gone in a flash, like tearing a page from a notebook. It feels Clayton slip away and it whimpers in terror, because it cannot follow him, and everything it feared of death is true. It's loosed, but still trapped in this world, only now it is alone. It can't find a form. It seethes and roils above the body that once sheltered it, and the whole room goes mad around it.

The Police is getting up, staggering toward her Daughter, who is running toward her, the big man moving to help them.

The Messenger is still filming – and everything his lens sees becomes more alive, more real. A window to the world, when it has been obsessed with doors. And maybe there is still a chance to rise from the ashes.

It reaches out with everything it has left and pulls the strings, and in the center of the maze, Marcus Jones steps away from his pillar and starts making his way toward them.

Seeing/Believing

Layla knows somehow that her mom can't see it. The man's limp arm twisting around on itself, becoming a black tentacle that snakes across the room while Gabriella is looking at her with heart-stopping love and relief. She doesn't see how it snags her round the ankle and yanks her off her feet.

Her mom fires her gun, and Layla covers her ears. It's like a fire-cracker going off inside her head. The window shatters, but the glass shards turn into crows, fluttering round the room. Jonno shrieks and swipes at the birds and then slams himself back against the wall, jabbing at his phone.

But even as the killer is dragging her mom across the floor, he's looking directly at her, at Layla.

'You can feel it,' he says.

'No,' she whispers. 'Fuck off.' But she can. This is what she does. Imagines other people. Steps into other roles. She *can* see it – all the tumult inside him. The dreams building up until they're eating him alive.

And then her mom blows Clayton's head off. Brain matter and blood and bits of skull splatter the pillar, but something else comes spilling out of the ruin of his head as Clayton slumps to the ground – a great cloud, like gray cotton candy condensing in the air.

Everything is going nuts. There are newspapers and crows fluttering around the room.

'Holy shit, holy shit!' Jonno yells, still filming. She sees how his phone makes the cloud bigger and darker and it makes her think about how the old gods needed people's faith to make them powerful.

Gabi is climbing to her feet, uncertainly, holding her head, looking for her daughter.

'Mom, I'm here.' She runs to her, TK following, and tucks herself up under her arm. TK does the same, although he has to stoop.

Her mother can't stop touching her face. 'Layla, I thought he was going to kill you. I thought you were dead already.'

'Come on, Mom, keep moving. You're goddamn Detroit PD, and you shot the bad guy. He's dead. Everything is fine now.'

Only it's not, not really, because she can see the storm building above their heads and feel the wild thoughts that dance through it like lightning.

'It's looking for somewhere to go!' she shouts to TK, because Gabi doesn't understand, she sags between them, shock or concussion, closing her eyes against the shit that is happening around them, paint flaking off the floor and lifting into the air, whirring into tornados of color. The garbage bags are dragging across the floor and something is lumping its slow way through the newspaper tunnels behind them.

Jonno turns in a half-circle, his mouth open, filming everything he can. Crows made of black glass circle over a dead woman with her chest torn open, and Layla doesn't want to look too closely at her, because she thinks she is definitely real and definitely dead.

She just wants to get out of here alive.

But the birds land on the woman's chest and peck at her skin.

'No,' Jonno shouts and runs at them waving his arms. 'No, get away from her!' Layla looks back and sees how the birds become misshapen feathery smears as they near the ceiling. The moment they're out of the camera's depth of field, they go out of focus.

'It's the phone,' Layla says. 'He's streaming it.'

'I told him not to,' Gabi says. 'I'm going to kill that knucklehead punk,' but it's all bluster, because she can barely stand.

'The old gods,' Layla says.

'What?' TK snaps. He can see it too. The wildness around them.

'You have to see to believe. The phone is making it worse, stronger, whatever. I have to stop him.'

She shifts her mom's weight onto TK, slips out from under her arm, and sprints toward Jonno, scooping up a half-brick from the ground. Which means she does not see the broken thing stagger out of the maze behind her, plywood angel wings hanging lopsided from its shoulders and a door lodged in its face.

All You Ever Dreamed

Jonno doesn't know what to focus on. There's so much happening. The dead man with the gunk pouring out of his head, like a mushroom cloud. That's not normal, right? He's pretty damn sure that's not normal. His phone keeps beeping with new messages. Nineteen missed calls. They'll have to wait. And he should try to figure out how to turn off incoming calls, because it's got to be draining his battery.

Stop fiddling. Film this shit. Even his troll is on his side for once. He wonders if he should be adding commentary.

'I'm Jonno Haim,' he says, 'and shit. Look, this is real. This is happening. All of this is real.' He pans across the room and sees the birds on Jen. 'No! No, get away from her!' He runs at them, waving his arms, still filming, always filming. They take off from her body, losing substance as they flutter into the air above him. 'Bastards!'

Concentrate. The detective. The dead guy. The volcano coming from his head.

'I'm trying!' Jonno shouts in frustration and then the kid, out of nowhere, smashes a piece of brick down on his wrist.

'Ow, fuck! What the hell did you—?' He's dropped the

493

phone. 'No, I need that. Cut it out. It's not a game.'

'I know,' she says and stomps down on it with all her weight. The screen splinters. But it's still working. She's what, all of a hundred and ten pounds? It's almost funny. He *almost* laughs, but he's too busy fighting her for it.

She raises up the brick, like Abraham in the Bible about to sacrifice Isaac, and he's God, and he won't let her, because he realizes *this* is his baby.

He punches her in the face and she falls back, dropping the brick. He snatches up his phone and turns just in time to see it. The most wondrous thing on earth.

A black angel steps out into the room with a door embedded in its face.

Jonno turns the camera on it and its wings erupt into flame, the halo flares into spikes of light, and the door begins to glow as if all of heaven is on the other side, shining through the cracks.

The angel reaches up his hand to touch his own cheek, in awe. His fingers reach up blindly for the handle, and close on the golden doorknob.

Everything to Everyone

'Come on, stay with me,' TK says, half-carrying the cop, semi-conscious, delirious. Not so out of it that she sees what *he* sees, maybe she's too sensible. But never mind all that, he is *not* going to see some other kid lose their momma to a monster.

'No, Layla!' the woman in his arms calls out, struggling. 'Lay, come back here.' She thrashes at TK. 'Don't let her go.'

'Easy there,' he says.

But when the idiot with the phone punches her daughter in the face, she reaches for her gun. Can't say he blames her.

But then none of that matters, because the source of the shuffling reveals itself. Some *thing* steps out of the labyrinth, ablaze, and even the cop sees it, and makes a sound in her throat.

Gabi sees Marcus shambling out from the passage of crusted newspapers toward them. She sees him burst into flame and reach for the door in his face, and she raises her gun to put him out of his agony. Then she wavers. She can't believe he's still alive. She should have checked when she found him. They need to get him to a hospital.

'Mom!' Layla yells, getting to her feet on the other side of the room. 'The phone. Get the phone. You have to stop Jonno filming! You have to trust me.'

And she does. Against every damn instinct. She turns, away from the fiery angel-monster, and trains her gun on Jonno instead at the exact moment a tidal wave of furniture crashes over him.

The chairs come when TK calls them, a whole bunch of them. Some of them once belonged to him, the killer, but not any more. They swarm across the floor, tik-tak, tik-tak, and smash Jonno off his feet, battering him to the ground.

Jonno flails against the furniture. Death by Ikea, he thinks before the hard wooden edge of a seat catches him on the forehead and knocks him out.

The phone goes skeltering across the floor and bounces off the leg of a chair, skidding toward her. Layla snatches it up and hits the stop button on the video app. The live feed cuts off.

Everything collapses, just like that.

The birds fall out of the air and shatter like so much glass, the whirling papers fall, the chairs stop moving and Marcus slumps, no longer ablaze, his fingers slipping from the door handle, his knees collapsing. No longer an angel, just a terrible mistake.

'What are you doing?' Gabi shouts at her, swinging her gun back to Marcus, slowly slipping to the ground.

Layla looks up at the dark cloud that has swollen to fill the entire room, hanging low under the ceiling. She can feel what's inside it, the hope and despair crackling through like static.

'You really didn't know,' she says. She is furious that anything could be so fucking stupid, so naïve. But this is what she does. Finds the empathy to step into even the most hideous roles.

She knows what it needs.

Layla turns the camera back on, pinch-flicks her finger over the screen to zoom in on Marcus's face and holds it there, long enough, just long enough for him to raise his head, for his chest to heave, for his fingers to reach for the door. The light behind it is shining again, a brilliant border. He closes his hand on the handle. The catch clicks. The door starts to swing open, just a crack. There is a blaze of gold and darkness whirling to meet it – the storm rush of the black clouds sweeping through the door. Away.

'Shoot the door, Mom,' Layla says. 'It's not Marcus any more. It's not anything.'

Gabi squeezes the trigger. Her aim is true.

Layla hits stop.

She presses delete.

Open

'Layla!' Gabi grabs her by the shoulders, turns her round, examines her for damage. A deep cut on a raised welt on her temple, already scabbing up, dried blood in her hair. Black and blistered skin on her shoulder, burned right through her jacket. Big eyes, dilated, shock that hasn't set in yet, because she's furious.

'You're okay,' Gabi says. It's as much a command as a question. Layla nods and then the anger drops out of her, like the phone from her hand, and she starts shaking, her hands over her eyes.

'Oh God.'

'It's okay. Come on, sugarbean, we're getting out of here.' She can't look back at Marcus. What is left of Marcus. Eighteen years on the force and she has never killed someone. And now...

Her daughter looks up wildly at the black smoke pouring over them, 'I thought it was gone.'

'It's all the newspaper. It's caught on fire. We have to get out.'

TK is pulling chairs off Jonno, unconscious beneath them.

He yanks him up by his arm and swings him over his shoulder in a fireman's lift.

'What about Marcus?' Layla says.

'Like you said, he's not there any more, baby. We have to worry about the living.' Even Jonno, although she would dearly love to leave him here. 'We have to find a way out.' Gabi scans for exits. The broken windows open to a twenty-foot drop. The fire-escape has been ripped away and hangs dangling from the brick. She knows for sure that there is an elevator shaft on the other side, which means there will be another staircase, probably.

Layla swabs at her eyes with the heels of her palms. 'Mom. I know a way.'

She reaches for her hand. Gabi can't remember the last time they held hands. Her daughter leads her to a bricked-up section of wall that juts into the room. It might hold cabling or it might be a vent. There's one of the damn chalk doors drawn on it.

'Oh, beanie, no. That's not...' Gabi can't stand it. This might be the last nudge over the edge.

But then she realizes that this one is drawn over an *actual* door. Layla shoves down on the bar handle and pulls it open onto a ladder leading down. There's light from above – a hatch open somewhere high above them.

'It'll be okay, Mom.'

'No, we don't know where it goes.'

'Trust me.' Layla's face is bright and open, her eyes shining. She's never looked more sure of herself.

She surrenders to the certainty of the young woman, suddenly a stranger, as if all the potential in her has come into bloom.

'All right,' Gabi says, gruff. 'All right. But I'm going first.'

She rattles the ladder as hard as she can. It's built solid. She steps down onto it and shoves away, with all her weight. It doesn't budge.

It's an old chimney. She can see patches of light below them, where bushes have pushed their way in between the brickwork. They might have to fight their way past the branches, but at least they'll be out.

'All right,' she calls up.

Layla steps onto the ladder above her.

There's water running down the bricks on the inside and moss growing in the cracks, with tiny purple flowers blossoming in defiance of the cold.

They climb down, all of them, one step at a time, closer and closer to daylight.

AFTER

Mind Bleach

In the matter of the death by shooting of serial murder suspect Clayton Broom

 Official Report Filed #261114/4438 Homicide Department, November 30, 2014

Lead Investigators: Detectives Luke Stricker Badge No. 531 & Gabriella Versado Badge No. 866

Report filed by: Internal Affairs Investigator Detective-Sergeant Farokh

Date of incident: Wednesday, November 19, 2014

Location: Fleischer Body Plant, Detroit

Additional materials attached:

A full report of events leading up to the death of Clayton Broom, as reported by Detective Versado

Complete set of case notes

Video file recorded by private citizen, Jonathan Haim

Witness statements by Layla Stirling-Versado, Jonathan Haim, Thomas Keen

Evidence Tech documentation of the scene

Ballistics report

Forensic lab reports

Phone records

EPA report on chemicals present at the Fleischer Body Plant

Medical examiner's report on Jenefer Quillane

Medical examiner's report on Clayton Broom

Medical examiner's report on Officer Marcus Jones

Cyber-crimes analysis of video footage material

DPD Psychologist Dr Elle Weir's debrief and evaluation of Detective Versado

Final Notes:

This investigator finds that there are still many inconclusive and disturbing aspects around the events that led up to the death of Clayton Broom and the shooting of Marcus Jones.

EPA examination of the building and blood tests have proved inconclusive on possible hallucinogenic toxins.

However, the witnesses' testimonies, interviewed separately, confirm that many of them experienced vivid and subjective hallucinations consistent with psychotropic drugs. Speculation about whether Broom was able to induce mass hypnosis or hysteria is irrelevant at this point. PTSD has also been put forward as a possible factor; all witnesses had seen one or more of Broom's victims.

The footage filmed by 'citizen journalist' Jonathan Haim has been largely discounted as a reliable record of what transpired.

Cyber-crimes conclude that the footage was doctored in-camera, using a more professional version of live-filtering effects software that is widely available. They have been unable to identify the exact software because the footage on the phone was deleted, even though there are multiple recordings of the live-stream online. Mr. Haim continues to deny any manipulation of the footage, which is shaky and dark and hard to discern.

Haim has confirmed that he purchased the crime-scene photographs used in his previous videos from Detective Michael Croff. An investigation against Detective Croff is pending.

The footage has helped to confirm that Detective Versado did warn Broom before shooting him the first time, in the arm (refer to audio on video footage at 41:56 and ballistics and ME reports) and that she was prone at the time of the shooting and under direct physical threat when she made the fatal head-shot (refer to audio and video footage at 43:18 and ballistics and ME reports on bullet trajectory).

Apart from the mutilated body of Officer Marcus Jones, none of the other 'art works' on the scene contained human remains. The autopsy reveals that Officer Jones died on Monday morning, from a combustion nail gun to the head, two days before Detective Versado discharged her weapon into the corpse while attempting to shoot Broom.

A cat belonging to Layla Stirling-Versado was recovered, alive, from the scene.

The psychologist's report indicates that Detective Versado was under extreme personal and professional duress when the shooting occurred.

The evidence that would have been brought to bear against Mr. Broom is very strong and likely would have led to a conviction (please refer to case notes attached), including, most compellingly, a clear fingerprint on the clay wrapped around the remains of Ms. Spinks, which has since been confirmed by forensics as his right thumbprint.

We have to consider the public perception of this case and Detroit's police force in general. There is little doubt in the public eye that Broom was guilty of the heinous crimes and that Detective Versado acted in good faith, even heroically.

We must also consider the public hysteria around the more gruesome aspects of the case.

I believe a definitive statement from the DPD, laying out the facts as set out in this report, will put a great deal of this hysteria to rest.

I hope this submission will assist Internal Affairs in making an informed and fair ruling.

It is this investigator's considered opinion that Detective Versado was justified in fatally shooting Clayton Broom under the circumstances described in these reports.

My recommendation is that she be commended for her actions and reinstated to her full command, after a mandatory period of counseling.

I am Jonno Haim, the last person who spoke to the Detroit Monster alive. Ask Me Anything.

submitted today by <u>JonnoHaim</u>

The events you've seen on Jonnoh.TV are a real record of events as they happened. There was no filtering software or effects added. Here's the <u>link to The Fleischer Footage</u> and the <u>relevant discussion forums on /x</u>, which includes the frame-by-frame stills. Help get the truth out and <u>fund my documentary on Kickstarter.</u>

UPDATE: I have a very hectic media schedule. Sorry if I can't get to all your questions in this hour. I'll do another AMA soon or you can continue the discussion on <u>my website.</u>

<u>top 200 comments show 500</u>
sorted by: **best**

[–] **xsyntz** 2677 points
Don't you think it's unfair that you're propheting off Jen Q's death?

[–] **Gal00t** 2394 points 1 year ago
  Best. Typo. Ever.

[–] **Jonno Haim** [S] 4841 points

If you knew how much I loved her, you'd know what a shitty question that is. She died right in front of me, remember? I miss Jen every single day. As soon as the documentary is wrapped up (the soundtrack uses a lot of her tracks, btw), I'm looking to launch a new Kickstarter to create the Jenefer Quillane Music Academy in Detroit. Maybe you'd like to chip in? ;)

But seriously, if you've seen the footage that was live-streamed, that has been cached, you'll know it's not fake and you'll know I'm not a prophet, I'm a disciple. All of you are. It lives on in all of us, everyone who has seen it. I'm the messenger.

load more comments (1,060 replies)

[–] **Nothingmonstrd** 1369 points

In your interview on You Can't Handle The Truth [click to watch on YouTube] you insinuated that the authorities are trying to cover this up. Do you really believe that? Don't you think you're hurting your cause appearing on shitty conspiracy video podcasts? This is the same channel that did a special on how the Twin Towers were brought down by an alien ball. Not exactly helping your credibility?

[–] **Jonno Haim** [S] 4661 points

I called them out on it to their faces. They're scared. They're trying to hold on to the world they know. It's up to us to show them what lies beneath. And I'll get the word out wherever I can. To whoever will listen. You think I haven't seen the skit about me on The Daily Show? But I am NOT A JOKE and this is REAL.

load more comments (855 replies)

[–] **CaptainFluffyPants** 1300 points
Isn't this just like the Russian Mutant? SO FAKE?

[–] **Jonno Haim** [S] 2122 points
In that the Russian Mutant is a clever bit of visual effects work and the Fleischer Footage really happened? I'm going to say no. It's not like that at all. To all the skeptics out there, cos this tedious question just keeps coming up please show me the video filters that can create those effects live! I've had various visual effects experts in Los Angeles and in France analyze the footage independently of the police's so-called experts and they'll corroborate that it's the real thing, unadulterated, undoctored. This is NOT Internet urban legend shit. This is not spooky noodle!

load more comments (1,638 replies)

[–] **Laughing_Toaster** 2093 points
I think you mean 'Creepypasta'. Do you have any contact with the other survivors?

[–] **Jonno Haim** [S] 3487 points
I'm under a court order that prevents me from naming them or talking to them. Which says a lot, I think.

509

load more comments (187 replies)

[–] **Goraan** 2049 points
Isn't that because one of them, Mystery Girl, is a minor and she has a reasonable right to privacy? And didn't you physically assault her?

[–] **Jonno Haim** [S] 3655 points
Yes. One of them is a minor. You can see a glimpse of her at 47:02-37:11 in the footage. She's also the one who deleted the footage, making it impossible for me to prove everything.

load more comments (596 replies)

[–] **GeekofSolitude** 6752 points
We <3 Mystery Girl.

[–] **Jonno Haim** [S] 7454 points
I don't get this obsession with her. I know you want to romanticize her and turn her into this big hero like the Hunger Games or whatever, but she was a dumb teenager who wandered in by accident. It's a miracle she didn't get everyone killed.

load more comments (2,541 replies)

[–] **RavenSara** 2041 points
What about the Homeless Hero who saved your life?

510

[–] **Jonno Haim** [S] 3257 points
The guy who beat me unconscious with a chair? You think I should thank him for carrying me out of a burning building? I don't know. He declined to be interviewed for my documentary, which you can help fund, by the way, assuming the city of Detroit doesn't try to sue me again.

load more comments (461 replies)

[–] **Anonymous835** 4100 points
You make it sound like a vendetta.

[–] **Jonno Haim** [S] 9383 points
It is. The same way it's always been against people who dare to speak the truth against power. Ask Galileo or Aristotle or Martin Luther King. I'm a heretic and they will go to any lengths to stop me.

load more comments (3,853 replies)

[–] **Dakegra** 1998 points
That sounds very serious! Are you safe?

[–] **Jonno Haim** [S] 9264 points
I'm just saying if I suddenly die in a car crash or a freak cinema shooting, ask questions. A LOT of questions.

load more comments (5788 replies)

[–] **Oolex** 6102 points
Was it real?

[–] **Jonno Haim** [S] 6868 points
Yes. It was all real. It lives in me now. If you've seen it, there's a splinter of it in you too. We can change the world. You just have to open the door.

load more comments (8,641 replies)

UPFEED: 10 Reasons The Homeless Hero Is More Bad-ass Than Anyone You Know

1. When he was fourteen years old, he shot the man who stabbed his mother to death, Wild West revenge-style.

'It's on my record, you want to look it up. I don't want to talk about that. That was some sad, messed-up shit.'

2. He carries a home-made machete hidden in his walking stick.

'Haven't had to use it. Usually it's enough to show it to someone.'

3. He really hates it when you tell him he's a hero.

'Who the fuck saying that?'

4. He was a slumlord when he was thirteen, renting out rooms in an abandoned building.

'I was looking after my friends.'

5. Speaking of friends, his best buddy, Ramón Flores, got killed by notorious serial killer, Clayton Broom – The Detroit Monster, who stuck a toy head on his body. (click for pics)

'You think that's something to brag about? What's wrong with you?'

6. He tracked down the Detroit Monster and tipped off the cops. (click to listen to the police hotline calls)

'You think I was gonna let the bastard who did this to my friend walk away? Hell no.'

7. He's very modest.

'I had nothing to do with it. It was my higher power.'

8. And grumpy. (He also helps out ex-offenders at the local church)

'Screw you and your stupid questions. I'm a busy man. You see those people out there, they waiting on me to help them type up their CVs. Wasting my time like this. Yeah, I type. I can do sixty words a minute.'

9. He tried to take down the Detroit Monster by himself.

'It wasn't like that. I thought maybe I could take it on, take it into myself, you know. I could carry it inside me and I wouldn't let it break me the way it broke him. Shit I've seen in my life, stuff I've been through, ain't nothing I can't handle. I could have taken that on. In a way I did. Part of it's in me. A dream doesn't have to be bad. It's what you do with it. Like I'm building me a house. That's my dream right there.'

10. Ain't nothing he can't handle.

'We done here?'

<u>Click here to donate to Help Buy The Homeless Hero a House Fund!</u>

MORE UPSTUFF:

If you liked this, you might also want to check out:

5 SERIAL KILLERS EVEN MORE SCREWED UP THAN THE DETROIT MONSTER
10 SIGNS YOUR GIRLFRIEND MAY BE A PSYCHOPATH
22 CELEBRITIES WHO ARE TERRIBLE PARENTS

The Things that Follow You

Layla's gotten used to it. Being *that* girl. The one who knocked Travis's teeth out. The one whose mom killed the psychopath. And of course the rumors swirl that she's Mystery Girl in the video.

Cas's dad helped with that. Faked surveillance footage from a convenience store that showed she wasn't even there at the time. Bumped it up in the search results, bought opinions in bulk from an Indian company that uses English-speaking students for one cent per comment with their own choice of words to cast doubt on the theory in the forums on Reddit and 4Chan. Andy Holt is convinced the human touch is going to be what sets Walled Garden apart from other reputation management services. Maybe he's right.

She did spend a few months in Atlanta with her dad while it all blew over. She actually got on with her step-sibs, Julie and Wilson, and had them performing a Christmas play with a Transformer as Santa Claus and Wilson in reindeer horns making hee-haw noises, which made her step-mom thaw a little, although she still treats Layla like she's a pack of rotted dynamite that might go off at any moment.

515

They took the little ones to Six Flags, which was great, but her dad took her on her own to an experimental re-imagining of *Othello* with puppets that she had to explain to him afterwards over dinner. Just the two of them, and it felt like old times, back when they did finicky craft stuff together, or went out into the woods to look at the stars with binoculars.

And she met a boy. Armand. Who is seventeen and wants to study molecular science, but still likes video games and movies and weird theater. She can't handle art galleries any more, but she took him to see the *Othello* remake after she'd seen it with her dad. They messed around, but didn't have sex. It was intense, like love, even though they never said it and they didn't talk about what had happened to her, although they have since on both counts. He's promised to try and visit over the summer, because she's come back to Detroit.

She missed NyanCat, and after much fiery family debate, with Gabi threatening to pack her off to her grandparents in Miami, it was decided that what she really needed was stability and familiarity, at least until she finished school. So she was back in time to start in the new year.

They talked about transferring her to a different school, switching to her dad's name only. But she likes being Layla Stirling-Versado. She's proud of her mom, even if things are sometimes fraught between them, and they're both seeing psychologists once a week to try to deal with what happened, which they can't agree on and probably never will.

Cas is Cas, although she's more open now. It's easier when you're not living underneath the weight of a secret. She even gave a talk in lifeskills about sexual harassment. It was awkward, but a lot of kids came up to her afterwards to tell her how brave she was. They're veterans, the two of them. Scarred, but alive.

So, let the rumors fly. Bring on the Mystery Girl fanmail, which she dumps straight into the trash. She can handle it.

This is the way the world is now. Everything is public. You have to find other people who understand.

You have to find a way to live with it.

Acknowledgements

I've had many generous guides to the city of Detroit, beyond the evocative ruin porn and doom on the news. I'm grateful for all your personal insights, and I hope you'll forgive me the artistic liberties.

Anna Clarke was the best kind of well-connected fixer, who brought her own journalist's eye to the places we visited and people we spoke to, and read the manuscript when it was done.

Robert-David Jones introduced me to the arts scene, told me wild stories (including the one about the séance), took me dancing in Eastern Market and drove me around town in a big black mortuary van.

The NOAH Project at the Central United Methodist Church allowed me to work in their soup kitchen for a morning. I'm grateful to all the people who were willing to sit and talk to me about their lives, especially James Harris, who gave me permission to use aspects of his personal history. You can donate to NOAH to help them continue their work via their website http://www.noahpro-jectdetroit.org/.

Julia Cuneo arranged for me to visit the Detroit Arts Academy and hang out with the students, who were all the best kinds of surprising and awesome. Thank you all for being so open. The Mosaic Theater School gave me a back-stage pass to their performance of *Hastings Street* (and roped me into the warm-up exercises). Thanks especially to Ta-Shaun and Shennell for our chats online about the perils of being a theater geek.

Sergeant Robert 'Bubble' Haig advised me on police procedure, let me read an early draft of his memoir, *Ten Little Police Chiefs,* about his long service in the Detroit Police Department, lent me his dead baby in the basement story, and, along with Commander Joseph O'Sullivan, gave me invaluable feedback on police procedure in this novel. Any errors or discrepancies are mine.

Keith Weir and Randall Hauk made introductions possible to homicide detectives William Peterson and Paul Thomas, who let me take them to lunch. Thanks especially to Sergeant Kenneth 'The Reverend' Gardner, who took me to visit Beaubien, and everyone at DPD Homicide. I appreciate your personal perspectives on the very fine and very difficult work you do.

Zara Trafford and Amanda Stone helped me to make invaluable connections. Sherry Sparks introduced me to Pewabic Pottery, Saladin Ahmed took me to a concert with his family, Dean Philip shared stories about real estate and new journalism, Norene Cashen Smith provided a poet's insight and pancakes, Clinton Snider talked dreams and art and took me round the Powerhouse District, and Scott Hanselman demonstrated diabetes treatment over Skype from Portland.

Photographer and artist Scott Hocking let me hijack him for the day, introduced me to the DelRay Angels and the border patrol, burial mounds and ghost factories, and told me about finding the body in the ice, which I couldn't squeeze into the novel.

Mickey Alice Kwapis from the Detroit Academy of Taxidermy explained how to peel a really gross orange and lent me the kangaroo story, and Chef Wylie Dufresne of WD50 walked me through the particulars of using meatglue. I have taken liberties with science. Cynthia Duncan Eñi Acho Iya of AboutSanteria.com candidly discussed her faith, dispelled the easy clichés and introduced me to broken heads.

Thanks Danah Boyd for the thing you weren't supposed to do, and Scott Westerfeld for facilitating, to Katherine and Kendaa Fitzpatrick for your personal insight into growing up bi-racial, and Janee Cifuentes for the Cuban leads.

Megan Abbot, Anna Clark, Anne Perry, Emma Cook, Matthew Brown, Helen Moffett, Sarah Lotz and Emad Akhtar all read early drafts of this book and helped to shape the beast.

Behind the scenes, I owe everything to my agent, Oli Munson, for making it happen. Thanks to Jennifer Custer, Hélène Ferey and Vickie Dillon at AM Heath, as well as everyone at Blake Friedmann, also Lawrence Mattis at Circle of Confusion.

I'm grateful to Julia Wisdom, Joshua Kendall and Fourie Botha for your faith and perspective.

On a personal level, I'm thankful for my friends and family, especially Dale Halvorsen, Nophumla Nobomvu, Craig Madeley, Monene Watson, Roxy and Ella, Sarah Lotz, Keitu and Matthew Brown, whose love and friendship mean the world and make all things possible.

This book is what it is because of my editor, Helen Moffett, who pushed the story harder and higher, and caught me when I fell.

Thank you.

Behind the Scenes of

Broken Monsters

- Photos from Lauren's research trip to Detroit
- Reading Group Questions
- An Interview with Lauren

The Packard Plant, Detroit. 'The number one
Death-of-America pilgrimage destination.'

'Shakespeare would have it wrong these days. It's not the world
that's the stage - it's social media.'

'She keeps looking back in the mirror, hoping to see her mom, who has gone now, disappeared into the terrible building with its blacked-out windows and broken glass.' (Fisher Body Plant, Detroit.)

'The window of Rocket Coffee gives Jonno the perfect view of the Michigan Central Train Station. The Acropolis of Detroit. Some genius suggested preserving the iconic ruins. That's what everyone's here for, anyway. To gawp at the broken buildings and take their portraits.'

'I'm sorry Jay Woody. I didn't mean for this to happen.' Interview room. Former police station on Beaubien, Detroit.

The old precinct on Beaubien, Detroit.

'Party Animal House.' The Heidelberg Project, Detroit.

'They end up at an apartment block in the city centre at three in the morning . . . a man leans out an upstairs window and throws the keys, attached to a plastic bag so they come parachuting down.'

'In front of her is the kiln and whatever's inside. It's huge, shaped like a sarcophagus, with a curved roof and chalky white bricks, scorched in places, and gas canisters and pipes down the side. It's framed in black iron, with a metal rod handle, and rails to pull it out on, marked with yellow and black hazard stripes. Old-school industry, this.'

'"This city," he says, inspired, "this city is all about the people, who have to burn against the dark. It's the bright against the blight."'

Reading Group Questions
– For Discussion:

- Who is Clayton Broom to you: despicable monster or flawed human or something else?
- In *Broken Monsters*, Detroit is as alive as its characters. How did Lauren's depiction affect your ideas about Detroit?
- The power of social media is seen to full effect and full impact in this book. Did it make you question how you use it? Do you think this was the author's intention?
- What did you think of Cas and Layla's 'catfish' experiment? Dangerous and stupid? Heroic and brave?
- The mother-daughter bond is integral to this storyline. How did their developing relationship affect you as a reader?
- Who was your favourite character? Why did they resonate with you? Who was your least favourite? Why? Do you think some characters' compromises were more reasonable than others? Who are the broken monsters of the title?
- How do you feel the author portrays the Detroit police force?
- What did you think of the ending?

An Interview with Lauren Beukes

How did writing *Broken Monsters* compare to writing your previous novel, *The Shining Girls*?

It was difficult, because the stakes are raised every time and I try to push myself harder, to write a better book than the previous one. The person with the most unreasonable expectations of my work is . . . me. But I'd rather be ambitious and fail than resort to a formula. I want to write the kind of books I'd like to read and I'm a really, really demanding reader.

It does help that there is physical evidence on my bookshelf that I have been able to do this before. It's lonely, stuck-in-your-head work with imaginary people, but when it works and the words flow and I surprise myself or someone writes a good review online, it makes it all worthwhile.

It feels like a terrible privilege to be paid to make up stories, to create a world and lives that other people will want to inhabit for a while.

Clayton Broom, though terrifying, is not your typical amoral serial killer. How do you feel about him – should he be wholly blamed for the atrocities he commits?

Clayton is a very damaged man who got lost in a bad place and found a terrible vision. I think a lot of people might have ended up in that situation.

When we describe someone as 'monstrous' we are trying to say they are more than (or less than) human. But humanity has to allow for even the most despicable acts. We are all capable of those things in the darkest corners, in the worst circumstances.

The book is about broken people – and we're all a bit broken inside, it's how we deal with it. The monsters are ones of ambition and pride and fear and naivety and I wanted to treat that with compassion. The killer does terrible, terrible things, but what drives him is ultimately very human – that desire to be recognized, to be seen, to feel known.

I think it's telling that even the monsters are broken. They don't quite work. They're not fully-functional monsters, because the humanity is still there, underneath. Drowned, perhaps, by unspeakable acts. Irredeemable, maybe, but still there.

How did your research trip to Detroit help to shape *Broken Monsters*? Were any of the characters based on people you met there?

I hadn't been to Detroit before, but I'd seen any number of evocative photographs of decay taken by urban explorers. It seemed like a haunted place, but I know from experience growing up in Johannesburg that the most blighted and desolate parts of a city are still somewhere people live.

I wanted to get underneath the ruin porn façade, the same way I was interested in exploring the boarded-up buildings in Hillbrow in my Joburg novel, *Zoo City*. Detroit is interesting for being such a symbolic place. It represents the birth and death of the American Dream, it's supposedly the most violent city in the US, it's the ground zero of foreclosures and the financial crisis. You can hold up the city as a symptom of everything that's wrong with America (or the world).

The reality is that it's a lot more than that. Symbols have unexpected depths that defy easy clichés and this can be very uncomfortable. We want things to *mean* something. But cities (and people) are much messier and more complicated.

I read a lot about Detroit, following people on Twitter, and blogs like CurbedDetroit or PositiveDetroit, keeping up with news stories, reading books including Charlie leDuff's *Detroit: An American Autopsy* and Mark Binelli's *Detroit City Is The Place To Be* and my favourite, John Carlisle's *313: Life In the Motor City*, which features wonderful biographies and photographs of ordinary people.

I also went there on two separate research trips just over a year apart, at the beginning of the novel, to get a sense of the city, and after I'd finished the first draft, to fill in the gaps.

I used to be a journalist and I know that real life is often weirder than anything you can make up, and the details matter. The personal perspectives on the city cracked it open for me.

I interviewed journalists and artists and photographers, got yanked in to doing warm-up exercises with a teenage theatre troupe, "infiltrated" Detroit Homicide with a box of donuts and walked one of the detectives through my case and talked about how the procedure would work at each stage and fed him the clues (he cracked it), drove around with photographer Robert-David Jones in a funeral home van, visited the Packard Plant and Secret Beach on Belle Isle and secret parties in Eastern Market and an abandoned theatre with rotting curtains and a velvet chair pulled from its row like a rotten tooth. I also worked in the soup kitchen at the NOAH Project for the day and sat and ate lunch with people like the inspirational volunteer James Harris, who were all happy to share their stories, to give me their perspective on Detroit.

I interviewed Chef Wylie Dufresne on the phone about how to use meatglue, spoke to a santeria priestess about misconceptions and bad heads. I got the low-down on living with diabetes from my friend Scott Hanselman, and interviewed a real taxidermist, Mickey Alice Kwapis who showed me her house and her work space over Skype.

My interviews and experiences provided so much rich detail and personal insights and stories I couldn't have made up, from Mickey's skinned kangaroo story to James Harris's memory of being an "abandominium" landlord when he was 13 to hearing about how female police officers' bra sizes were leaked to the entire department when they were measured for bullet-proof vests or Detective Bob Haig's story about a basement full of dead babies that turned out not to be.

Broken Monsters addresses a huge range of issues from provocative art to the dangerous world of social media – what inspired you to bring these themes into the novel?

Some people see psychologists, I work my issues out on the page. I was interested in art and social media, id and dreaming and reflection and what we make of the representations of ourselves and what we put into the world.

I live a good chunk of my life online, as many of us do now in the wilder-than-you-could-have-imagined 21st century where we have killer robot drones in the sky and the whole world in our phones, and I wanted to write about how amazing that is and how terrifying.

The novel follows my personal interests, news stories I've been upset by about teen bullying, teenage rape victims who were slut-shamed and committed suicide like Reateh Parsons, creepypasta urban legends, creativity, ambition, broken masculinity, the idea of identity, of a projected, idealized self.

It ties into art. I collected a lot of images on my Tumblr of art featuring distorted or obscured faces. It's exploring who we are, who we want to be, how much we need to be recognized, acknowledged, seen, how much those wretched "likes" matter.

In a world that is so traumatized right now (and throughout all our history, because humans are special like that) art, fiction, stories allow us to look at the unbearable and maybe see it in a new way. We can turn off the news on Gaza or Boko Haram or Syria or the Ukraine, because it's too much. Art gets past our defences.

I'm not much of a fan of shock jock art or ill-conceived concepts. I've seen way worse on the Something Awful forums back in 1994, let alone on the Internet now. When Two Girls One Cup exists in the world, how are you going to top that and is there a message in breaking taboos, in pushing grotesqueries to the utmost?

I like art that manages to find humanity in the awfulness, compassion, humour. Relentless nihilism is a bit tedious and genuinely doesn't get at the complexity of being alive in the world.

To break out that Nietzche quote about how you shouldn't stare into the abyss: I believe art has a moral obligation to confront the unknowable, and, hey, the worst thing you'll find looking back is. . . us.

There's only us and everything we are capable of, all the wonder and whimsy and grace and horror and terror in the world and we have to be able to look at it. Art is a handy lens to do so.

There are so many wonderful characters in *Broken Monsters*, each with their own distinct voice. Who was your favourite one to write and who was the most challenging?

Layla was the most fun to write, she came through very easily and I remember well that confusing heady mash of absolute self-righteous certainty and crippling self-doubt of being fifteen. You take that seed of your personality or your memory and you grow it into a tree, so that the character becomes uniquely herself.

I think it helps that I live a fair bit of my life online, which is a young space generally, and that I interviewed Detroit teenagers about their lives and their perspective. The quote about how social media is the stage and life is what happens in the wings preparing to put on that performance came out of a group discussion I had with a class of ferociously smart teens.

Clayton was the most difficult, establishing exactly what he wanted, how he saw with his new eyes, exactly what his vision was and what that meant for him – a world laid bare in its symbols and definitions and possibilities.

Jonno Haim, possibly even more than Clayton, will evoke a strong response from your readers. How did you want people to react to him?

Hopefully with some empathy. He's not entirely a bad guy, he's just doing all the wrong things because of pride and ambition and fear of being a failure. Like Clayton, he's desperate to be recognized. It's a very ordinary desire but it can turn very ugly.

There are some exquisitely dark scenes in *Broken Monsters* that make the reader feel like they are retracing their own nightmares. Did you have disturbing dreams when you were writing the book?

No. But I have since! I did raid the dream diary I kept as a twenty-something for weird imagery and a sense of dream logic. The flower lamprey on the side of the house is something I really dreamed.

Was it a challenge to portray an authentic police procedural alongside the more supernatural elements of the novel?

It was a finely managed process to let the strangeness seep through, like rising damp or black mould until you can rip right through that thin wallpaper. My editors were incredibly helpful.

Can you tell us a bit about what you're working on next?

A new novel or two, comics, screenplay adaptations of my previous books. I think I'm done with serial killers, but I can almost guarantee that my new work will be strange and fantastical and genre-blending and trying to get a handle on who we are in the world.